PART ONE

CHAPTER 1

Lake Ronkonkoma, Long Island, New York.
September 7, 1988, 6:15 a.m.

The digital alarm clock bellowed its obtrusive melody pulling young William McCabe from his peaceful slumber. The clock, given to him as a birthday gift just months earlier. Now it stood on his nightstand, and the red glowing digital numerals were a symbol of adulthood. It had a job and a purpose that reached far beyond just waking him at a predetermined hour. It was his key to the door that would usher him out of childhood and away from the ritual of having his mother stir him from sleep. It was a symbol of responsibility and maturity. This symbol was lost on William as laziness got the better of him, he reached over, punched the snooze button, and bought himself nine more minutes of semi-tranquil sleep.

Just as promised the alarm came back for a second attempt exactly nine minutes later. Ignoring the notification again was not an option. Mrs. McCabe would only let the charade carry on for so long, before using her method of bringing her son to a state of alert awakening. A cup of cold water dumped on his sleeping head.

She expected more from her second son; he was entering Junior High School and time was no longer a luxury item stored in excess. William's vocabulary was about to grow, words like; "mid-terms" and "finals" and "GPA" would all work their way into his daily life. They all played a role into another word he choked on whenever it left his lips, "College."

That word hung over him like a dark cloud of responsibility. The pressure of getting the best education and the best job to gain the best life weighed on his thirteen-year-old mind. This burden lay heavy on his tired shoulders.

Groggy and still half asleep William rolled from his bed to the cold cement floor of his basement bedroom. The secluded locale gave him the privacy he felt he deserved. He believed he earned this privilege and would need it entering into his new adult life. The lack of windows also cut off any outside sunlight, creating no difference in illumination between 12 noon and 12 midnight. The lack of natural light was a small price to pay for shedding the main floor bedroom he had shared with his older brother next to his parent's room. With the basement now converted into a living space, the two boys were each granted the rare luxury of individual bedrooms and a shared bathroom. The basement arrangement was cruel and simplistic, but the boys could muster no complaint, they had their semi-private living quarters. They were living as virtual roommates sharing an eclectic urban apartment.

This particular morning William had the entire subterranean level to himself. Danny, his older brother by four years, was already in High School. By this time of day, he was already at school, sitting in Homeroom. Homeroom was the abbreviated pre-first period class dedicated to the taking of attendance and the hurried, panicked shuffle to complete every neglected homework assignment from the

CHAPTER 1

previous day.

Right now, however, William had the bathroom all to himself. Bathroom occupancy never posed a problem in the past. William had an almost non-existent emphasis on personal hygiene, but this William was a new man, and he was reborn and dedicated to taking a shower every morning. As the social circles would dictate, it was no longer OK or cute to leave the house donning hair depressed down and rancid breath. So, as maturity would have it, morning showers took the place of the every other night bathing that used to be his usual, forced ritual. In the past, when left to his accord, bathing was only for those special occasions. These events included Easter service at the local Catholic church or the rare family function that included dining at a restaurant, the kind with cloth napkins and glass plates and cups.

The first day of school had always brought with it the bonus of finally being able to wear all those new school clothes purchased at different intervals throughout the summer break. They spent their time during that beloved vacation standing vigilant in the closet, almost mocking you, daring you to take them out for a spin. Challenging you to let the warm summer air infect them or the fresh dirt of the backyard soil their perfection.

Now it was revenge time, the clothes were fair game, the entire new wardrobe was available for wearing. Excluding nothing, not even the brand new white Reebok sneakers, still in the box. They gleamed with a cleanliness that they would never see again in their short life. So pristine and elegant, the Union Jack emblazoned box that held them captive also contained that combination of a leather and rubber smell. With the box lid removed, that unique smell was free to disperse into the waiting air like so many ceremonial doves.

The early September temperatures hadn't quite surrendered their warm summer air just yet so a T-shirt would serve as an adequate clothing option on this first day of school. Not just any T-shirt would suffice, after all, today was the first day of Junior High School. This year was the beginning of a new era, new friends, new experiences, and to an even higher degree, the age of impressing the girls. This particular day called for William's favorite addition to his new T-shirt ensemble, the sea foam green Ocean Pacific T-shirt. This shirt was the one with the larger than life wave and surfer screen printed on the back and the simple "OP" on the front where a chest pocket should be. Joining the T-shirt was a new pair of jeans, with a pinch-roll cuff and the white Reeboks. The preparation was complete, as William headed to the corner to catch the bus.

The regular cast of characters assembled at the corner of Union and Pine. Leading the charge was Jason Cosimo, the perpetual wise ass. The only time Jason wasn't cracking jokes at other's expense was when he was talking about his beloved New York Rangers. Hockey season wasn't slated to start until next month, so it was open season for a continuous, vicious onslaught of insults. Everything was on the table, mother jokes, ethnic stereotypes, and the ever popular ridicule at whatever clothing you happened to be wearing. He was relentless, never showing any sign of letting up. Only the World War II bombing of Dresden would hold a comparison to the barrage of verbal insults emanating from Cosimo. It was a wonder he had any friends at all. One did have to acknowledge his keen wit and advanced use of the insult library. He was a marvel for the ages, quicker to the draw than most kids twice his age.

As William trudged to the corner, Jason jumped down off the fire hydrant that was serving as his pedestal. He was like a sentry, waiting, remaining on guard, staying vigilant looking for that first brave soul to leave the safety of cover and cross into his line of fire.

"Nice snot green shirt McCabe, did you sneeze that one out this morning or have you been working on that all summer?" mocked

CHAPTER 1

Jason.

"Go screw yourself, Cosimo."

"That would mean I would have to stop screwing your mother, wouldn't it?"

A rhetorical question, but still Jason waited for a response, waiting for William actually to answer the question. Would he have to literally stop having sexual relations with his mother to then engage in other relations with himself? Such was the insanity of being a thirteen-year-old kid in this suburban New York neighborhood.

The bright yellow school bus lumbered to the corner before making its scheduled stop. The brakes hissed and popped with the creak of the hinges of the door as Ms. Carmichael, the district's most senior driver, swung the handle forward. She was a weathered woman, beaten down by life. The two-pack-a-day cigarette habit was showing its effects on all her features. The glisten in her eye only showed itself on the rarest of special occasions and the first day of school was one of them. She could smell the fear emanating from the prepubescent pores of all the new recruits. She took solace in that these fresh new Junior High faces just might have a worse day than she would, at least just for today.

Her great pleasure showed in her over the top jovial greeting, "Welcome aboard kids, please… make yourself at home. Pick any seat you want."

Not missing a chance to contribute to the situation Jason Cosimo chimed in, "Any seat? Then I pick McCabe's mom's seat."

Turning to William, Cosimo felt the need to explain his vulgar insult, "McCabe, that means your mom's ass, I choose your mom's ass."

Having enough, and feeling the need to reestablish her alpha role in the tight confines of this golden district vehicle Ms. Carmichael snapped, "That's enough of that! Grab a seat and shut up!"

PART ONE

Cosimo, without hesitation, grabbed a handful of William's rear end and gave a violent squeeze. William turned, shoving Cosimo away yelled, "You're an asshole!"

This comedy routine was a welcome change for the rest of the comatose passengers of Route 6B on its way to the Junior High School. A few let out an audible laugh, but most just peeled their faces away from the window for a brief second and gave a slight grin, one almost as inconspicuous as the Mona Lisa herself.

William, feeling agitated and angry more than embarrassed, found an empty seat at about the halfway point on the passenger side of the bus. Cosimo continued to the back of the bus. William's relationship with Jason Cosimo was fragile at best. Cosimo's older brother Mark and William's brother Danny were friends, had been since elementary school. The assumption was that the families would continue the lineage of friendship, but Jason Cosimo just wasn't the type of person William enjoyed spending prolonged periods of time in the company of. They got along for the most part, but their social interaction was usually relegated to pick up street hockey games and neighborhood-wide games of Manhunt.

William was happy to rid himself of the burden of Cosimo. He was similar to a bad case of diarrhea, always an amusement when it was happening to someone else, but not so funny when you became its latest victim. Besides, William's best friend since kindergarten would be boarding at the next stop.

Kenny Springer lived just around the corner from William but made the bus stop in front of his grandmother's house his regular morning boarding station Mondays and Wednesdays. Kenny's father worked the overnight shift for the Long Island Rail Road, and his mother had the first shift as a nurse at the Stony Brook University Hospital those days. Kenny spent these mornings at his grandmother's house, arriving at 5:00 a.m. The early start meant that Kenny had to be up and out of bed by 4:30 a.m., but it also included a home-cooked meal, prepared by his grandmother, that would please the hungriest of recipients. Eggs, pancakes, bacon, sausage; you name it, it was there. It was a spread fit for a king. With such a full breakfast, this meant that by half-way through the day Kenny had to excuse himself for an emergency bathroom visit. The general population bathroom offered little to no privacy so he would always retreat to the cleaner more private bathroom facilities of the nurse's office, feigning some mild illness or injury. He thought he was fooling everyone with this stunt, but everyone knew his secret.

The bus came to a stop at the corner of Union and Maple Avenues, and Kenny boarded, carrying a book bag that was larger than he was. He navigated his way up the narrow staircase and past Ms. Carmichael. Kenny looked up, scanning the top part of the faces that just cleared the bus's oversized seat backs. He was like a hawk scanning a field for his dinner. Locking eyes with William, Kenny moved quick and with a lot more grace than he exhibited during his initial boarding process. He was eager to meet up with his friend and discuss their plan of attack for surviving the first day of Junior High.

Right on cue, from the rear section of the bus, the irritating shrill voice of Jason Cosimo shouted out, "Hey Springer! I hear the nurse's bathroom is exceptionally clean here, so please feel free to blow it up with your blitzkrieg of a shitstorm."

Kenny's face turned red with a combination of anger and embarrassment. Wasting no time, he slid into the seat next to William, hoping that no one would make the connection, or follow what it was that Cosimo was saying. Given the zombie-like state the rest of the bus's inhabitants displayed, it was safe to say that the jab went unnoticed.

Recouping from his first verbal assault of the day from Cosimo, Kenny gathered himself and turned to William, "You ready?"

"For what?" William replied.

"It's our first day, the first day of Junior High. We are no longer elementary school kids. We are like men now. Look, I packed a first-day survival kit. Want to see?"

Not waiting for a reply from William, Kenny started pulling out items from his oversized book bag, "Binaca, just in case girls want to make out in the hallway."

Turning to face William with a serious expression he continued, "They do that you know. Junior High School girls, they love making out with guys in the hallway, it's a proven fact."

Kenny loved attaching the footnote of "It's a proven fact" to everything, whether it was a fact, proven or not.

Kenny continued, "Extra deodorant, in case we get a little smelly and sweaty."

"We?" William asked. "Kenny, I don't care how sweaty I may get, for whatever godforsaken reason I may get sweaty, I am NOT sharing roll on deodorant with you."

"So you're saying I should have gotten the spray kind?"

"No, it's fine. What else do you have in that magic bag of goodies?"

Kenny continued to empty the contents of his bag onto the empty seat space between them, "Breath mints, extra underwear, fruit roll-ups, extra shoelaces, and ChapStick."

"Well, Ken, you are certainly prepared for Junior High, no one can ever say otherwise. Let me see your schedule again so we can try to coordinate our day."

Kenny's face fell and turned white, "Oh no! I forgot it at my grandma's house."

William shook his head, "I stand corrected."

As the bus worked its way closer to the school, a long series of dramatics continued to play out. Kenny was bringing himself to the verge of a panic attack while William assured him that his homeroom teacher would have an extra copy of his class schedule.

CHAPTER 1

All Kenny needed to do was remember where his homeroom was, which was easy since it was all split up in alphabetical order. William also reminded him that Jennifer Sprague would most likely be in his homeroom class he just needed to ask her. A task that was remarkably easy since she was sitting three seats behind them on the bus, but also somewhat difficult. Jennifer Sprague was one of the most popular and prettiest girls in the entire district. Talking to her usually required a membership on one of the major sporting teams or at least, the muscle tone that resembled a 32-year-old professional athlete. Kenny was not in either one of those categories.

Mustering the courage, and due to severe desperation, Kenny slid to the aisle and maneuvered with care back three rows until he stood above Jennifer, who was deep in conversation with Melanie Breckenridge. Instead of the polite "excuse me" Kenny opted for a more ominous approach of just standing there, hovering until Jennifer noticed him. This move did work after a few minuted but not the way Kenny intended. Jennifer hit a break in her conversation, turned. She expected to see the passing trees flying by the window across the aisle. The close, hanging, pale face of one Kenny Springer threw her back in fear.

"Ah… Oh God Kenny, you frightened me," She exclaimed, doing her best not to show how much he did frighten her.

Kenny struggled through what no English teacher in the world would call a complete sentence, "Um… Hey, Jen. Um… I was wonderin' maybe, if you knew, like, where, homeroom is?"

"My homeroom?" Jennifer asked.

Again, Kenny struggling to string words together to form some semblance of a cohesive thought, "Yeah, Um… The thing is, you see, I kinda sorta forgot mine. And you know, we got like close last names and stuff. I just thought like maybe you knew."

In an odd turn of events, Jennifer was able to decipher what it was Kenny needed and was happy to help out, "Room 146."

She paused before continuing, "And Kenny, I think the homeroom teacher will have extra copies of your schedule."

"Um... Thanks a lot, Jen. See you there?"

Even though Kenny finished the sentence with the higher inflection indicating that the "see you there" wasn't a statement but a question it went unnoticed, and Jennifer turned back and continued her conversation with Melanie.

Kenny turned to head back to his seat, feeling a lot more confident than he did when he started this venture. He only got one and a half steps into his graceful return to his seat when a loud, boisterous laughter radiated from the back of the bus, "Shot down again, huh Springer?"

Kenny paused, then realized that getting into a war of words with one Jason Cosimo would be futile, so he continued back to his seat, ignoring the existence of that annoying mouthpiece named Cosimo.

Getting back to the welcoming space next to William, Kenny let out a sigh of relief, he had done it, accomplished his mission.

William addressing the Cosimo comment asked, "Is there anything that happens anywhere that Jason Cosimo doesn't see and comment on?"

Not waiting for a reply William continued, "So, you get the room number?"

"Sure did."

"Well, what is it?"

There was a long pause, and a blank stare on Kenny's face, "Shit! I forgot what she said."

William trying to be sympathetic by holding in his laughter was busting at the seams, "You forgot what she said? How retarded are you?"

"One forty-something," Kenny was now looking up at the fire

escape hatch located on the bus ceiling attempting to clear his mind.

William, just sat there, stoic, giving Kenny the much needed quiet and space to pull from the archives of his brain what it was that Jennifer said. It was there somewhere, even if young Kenny didn't retain it, his brain did.

Finally, after some deep concentration, Kenny broke his staring contest with the bus ceiling and shouted out, almost a little too loud for the morning bus, "ONE FORTY-SIX!"

Crisis averted.

CHAPTER 2

Navigating the complex labyrinth of locker filled hallways and classrooms was no easy task for the average new student, but William McCabe was not your average new student. He spent the second half of his summer vacation studying the map of the school's maze-like layout. He knew every inch of that building, down to the location of every water fountain; he felt you never knew when the situation might call for some emergency hydration.

Arriving in Homeroom with plenty of time to spare he had his pick of seating. The chair selection ritual was a risky game of strategy. Too close to the front would be social suicide, too close to the back would label him as a trouble maker. A designation William did not need, especially with the added weight his last name carried with it. Danny McCabe, William's older brother, was a decent student grade-wise, but he had a reputation as a raucous type. Danny had a motley crew of misfits and derelicts as friends. They were all good and decent kids but avoided trouble with little efficiency. William feared his new teachers would see him as "that troublemaker Danny McCabe's kid brother." He was his own man attempting to get out from under his brother's shadow.

Homeroom was uneventful, a central crash course in Junior High protocol and a chance to catch up with old elementary school acquaintances. The district was huge in comparison to the other school districts on Long Island. Seven elementary schools pooled into two Junior High Schools, which in turn combined into one massive High School. With so many new faces around William struggled to find just one he knew. Luckily, Jerry McMurray was in his Homeroom, Jerry and William were in the fifth grade together, even sharing a bus seat on the field trip to the Cold Spring Harbor Science Labs.

William spent the rest of the shortened period engaging in some polite chit chat with Jerry. The typical "How was your summer" variety. Shortly after running out of things to talk about the clamorous, electric sounding bell rescued them from the awkward silence. Which was only a bell in name, it sounded more like the alert sound that would signify a game show contestant's to attempt to answer a question.

The rest of the day passed with no significant problems or events. It was Introduction to Basic Mathematics, US History, Earth Science, English & Literature, etc. All the same boilerplate speeches delivered by the teachers. Each teacher was a clone of the one before. Each presentation was the same as the one before it. "This is what I expect" "This is how I grade" "I'm fair to you if you are fair to me" and so on.

Then came the sixth period, time for something a little different. William knew picking German as his foreign language option was more than a bit unorthodox but Spanish, Italian or French just sounded so dull. William recognized no one in the class, not a single person from his elementary school had thought like he had. "I'm sure they were all enrolled in Spanish, like lemmings walking off a cliff," William would think to himself.

CHAPTER 2

Again he arrived early and had his choice of seating found something that just felt right, about mid-room. He made himself as comfortable as the situation would allow. William was great when it came to socializing with established friends, but he was quiet, reserved and shy when it came to saying the slightest of greetings to someone new. One by one, the other kids filed into the classroom. It was an odd assortment of students; every school caste system had representation; the nerd, the burnout, the skater kid, the jock, etc. William never felt he fit into any particular group, and he wasn't popular by any means, but all the popular kids knew him. He wasn't a jock but proved to be a talented goalie in the area hockey leagues. William didn't smoke or keep his hair too long or enjoy heavy metal, but the burnouts seem to be cool with him too. The skater kids thought he was OK, but that was all hinged on the decent Rollerblading skills he possessed from years of playing Roller Hockey. He blended in, and he didn't make waves, he didn't irritate anyone, and moreover, he didn't make too strong an impression on anyone.

The Introduction to German class started with little fanfare, business as usual. The teacher a large framed, goatee-sporting man who called himself Herr Werner, "Herr" being the German equivalent to "Mr."

"Guten Morgen" Herr Werner bellowed.

The class remained still, not knowing what the broad educator was looking for exactly, acknowledgment, maybe? After a few seconds of silence, a student from the back of the class spoke up, "Guten Morgen?"

It was more a question than anything else, the reply pleased Herr Werner, if even by accident. A big smile stretched across his square jowls like the slow, gradual movement of the sun ducking behind the horizon on a beautiful summer evening. Once the grin reached the limits on Herr Werner's face, he gave the one brave student in the back of the room an exaggerated wink and replied, "Sehr gut!"

Herr Werner began explaining to the rest of the class what exactly just transpired between himself and his unwilling counterpart in the back of the room. It was, as he called it "Basic Conversational German" He had said, "Good morning" and the student replied in kind, to which Herr Werner returned "very good." There was a collective "Ah" that filled the room in unison.

As Herr Werner turned to begin writing the first collection of German words on the board, there came an aggressive rap upon the door. Herr Werner, dropped his arms, tilted his head to the ceiling as if questioning the heavens, looking for a reason for such an untimely interruption. Giving up on hearing an explanation from the tiles above his head or the Heavens, he turned and looked at the closed door and yelled, "You may enter!"

A young pimple faced boy entered with a slip of paper ready, like a sword drawn in battle, expecting the worst and prepared to defend himself with this official document. His shaky hand raised it and with care, delivered the paper to Herr Werner.

"What is this?" Herr Werner asked.

The boy with the bad skin mustered the courage to reply, "Um… this girl here, she is like new, and she is kind of in your class this period?"

William, like the rest of the class, was so intrigued about the interaction between the boy and Herr Werner that they did not notice the girl standing in the doorway. Herr Werner was too busy correcting the young man's poor sentence structure to see the girl himself.

Finally, when Herr Werner felt he had made his point with the boy, he signed the document. He then handed it back to the youth and excused him by letting him know, "You may leave now. This young woman is now in my care for the remainder of the sixth period, it is official, a job well-done sir."

Herr Werner turned and got his first look at the young girl. She was short in stature, dark complexion, and short haircut gave a boyish look to her. The jeans, sneakers and white T-shirt added to the subtle masculine look of this young hoyden.

When Herr Werner finally addressed her presence, it was again, in German, "Wie gehts?"

The mystery girl was too occupied sweeping the room at all the leering faces to know that someone was speaking to her, in any language.

"Wie gehts?" Repeated Herr Werner.

"Huh?" The girl replied.

"How are you doing?" Herr Werner was finally revealing the English counterpart of his question.

"Oh, um, I'm OK."

"Good, now you may relocate to any available seat of your choosing."

Without any further conversation, in English or German, the girl scanned the room and immediately eyed the empty desk positioned right in front of William. Showing the slightest grin on her young face, she made a quick move to the open seat. She threw her book bag down on it as if staking a flag in a foreign land, claiming it as her own.

William could smell the subtle scent of femininity. It wasn't perfume; it was just the smell of her. The soap she used or the shampoo or laundry detergent. She may have had the androgynous haircut and dressed like a boy, but there was no doubt in William's mind; she was 100% girl. He became focused on the freckle on the soft skin on the back of her neck. William had been this close to girls before, he knew he must have, but never had he taken any time to notice the small details that create the biggest differences between the sexes.

Herr Werner wrapped up his introductory expectations and his plan to invade these young minds and sculpt them into little German speaking geniuses. He used the term "invade their minds" completely not seeing the insensitive nature that it implied. After all, it was the German's invasion that started two world wars.

There were almost ten minutes left of class time before the intrusive bell would summon them again to proceed, in a military style, to their next class. The new girl took this opportunity to turn around in her seat and face William and make a formal introduction.

"Hi, I'm Amanda. I just moved to this school district. What's your name?"

"William."

"Cool, I like that name, you mind if I call you Will?" Amanda gave an extended smile, showing off two rows of perfect teeth.

"No… I don't mind."

William never preoccupied himself with girls; he always figured there would be plenty of time for that stuff later. He liked one girl in the sixth grade, but if he was honest with himself, he wasn't sure what that meant or what it entailed. There was a sixth-grade dance at the end of the year. William had mustered up all the courage he could find, even borrowing some from his friends, to approach Stacy Miller and ask if she wanted to go to the dance with him.

Stacy had a tall, slim body with long straight blonde hair and eyes so blue they resembled the swimming pools William had seen during the family vacation to an upscale resort in Florida.

William was still just 12 years old. The fantastical world of the female species had not yet manifested onto his everyday radar. He appreciated the beauty of the female stars on TV. He knew Loni Anderson was gorgeous, and Madonna was sexy, but he just didn't know his role in this complex game, this theater of sex. He wanted to join in with the guys and their shared stories of girls and sex, none of it based in fact, but he had no frame of reference, nothing to go on. The few exceptions were the times he and Kenny commandeered Kenny's older brother's pornographic magazines for a quick afternoon peak while his brother was at work. Even at his young age and inexperience, William had the foresight to see that the actions taking place in those magazines were far removed from the real world. In fact, they only left him with more questions than answers.

In his neighborhood, perceived sexual prowess was everything, no matter how made up it might have been. It was more of a game of knowledge than a game of actions and William was so far behind. So he convinced his friends and himself that he was in love with Stacy and her in love with him.

The charade continued all the way through the rest of the sixth grade. William even telling his friends that he was going to the dance WITH Stacy, when in reality her answer to him was, "Um… we can just meet there and maybe dance a little if you want."

It wasn't a "No" but not a "Yes" either, and not a "Going with."

What he saw in Amanda was different from what he saw in Stacy. Amanda looked him in the eye when she talked to him. The smile on her face was genuine not forced. She was about as real as anyone William had ever met. She radiated truth and honesty. It was evident she knew how to lie but would never exercise that knowledge to anyone she saw as important or worthwhile.

Amanda continued the small talk with William while he found himself studying her features. She had deep brown eyes, eyes that had mileage on them but held tight to the innocence of her youth. They were kind eyes, as long as you were kind to her. Her smile was one that didn't get too many chances to come out, but when it did, it relished the moment that let it out. She had subtle brown freckles that stretched across the bridge of her nose and cheeks. They were like faint stars in a sky just a little too bright, their full potential restrained, held back from view.

William was so focused on Amanda's features that he didn't realize that she was just looking at him. The rest of the world had become a blur around her; even her small talk had faded into the background. Amanda finished her thought, and she was watching him, waiting. That's when it occurred to William that she must have asked him a question and was waiting for his reply. A response that would never come because he had no idea what the question was. The puzzled panicked look on William's face served as a dead giveaway to Amanda that her answer would not be coming. She let him sit in his fear and confusion for a few seconds before finally breaking the awkward silence and bailing him out.

"What period do you have lunch? I asked," She finally repeated.

"Oh, sorry. Um… what period is this?" William stammered.

"Sixth."

"Oh, OK. Lunch? Um… seventh period, I have seventh-period lunch."

"That's next period, dumbass," Amanda teased.

"Dumbass" would prove to be Amanda's favorite term of endearment. She used it as often as possible.

"Oh, yeah, so I have lunch next period."

Amanda's face lit up, "Awesome, so do I! Want to sit together? I mean if you don't have anyone else to sit with that is. It's just that I'm still pretty new to this school and don't know anyone. You have been excellent and friendly so far that I just think it would be cool if I could sit with you during lunch. Maybe just until I make some new friends and stuff."

"Sure, I don't mind," William replied.

He had already run the investigation with his circle of friends, and no one had seventh-period lunch. He was void of companionship. None of his usual crew shared that same lunch period. It was already a late start for eating and sitting alone would only add to the misery.

Not missing a beat Amanda added, "Cool, we can walk together."

The bell rang ending German class and releasing the throng of students into the narrow hallways. They were all headed in different directions, except for William and Amanda, who were both making their way to the cafeteria for seventh-period lunch.

CHAPTER 3

Ronkonkoma, William's hometown, got its name from an Indian princess. Local lore stated that she had drowned herself in the town's lake in retaliation to her father's forbidding of true love with a white settler. She would return every year and claim one male soul as repayment for her lost soul. As much as everyone in the town loved to spin the tale as often as they could most of the residents didn't believe it, but some, unfortunately, did.

Most of the towns on Long Island had some connection with its first inhabitants, the Native Americans. Some names are so difficult to pronounce that the mark of a real Long Islander was their ability to correctly and phonetically pronounce them. Town names like Patchogue, Hauppauge, Quogue, Yaphank, and Massapequa.

It was mid-December, winter had begun, the cold freezing temperature started to awaken from its eight-month long slumber, like a hibernating bear. Real snow hadn't quite started yet, the occasional snow flurry had hit, but the island was still to get its first significant snowfall accumulation. The sure sign that winter had

PART ONE

arrived was the freezing of Lake Ronkonkoma, an event that started over a week ago.

It was a Saturday afternoon, and William and Kenny were riding their bikes back from the park where they spent the afternoon playing tackle football on the frozen grass. Each fall to the ground was on ice-infused soil which had a consistency close to concrete. The game had ended, and all its participants went in their respective different directions back to their houses. Kenny had something on his mind that he had been wrestling with for the better part of a few weeks now and finally dug up the courage to mention it to William during their ride home.

"So, William, what's going on with you and that Amanda girl?" Kenny asked.

"Going on? Nothing is going on, she's nice, we get along and eat lunch together. We're not dating or anything. She's in my German class, and we both didn't know anyone else in that lunch period, so we sat together, it's not a big deal," William answered.

Kenny was quiet for a while, gathering the courage to ask his best friend the next poignant question, "Do you like her?"

"No, Kenny, come on… that's just weird. It's not like that at all, we just have lunch together, that's it," William was lying.

"Well, what do you guys talk about?" Kenny was curious.

Without hesitation, William replied, "Believe it or not, hockey. She's a big Islanders fan, watches all the games."

Kenny, not making eye contact with William added, "OK, if you say so. I just figured we would both get girlfriends around the same time, and not this early."

"Ken, she isn't my girlfriend," William snapped back.

Kenny, on the defensive, answered back, "OK, forget I said anything."

Once the boys reached the far end of the park, they faced a

navigational dilemma. They could either take the road around the lake to get home or go on the solid ice block that now lay where the lake would spend its summer home. William, always the cautious one, opted for the longer road around. Kenny, just the previous day, overheard his older brother talking about some guys from the neighborhood who drove their cars out onto the lake at night. The adventure sounded thrilling, and it left wide-eyed Kenny eager to do the same, with bikes racing across the frozen water tundra instead of cars. The boys argued each of their cases for a few minutes. William's theory was that one would have to walk their bike across the ice, so any time saved in the trip distance was more than lost in travel time. Kenny believed that he could peddle his bike across the frozen surface of the lake. After some time, the two realized that they had reached a stalemate and decided to make a game of it. Each would go their individual way, and the one arriving at the corner at the end of their street first would be the victor. The reward would be the candy of choice for the winner paid for by the loser. On the count of three, the boys sped off, parting ways at the end of the street where the lake front park began.

William felt confident that even peddling at his normal riding speed would still assure him the victory, especially now with the evening winds starting to kick up. William knew that crossing the vast open expanse of the lake would not give Kenny the luxury of trees for optimum wind blockage. If that wind were a headwind, which William figured it would be, Kenny's trip would not be an easy one. Even with the elements of nature in his corner, William peddled his bike as fast as his legs could push themselves. The candy was a secondary prize, it was meaningless, a fifty cent consolation award. The real victory was in the bragging rights. Each boy knew those claims were guaranteed for at least three months of constant badgering, followed by a year, maybe even two, of peripheral and subtle jabs.

The daylight hadn't quite surrendered yet, it was still holding on but wouldn't for much longer. When William turned the corner, even from this distance, he could see that Kenny was not already there waiting. Pulling his hands from his handlebars and raising them in victory for no one to see but himself William coasted to a stop at the post that held the names of the two intersecting streets. The pole was holding him up while he took the few minutes he had to regain his breath and composure. He began to plan the order in which he would unleash his barrage of insults at Kenny, who should be turning that same corner in the next minute or two.

Those two minutes turned into fifteen, then twenty, that's when William figured there must have been some confusion about where the finish line was. Picking up his bike from the frozen ground he headed down the street under the illumination of the street lights, and he went to Kenny's house. Pulling into the driveway and dismounting his bike something felt different, it wasn't until William was on his third ring of the doorbell that the realization came to him on what was missing. There was no car in the driveway; he should have realized it sooner when he was able to ride his bike all the way to the garage door unimpeded.

The incredible advantage of a young mind is its innocence; instead of fearing the worst like any adult would in an unexplained circumstance, a child will just shrug their shoulders and be content leaving it unexplained.

William, for the second time, picked his bike up from the ground and headed home. Tomorrow was a new day, and he would find out the whole story from Kenny then.

That Sunday started no different from any other one before it until was until the late morning rap on the door. William still in his pajamas and cradling a bowl of Cookie Crisp cereal looked out the front bay window. Not expecting the person on the other side of the door to be for him he figured he could ignore it if he knew who it was. To his surprise, Jason Cosimo was standing there, bundled up in his winter coat and his knit New York Rangers cap on almost covering his eyes. William placed his cereal bowl down on the living room coffee table and opened the door. With a severe look of confusion on his face, he asked, "Cosimo, what are you doing here?"

"Didn't you hear?" Cosimo replied, "Kenny fell through the ice on the lake last night. I think he's dead!"

William's whole world just stopped, if there were any ambient noise at that moment William would never hear it, everything went white and blank. After what seemed like hours but was only seconds Cosimo spoke again, "Nah, dude I'm messing with you, he's alive, but he did fall through the ice. Some guy driving passed saved his ass."

William feeling both relieved that his best friend was alive but infuriated that Cosimo would play that cruel a joke on him uttered the only words he could think to say, "Stupid asshole!"

It wasn't clear if William was referring to Cosimo for playing that mean a joke or if he was referring to Kenny for doing something so stupid and causing him so much worry. The truth was a little of both.

William made a point of never cursing in or around his house. He was always afraid of the consequences that would follow if his mother or father ever heard him or the level of blackmail his older brother Danny would enact if he heard it.

"Relax," Cosimo replied, "Come on, get dressed. I'm heading over there to see him now."

Within fifteen minutes, the two boys were walking around the block to Kenny's house. This time, William noticed that there were cars in the driveway, and the house looked a lot more alive than it had twelve hours prior. Mrs. Springer saw the two boys approaching from the street and greeted them at the door, "Hello boys. I'm sure you heard we had a little accident last night."

Mrs. Springer liked to use words like "we" and "us" in situations like this, it was a weak attempt not to assign blame to anyone.

"I meant to call your mother William to let her know Kenny is OK, I'm sure you were sick with concern. He is upstairs in his bedroom. The doctor said he needs to stay in bed and rest for a couple of days then he will be right as rain. Just a scary close call is all."

"How did it happen Mrs. S?" Cosimo asked. He was never quiet or reserved while conversing with adults like most kids his age.

"Why don't you go up to his room, he will tell you the whole story," Mrs. Springer explained.

The boys raced upstairs barely kicking off their shoes before stepping on the carpet and headed down the hallway to Kenny's room. He was lying in his bed, blankets up to the bottom of his chin. Judging how tight the covers were around him, it was safe to say that it was Mrs. Springer's doing. The tight constraints of his Batman sheets kept Kenny swaddled like a baby in a blanket, except Kenny was thirteen.

"Hey guys," Kenny spoke from under the oppressive trap of bed sheets, "You have got to help me get out from under these blankets."

It took both boys pulling on a sheet corner and Kenny pushing up from the inside to break the covers free. Underneath Kenny was in sweatpants, a sweatshirt, and thermal socks. It wasn't until they questioned it that Kenny informed them that he was also wearing thermal underwear, all his mother's doing. Kenny, wet with sweat, pulled off a few layers and grabbed a glass of water from the metal folding table next to his bed that held a steaming hot bowl of soup. Kenny looked at the soup and then at his two friends and said, "She brought that soup to me an hour and a half ago. It's still steaming. Can you begin to imagine how hot it was when she first brought it?

It would have melted my face off, assuming it didn't turn the spoon into molten metal first."

"So what the hell happened?" William asked first.

"Well, so we made our bet, and I saw you take off, peddling your ass off, and I knew you meant business. I rode my bike down to the lake's edge and right onto the ice. I was right, by the way, you can ride your bike on the ice, it's totally possible, well… it was for a while. I slipped and fell pretty hard, but that was because there was this divot on the ice and I turned to avoid it. Anyway, I kept going on foot, walking my bike, I was almost to the other side. I had a tail wind the whole time, if I had a sail, I could have gotten away with not peddling or walking at all."

William looked down at the ground and let out an almost inaudible grunt.

"So there I am, walking across the lake with my bike and I can see the other shoreline, it's like ten feet away. I step and crack; I fall through the ice. At first, I got scared, but then I realize, I'm standing on the bottom of the lake. The water was only like two feet deep. I was so close to the shore it was still shallow. So I just start walking. My bike, by the way, gone. That went under too, and I wasn't going to go fishing for it, it was freezing in that water. So I walk about three or four steps, and now I'm like five feet from the shore. Then, this car, up on the road comes to this screeching stop. This guy jumps out and starts screaming at me. Saying something about 'The Lady of the Lake' and tells me not to move because she was 'going to claim her male soul for that year.' I mean this guy was screaming this over and over again. I was trying to tell him that I was fine and could walk to the shore, it was only a few feet away, I had my feet on the floor of the lake. But no matter what I say to this guy he keeps screaming, 'don't move, help is coming, the Lady of the Lake won't get you.' I had no idea what he was talking about; the guy was nuts."

"Speaking of nuts, how frozen were yours at this point?" Cosimo, always offering the most enlightened observational points.

Kenny continued his story, paying no attention to Cosimo's running commentary, "So, now I'm standing there. Just over knee deep in freezing water. Just a few feet from the land and now I have to stop and wait because I don't know what this crazy guy is going to do. He kept saying that help was on the way. How did he call for help if he was standing there in the road yelling at me the whole time? Sure enough, I start hearing sirens. Less than a minute later they closed off the entire, and its filled with fire trucks, police cars, and ambulances. I swear I think I even heard a helicopter flying overhead. It was crazy! So this fireman runs down to the water's edge and asks if I'm OK, I tell him yeah, I'm just very, very cold and that I can easily walk to the land. So he tells me to do that. It took me five seconds to get on to the land, but when I got there, that one fireman had turned to twenty people. No sooner did I put my first foot on the ground, they grabbed me, wrapped me in blankets and carried me into the ambulance. The whole time they are asking me a million questions. 'What's your name?' 'Where do you live?' 'What is your phone number?' 'Are you allergic to any medications?'. They rushed me off to the hospital, and they called my parents. They kept me there overnight just to make sure I was OK. They released me first thing this morning. Now I just have to stay in bed, rest and drink lots of fluids, and oh yeah, I get to miss school tomorrow. That's the best part."

William and Cosimo remained fixated on Kenny's big climatic finish of his story, both stunned and amazed. Again it was Cosimo who broke the silence, "So really Ken, how frozen was your ball sack? Will you ever be able to produce children?"

The other two boys ignored Cosimo's question. Kenny offered up his unfounded personal insight into the ordeal, "So I stole death from the hands of an Indian Princess; I guess this makes me immortal."

"Where did you hear that?" William inquired.

"It's a proven fact," Kenny replied with confidence.

CHAPTER 4

William arrived in German class early, as he had done every day so far this year, and Amanda entered fractions of a second before the bell rang, as she had done every day so far.

Herr Werner, never tiring from the same joke dispensed it once again, "Nice of you to join us, Ms. Flores."

"Entschuldigung" Amanda offered.

Learning how to say "sorry" in German was Amanda's way out of 90% of the trouble she would have ordinarily gotten into with Herr Werner. He was proud that some of his lessons were getting through to his students, no matter what the vehicle was that got it there.

Amanda grabbed her seat in front of William and spun her head around, "Will, what happened to your dork friend Kenny? I heard he fell through the ice on the lake. Is that right?"

"Ms. Flores! Bitte!" Herr Werner bellowed from the front of the classroom.

"Sorry," Amanda spun back around to face the front of the class. "I mean, entschuldigung."

William leaned forward and whispered in her ear, "I'll tell you about in lunch next period."

The two packed up their books and stood poised and ready, like Olympic runners in their starting block awaiting the pop of the gun. The bell rang, and they were off. The mad dash ended as soon as they passed the invisible barrier that was the door frame of Herr Werner's classroom. Next period was lunch, they had all the time in the world to get there, the rush was just to get out of Herr Werner's lecture space.

Grabbing their usual table in the back corner of the cafeteria the two sat across from each other. Amanda had this look on her face, a look of anticipation. That look faded pretty quickly as William finished the story of Kenny and the icy lake. She looked almost disappointed. William sensed her disapproval of the story's ending and asked, "Did you want Kenny to die?"

"No! I just thought it was going to be more dramatic than just falling through a few feet of ice a couple of inches from the shoreline. That wasn't a brush with death, Hell, that wasn't even a paint roller with death. He was about as close to death as you and I are to California."

Amanda always used California as a measure of distance to illustrate something being far. William figured this had something to do with her father living there. Her parents had divorced when she was still a baby. Amanda had no recollection of her real father. He was a photo that lived in an old shoe box under her bed or a voice on the other end of a telephone receiver when she turned ten. These days her real father had been diminished to a signature on a check that maybe came once a month. In his place was her stepfather. She never referred to him by name not even or as her "stepfather" instead he was just "that asshole married to my mother" or the shorter version "asshole." As far as William could tell in his conversations with

Amanda, he didn't do much in the way of work. The picture that she painted seemed he and Amanda's mom liked to spend their days with a bottle of booze in one hand and a cigarette or the TV remote in the other. Sometimes it was a bottle of alcohol, at times it was marijuana, and sometimes it was both at the same time. Not much else was on their list of "things-to-do." These were grown-up issues for which William had no frame of reference. He would offer up the symbolic condolences and the traditional "that sucks" whenever Amanda would tell him stories about her broken home life. Even she could tell that it was all too much for William to process and would always offer some silver lining to her stories, just enough to make William a little less stressed about his friend.

"Will, I want to ask you something."

"OK," William wasn't much for long responses.

"What do you think people think about us?" Amanda asked.

"I dunno, what do you mean?"

"Like do you think everyone in the school thinks we are, you know, like, dating?"

William was quick to shoot back, "No! We are just friends, why would people think that?"

Amanda was quiet for a second, then finally spoke, "Do your friends ever ask you about me? Do they ever say anything?"

The truth was they did, almost every day, sometimes in a teasing way and sometimes in an inquisitive way like Kenny had before his date with the icy waters of Lake Ronkonkoma. William had never lied to Amanda before, but he worried what line of questions would follow if he spoke the truth and answered her last question honestly. So, William did the only thing he knew he could at that moment, he lied.

"No, they don't say anything."

Amanda looked puzzled. She knew they had. There was no proof, but she understood human nature enough to know that the topic had come up, more than once. She hated that William was lying to her, but she understood his reasons. It was a huge issue to face dead-on, and she knew him well enough to know that he would avoid it at all costs.

Either way, she was going to press on, she had an aim and a goal, she reached the point of no return, and there was no going back now.

"Well, my friends think it, and they say stuff. Girls are like that, they communicate, more than you idiot boys do."

"Really?" William was faking his surprise.

"Yes, really. Girls communicate better than boys," Amanda offered, channeling her inner wise-ass.

"No, I mean about us dating."

Even just saying the words out loud gave William a small anxiety attack. He had some feelings about Amanda; he just had no idea what they were. This whole world of the opposite sex was foreign to him. In his eye, he had replaced Amanda's sex. She was no longer a girl. He tried to see her as a boy, this way he could justify their relationship to himself. She was a friend and nothing more, or so he convinced himself.

Amanda was getting a little irritated with William's fake ignorance, "Yes Will, they do. The entire school thinks we are a couple. Listen, I'm only going to get the balls to do this once, and every minute we talk about it, I think maybe it's not an excellent idea."

Now William was more than perplexed; he was downright lost, "What are we talking about again?"

"Here!"

Amanda stuffed an origami folded piece of paper in his hand. She stood up from the table and walked out of the cafeteria, leaving William sitting there, alone. His confusion had overtaken all his senses, including his ability to inner dialog because he spoke aloud

CHAPTER 4

his next thoughts, "What the hell was that all about?"

William looked up at the clock behind the steel cage on the aqua colored tile wall and saw that he had fifteen minutes left during his lunch period. Whatever message was on that triangle shaped, folded sheet of paper, William readied himself to receive it.

While he started to deconstruct the paper labyrinth, he began putting the pieces of the puzzle together. Starting with Amanda's line of questioning, like a police detective interrogating a witness, her frustration over his short rebuttal, and finally, the aggressive nature in which she delivered the mysteriously folded note. William was naive to the ways of the female, but this was too obvious to ignore. Amanda no longer wanted to be just friends. She wanted the rumors spoken by their classmates to be true, and she wanted to be William's girlfriend.

Taking a deep breath, he continued to unfold the complex form of communication. He began to worry he would make a wrong move and accidentally tear it, but his caution paid off. The paper note, now unfolded, remained intact. Gathering the courage to look down and read it shock and surprise filled William. There was no long epic tale woven through paragraphs of a profession of love. No poetry, no emotional sonnets or lyrics to love songs, just four simple words:

DO YOU LIKE ME?

William's heart began to pound faster and with more intensity than he had ever experienced in his life. He could feel his heart beating in his ears. His face got hot and red. His stomach began to churn with an uneasy feeling. He was sitting but yet uncomfortable. His emotions and feelings ran the gamut. On the one hand, a relationship with Amanda was what he had always wanted, from that first day in German class, but, on the contrary, it was almost exactly what he didn't want. Amanda had compromised the status quo. Could they ever continue to be friends no matter what his answer to that question scribed on that paper was?

The answer was of course "yes." William did like Amanda, a lot. He thought about her all the time, would spend full classes fixated on the nape of her neck, wondering what would happen if he leaned forward and kissed her there. He went home and lay in bed thinking about her and replaying his daily interaction with her over and over in his mind until he fell asleep.

The counterpoint hung over his head like a dark cloud of rain, just waiting for the worst time possible to dump its contents. He ran through the possible scenarios. What would his friends say? What would his parents say? What would his brother say? In the adult world, concerns like this never surface, but in the complex dramatic world of thirteen-year-old kids, other people's perception was the driving force in all significant decisions.

He took the note, folded it back up. He could never do the fold justice. His origami folding skills were cave drawings to her Renaissance works of art. He knew that it was impossible for anyone in the room to find out what was on that sheet of paper. He couldn't help looking around that cafeteria and feel the eyes of his classmates piercing through him, judging him as if asking him, "Well, do you like her or not?"

William needed time to sort all this out. Moving to this level was a huge step for him, was he ready for a girlfriend?

The next day William did all he could do to avoid running into Amanda before their predestined meeting time, their German class. William figured he could even stall in that class since talking was always forbidden, so in reality, he had until his seventh-period lunch before he had to face the questioning eyes of Amanda.

German class started on cue, as it always had, William arriving early and Amanda arriving late. The palms of William's hands began to sweat, and his pulse quickened as Amanda walked in and took her regular seat right in front of him. Something was odd about her entrance, she didn't even look at William, she didn't look at anyone, just straight to her seat, not saying a word. William was just waiting for her to turn around and ask him something, anything, but she didn't. The silence from her was worse than the question she asked through her pen and paper the previous day. Why was Amanda not acknowledging him? Was she mad at him? A million thoughts raced inside William's head. They ranged from the logical, "Maybe she was just embarrassed." To the illogical, "Maybe she can read my mind and can tell how uncomfortable I am with this."

When the bell rang signifying the end of class Amanda stood up grabbed her backpack. She turned to William and just said, "I'll meet you at lunch, I'll be a few minutes late."

William had a barrage of questions he wanted to ask her but instead settled on the simple reply of, "OK."

William sat by himself at the table in the corner of the cafeteria and waited for Amanda to arrive, she never did. In fact, she didn't appear for the next two days. A feeling of confusion and worry came over William, and he contemplated his course of action. He didn't know where she lived, he didn't know her phone number, he had no way to contact her outside the school walls.

His worry was reaching action taking status when on the third day Amanda showed up back at school. Not waiting for German class she hunted William down in the hallway and grabbed him sending him jumping out of his skin with a shriek of terror.

"Ha! Scared you!" Amanda teased.

"Where the hell have you been?" William asked, still breathing heavy from the fright.

Amanda looked down, "I was sick, but I'm OK now."

"What was wrong with you?" Asked William.

"Nothing serious, so what did I miss in German?" Amanda asked, making an apparent attempt to change the subject.

William followed her lead and allowed her to execute the subject change.

"Nothing," He offered.

"Cool, I got to run to class, I'll see you later," She proclaimed before running off down the hallway.

William had always heard about the mysteries of the female species, but this was the first time he encountered it. More than willing to put the odd behavior of Amanda behind him he shrugged and continued with his day.

German class rolled around again, and when Amanda showed up she plopped herself down at her desk turned around and said, "Hey Will, so that note I wrote you the other day? You can just forget about it. It's no big deal."

Then she spun around again. William was more confused than ever now. Does this mean he wouldn't have to invent some elaborate story to explain that yes he did like her, a lot? That he was so afraid of the idea of having a girlfriend that he would never want to be her boyfriend? He had no idea how he was going to sell that idea, so avoiding the topic entirely worked out perfect for him.

William trying to act the part of disappointment answered her with a simple, "Oh, OK if that's what you want."

"Yes, that's what I want right now. Thanks, Will, I knew you would understand."

The rest of the day carried on like any other day, they shared their lunch period together and talked about whatever was on their mind, except that note. It always stayed in the back of William's mind, what did he come so close to getting? Amanda was carrying on with a normal conversation, and William would just stare at her, looking like he was listening but all he had on his mind was that note and what it all meant. He did like her; he loved her. It was different though it was more grown up, not a typical thirteen-year-old crush. He wished he had the knowledge and vocabulary to express this to her. He wanted to know, was it returned? Was that note just a reaction? Was she just going through the motions? Was she looking to get involved in some relationship with the opposite sex out of peer pressure? Was it a poorly thought out plan of attack to address a simple school girl crush? Had he been already replaced in her heart with the latest teen heartthrob from the next great TV show aimed at your typical suburban adolescent girl? Is that all he was?

He would never know for sure, and for now, he would have to be content just being Amanda Flores best friend, a title he would wear with pride.

CHAPTER 5

William had a summer birthday, so he was always one age number behind most of his grade. He turned thirteen in August, and when eighth grade started, he was the same age as most of the kids in his class. As the school year continued, everyone jumped up to fourteen leaving William behind in his age thirteen group. His young age always made him feel left behind; he had done all the math equations in his head already. He would be the last to get his driver's license, the last to get to see an R-Rated movie, and the last to be able to buy alcohol.

Things started moving at a rapid pace for William and his cast of friends. Seventh grade gave way to the summer vacation with little fanfare. Like every other kid on Long Island, William's summer was always filled with activity but never getting anything done. The boys spent their days shagging fly balls, swimming in Kenny's oval shaped above ground pool or playing Stickball against the red brick wall of the elementary school.

Every activity ended the same way. The boys, sitting on the curb in front of the 7-Eleven drinking Big Gulps and talking about the things thirteen-year-old boys will talk about, sports, cars, cartoons and most significant of all, girls.

The end of the summer vacation came the same time every year, but it still always seemed to sneak up on the boys like that pesky Jack-In-The-Box that still gave a start to the most seasoned crank turner. The last day of this prized hiatus had arrived, and the boys had taken up residence in their normal spot on the curb. William was sitting on the curb while Kenny was laying on the grass behind him; Jason Cosimo was standing above them like a giant shade tree.

Cosimo broke protocol and deviated from the traditional group approved topics, "McCabe, what was the story with you and that girl last year?"

"There was no story," William answered, "We were just friends, that's all."

Cosimo always reaching to find the limit of what was appropriate and then stepping beyond it asked, "You boink her?"

Kenny, still laying in the grass with his eyes closed absorbing the sun let out a chuckle, "Boink?"

"Yeah," Cosimo replied, "You know, do it, sex?"

William showing his age and his lack of knowledge with the opposite sex blurted out, "Eww, that's gross Cosimo."

Kenny offered up his own sage advice, "Actually William it's not gross. I hear it's supposed to be the best thing in the world. I for one can't wait until I find a girl who will let me do sex with her."

"'Have' sex you imbecile, not 'do' sex," Cosimo corrected.

"Whatever, as long as I get to do it," Kenny continued.

William was happy that the interrogation shifted away from his and Amanda's relationship and onto Kenny's misuse of prepositions.

Cosimo, still standing, began to command his friends like a General about to enter battle, "So tomorrow is the first day of school, what's the plan?"

"Plan?" Kenny asked.

"Are we just meeting at the bus stop like we always do or should we rendezvous at McCabe's house, which is the halfway point?" Cosimo posed.

"Cosimo, does it matter? You never sit by us anyway, you always just go to the back of the bus," William pointed out.

"Yeah, but this year we are eighth graders, we are the senior level students at the school, no more sneaking into the back seat, we own the back seat. Let the punk seventh graders sit up front," Cosimo stated, delivering an inspirational speech.

"Cosimo, it's eighth grade, it's no different from seventh grade. In fact, none of this matters until we get to High School. That's where life begins for us," William noted.

Still laying in the grass with his eyes closed facing the sun Kenny added, "He's right," Feeling outnumbered Cosimo agreed with the other two boys, eighth grade was just dress rehearsal for the real show, High School.

Just as the friends predicted, eighth grade was an exact clone of the seventh grade and passed like a high-speed train flying through a European countryside. William and Amanda continued their friendship. They only shared the one class together that year, German. William began making more time for his guy friends but always kept a special place set aside for Amanda. She never spoke of the note she gave him that day, and he never felt the need to bring it up. They both lived content keeping it pushed into the back corner of their minds.

At one point, Amanda started dating some other eighth-grade guy that William had never seen before. He would pass them in the hallway; she would always say hi to him, but with her hand interlocked with someone else's, William never felt comfortable returning the greeting. It wasn't as if he had any animosity toward her, after all, he was the one who let her go. He was the one content not to mention the note or never answering the question it asked.

Fall had passed and brought winter with it. Soon the snow melted, and the spring temperatures began to ease in. It was one of these unseasonably warm days that William went for a walk outside in the courtyard after he finished his lunch. He needed some time to himself. Life was moving so fast for him right now, so he made a point of inserting these little checkpoints from time to time to just slow life down and reassess his progress. The blacktop paved courtyard outside the cafeteria was legal grounds for students who finished their lunch early and wanted some outside time. Usually, an impromptu stickball game would form if Mr. Nelson, the baseball coach, were around to serve as the designated pitcher. Today was not one of those days, so the area regularly reserved for the game was now an open space for socializing. William walked through the makeshift stickball field and continued to the far corner where a bank of garbage dumpsters lived. These dumpsters served as the territorial border for students on lunch break, roaming past this invisible line was grounds for detention. William was about to turn around when he saw an unattended backpack leaning up against the side of the end dumpster. He figured a student left it behind on accident, and he was going to do his civic duty for the day and return it to the lost and found. William walked just beyond the boundary to retrieve it. He figured no disciplinarian would hold him guilty of extending the legal limits of the outside courtyard if it were for a good cause. He reached the abandoned satchel and bent down to pick it up; that's when he got struck in the gut. It wasn't a real punch from a fist, but it might as well have been. Around the backside of the line of dumpsters, he saw Amanda with her face locked in a violent exchange of lips and tongues with her unknown boyfriend.

CHAPTER 5

The sight was a figurative punch of course, but still, William felt the wind knocked out of him. Struggling to regain his breathing he hit his knee on the side of the dumpster. The sound startled Amanda and her partner in kissing crime. They turned to look in the direction of the noise, but it was too late. William had executed a hasty escape, avoiding detection.

The next day in German class William avoided making eye contact with Amanda hopeful she wouldn't talk to him and force him to display the anger and hurt he had inside. He was rational enough to understand that he had no cause to be angry at her. She professed her interest in him a long time ago; William did not reciprocate it. She did her part; he was the one that failed. She was free to pursue any relationship she wanted, with anyone she saw fit. Amanda was acting within her social rights. All this made sense to William, his rational mind could process it and make peace with it, but his emotional mind was angry and hurt and wanted to lash out at her.

Like clockwork, Amanda entered German class, she again was sitting in front of William, Herr Werner was content with letting the students choose their own seating, as long as they behaved themselves. Due to the small enrollment, the German foreign language brought, it was the same class members from last year.

Amanda grabbed her seat and swung around to face William, "Hey Will!"

"Hey," Was all he could gather the nerve to say back.

"What's wrong?" Amanda asked in a playful tone.

"Nothing is wrong," William's response was more rash than he wanted it to be.

"OK, if you say so," Amanda sensed something was wrong. It was clear that William didn't want to talk to her about it or anything else. She just turned around in her seat and focused on Herr Werner's German lesson for the day.

William's anti-social behavior towards Amanda continued for the rest of the week and the week that followed. Amanda continued to give him space. She understood the importance of needing room to work through issues, she was still unaware that she was the cause of William's sour mood.

By the end of the second week, Amanda felt she needed to approach William and solve this mysterious behavior. After the final class had ended that Friday Amanda waited for William to exit the school, she stood vigilant, on guard awaiting his arrival. Her patience paid off. Shortly the back door of the school swung open, and William was walking out to his bus.

She stood in his path to stop him, "What has gotten into you lately?"

William avoiding eye contact answered, "Nothing is wrong, now please move or else I will miss my bus."

"I'm not moving until you talk to me, you will either have to push me out of the way or miss your bus."

She knew there was no way William would resort to any violence, especially toward her. He pleaded his case for her to move and continued his false assurance to her that nothing was bothering him. It didn't work. Amanda stood her ground until William could hear the engines of the line of buses pull away and grow faint in the distance.

Now angry William yelled at Amanda, "Look what you did! You made me miss my bus! What's the matter with me?"

"What's the matter with me? What's the matter with you, that's what I am trying to find out."

"I told you a million times, nothing is wrong with me, just drop it, OK?"

"Drop what William? What do you want me to drop?"

"Nothing, please, just stop I don't want to talk about it."

CHAPTER 5

"I'm not going to drop it, you are my best friend, and you don't want to speak to me anymore, I need to know why."

"I'm your best friend?" William yelled at her in an accusing tone, not so much as asking but looking for clarification.

"Yes, you are. You are the only person in this whole school who's opinion matters to me," Amanda's eyes started to moisten with tears, and her voice became shaky.

William's anger and hurt had reached a level he could no longer control. He blurted out, "I saw you! I saw you making out with that guy! Behind the dumpster, I saw it!"

A look of shock fell over Amanda, this was not at all what she expected to hear from him. She looked down at the ground, staring at her feet she just said, "Oh."

"That's all you have to say? 'Oh'? Who is he? Are you like in love with him?" Finally, William said something he hoped he would never say, "What about me? What about that note you wrote? I thought I meant something to you."

The tear build-up in Amanda's eyes started to intensify, one even broke free. Amanda avoided wiping it in fear that would bring attention to it. She thought if she just let it fall and run down her cheek William would never notice, but he did.

She finally spoke, "William, I'm not sure what you want me to say. You never replied to that note."

"You told me to forget it, and not to reply," William protested.

"I only said that because I could tell that the whole thing made you uncomfortable."

"It did make me uncomfortable," William confessed.

Amanda knocked back with a simple one-word question of her own, "Why?"

"Why?" William repeated, "Why? Because I didn't know how to react. I didn't know what to say. I have never had anything like that happen to me. I didn't know how to handle it."

Amanda was calm now, the yelling had ceased, "Do you know how to handle it now?"

"No. I don't," William admitted.

Amanda thought for a second and asked, "What if I gave that note to you for the first time right now, what would you say?"

"Yes," William answered.

"Yes?" Amanda repeated his answer in question form.

"Yes Amanda, I do like you. I just have no idea what that means. You are my best friend, I feel so comfortable around you. I can tell you anything. I never have to lie or make shit up just to impress you. I can talk about hockey one day and confess my secret love of Cher's music the next. You are everything I ever wanted for a best friend and all that could go away if we dated. One stupid fight over one stupid thing and we break up, and I never get you back as my best friend, ever. I would rather suffer from the pain of seeing you kiss a million other guys that aren't me than have a life that doesn't have my best friend Amanda in it."

Amanda took a minute to process everything she just heard. Finally, when William thought she was going to say something, she leaned forward and grabbed hold of William and hugged him so tight.

While holding him tight, she whispered in a soft voice low enough for only William to hear, "I missed you, I missed my best friend Will, don't ever do that again."

William liked having his friend back but was still confused on where they go from here. So he asked, "Now what?"

Amanda didn't answer right away, she was just as confused as William was. Finally, she spoke, "I don't know. I can't lose you as a friend. That much I do know. Let's just work on being friends, for now, if something more comes out of it, we just take it slow and be careful with each other's feelings. Deal?"

"Deal," William agreed.

There was a quiet reserve between the two friends for a few minutes. It was Amanda who finally broke the silence, "Wow, that was a quite the adult conversation, wasn't it?"

CHAPTER 6

The summer after eighth grade arrived with little fanfare just the previous ones had. The only difference for William and his friends was this was the last official summer before High School. The time the boys had together was dwindling down. They knew that as soon as High School ended the friends might begin the inevitable drift apart like two kayaks stuck in different currents.

Sticking with the German foreign language elective was a sure way William would have at least one class with Amanda. Their new arrangement was working out fine so far, in fact, William had started to take an interest in other female classmates, and a few female classmates began to take an interest in William. He was maturing, growing into his body. His voice was changing, and his body was filling out. He was always a tall kid, but now he was becoming less scrawny, he was putting on muscle tone. Little wisps of hair began to decorate his upper lip. No freshman ever realized how ridiculous this looked, and they all refused to start shaving in hopes that the thin segments of hair would blossom into a full-fledged mustache that would make Tom Selleck himself proud. This rapid growth of facial hair would never come to fruition, the hairs on the lip remained few, so few that one could count them by hand.

Along with the poor excuse of a mustache, the boys also began to grow something else on their faces, zits. The never ending battle with hormones and oily pubescent skin waged on. In spite of all the obstacles nature was throwing at William, he was able to maintain decent looks. He was quiet and shy, not the most social of kids and that is what stopped him from being popular. He possessed the looks to be one of the popular kids.

Getting back to school excited William. It wasn't that he enjoyed the workload, he was looking forward to seeing Amanda again after the summer hiatus. There was a new German teacher in High School, Mrs. Kraus, or Frau Kraus.

Sitting behind a desk located mid classroom William waited with bated breath for Amanda to enter that classroom door. He was still staring at the door when a voice rang from behind him, "Will!"

He turned and looked; it was Amanda's voice, but the person standing in front of him wasn't Amanda, not the awkward boyish girl with short hair he knew in Junior High School. This person standing before him had long beautiful curls of hair that cascaded off her head like a secret hidden waterfall in some remote exotic jungle. The body of the mysterious girl stood at least four inches taller than he remembered Amanda standing, although she still stood shorter than the majority of her female freshman counterparts. Her body was no longer a collection of straight lines of similar lengths; now it boasted a series of curves that intersected at every location like a complex wiring diagram. When William looked even deeper, he swore he even saw the slightest glimpse of eye makeup. The eyeliner accentuated the full brown, glassy circles that sat equidistant on either side of the cutest of button noses. The dead giveaway that the body standing in front of him did indeed belong to Amanda were those perfect, straight teeth. They were the same ones he noticed that first day she disrupted Herr Werner's class with her first of so many late arrivals. It was Amanda all right but in a different shell. William always thought she was attractive, but this was different. She would never reign supreme over the cheerleaders and popular girls, but she now had a look, a look that appealed to William. She was a woman, or at least on her way to becoming one, either way, she was on the road to adulthood, maybe even a few miles down it.

Sensing his confusion, Amanda asked, "What are you looking at Will?"

"I didn't even recognize you," He felt his voice crack mid-sentence.

"Yeah, I let my hair grow out. I hated that boy haircut my mother always made me get."

The reunion was short-lived, their new German teacher entered the room and told them all to sit, in German, when no one moved she knew she had her work cut out for her.

Amanda grabbed the open seat in front of William and immediately spun around to face him and proclaimed, "Just like old times, huh Will?"

William grunted an answer, it was more of a sound than a word, in any language. Amanda turned and pulled her hair to the side exposing the nape of her neck. The body was different, but it was still the same neck William looked at all throughout Junior High School. This body was more mature and more beautiful.

William whispered to himself, "This is going to be a long year."

CHAPTER 7

Freshman year was a good lunch year for William. He shared his fifth-period lunch with Kenny and Cosimo. This scheduling alignment made for a fun-filled and exhausting lunch period, usually never leaving William enough time to finish his meal.

The three friends showed up at different times and waited for the full reunion before securing a table. Once seated they began to compare their notes with each other about their classes and the High School experience as a whole. William was mid-sentence when Kenny broke in with an over exaggerated sense of urgency.

"Oh William, I forgot to tell you, guess who is in my Social Studies class?" Kenny asked.

"Ken, I have no idea, Andre The Giant?" William answered in a sarcastic tone.

"Andre the what? Wait, what are we talking about? No, there is no giant in my Social Studies class, why would you guess that?" A confused Kenny stumbled through his thought.

Cosimo and William always shared a laugh when it was at

Kenny's expense.

Kenny, giving up on trying to figure out the riddle just pressed on, "Your friend, Amanda. Man did she get cute."

This revelation stirred Cosimo from his staring contest with his ham sandwich, "The Flores Girl is cute now?"

"Yep, She has long hair now, and I think she got boobs," Kenny added.

"Jesus Ken, why do you have to say shit like that in front of me?" William pleaded.

Cosimo jumped in with his addition, "Damn McCabe, you kinda screwed the pooch on that one. You should have nailed her when you had the chance, now she will never want to fuck you."

"Cosimo, you are a dick. We are just friends, nothing more. I saw her already, and yes she looks a little different. But it's no big deal," William tried his best to sound convincing.

Cosimo sensing William's cover up called him out on it, "Bull! Shit! I call bullshit. If you say it's 'no big deal' then you wouldn't mind if I lay the pipe to her, would you?"

The question was again rhetorical, and William was not about to answer it. After a few seconds, William offered a reply that he thought for sure would shut Cosimo up.

"It wouldn't matter Cosimo; she wouldn't let you within five feet of her."

Cosimo quick to retort, "Well, it's a good thing I have a six-foot penis."

William once again failed at outdoing Jason Cosimo.

The banter between the friends was a standard ritual. To the stranger, one would think William and Kenny hated Cosimo and vice versa. The truth was they had grown almost to enjoy hanging around with him. For all his flaws, he made them laugh. Each boy played a role in the unique dynamic they had. Kenny and William

CHAPTER 7

were the better friends, where Cosimo was more of a pest. Now he took on more of a court jester role.

The conversation William had with his two friends was resonating over and over in his head during the next few days. He kept looking at Amanda a little too long, and sometimes she would catch him and call him on it. William would always play it off as if he was just tired and "looking into space." If William wanted to keep his best friend, he would have to learn to snap out of it.

A strange turn of events unfolded one late fall afternoon that brought Amanda into a different light for William. A light that would change the way he looked at her forever.

Frau Kraus had split the class up into groups of two to practice basic conversation skills. She allowed the class to pick their partner. As it had become custom, William and Amanda teamed up. They were running through an exercise when Amanda kept forgetting the German word for "lunch."

William, thinking he was playful, finally gave up and said, "Come on stupid, you know this."

The smile immediately retreated from her face which was growing red and fierce, and she exploded with a never before seen fury, "Fuck you, William!"

She threw her textbook at him almost hitting him square in the head, grabbed her bag and just walked out the door. Frau Kraus' calls to her went unheard or at least ignored. Frau Kraus looked at William as if expecting an explanation, but he had none.

He pitched a deal to Frau Kraus, "Let me go get her, see if I can talk to her and figure out what I did."

"You have five minutes," She commanded.

William grabbed his bag; he wasn't sure if he was going to make Frau's five-minute deadline and didn't want to risk having to come back to the class for his things.

PART ONE

He exited the classroom and scanned both ends of the hallway. At first glimpse it seemed empty, it wasn't until his second scan he saw two feet sticking out from behind a row of lockers. He walked down, and when he entered the clearance, he could see Amanda sitting on the floor with her head in her hands. He slowly approached her and stood over her for a minute, hoping she would acknowledge him first before he would have to say anything. She didn't.

"Hey, are you OK?" William was careful.

"Don't ever call me that," Amanda still had a terse tone.

"Call you what?"

"Stupid, don't you ever call me that again. Not you, anyone but you. You never get to call me that. I need you to promise me," Amanda lifted her head from her hands and looked William in the eyes, so deeply he felt her looking into his soul.

"William McCabe, I need you to promise me that you will never call me stupid again."

"Yeah, I promise, Amanda I'm sorry I was kidding around, I didn't mean it."

"I know you didn't mean it. You have to realize that you don't understand everything about me, and you also don't understand the important role you play in my life. You're different than they are, I need you to be different than they are, that's why you can never call me that. OK?"

"OK," William was feeling confused but couldn't help to feel a small sense of relief that Amanda was no longer angry at him, at least he didn't think she was.

He slid down the wall into the area next to her. She rested her head on his shoulder.

"You mean a lot to me, I need you to know that," Amanda finally spoke.

"You mean a lot to me too."

CHAPTER 7

The two sat in silence for a while. William still had a million questions about her outburst, and he weighed them carefully in his mind. Should he ask them now? Should he wait? She had called him "dumbass" a million times, how was that any different? He was still contemplating his best course of action when Amanda spoke.

"Sorry I threw the book at your head."

"It's OK, you missed."

"William?" Amanda sounded vulnerable, "You are my best friend, you know that, right?"

William could feel his heart race; they had shared the "best friend" proclamation to each other many times before, but this one sounded different. This one rang of honesty and her need for a higher level of closeness with him. His adolescent mind couldn't quite grasp all this yet. Amanda was so far beyond him in maturity. She understood the love between two people was more than making out behind garbage dumpsters or holding hands in crowded school hallways. She realized she loved William, for him, for his friendship, his honesty, and his loyalty.

The days that followed were good ones; Amanda was feeling particularly close to William. She would seek him out in the hallway and walk him to his classes. She spent more time with him than she did with her boyfriend, which wasn't much of a relationship William figured out.

William enjoyed the attention and extra time Amanda awarded him and had no intention of messing it up. He still had questions about her outburst but was loyal to her wishes. In time he hoped she would offer the full explanation of her actions without him having to ask her first. It didn't matter right now; the two were close. They even spent one afternoon when the sun was unusually bright in the sky walking home together. Their bond was growing, and they both enjoyed each other's company. They started to establish a schedule. They would plan to meet up between specific classes if the time allowed. They would accompany each other to their classes, depending who had the closer geographical location dictated who would host the walk.

Amanda was spending so much time with William that her boyfriend, in a jealous fit, broke up with her. William only found out about it a week after it happened when Kenny, his resident school gossip purveyor, told him during lunch. William understood why Amanda didn't mention this to him; they had an agreement. Talking about other relationships was off limits, forbidden. He understood it, but he was still perplexed. She hadn't broken at all from her cheery demeanor, and this happened a week ago. In fact, she didn't seem fazed by anything during their time together.

It was early winter, and the class day started as it always had. Nothing in the air to signify anything was different. There was no reason for William or anyone to suspect that today should be any different from any day that proceeded it. They would have been wrong.

With the air of the book throwing incident still lingering like a long since eaten apple pie that still leaves the faintest of aromas in the kitchen, Amanda entered the classroom. She didn't march in and slam her books down on the desk. Amanda didn't spin her head around almost slapping William in the face with her long curly locks. She didn't do any of her usual routines. She trudged in, placed her books on her desk using slow and careful movements, took her seat. She was silent, not saying a word to anyone, not even William.

William leaned forward and whispered in her ear, "Are you OK?"

Not turning her head Amanda answered, "I'm OK Will, just not having a good day, that's all. I just need some space, sorry."

"It's OK, I understand," William was lying, he didn't understand at all.

CHAPTER 7

This drastic mood change lasted the rest of the week and two days into the next week. In time Amanda returned to her cheerful fun loving self. William added this to his growing list of questions. One day he hoped all of his questions would get answered.

The school year continued to play out never deviating from the script. The typical cast of characters playing their natural roles. The mundane days began to melt into each other. It was hard for any of the students to know what day it currently was. It was a series of uneventful events followed by more routine events. The students all wished they were somewhere else, or sometime else. Anything was better than being a Freshman in High School.

Amanda was her old self again. She never offered any explanation for her sudden and drastic mood change, and William was more than happy to put it behind them and keep moving forward. The book throwing incident was behind them now. William didn't dwell on it and gave up finding out exactly what happened that afternoon.

It was spring, and the change in Amanda occurred again, it came without warning and stayed a few days before once again leaving. Women were different then men, William knew this and understood it, but this was more confusing than he had ever anticipated. His confusion began to overtake his logic, and he did the most illogical thing he could have. He sought the advice of his two friends, Kenny Springer, and Jason Cosimo.

In the midst of their typical lunch comedy routine, William broke character and asked, "Hey guys, so there is this weird thing that Amanda does now and then."

Cosimo, always working dirty was the first to contribute, "You mean like some swirly thing with her tongue when it's down your throat? That's common man, just go with it. They say a girl who knows how to use her tongue when she gives you a French Kiss gives great blowjobs."

"Cosimo, come on! I'm serious," William contested.

Kenny, always the voice of reason, restored order, "What kind of weird thing?"

"I don't know; it's hard to explain. Every few months Amanda gets all weird, quiet and sad. Then after a few days, she is fine again."

Once again Cosimo digging to the bottom of the barrel offered his hypothesis, "Bleeding vagina, I read about this. Blood comes out of their vagina for like a month straight, and it messes with their moods."

"Cosimo, you are an idiot," Kenny chimed in, "What you are referring to has a name, it's the female menstruation cycle. It's a marvelous wonder of the human body. But where Jason's misinformation lies are in the length of the menstruation period, it's not a month; it's only for a few days. Besides, it's clear this isn't what is going on with Amanda, the cycle happens every twenty-eight days, and this sounds like it's a lot more infrequent."

Since Kenny's mother worked at the University Hospital, Kenny fancied himself as the resident medical expert on everything.

He punctuated his last medical entry with his signature, "It's a proven fact."

William left the cafeteria with more questions than he had when he arrived. One of those questions was, "Why am I friends with those dolts?" A riddle he asked himself often.

The mystery of Amanda would remain unsolved for the rest of the school year. Freshman year came and went almost as fast as the summer vacation that followed it.

CHAPTER 8

There weren't many jobs William could legally have at his age, so his father had to secure him a way to make a little extra money over the summer. Mr. McCabe used an undisclosed acquaintance to procure some mild form of employment for his son. William's services were loaned out to be the official lawn maintenance provider for an elderly gentleman who lived on the affluent north shore of Long Island. The man's name was Mr. Benjamin Bauer.

Mr. Bauer was a seventy-six-year-old man who had a large aging house that sat stubbornly in the center of an even more aging plot of poorly landscaped land. It was hard to imagine at first glance that this estate was once considered beautiful. When you looked hard enough you could almost see that the old girl still had some life in her, all she wanted was a little love and care.

Every Saturday morning William would be driven to Mr. Bauer's house for his weekly ritual of taking the surprisingly modern ride-on mower out of Mr. Bauer's garage and firing it up. His job was simple; he was to bring the overgrown blades of grass that adorned the property down to a length that the neighbors considered appropriate and reasonable.

It was an easy enough job that could have been completed in half the time it took him. Mr. Bauer made a habit of coming out of his house to flag down William mid-mow to offer him a cold glass of iced tea and encourage him to take a break. After about the third time this interruption occurred, William began to realize that good old Mr. Bauer had more interest in some companionship and conversation than he had in actually getting his lawn cut. Mr. Bauer's wife passed away five years prior, and all the Bauer children were moved out and had families of their own leaving Mr. Bauer in need of some company, he wanted to talk to someone. He spent most of his time lonely and bored, glued to the old faded high-back woven fabric chair that sat directly in front of the television. The television was relatively new in comparison to everything else inside the Bauer house. It had obviously been a gift from one or all of the children to help alleviate the guilt they felt for not spending any time with their lonely father.

William enjoyed listening to Mr. Bauer tell stories about his life. Benjamin Bauer was a lifelong military man and took up arms to fight in World War II as a First Lieutenant while in his early 30's. He spun fascinating tales of his experiences fighting overseas. William wasn't entirely sure that all of his stories were true, but he liked hearing them anyway.

One particular hot July day, while William was sitting at the small kitchen table sipping his iced tea, Mr. Bauer began to tell one of his stories. He had a flare for the dramatic and spoke like he was reading for a movie role.

"It was January 1945, Belgium, we had just broken through the thick forest at Bastogne. It was a hellish fight, I lost a lot of good men in those woods, a lot of good men. Anyway, we reached Bastogne and camped the night. The next morning I awoke to a beautiful sunrise, I remember thinking to myself this is going to be a good day. I was wrong, dead wrong, the Krauts bombed the shit out of us, but I survived so I guess it was a good day after all."

This is the way Mr. Bauer's stories went. As the summer wore on and neared its inevitable end, William knew his days and talks with Mr. Bauer would come to an end as well. On William's last day, Mr. Bauer again called him in for some iced tea and again spun a wild tale of his European adventures during the war.

"February 1945, somewhere in the forests of Germany, I took my men on patrol through some still heavily contested areas when we came across something we had never seen before. It was a large disk propped up at an angle facing the sky. It stood alone in this clearing about six kilometers from the nearest town. The thing must have been ten stories high. I had no idea what to make of it, so I called it into the top brass. They told us to guard it, and they would send some 'experts' out at first light to check it out. So me and this young private, what was his name? Jones? James? It was something with a 'J.' Nice kid, a Catholic, he would eventually get blown to bits as we got closer to Berlin. Anyway, so as I was saying, this kid and I, we sit there all night, and the thing of it was, we were sweating our balls off. It was sub-zero temps, snow falling from the sky and here we were this kid and me, and we weren't cold at all, we were hot. Then I start to have this funny taste in my mouth like I'm sucking on a screw or something metal. Wouldn't you know it, the fillings in my teeth were melting! I kid you not. We were guarding some Kraut microwave dish, and the heat radiating off of it was cooking us alive! I couldn't believe it. That's the God's honest truth."

Another fascinating story delivered by Mr. Bauer. He never disappointed William. Once he had ended his latest addition to the summer-long Chronicles of Mr. Bauer, he sat quietly looking down at his coffee.

William spoke first, "Thanks again for the iced tea Mr. Bauer. Guess I should get back to the lawn."

Mr. Bauer looked out the window to his expansive yard and squinted for a while. He finally broke his silence, "Kid, forget the lawn today. You worked hard all summer, and I hoped you learned something about an honest day's work and making an honest wage and all that shit. There is something else I want to show you."

He stood up from the table and walked into the adjacent room. William stayed seated at the table. It wasn't made clear whether or not he was supposed to stay and wait for Mr. Bauer to bring him what he wanted to show him. Or maybe he was meant to follow him into the other room to see this mystery thing.

William wouldn't have to wonder for too long. The faint voice of Mr. Bauer could be heard talking in the next room. He wasn't aware that William didn't follow him and was speaking to him as if he was directly behind him. William jumped up and quickly joined him in the next room, and Mr. Bauer was never the wiser.

"You see this kid?" Mr. Bauer asked picking up an old sepia toned photograph not short on scratches. The photo was of a man, sitting in an Army Jeep with piles of cement rubble lying amidst the background. "This is me, August 1944. We just liberated Paris, and this is what it looked like. Damn Krauts bombed it to Hell. But she was still there, the old girl held up. They are stronger than us, don't forget that. Women, they are always tougher than men, they always bounce back."

Mr. Bauer's voice began to trail off as he spoke that last part. William understood why when he picked up the faded photograph of himself and his bride taken on their wedding day.

He composed himself and spoke again, "She was beautiful, smart and she loved me, go figure."

CHAPTER 8

He turned and faced William, "There aren't many perfect ladies out there, you're a young kid, you think you have your whole life to find one, but you don't. Time sneaks up on you. When you find that one, you go get her. Even if you have to run and chase her down, you go get her, never let her get away."

William let Mr. Bauer's words resonate with him for a second, then spoke, "Thanks, Mr. Bauer. For everything. You are a great guy, and I really enjoyed working for you this summer."

Mr. Bauer smiled, "It's been a pleasure having you here."

He gazed out the window at the lawn again and said, "The old girl hasn't looked that good in a long time," He paused, "Maybe it's time I put her up for sale, let someone else get some use from her. Maybe it's time she makes some other family happy."

Mr. Bauer enjoyed talking about his beautiful estate as if it were a living woman. He held out his hand for William to shake it and when he did Mr. Bauer had a folded up bill in his palm than he subtly slid into William's hand. When William looked into his hand he saw the face of Ben Franklin, Mr. Bauer just gave him a hundred dollar bill.

William started to protest, "Mr. Bauer… I Can't"

"Shut up kid; you've earned it."

Mr. Bauer, a decorated war hero, turned lonely old man passed away later that winter.

CHAPTER 9

Jason Cosimo started the Sophomore year with a declaration, "This is the year Jason Cosimo loses his virginity!"

He was so sure of it that he announced it to everyone sitting on the bus awaiting transport to the school. He even grabbed hold of William and Kenny and made an even more robust proclamation.

"In fact, this is the year we all get laid, think positive boys. We will all lose our virginity together. Wait, that didn't come out right. You know what I mean," The faux pas embarrassed Cosimo for a few seconds. It was rare to see Cosimo get fed a slice of humble pie, William and Kenny savored it while they could. It was going to be short-lived.

It was an absurd claim for him to make, he had no prospects that could assist him with this goal. Cosimo barely talked to any member of the opposite sex, ever. Kenny had done a little better in the complex world of girls, but it was William that fared the best. It had nothing to do with his charm or witty personality, he had little of both, it was more based on the perception that he and Amanda were a couple. In High School, nothing made a boy seem more desirable to girls than the idea that he was with someone else. High School girls were catty and very competitive, girls would flirt with their best friend's boyfriend all the time.

The rumors often spread that Amanda and William were a couple and sophomore year didn't do much to rectify that false report. They shared four classes that year and would be, for the most part, inseparable. They were reunited for lunch, once again and their social bond continued to grow.

Summer's end brought with it a series of changes in both William and Amanda. William began to find interest in other girls, letting some of the emotional grips Amanda held on his heart slip away. He touched his toes in the water that contained those "other fish" that he heard talked about so often. His first catch in that sea was a girl named Beth Glaus, she was a short fair-skinned girl with golden hair that shone like a teasing sun filling the sky on a cold winter day. She was physically beautiful, more beautiful than William thought anyone interested in him should be. She was perfect as far as anyone else could see, but William found a few fundamental flaws in her. Beth wasn't fun to hang around with, she wasn't that great to talk to, she lacked any personality. Beth was dull and void of any sense of adventure and excitement. In other words, she wasn't Amanda. William found enough other reasons to maintain a relationship with Beth. Most of those reasons had to do with the jealousy and envy his friends exhibited at his ability to "land a hottie" as they so often put it.

The new year brought a change to Amanda as well. It was subtle at first. If William and Amanda didn't share an unusual amount of classes, he might not have even noticed it. Amanda was beginning to show signs of slight disrespect for anyone in a position of authority. She was still sweet and charming to William, and to most of her friends, she was always loyal to them and their friendship.

William first witnessed the change one afternoon in their math class. Amanda occupied the desk immediately adjacent to William's right side. They always made as much of an effort as they could to sit close to each other, and when classes did not restrict them to assigned seating, they took full advantage of it. The school year was still in its infancy and teachers, and students were all engaged in a playful bout of getting to know each other's limits and boundaries. Mr. Christiansen, the math teacher, was very unversed in the world of high school politics. He had a profound almost obsessive love for mathematics and wanted so desperately to spread his passion to the young sponge-like minds of the adolescents in his class. Mr. Christiansen gave each class 100% of his time and attention in the space between the bell chimes dictating the start and end of his class. Mr. Christiansen wasn't much for discipline; he believed that students would act the age you treat them. If regularly treated like elementary school kids they would act accordingly. His philosophy worked for the majority of students.

Amanda walked in before the bell chime that signified the start of class, she grabbed her seat next to William and immediately turned and spoke.

"You will never believe what I just found out," She exclaimed.

"What?" She had gotten William's attention.

"Frau Kraus, she was at Woodstock, she was a hippie!" Amanda revealed as if she was sitting on some secret plans for a new destructive weapon.

Somewhere in the background of Amanda's dispelling of the secret life of Frau Kraus the bell rang to signal the official start of Mr. Christiansen's mathematics class. Unaware or uncaring of the call to surrender to Mr. Christiansen's time, Amanda continued with her story.

"You think she still smokes pot at night? I bet she does. I can't believe she was a full-fledged hippie!" She spoke with wild-eyed amazement.

"Amanda! The class has begun, please be quiet," Mr. Christiansen interrupted.

"Wait, I'm almost finished telling my story," Amanda snapped back.

The ambient buzz that floated around the class came to a screeching halt like a car locking up its breaks to avoid an accident.

"Excuse me?" Mr. Christiansen answered back almost immediately.

Not missing a beat in this back and forth battle of control, Amanda replied, "I said give me a minute, I'm telling Will a story."

William could feel himself slide down behind his desk as if making himself those few inches shorter in stature would render him invisible. At this point, he was no longer making eye contact with Amanda.

It was Mr. Christiansen's time to lob back, "Amanda, I do not want to have to ask you again."

"Then don't!" Amanda now in full disrespect mode.

The verbal exchange would have gone on all afternoon like a tennis match between two pros each executing their volley over the net. Mr. Christiansen eventually ended the competition by excusing Amanda from the classroom and invited her to step outside with him, to which she complied. As she stood up, Mr. Christiansen added one more serve.

"Bring your stuff with you."

It was evident to everyone in attendance that Amanda would not be coming back for round two, she fought a good fight, but eventually the authorities won.

While Mr. Christiansen and Amanda remained in the hallway

outside the classroom debating topics known only to them a hushed buzz fell about the room. Kids loved seeing confrontation that did not involve them. It was a spectator sport, even more so when there was a teacher involved.

The door to the classroom reopened, and everyone waited with bated breath, who would emerge victoriously, all the money was on Mr. Christiansen, but could Amanda pull off the underdog upset of the year? Would she return lifting Mr. Christiansen's scientific calculator aloft in victory? Perhaps they would both return, reaching some middle ground peaceful truce. Within seconds the door reopened, revealing all.

Alas, the smart money wins. Mr. Christiansen reappeared solo, no Amanda in sight. The underdog victory or peaceful truce would have to stay in the Hollywood scripts for today.

"Ok class, we have had enough disruptions for today. Let us continue with today's lesson," Mr. Christiansen successfully attempted to restore order.

A hushed tone immediately fell over the remaining students still sitting in their desks. They were all afraid there would be some fallout from the Amanda incident. Did it put Mr. Christiansen in a sour mood for the rest of the day? Did her outburst and consequent punishment count as a warning for the remainder of the group? Would the rest of the students be starting with one less warning today because of the actions of one fellow classmate? That hardly seemed fair or diplomatic. Mr. Christiansen was a math teacher; he dealt with numbers and facts and figures. He wasn't a political science or social studies teacher who understood the policies of diplomacy and democracy.

None of this mattered, of course; the remaining students were on their best behavior for the rest of the class. The lesson taught and learned that day had nothing to do with fractions and whole numbers it had everything to do with Mr. Christiansen's tolerance threshold.

Class ended, same as it began, with the sound of the electronic bell. The students gathered their belongings and headed for the door. The movement of students passing through the doorway began to slow down, and this caused some congestion behind them. As William neared the door, he could see that everyone exiting the door did a double take to their right, and when his turn came, he saw why. Amanda was standing there outside the door, waiting. When she saw William, she smiled and picked herself up off the wall in which she was leaning on.

"Will! Can you believe that asshole?" She began.

William was not going to be taking her side on this one, "What the hell was that?"

"What?" Amanda tried to play it off as normal, "He was a dick."

"A dick? He is the teacher; the class began, he told you to be quiet. Amanda this is all standard procedure in a classroom. You were the one in the wrong, not him."

"Will, you're siding against me? I thought you were my friend," Amanda replied in a more hushed tone.

"I am your friend, and that's why I'm telling you this stuff. You can't do shit like that. You will get in trouble."

"So what Will? So what if I get in trouble? What fucking difference does it make? I was talking, and he interrupted me, he was the asshole; he was wrong not me. Just because he is an adult doesn't mean he always gets to be right. It's common courtesy not to interrupt someone speaking. I was right he was wrong. Besides, he gave me the classwork; I just had to do it in the hallway. It's not like I got detention or anything. But, I'm not allowed to sit next to you anymore. He says I talk too much to you. He's a dumbass."

William took a minute to process everything before speaking,

"Amanda, just don't do anything like that again, Ok?"

"Fine, let's just go to lunch."

None of this seemed to faze Amanda at all. She was more than content to continue her day and her career at the high school as if none of this occurred.

CHAPTER 10

William brought a handmade, hand packed lunch to school almost every day. On rare occasions he would buy a school lunch, mostly on pizza or grilled cheese day, those were his favorites. Amanda, on the other hand, purchased the school lunch every day, she never opted for the packed, bring your own lunch option. William saw the purchasing of the over processed meal from the school's cafeteria as a luxury, almost a delicacy. For this reason, he had the utmost envy of Amanda's lunch-buying habit, and would often lament about how lucky she was.

The school cafeteria was always loud with the constant clatter of plastic trays, and the volume of each student turned up a few too many levels. It was as if a day of deprived, loud, out of turn speaking needed to be rectified all within that forty-minute session. Speaking in a loud tone wasn't even good enough for most of the students, they had to resort to an all out yell.

William was waiting for Amanda at their usual table. It was nearest to the large plastic garbage pail on wheels that served as the communal dumping point for all the unwanted lunch remains. The table was always empty because most kids hated the awful stench that arose from the plastic beast of a barrel that stood ominously in the back of the cafeteria. The smell bothered William too, but he was willing to sacrifice one sense for another. Due to its secluded locale, it offered a luxury not found at any other table in the place, quiet. Amanda returned from the cafeteria kitchen with her turquoise tray filled with the most liberal definition of food one could imagine. The contents of the platter never mattered, the recipients of the food were not culinary experts, but a bunch of self-absorbed teenagers that never even noticed the object they were consuming.

She had one item on her tray that caught William's attention, a squeeze ice pop. On special occasions, the school found it within their budget to offer the treat for free to anyone brave enough to purchase a lunch. The treat otherwise cost seventy-five cents. Amanda knew that this particular frozen treat was a favorite of William's. She smiled at him when she saw his eyes locked on it. Either Amanda was going to give it to him, in a generous gesture, or she was going to be spiteful and use it for blackmail reasons. She must have read William's mind because as she approached the table, she put his concerns to rest.

"Yes, dumbass, it's for you," She teased.

William tried his best at playing dumb, "What?"

She didn't even grace his question with an answer. Instead, she threw the frozen goodness on the table in front of him.

When she sat down across from him, he thanked her. He again took the opportunity to tell her how lucky she was.

"I wish I could buy lunch every day," He said in a somewhat whining tone.

Amanda ignored William's complaint. He then followed it up with another whining statement, "You are lucky."

Amanda stopped eating, put her combination fork and spoon

utensil down and slowly looked up at him. There was a hint of anger in her eyes; it reminded William of the look she had given right before she threw the book at him in German class. He retraced his steps, had he called her "stupid" again without realizing it? Where did he go wrong? He quickly panned the contents of the table to make sure it was free of books or any other object that could serve as a projectile weapon. The only thing he saw was the tray, that turquoise tray; he quickly weighed how badly it would hurt if flung at his head, he cringed.

There would be no throwing of dishes or books. Amanda just calmly looked at him and said, "Don't talk like that."

Once again, William felt confused, "Say what?"

"That I'm lucky."

"Well, you are, you get to buy lunch every day."

Amanda reflected in thought before continuing, "Will, I want to share something with you that I have never told anyone else, ever. You are my best friend, and I don't want this getting around. OK?"

"OK," William confirmed.

She continued, "I buy lunch every day because I don't have parents that care enough about me to make me lunch. In fact, they don't care enough about me to make me breakfast or dinner either."

William remained confused; he could not fathom an existence where a parent did not supply any meals for their child. It was so far outside his realm of understanding. He wanted to be sympathetic, but he needed further clarification. So he kept the topic alive, even after everything in his gut told him to let it die a quiet and peaceful death.

"What do you mean?" He asked.

Amanda was also hoping he would let it die, and when he didn't, she figured since she had brought them down this road, it was near impossible to turn back around and take the safe road. She owed him a deeper explanation.

"Well, the thing is Will, my mom and that asshole she married, they don't do too much of anything. If I want anything, I have to do it myself. I get myself up in the morning; I make some toast for breakfast before heading out the door."

William ran a quick comparison of his regular morning routine to what Amanda just revealed to him. He began to ask the questions that would clearly outline the radical differences between their mornings.

"So your mom doesn't make sure you are up in the morning?"

"Nope."

"She doesn't have breakfast made or at least some cereal put out for you?"

"Nope."

"She doesn't ask about homework or tests or anything like that?"

Tiring of giving the same response Amanda made an attempt to sum it all up for William.

"My mother and that asshole are still in bed sleeping when I leave for school. She doesn't even know when I leave. In fact, they are both probably still sleeping in bed right now. If not they are planted on the couch in front of the TV with a bag a chips and smoking pot. They have no idea if I have a test, a quiz or homework. If I need anything signed by her, I sign it myself. She has never signed anything for me. No tests, progress reports or permission slips, this school has no idea what her signature looks like, making it easy for me, I didn't have to copy it, I could just make one up. I would love cereal, but we don't have milk in the house, ever. If we did, it would spoil, the idiots would leave it on the counter. The only thing we have is bread and a somewhat working toaster. I make toast for breakfast, and she sure as shit isn't making me lunch the night before and packing in a brown bag for me to take to school the next day. I buy lunch every day because, in her infinite wisdom, she realized that I qualify for the free lunch program. Bonus, she does shit, and the state feeds her kid at least one meal a day. I come home after school and go right to my room. I do my homework and then come out and pick at any scraps of food they might have accidentally left behind after feeding their faces. That is my day Will, that is how I eat. So you will have to excuse me when I get a little pissed off at you when you say, 'I'm lucky.' I look at your lunch there, your mom made that sandwich for you, with you in mind, packed the contents of that brown bag to fit your needs and wants. I'm sure breakfast and dinner are very much the same for you. Meals prepared for you by a woman who very much gives a shit about you and your nutritional needs. The reality here Will is that you are the lucky one, not me. My life sucks."

William was speechless. He knew he needed to say something but with such a delicate topic as this, it would have been so easy for his adolescent mouth to say the completely wrong thing. He did the only thing he could think to do; he looked down at his sandwich, half eaten, picked up the uneaten portion and lifted it slowly to Amanda in an offering of peace.

Amanda smiled and said, "Thanks, Will, I think I will take you up on that."

She took the sandwich half from William and bit into it. She tasted the love and care of a healthy family life. A nurturing that went into making that luncheon delight. Watching her pleasure, William felt pity and sorrow for her.

"Sorry," he whispered.

She immediately felt regret for making the only person who cared about her feel that sort of guilt; she spoke again, "Will, I'm sorry. That was too much to lay on you. It wasn't fair of me to tell you all of that. You have a good a life; you should never be ashamed of what you have. You deserve it all."

Sensing Amanda's discomfort in discussing this part of her life William steered the conversation away from the potential road hazard and back onto a safe path.

"Did you do Frau Kraus' homework?" He asked.

"Yeah, it was pretty easy," Amanda replied.

She was glad to see the conversation shift gears as well. It was a hard thing to verbalize. She was embarrassed by her mom and her stepdad. She often wondered why they couldn't be more like everyone else's parents. They never attended school functions, and they would never schedule a parent-teacher conference. They took no interest in Amanda or her life. The reality of her life was painful to dwell on. She did everything in her power to push the real world back into the corner recesses of her mind.

That was Amanda's home life, it was beyond broken, it was beyond fixing, it just was. She was a strong person and made a promise to herself every day that she would endure all of this, and she would be better because of it. She swore she would have children of her own and when she did she would cherish every minute of their lives. She would love them and care for them and provide for them in all the ways she was never cared for, loved for and provided for, her own life's success would be her ultimate redemption.

Later that night at the McCabe house a call had rung out from the kitchen to gather everyone for dinner. William was in his basement bedroom and immediately ceased with his homework assignment, pulled off his stereo headphones and darted up the stairs to the waiting meal prepared by his mother. Playing out the events of the day he took stock in his life, and all the complaints he issued about what his mother made for dinner seemed selfish and silly. He stared at his mother while she scooped the contents of the big cooking pot into the smaller serving dishes on the table. She then scooped the contents of the small serving dishes onto the plates of William and his brother. He was proud of this life, proud he had everything he had. He did feel guilty, though. Why had he been rewarded with so much? Why was his life so much different from Amanda's? She deserved it just as much as he did. He was confused but more than that; he was thankful.

"Thanks, mom," He professed to his serving mother.

"For what?" She had been a busy server to her family for so long that she never felt it warranted any level of "Thanks."

"For dinner, for breakfast, for making my lunch every day. It's a lot, and I never say thank you, so thank you," The words of appreciation flowed from William as effortlessly as the rainwater that ran alongside the curb in front of their house and into the storm drain that swallowed so many tennis balls.

"Oh dear, you are quite welcome. Are you angling for something?" His mother was suspicious of this unprovoked onset of politeness.

"No mom, I just realized how much you do and that maybe everyone doesn't get the same treatment as we do, that's all."

Kicking back into teenager mode William added, "Can't a guy thank his mom for dinner without getting the third degree?"

"Yes William, a guy can. Thank you for appreciating me and everything you have, now eat before it gets cold."

CHAPTER 11

The first warning bell of the day sounded, it meant that all the meandering students in the hallway had six minutes to get to their homeroom class. William was already at his Homeroom. He was standing outside his classroom, in the hall with his back leaned up against a row of lockers. He was facing Beth, as they jointly sent out the signal to the rest of the school that they were officially a couple. The ceremonial offering of William's school jacket to Beth was the marriage proposal of the High School couple. The jacket was to be worn by Beth during periods one through nine, after which it would be returned to William to not cause any stir with either his parents or Beth's. The presentation of class rings would not be until senior year; then they would replace the jacket as a symbol of togetherness.

When a girl was seen walking the halls with a jacket four sizes too big it was a symbol to all that she was unavailable, officially off the market. Clearly embroidered on the left side of the jacket front was the name of her suitor. Beth wore William's jacket like all the other girls did, sliding off the back of her shoulders, arms through the sleeves and the bottom snap fastened to keep it from falling off her back.

She stood abnormally close to him in the hallway, her face so close to his, he could see every detail of her pale skin. She always positioned herself close to his face, and her eyes would dart back and forth from his eyes to his lips. He could smell the minty aroma of the chewing gum that laid pressed between her back teeth. Her index fingers were hooked into the front belt loops of William's jeans to assure that he couldn't escape, he was like a dog on a leash. William awkwardly rested his hands on Beth's hips; he could tell that she was pleased with his offering of a public display of affection.

It was the last day of school before the Christmas holiday break. Beth was a fan of "baby-talk." William hated it.

Beth always ended her sentences with an upward inflection in her speech, making everything sound like a question, even if it wasn't.

"What am I going to do without my little wubsy bear?" Beth asked using a fake speech impediment for an additional cuteness effect.

William had no idea what a "Wubsy Bear" was, but he was never going to inquire about it. The answer was one that he didn't need to know or one he felt Beth had no answer for.

"You will be fine," William answered.

"You better think of me every day I'm gone, I will be missing you," Beth again using a child-like voice.

"I will," William again answered not playing her baby talk game.

William was unmistakably distracted; his mind would wander more and more when he was with Beth. She was sweet and very attractive but he just never felt that personal connection. Beth sensed his wandering mind; she could feel it, he did not want to be there with her, right at that moment.

CHAPTER 11

"What's the matter?" She asked momentarily dropping the baby-talk voice.

"Nothing, I'm just tired."

"Just tired" was the safe answer for William to retreat to when he didn't want to talk about anything.

Beth thought for a second, then spoke, "I want to ask you something. I was going to wait until I came back from Florida, but I want to know before I leave. What is going on with you and that Amanda Flores girl?"

The question blindsided William, "What? Amanda? Nothing, she is just a friend of mine."

"I just don't want you cheating on me," Beth added.

"Cheating" was a relative term for sophomores. "Dating" was a very simple practice at that age. It consisted of walking your significant other from class to class with fingers interlocked and stealing the occasional kiss in any of the crevasses that were out of the line of sight from any passer-by. When Beth insinuated that William was cheating, she was essentially asking if he had been escorting another girl to class. She was accusing of finding extra time during the school day when not with her, to grab a quick kiss on the lips of another woman. The logistics of her accusation were impossible at best.

William didn't bore her with all of that. Instead, he opted for the simple approach, "I'm not cheating on you, Beth."

The idea of being seen as a two-timer and a womanizer appealed to William as he played out the scenario in his head, before being brought back to earth by Beth's incessant nagging.

"William, I do not like that Amanda girl," Beth was not going to surrender the topic easily.

"Why not?" William realized that asking that question was only going to invite an answer he didn't want to hear.

"I hear things about her," Beth moved to a more whispered tone.

"What 'things'?" Again William was setting Beth up to deliver something he didn't want to hear.

"I hear she has sex with teachers. I heard she was like really poor so she will show guys her private area for five dollars, and for like twenty dollars she will go all the way with a guy. William, basically she is a slut, and I don't like my man hanging around her. It looks bad," Beth was proud of herself, she had delivered the inside scoop on some High School rumors.

William thought he would be torn in his loyalty, that it would be a difficult choice, his friend Amanda or his girlfriend, Beth. As it turned out, the decision was not a hard one at all.

Without letting the silence linger too long, William lashed out, "Beth, who the fuck do you think you are? You don't know her; you don't know anything about her. All that made up crap you just spewed is horseshit. Lies that you and your fucked up prima-donna friends sit around and make up. You don't know her because she isn't anything like you or the fake assholes you call 'friends.' You need to come off that artificial high horse you think you are on and realize that you aren't better than anyone else, and most certainly not better than Amanda Flores."

Beth was at a loss for words when she regained her senses all she could string together was, "William McCabe, we are through."

A crowd had gathered during William's outburst, and he was speaking louder than he thought he was. He didn't care; he had hit the point of no return and honestly had no interest in returning.

"Beth, take my jacket off before you stain it with the shit coming out of your mouth, and you stink it with your fucked up air of pretentiousness!"

On cue, the bell sounded to start homeroom. Beth violently pulled the jacket off and threw it at William.

William chuckled and said aloud to no one in particular, "At least it wasn't a book."

By the time classes resumed after the holiday recess word had spread of the break-up and the fight in the hallway. Neither William or Beth were members of the elite, popular kids in the school, so news of their demise wasn't bound to hit the front page, it barely made news at all.

Amanda tracked William down that first day back like a hound sniffing out a fox. She finally found him between first and second periods at his locker making an exchange of books.

"Will, I heard you and what's her face broke up. What happened?" Amanda asked with just a little too much excitement in her voice.

"Amanda we have like four classes together, you didn't have to seek me out first thing. I'll see you in Math class; we will talk there."

"Like hell we will, that crazy Mr. Christiansen won't let me talk to anyone anymore."

William laughed, "Oh yeah because you told him to go fuck himself."

"I did not tell him that!" Amanda protested.

"Not in those exact words, but you sort of did," William explained.

"Fine, I will wait for lunch, but I want the whole story," Amanda turned and left not giving William a chance to protest her request.

William called down the hallway to a quickly escaping Amanda, "There is nothing to tell Amanda."

It was too late, she moved down the hall and away from his protest.

William weighed his options, and he knew Amanda was going to want to know what caused the break-up, but there was no way he could tell her about the rumors and what Beth had said. He still weighed this when Amanda emerged from the kitchen in the back of the cafeteria with her tray of food. It was Spaghetti and meatball, yes meatball as in singular, one meatball. Amanda hated Spaghetti day;

William knew this and had already prepared himself for the lunch swap routine that had become customary between the two friends. Personally, William wasn't too fond of the Spaghetti either, but he played up how much he loved it so that Amanda would be willing to swap. It was one of a few subtle victories William held in pride. He wanted to do everything he could to make her life just a little more enjoyable.

With no words spoken Amanda arrived at the table, slid the tray in front of William and took his sandwich.

"You are lucky to have a friend like me, I have no idea why you like that stuff so much, but if it makes you happy you can have it," Amanda might have known what William was doing, but she never let on.

She continued, "So, what happened?"

William thought, he made one last ditch effort to get out of the situation, "We made a pact; we aren't supposed to talk about the other people we are in a relationship with."

Amanda quickly offered up an answer, "One, you made that pact, not me. I don't mind hearing about your lady friends. Two, you aren't in a relationship with her anymore it seems, so all bets are off."

William began to cave, "I don't know, we got into a fight and broke up. It's not that big a deal. I don't even care. She was boring anyway."

"What was the fight about?" Amanda asked playfully.

"Honest, Amanda I don't remember."

"Come on Will. There is no way you don't remember what it was about."

"I don't, can we please just drop it now. I don't want to talk about it."

Amanda saw something in William; he was hiding something. Her interrogation was playful banter at first, but now it had a purpose,

CHAPTER 11

some bigger meaning.

"Will," She paused until he looked up, "What was the fight about?" She asked him placing emphasis on every word and pausing between them.

"Amanda, drop it," William had a stern tone to his request.

Amanda stayed quiet for a second, as she played out all the possible scenarios. Then she landed on something, and she knew she was right, as soon as it crossed her consciousness. Amanda was looking down at her swapped sandwich, and her gut told her all she needed to know. She slowly looked up to see if William was still looking at her. He wasn't, he had turned his attention back to his spaghetti.

"Will?"

"What?" William still sounded agitated.

"Thanks."

William felt embarrassed, she saw right through his guarded secret. She was the only one who could pierce his armor like that. It didn't take much; she knew him better than she had ever known anyone or anyone had ever known him.

Officially letting his guard down for a brief moment William spoke, "She was a stuck up bitch, she doesn't know anything, and she will never know me."

Amanda didn't know what Beth said about her, but she could clearly deduce that she was the cause of the fight and the eventual end of the relationship. She knew that whatever mud Beth Glaus slung, William did not put up with it. He took a stand and placed his friendship with her over his relationship with this girl.

Moments like that felt like a million handmade sandwiches packed in a million brown bags by a caring and loving mother. It made Amanda smile, a real, genuine smile.

CHAPTER 12

It was customary for William and Amanda to part ways at the end of the school year with plans to reconvene on the other side of the summer break. Their relationship had been growing at a rapid pace. They had now discovered that they did not live too far from each other. In spite of their proximity, it had been decided early on that there would be no need to keep in touch or to see each other over the summer.

William had made the assumption that the same deal would be in place this summer, so when he met up with Amanda after his last class of the day, he was prepared to say his good-byes. She was waiting at her locker when he arrived, and he could tell she had something to say to him.

"What's the matter?" William asked her.

"Can we get together over the summer?" Amanda was never one for dancing around her thoughts.

"Um… sure I guess so, why?" William was showing his confusion.

"It's just the idea of not seeing you all summer that bothers me. It's not like we have to hang out every day or anything, I know you want to see your friends and stuff, I just thought a day or two here and there. I could ride my bike to your house, or we can meet somewhere else."

"Yeah, that's fine, we can do that. You can call me when you want to hang out," William still had the sound of confusion in his voice, no matter how hard he tried to disguise it.

Amanda sensed his hesitation and gave him an option, "Will, we don't have to, I know we don't usually see each other over the summer, I just thought it would be fun is all."

William realized that his confusion and hesitation was becoming evident in his speech, he gathered himself and offered a reassuring confirmation, "Amanda listen, we can totally hang out over the summer. I would love to, just call me, OK?"

"OK," Amanda answered as she threw her arms up around William's neck. He had grown so much since they first met four years ago it was hard for her short stature to reach him.

Summer rolled on, one day sliding into the next a continuous cycle of days and nights circulating and never changing like the ornamental animals on a carnival merry-go-round. William continued to think about the new pact he made with Amanda, and he replayed it over and over in his head. He had to remind himself that the deal was she was to call him, not the other way around, but why hadn't she called yet?

William was sitting on the couch one day when the phone rang; he stopped thinking it might be Amanda, so he let his mother answer it.

Moments later a bellow rang out from the kitchen, "William, it's for you."

Still thinking it was Kenny or Cosimo, he pulled himself up from the sofa and lumbered into the kitchen. His mother had placed the

CHAPTER 12

bright yellow phone receiver on the back of the kitchen chair closest to the wallpapered wall of the McCabe's kitchen where the phone was mounted.

"Hello?" William spoke into the banana looking device.

"Will?" A voice that was not Kenny or Cosimo came from the other end.

"Yeah?" William was still searching his mind trying to place the caller.

"It's Amanda you dumbass," The voice finally revealed.

"Oh, man you sounded different on the phone. What's up?"

"You sound different too," Amanda replied back. They had both had the same revelation; they had never spoken to each other on the phone in all their years of knowing each other.

Amanda continued, "I have nothing to do tomorrow, and I would love to get out of this house, want to go to the beach?"

"The beach?"

William's confusion was warranted. Even though they technically lived on an island, one that had some of the most magnificent beaches in the Northeastern United States, their geographic location was the essential dead center of the island. Long Island is not overly spacious in its width. On average it was about twenty miles from the North Shore to the South Shore, so that meant that, at any given time, anyone on Long Island was at most ten miles from the closest beach. Ten miles was nothing, to the owner and operator of an automobile, which both William and Amanda were not.

So William asked the obvious question, "What beach?"

"Lake Ronkonkoma," She replied as if that was the obvious answer.

The lake was massive and was indeed water, and one could swim in water, so it wasn't too difficult of a deduction to make that it did have a beach. William lived in the neighborhood of that lake his whole life, and he never knew it to have a beach, but maybe he was wrong.

"Lake Ronkonkoma has a beach?" William made an attempt to clarify.

"Yes. It's not that big, and it's supposed to be for residents of this community over there, but we can get in, and it's close enough to ride our bikes," Amanda explained.

"Huh, well. I never knew it had a beach, OK, let's go, what time do you want to meet?"

"Nine, at the gate by the park, from there I'll show you how to get to the beach."

"Cool, it's a date," William quickly realized that the common phrase he would use with any of his guy friends had a slightly different feeling when used with his female friend.

He quickly tried to repair his faux pas, "Not a date, I mean like not in that way. You know what I'm saying. I'll be there is all I was trying to say."

William could hear Amanda laughing on the other end of the phone call, "Goodbye Will, I'll see you there tomorrow."

He heard the click of the disconnection signifying the phone conversation had come to an end.

It was five minutes to nine in the morning when William arrived at the gate at the park entrance, and Amanda was already there. Her bike was leaning up against the fence, and she was sitting Indian style on the grass. Amanda was wearing a loose fitting tank top and some hand-cut jean shorts; her bathing suit was obviously underneath. William couldn't help but wonder what kind of swimming garment she would be wearing, a modest one-piece or a revealing bikini, both had their pros and cons. The pros of the bikini were its revealing nature, showing more than William was ready to see, the cons of a one-piece, it wasn't a bikini.

CHAPTER 12

Upon seeing William Amanda stood up and grabbed her bike off the fence. When she stretched her arm out to grab hold of the handlebars her tank top lifted just enough for William to notice the smooth dark skin on her midsection, she was wearing a bikini.

The two friends had exchanged the traditional pleasantries and greetings before Amanda showed William a secret path through some trees that lined the edge of the park, separating it from the lake. When they came to a clearing, William could see traces of light beige sand and heard some distant voices and laughter.

"I'll be damned, there is a beach," William exclaimed.

"Told you there was," Amanda liked knowing something William didn't.

The beach was as Amanda described it, not very large, spanning about twenty yards from end to end and about five yards deep. As best as William could tell it wasn't entirely private, it seemed attached to a parking lot and a small collection of tennis courts. They stood their bikes up against a tree at the edge of the wooded area and made their way to a vacant spot on the carpet of soft sand. They threw down some towels to lay on, and William pulled off his T-shirt and kicked off his sandals. He then waited patiently to see what mysteries Amanda was going to reveal when she shed her outer layer of clothing.

She unbuttoned the jean shorts and shimmied them down her short legs uncovering a part of her that William had never seen, her rear end. The bottoms of the bikini had ridden up and exposed a little more than she would have liked of her backside. She quickly pulled them back into place and turned to see if William had noticed. He did his best to quickly dart his eye line out to the lake and away from her body, but it was obvious he saw. Amanda blushed and left the moment alone.

She pulled the tank top off next, William still reeling in embarrassment for being caught looking at her, played it safe and maintained his focus on the water in front of him. There would be time later to see her bare stomach, and maybe even the slightest hint of cleavage that so perfectly formed at the mid-chest level as the bikini top did its job in securing her breasts.

Needing to clear his mind William stood up and quickly moved toward the water without giving any fair warning to Amanda that he was doing so.

Amanda never strayed from her towel spread out on the sand. She was there to work on her already dark complexion, besides she thought the lake was polluted.

At one point, she yelled out to William, "You know that the lake is cursed, it takes one male every year, it almost got that dumbass friend of yours, Kenny."

William called back, "Kenny almost died because he dared to defy me and attempted to beat me in a race, he should have known better."

Amanda laughed and lay back down to continue to soak in the ultraviolet rays given out by the sun, like a mall Santa gives out mini candy canes.

Eventually, William emerged from the water like a tadpole completing its frog metamorphosis. He made his way up the sandy beach to where Amanda was lying. She had sunglasses on so William couldn't see if her eyes were open, so he kept his gaze on her body quick and disguised.

After toweling himself off he sat down beside her, he pointed at her outer thigh, "How'd you get that?"

Amanda sat up and looked at William; he nodded his head toward her leg as if the act of picking up his hand and pointing a second time was too much effort.

She looked down to see what William was referring to and noticed it for the first time. A small patch of purple sat hidden on her thigh. Amanda gave a laugh, but it wasn't her regular laugh, this one felt very rehearsed.

"I banged my leg on my dresser the other day; I didn't even know I bruised it."

"Now who's the dumbass?" William asked as he lay down to take his turn in grabbing some of the piercing sunlight before it slid down under the horizon.

As they both lay in the sun, William felt Amanda's barefoot brushing on his. To her, it was a simple sign of physical affection, to him it was an overtly sexual connotation. He loved how it made him feel but hated that he would never act on it.

"Thanks for hanging out with me today, I needed this," She added.

CHAPTER 13

By the time Junior year arrived everyone was on autopilot. They were all keeping their eyes on that one big prize that still hovered over them, but now it was just a year away. Everyone had different paths they wanted to explore. Those who had the means would aim for college, those who didn't would try to find work. They had one more year to figure out which path they were going to get on and where that path might lead them. A year seemed like a long time, but it was still there, lingering like the odor of rotten food that had long been discarded but left a small reminder of its existence behind.

With the move up in grade, there were new liberties allowed. Juniors and Seniors were allowed to leave campus for lunch. There were a few options available within walking distance of the school. A deli that sat at the five corners intersection, named this because it was where five different streets intersected, and a pizzeria right behind that. No matter where you found yourself on Long Island you could be assured that you were never far from a pizzeria or a deli, and such was the case for the High School.

PART ONE

The deck felt stacked, once again William and Amanda would be sharing a lunch period, this time, they would have some company. Jason Cosimo also drew fourth-period lunch. Cosimo had another collection of friends that he would sit with and would only shoot William a quick nod of the head in passing. He could tell that William wanted the time alone with Amanda.

William was still bringing lunch almost every day, so he very rarely took advantage of the open campus policy that was in place. On the nicer days and sometimes on the not so nice days he and Amanda would still head outside, even if just in the open courtyard behind the cafeteria.

The school year was still new, and everyone was still working to figure out their routine and establish new friendships. The summer heat was still lying dense in the air; most students took advantage of the warm temperatures and congregated outside after their lunch. William and Amanda were no exceptions. Amanda was going through one of her quiet moods again as the two friends sat on the curb outside.

William spoke first, "Are you OK?"

"Yeah, I'm sorry Will, I know I just get quiet sometimes. It's not you I just have a lot of shit going on at home."

This admission was the first time Amanda opened up about the cause of her mood change. The door was open for William to step through, all he needed was the courage to do so. William was still very much afraid of what discoveries existed on the other side of that door. He knew Amanda lived in a world very different from his. Would his young mind even be able to understand the suspected atrocities that went on once she left the friendly confines of the school? He wondered how bad it would get. She seemed so content on most days, was that a fake face she put on for her friends at school? Maybe things weren't as bad as William imagined. He had known kids growing up with parents who were not the most loving and nurturing, perhaps that was the case with Amanda. Maybe her life had been so bad for so long that she just became numb to it all. Whatever the case was, there was an opening in front of William; he could choose to walk through and get a glimpse of Amanda's world. His fear got the best of him as he only slightly peeked inside that door.

All he could gather the courage to say was, "I'm sorry."

"It's not your fault," Amanda reassured him.

Almost on cue, Jason Cosimo walked over, although his walk was more of a strut. He was trying to appear bigger than he was.

"Hey, numbnuts," He called out looking directly at William.

"Hey, Cosimo."

"Are you going to introduce me to your lady friend?" Cosimo asked.

William just then realized that Amanda had never really met Jason Cosimo. She had met Kenny a few times but never Cosimo. It had become clear why there was still some balance left in his life, the two most extreme forces he knew had not yet crossed paths. What would happen? He felt like a chemist mixing two potentially dangerous chemicals together for the first time in hopes that something great would come from it while risking a massive explosion.

"Amanda this is Jason Cosimo, Cosimo, this is Amanda," William spouted out the introduction with little fanfare.

"Pleasure to meet the young woman who has stolen my friend's heart," Cosimo said while extending his hand.

William sank even lower than he already was on the curb. Amanda didn't seem alarmed by Cosimo's comment, and William wasn't even sure it registered.

There was an awkward silence that hung. William interrupted it almost right away, "Jason lives in my neighborhood," He added.

"McCabe. Come on. Do I just live in your neighborhood? We

aren't friends?" Cosimo chastised William.

"Yes, I guess we are friends too," William moaned.

"Don't sound too thrilled about it," Cosimo added with a sense of sarcasm sprinkled on top for good measure.

Cosimo continued talking to William, "So McCabe, are you and Springer playing hockey today?"

The boys of the neighborhood loved playing street hockey so much that they played year round, in all seasons and all temperatures and all weather conditions. The warm summer air or the fact that hockey season was not due to start for another month didn't stop the boys from playing their favorite game. Active participants never mattered much either. They could play a full five-on-five game with goalies or just something as simple as two of the boys taking shots on an open net. There was no big neighborhood game scheduled to be played that day so what Cosimo was asking was if the three of them could get together and play.

William had no reason to not play so he answered in the affirmative, "Sure, we can play."

At the second pause in the conversation, Amanda stood up.

She excused herself, "Sorry boys, I have to get going."

"Where are you going?" William inquired.

"I just have to go," Was all Amanda had to say.

She took a few steps back to the school when Cosimo figured she was out of earshot.

"Moody bitch isn't she?"

It didn't take too much for Jason Cosimo to shed his polite outer skin. The words were barely out of his mouth when he felt a shadow move in from his right. Amanda was on him like a hawk who just spotted prey in a field.

"What the fuck did you just say?" She was using a boisterous tone, and it began to draw the attention of the other students in the

CHAPTER 13

courtyard.

Cosimo, realizing he had been caught red-handed, stumbled for some plausible excuse for saying what he said. He thought he would use the "I was only joking" bit, but he was a little too prideful to let this girl back him down, especially under the watchful eyes of a courtyard of fellow students. He decided to stand and face the music, he was at the point of no return, besides she was a pint-sized girl, what could she possibly do to him.

"I said you were a moody bitch."

The last syllable of his sentence barely left his mouth before Amanda's open hand was across it. A loud slap rang out all the way to the nursing home that lay just beyond the sports fields that lay just beyond the school.

Cosimo didn't need a minute to assess what just happened; he knew it right away.

He yelled, "Fuck! You stupid bitch!"

"What did you call me?" It was rhetorical, but Amanda asked it anyway.

"Stupid, I called you a stupid bitch."

Cosimo was just a glutton for punishment at this point. He should have just cut his losses from the beginning and apologized for the first comment; he should have turned the other unslapped cheek and walked away. It would have gone a long way to salvaging the remainder of his pride. Getting slapped in front of your peers was a social death in High School.

William had flashbacks of when he called Amanda stupid, and he cringed at what might happen next, which was the appropriate response. Amanda pulled her foot back and swung it forward, channeling all those hours of youth soccer, and landed the toe of her right sneaker squarely between Jason Cosimo's legs. The sound was a lot less than the slap, but the pain far surpassed it. What the kick lacked in its audible impact it made up for with the collective gasps and ah's that emanated from the growing mob, especially the male onlookers.

The kick didn't miss or even just skim its intended target; it was a direct hit. Amanda was precise with a soccer ball and, it seems, equally as accurate with the male testicles. The pain was minor at first, so much so that Cosimo thought that, by some freak of physics, she missed or by even some more freak twist of anatomy his testicles were impervious to pain. Both very flawed theories because the pain eventually arrived, like a rock band who only took the stage when they felt the moment to be right. It was a wave of pain that affected areas of Cosimo's body that were not anywhere near the impact zone. His stomach began to turn with the threat of returning the lunch that was given to it just moments earlier. His eyes began to water, and his head began to throb with pain, as his breathing became labored, and finally his legs lost their ability to keep him upright. He fell directly to his knees, which when hitting the hard concrete ground caused a secondary wave of pain that in turn toppled him to his side. He immediately curled into the fetal position as if returning to his mother's womb would make all of the pain go away. It didn't.

Amanda almost instantly felt guilty for her actions. Not because she felt regretful for hurting Cosimo but because she injured William's friend. She turned to William whose mouth was still a gasp with disbelief.

"I'm sorry Will," Amanda almost had tears in her eyes.

William having a moment of clear thinking reacted quickly, "Amanda, get out of here, someone is bound to tell a teacher, and you will get screwed. I'll take the blame for this."

Amanda froze, she didn't know what to do.

William yelled, "Amanda, get the fuck out of here, I'll take care of this."

CHAPTER 13

Amanda had never seen William yell at anyone, especially not her. She was almost afraid of him at that moment, but she turned and ran.

Quickly William dropped down to the ground beside Cosimo, "Jason, you got let me cover for her. Tell them we were goofing around, and I accidentally hit you in the nuts."

"No fucking way, that bitch is going to pay for this," Cosimo was relentless.

William thought for a second, "Name your price."

For the first time since Cosimo's genitals met Amanda's foot, he stopped wincing and rocking on the pavement. He was giving it some serious thought.

"Your Gary Carter rookie card," He finally spoke.

"Fuck you, come on be serious," William loved that card. Gary Carter was the catcher for the World Series-winning New York Mets of 1986; he was also William's favorite baseball player. He searched for that very first baseball card of his for almost a year until he found it at a small hobby shop in Toms River, New Jersey while visiting cousins. It was in pristine conditions, sharp corners, no creases or discoloration.

"The Carter rookie card or she goes down, detention maybe even expelled."

"You provoked her, I'll give you his second-year card," William began to haggle.

"The Carter rookie or nothing," Cosimo drove a hard bargain.

William looked up he could see the gathered crowd start to dissipate meaning only one thing, some faculty member was on their way, and his time was running out.

"Fine, you got a deal. We were goofing around, and you were showing me a new wrestling move, and you accidentally got hit in the balls, that's the story we are going with, OK?" William only had time to run through the story once before some teacher he had never seen before emerged from the remainder of the crowd of witnesses.

William and Cosimo ran through the story as rehearsed and the teacher bought it. Those who witnessed it were more than willing to allow whatever deal the two boys struck stay undisturbed and would never tell anyone who the real testicle assaulter was.

At the conclusion of lunch William immediately darted off to find Amanda. He would eventually find her sitting on the ground in front of the school later that day.

"Hey," William offered as a formal greeting.

Amanda looked up, half squinting to protect her eyes from the sharp rays of the sun that lived just behind the towering figure of William standing over her.

"How's your friend?" She had a genuine concern in her voice.

"He'll live, are you OK?"

"Yes, Will… I'm so sorry about that. I hate violence, I do. I never want to hit anyone or hurt anyone ever in my life; it's not me. I'm so messed up, and I don't know what is wrong with me."

"Come on Amanda; you know as well as I do that Cosimo had that coming, has for years."

"It's not that Will, It's my life, it's so shitty and so messed up that I try so hard to keep it so far from you and everyone else here. This school is the only place I am happy, the only place I feel loved and at peace, and when the messy side of my life works its way into this part of my life, I hate myself. Will, right now I hate myself."

Amanda gave William a lot to handle, and he wasn't sure how to do it, so he kept it honest, "Maybe you should go talk to someone, like a guidance counselor or something."

"I'm thinking about it. I'm just afraid of what will happen if I do."

"Happen? What do you mean?"

CHAPTER 13

Amanda was silent. She was looking down at the ground. She was watching a colony of ants marching in succession from the bed of grass to her right to the small mound of dirt that lay a few feet away in the crack in the pavement. William's question still hung in the air, waiting for some reply or answer.

"Nothing, can we talk about something else?" Amanda finally asked.

William still had his concerns but honored his friend's wishes.

"Did you get in trouble?" Amanda asked, referring to William taking the blame for the Cosimo injury.

"Na, he owed me one, I just cashed in on it, no big deal, he is fine, I covered for you," William explained.

Again Amanda drifted to a far off place in her mind before finally standing up on the curb unannounced and stepped forward to give William a firm, tight hug. It took him by surprise, but he enjoyed it and slowly put his arms around her neck. Amanda was a lot shorter than he was and her face fell even with William's chest. The two had stayed in that locked position for a few seconds before Amanda spoke, "You are the only person in this world that cares about me."

"I'm sure that's not true," William began to protest.

"If you only knew."

William didn't know, part of him was glad to be in the dark about what her life was really like. It was a safe place for him to be. At the same time, he knew one day he would need to find out what was really going on with Amanda once she left him and the school at the end of the day.

CHAPTER 14

The weeks following the Cosimo kicking incident went by without any further mention of the assault. Amanda was back to being her upbeat self. There was even a tense moment in the cafeteria where she and Cosimo crossed paths. Amanda avoided eye contact, and that was enough for Cosimo to feel he had bested her in his imaginary round two of their bout. It was clear that the two would live in a peaceful coexistence for as long as they shared the friendship of one William McCabe.

William was beginning to forget about the dark cloud that he knew existed over Amanda's head. He began to see that her outbursts and sporadic bouts with authority were her way of dealing with the bad things that went on once she left the security of the school grounds. She was lashing out at teachers and other students as a defense mechanism. Her mood changes were usually safe indicators of a bad day at home. William began to read her more efficiently and do his best to ease the anxiety that seemed to follow her around.

William wanted to know more about her horrible life, and he

wanted to help her, but he knew his ability was limited and that frustrated him. William dealt with it by pretending it didn't exist, and when it would rise to the surface of his consciousness the wave of guilt that it brought with it was crippling. How could he sit by idly while his friend was living in what he only could presume was a life so far worse than his? The guilt weighed on his young shoulders until he pushed it back down again. This avoidance only served as a short term cover, and he knew it was just a matter of time before the guilt would come back again, and the process would repeat.

William and Amanda also shared a math class together, they both struggled in the subject and would often get bored of it quickly, and that usually led to socializing in the back of the classroom. Their teacher, Mr. Mangatto was what the students believed to be a borderline functioning alcoholic. The borderline part was not the alcoholism, there was no doubt, he was an alcoholic, the functioning part that was what they considered borderline. He routinely missed at least one day a week due to "illness." When he was present, it was usually wearing the same clothes he had on the previous day and smelling of something that more closely resembled a homeless man than a math teacher.

William and Amanda had Mr. Mangatto for the third period. This early time worked to their advantage if he was on school grounds that early he would be barely awake. He would scribble an in-class assignment on the board and play the role of teacher the best he could.

The students never dared to speak of their concerns with Mr. Mangatto's behavior; that was because you could pass the class with little effort. Just show up, pretend you are participating and remain quiet and non-confrontational and the magic "A" would appear next to your name in his grade book. It was that easy.

The district might have known about Mr. Mangatto's condition,

CHAPTER 14

but he was tenured and without any registered complaints from students or student's parents they never felt the need to act.

Such was life in third-period math class.

The cooler fall temperatures began to settle on Long Island. Winter was still in the distance, but it was making its presence known, like a cargo ship on the distant horizon that gives the obligatory sound of the horn when moving in closer to the shore.

Amanda was not present at the daily rendezvous point that she and William had designated at the start of the year. William just assumed that she was late or taking another sick day and moved on with his usual routine.

While William was sitting, bored, in Mr. Mangatto's class Amanda finally arrived, late. William immediately perked up when he saw her enter the room and hand the tardy slip to the half comatose teacher behind the desk. William was like a dog waiting at the front door for his master to walk in, tail wagging, panting with excitement like he had so much to fill her in on.

When she got closer to her desk and settled in William spoke in the loudest whisper he could, "Where were you this morning, I waited for you, and you never showed."

"I was running late, sorry," Amanda seemed different.

"Are you wearing makeup?" William asked.

"Yes, I am. I'm a girl, or did you forget. Girls sometimes wear makeup," Amanda was snippy but kept her voice to an appropriate whisper.

"Sure, girls wear makeup, but you don't. And I have to say; you are wearing a lot."

"Shut up William," Amanda wore a half smile through her cosmetology attempt.

She was not in a great mood, but she knew she couldn't get mad at William anymore, they had come too far in their friendship.

"If I'm being honest, I don't like it. I think you put too much on," William continued his prodding.

"Will, we will talk about my makeup later, please," Amanda's patience had run out.

Later on, that same day while eating lunch together William began the annoying prodding again.

"So why the makeup? You trying to impress a new guy or something?" He asked.

"No, that's not it at all," Amanda's tone remained calm.

"So why?" William asked again.

"Finish your sandwich, I want to go for a walk," Amanda avoided answering his inquiries.

While walking across the courtyard that lay just outside the cafeteria windows, Amanda was quiet.

"What's going on Amanda?" William asked.

She stopped walking and looked up at him; her big brown eyes were like two brown gems laying on the edge of a serene pond.

"My stepfather slapped my face so hard this morning that it left a bruise on my cheek so bad that I needed all this makeup to cover it up," The confession blindsided William.

"What?" His blood began to pump harder. There was an anger boiling up inside him so intense that it frightened him. He was at a level he had never seen before. This anger was different, not the one he would get at his brother for digging around in his room; this anger was reaching a new dimension.

He continued, "What the fuck is wrong with that guy? Why would he do something like that?"

"William, this isn't the first time he has done this. In fact, he has been hitting me or calling me stupid or just neglecting me for as long as I can remember."

William was at a loss for words, "But... why? I don't understand."

CHAPTER 14

He did understand, in fact, a lot of things all started to fall into place. Amanda's sensitive nature to the word "stupid" the bruises she claimed came from clumsy behavior, the extreme mood swings and her constant reference to her "messed up" home life.

Amanda continued, "It gets bad for a while, but then it will get better too. I guess I always think that it will eventually stop, but I'm starting to think it won't. He's a fucked up person, Will. He's evil, and I hate him."

William was still searching for his words, and his emotions were a raging storm tossing a boat about in the waves. There were no words in the only language he spoke to articulate what he was feeling. This bred frustration in him and his voice shook when he finally did speak.

"What about your mother?" He asked.

"What about her? If she isn't drunk or high, she is ignoring it, Hell she will help out sometimes. Will, I'm sorry to put this all on you, it's not fair. I've always wanted to protect you from this part of my life, but I need you now. If I don't talk to you about this, it will boil over, and I will start to take it out on you, like when I threw that book at you. It boiled over, and I lashed out. I'm so close to losing it again that I can't let it affect my friendship with you. You have to understand something Will; you are the only reason I'm still alive."

"What? What do you mean?" William was perplexed.

"If not for you Will I would have run away, or killed myself or worse, killed that prick who thinks hitting a kid makes him a real man. My life is hanging by a thread, but as long as that thread stays intact, I have a chance. Will, you are that thread."

"Amanda, I…" William was stammering.

"Will, you don't have to say anything, you don't owe me anything. You have done so much more than you could ever realize."

"I just don't think that I have. I need to help you. You're my best friend, and I can't sit by and pretend that none of this is happening to you. I want to kick that guy's ass, I want to pull you out of that place, I want to make sure no one lays a hand on you again."

"You can't. I didn't tell you this to make you feel like you have to rescue me. That's not my intention. I just need you for support. I will work this all out."

"How Amanda? How will you work this out?" William was getting angry now.

His anger was getting directed at her, but it was rooted elsewhere.

"This isn't something you take on alone. What's going on is something that is bigger than you, bigger than me, bigger than both of us. We need to tell someone. We need to get you out of that house, out of that situation," William exclaimed.

"Will, I can't just leave, where would I go?" Amanda asked.

"I don't know, come live with me. Anywhere is better than there," William was getting more excitable.

"Live with you? You think your mom would let some girl she never met come live at her house with her son?" Amanda made a good point.

"Well, we will tell her what's going on, then she will be alright with it," William was trying to interject logic into his idea.

"I think that's kidnapping," Amanda was beginning feel a lot better unloading her secret.

"What? Are you making jokes? Amanda this is serious. We need to do something. Because I'm one second away from going to your house with a baseball bat and cracking it over that prick's head," William was still enraged.

Amanda took a more serious tone, "William, don't you ever act on anything like that. If you ever go over there and confront them about any of this, I will never talk to you again. I mean it. I don't need you getting involved. He is a dangerous person, and the situation is even more dangerous."

CHAPTER 14

"I understand that that's why you need to get out."

"Will, I've been dealing with this for a long time now. I know you think I'm unreasonable, but I need to sit tight. I will get out. I can last one more year, and I will go off to college, and I will never see those assholes ever again. Just please, continue to be my rock for the next year. I will get through this; I won't let them win. Everything will work out, just give me one more year. Please."

William felt caught between the adolescent world he belonged in and the adult situation that blindsided him outside his high school cafeteria. The kid in him wanted to crawl into some corner and shut his eyes and go back to a life where these bad things didn't happen to anyone, especially the people he loved. The world was a hard, hard place and he was just starting to see the extent of its cruel reaches. He saw stories on the news of the atrocities that took place, but to him, that was someone else, someplace else. They were stories on the TV, it wasn't real, but now reality was standing in front of him. Amanda wasn't a news story on the TV she was his best friend.

His gut told him to tell someone, that the situation Amanda was in was dangerous, and it was only going to get worse. He knew that saying something to someone would set a chain of events in motion that would most likely have her removed from the house but not under her terms which would be the end of their friendship.

His naive look on the world wanted to trust her and give her that one more year to work this out on her terms. He began to rationalize it to himself. Maybe she did know best. Maybe it was best to let her control the situation and deal with it.

"Amanda, I don't know what to do with this," William finally confessed.

"You don't do anything, that's what I'm asking for you to do," Amanda pleaded.

"Jesus Amanda, how am I supposed to pretend I don't know any of the things you just told me?"

Not acting on it and ignoring the issue made William feel weak. He didn't know what his role was supposed to be. Proving his masculinity was not something William ever felt he needed to do. If he was honest with himself, Amanda was giving him a way out. He hated confrontation, and her plea gave him the opportunity not to have to get into a confrontational situation.

William looked down at the cracked concrete below his feet. He knew that all the debating wouldn't change the outcome. He was going to concede to her wishes. It's what his safe side wanted, but his gut told him that he needed to do more. If anything happened to her, he would never be able to live with himself.

"Fine," The one simple word finally escaped out of his mouth.

"I know you want to protect me, and I love you for that. I just need you to trust me on this one. I can handle the situation, and I know what I'm doing. One year, just give me one more year, then we graduate, and I go to college. I will be out of there, and I will never look back. Just please support me, be there for me," Amanda was calmer now, she was speaking in a tone that made William feel better about his compromise.

"Amanda, I will always be here for you, you know that," He offered.

"I do, I do know that. You are the only one I can count on, so please, don't let this get weird between us. I'm not a victim here, and I don't want your pity or any of that. OK?"

"OK," William answered.

CHAPTER 15

The winter months rolled in quickly. The cool nights of autumn gave way to the brisk cold nights of winter. Amanda's life had become relatively calm in the months since her secret confession to William. There was peace in her, the airing of her secret cleared her conscience. She felt a weight had lifted, but the weight didn't lift at all, it still existed, it just shifted. It moved partially from Amanda's life to William's. His knowledge of her home life ate at him, his reluctance to do anything about it churned a heavy guilty feeling that festered in his gut and his mind.

He knew where Amanda lived; he spent too many nights laying in bed, staring at the ceiling playing out a course of events that led him to her house. He would confront her stepdad maybe even get physical with him, and he would grab Amanda and take her away from that evil place forever. Irrational things played out in his mind, from the safe confines of his house in the even safer confines of his bed. They were still kids; this wasn't fair. They were supposed to be talking about their favorite TV shows or having silly crushes on each other, not dealing with this. Why did these people steal away her childhood? What made someone do something like that?

The more William let those thoughts dance around inside his head, the angrier he got. He could feel his fists tighten as if they had a mind of their own and were not under his control.

Kenny had a late summer birthday, and his parents had the option to hold him back when registering for kindergarten, which they chose to exercise, so he was always the oldest kid in the class. Kenny's age came in very useful during his Junior year. He was the only one of William's friends who could legally drive a car. His driving privileges were limited. He was allowed to travel to and from school and work. All other driving must be with a licensed parent or guardian in the vehicle.

The vote was unanimous, Kenny would be driving to school every day, and bringing William and Cosimo with him. Kenny's generosity spared the boys the added hassle of being at the mercy of the school bus schedule and all the additional stops between the school and their houses.

Kenny's car was only a car by the most liberal definition allowed by the state of New York to successfully register a vehicle. It was a 1979 Ford Fairmont that lived its previous life as a taxi, a fact that remained hidden from Kenny until after he had purchased the car. He had it displayed proudly in his driveway. First, he gave it a thorough washing followed by a detailed waxing, and this was where he made a startling discovery. Faintly seen on both the driver's and passenger's door panels were the remnants of the glue adhesive backing. The faint ghost of the vinyl letters that were visible spelled out "All County Taxi" followed by the phone number to the now defunct establishment.

Kenny immediately sighed and let out a simple, "Shit."

The car had clearly logged more miles than the modest odometer

CHAPTER 15

had let on, and when one lie is present on a used car, you can be rest assured there is much more still hidden in the weeds.

From that day on the car became a perpetual lemon for Kenny. Just when he thought he worked out all the bugs, a few more would show their ugly selves.

The issues ranged from the not so bad, a bad spark plug or a broken fan belt to the more severe. The bigger issues left Kenny stranded on the side of the road on more than one occasion.

On its functioning days it would taxi the boys to and from school, today the old girl was in perfect working order. "Perfect" was a relative term when talking about Kenny's car. It still had a laundry list of problems, but none of them significant enough to hinder the basic functionality of the vehicle. If it could get them to school, it was considered to be in perfect working order.

This particular morning found William in a mood that was less than agreeable, so he was delighted to see that Jason Cosimo would not be joining them on their morning commute. William had been having a hard time dealing with the burden of knowing what was going on at Amanda's house. It had been a few months since her confession to him, and the knowledge still haunted him. He could never let her know how it was affecting him, the guilt she would feel would only compound her situation even more. He wanted to be a rock and strong support for her; that's what she needed, and that's what he was going to give her.

Kenny broke the morning silence first, "You know that chick Melissa? She's in your biology class."

"Um… yeah, I think so," William wasn't much for noticing girls or anyone these days.

Kenny continued, "Well, word around the rumor mill is that she thinks you're hot and wants you to ask her out."

"Ken, come on… she's gross, she's got that gap in her front

teeth, it's horrible to look at," William was never this mean. The stress was breaking him down to a point where lashing out at other people served as a pacifier that only compounded his guilt later when realizing what he had done, and it made him hate himself.

Kenny dropped the subject, and the car remained quiet the rest of the way to school.

William's mood didn't change once school began; Amanda was absent. Her truancy added to the stir of thoughts and emotions already swirling around in his head like a small ship, tossed by the waves of a storm.

Biology class started, and nothing was further from his mind than the morsel of gossip Kenny filled him in on this morning, that was until Melissa walked into the classroom.

"Hey, McCabe. You're an asshole; you know that?" Melissa's anger ran red hot.

William was trying to catch up with the confrontation already in progress, "Did I do something?"

"I heard what you said about me. You think my teeth are gross to look at," Melissa snapped back.

A range of emotions and thoughts flowed through William. He was embarrassed for what he had said, and he was angry at Kenny for sharing it but most of all he found himself not caring about the situation he was in at that moment. He couldn't help but to remove himself from this confrontation, mid-confrontation, and keep his thoughts on Amanda. With Melissa still yelling at him in the background, his thoughts were locked in on Amanda and her well being. He finally snapped out of his wandering thoughts when Melissa threw her hand down onto the top surface of the desk in front of William.

"Are you even listening to me, McCabe?" She screamed.

William's attention joined the rest of the onlookers and focused

CHAPTER 15

in on Melissa's rage.

"I am now," William still appearing unfazed at the scene playing out right in front of him. He contemplated denying his words, or even downplaying them, but that seemed useless. She had unquestionably believed what she heard securely enough to confront him about it.

"I'm sorry Melissa. I am an asshole; you're right," William admitted defeat right away hoping it would put an end to the situation.

"You're sorry? That's all you have to say?" Melissa was stirring him, and she wanted something more.

William obliged, "Yes that's all, it's a fucking apology, is there something more in the world of admitting wrong that I'm missing? Do you want me to bake you a cake? I said a shitty thing about you, and now I'm apologizing, you either accept it or don't. I don't know what to tell you."

Melissa feeling bested gave one more jab before surrendering, "Fuck you, William McCabe. I can't believe I ever liked you."

William's remorse had increased tenfold, and he was beginning to hate the person he was becoming.

He hung his head low and muttered so only those closest to him could hear, "I can't believe you did either."

Reaching his limit on confrontations for the day, he thought it would be best to fake a sickness and head home. The stars were not in his favor when he came across Kenny in the hallway on his way to the school nurse.

"What the fuck Ken? You told that chick I said her teeth were gross?" William lashed into his best friend.

Kenny, not knowing what transpired, tried his best to put the pieces together in his head, "Um… shit. Well, Jackie asked me to talk to you about it and then asked me this morning if I did. I told her you weren't interested, and she kept asking why. I couldn't think of a lie, so I told her what you said. She promised not to say anything, and I guess she lied."

"Why would you tell her that Ken? That's the worst thing you could have told her. There are a million lies that would have been better. Hell, I would have been OK with you telling her I was gay. She went nuts on me in biology. Wait… who the hell is Jackie?" William's mind was racing faster than he could control it.

Kenny could see the near breakdown status in his friend's eyes, "Jackie. The girl with the huge breasts that I've been in love with since the fifth grade. She is Melissa's friend, and I wanted to get on her good side."

"You sold me out because of a girl? Jesus Ken, I can't tell you anything anymore."

Kenny changed gears on the conversation, "Well William, to be honest, I thought it was a very mean thing to say in the first place. Melissa is a very friendly and sweet girl, and up until today, I thought my friend William McCabe was also a very friendly and sweet guy. I thought it would be a perfect match. I was wrong. Something has gotten into you lately. You are not yourself, and you're mean, and you are always in a bad mood. We've been friends since kindergarten, and I've never seen this side of you."

For a brief second, William thought about confessing what he knew about Amanda but felt it best not to, "I have a lot of shit going on, it's hard for me to explain."

"You can try," Kenny was trying to be supportive.

"No, Ken, not this time. Listen I have to go home, I don't feel well and this day has not been that great.

Before Kenny could object, William was walking out of the school and heading home.

Kenny called after him, "Do you even have a hall pass or an excuse or are you just cutting the rest of the day."

William offered no reply.

CHAPTER 15

The next morning Kenny showed up in front of William's house, as he always did and to his surprise, William was there, out front waiting.

William spoke first once entering the car, "Kenny listen, I'm sorry about yesterday. I got pissed off because you told that girl about what I said, but the truth was I should have never said it, and it was good that I was held accountable for it. It was a hard lesson for me but one I deserved. Now I got to find this Melissa girl and make that right too."

Kenny reflected for a second on what William just said. Kenny was an old soul, he fancied himself to be wise beyond his years and never liked being grouped in with the rest of the teenagers. He felt their intellect was still years behind his.

Finally, he spoke, "'Be the change you want to see in the world.' Gandhi said that."

"Kenny I don't think that applies, but thanks for making an effort."

Kenny continued, "You know if you ever want just to talk about stuff, I have been known to be a good listener."

"Thanks, buddy, I'll be fine," William just wanted to go back in time and change everything about the past two days.

In reality, he wanted to change a lot more than just the past few days; he wanted to change what he knew about Amanda. It wasn't selfish, he didn't like knowing it, but part of him was glad he did, he was now in a position to act. He made his promise to her that he wouldn't but as each passing day came and went the urge to act built-up and grew. He had no idea what his options were, but he knew he wasn't strong enough to sit by idly while his friend was living in constant danger.

Once he entered the school, he raced to his normal morning meeting spot hoping Amanda would be there. He let out a big sigh of relief when he turned the corner and saw her standing there, leaning up against the wall, waiting for him.

"Thank God you're here today, I have to tell you what happened to me yesterday," William called out as he approached a waiting Amanda.

When he got close enough, he noticed something out of place. Where Amanda's arm had normally been, had been replaced by a large white block of plaster. It was a cast.

Ceasing all other thoughts William focused his attention on the medical apparatus now living over her left arm, "What happened?"

"Nothing, I fell down the stairs. I'll be fine; they said it was a clean break and will heal perfectly," Amanda explained.

William stared at the broken appendage; he didn't believe the stair story. Amanda knew he wouldn't, but she had to try.

"That son of a bitch, he did this, didn't he?" William's anger was pouring through his veins.

Amanda didn't answer, which, in William's eyes, was a confirmation.

"What happened?" William's question was less of an inquiry of concern and more of an interrogation.

Amanda thought about lying or just not telling him, but she knew he was already in too deep. Keeping him in the dark was pointless, "He pulled me by the arm. I yanked away, and he shoved me into the wall at the top of the basement stairs. I lost my balance and fell down the stairs and broke my arm. He was drinking again; it's only bad when he drinks. Please, I'm almost out of there, don't say anything to anyone, please."

The rage boiled up inside him, "Amanda I can't keep turning a blind eye to what is going on. We need to do something."

"Please Will, just a little longer, that's all I'm asking for," Amanda pleaded.

CHAPTER 15

William refused to commit to anything and was eager to move on so he could weigh his thoughts and any possible actions on his own.

"Come on; we have to get to class," He finally spoke.

Arguing with her was useless, she had her plan and was going to stick with it, no matter what. William wanted a change to happen, and he knew it wouldn't happen on its own, or on her terms. He needed to act, the weight of a thousand choices pressed on his shoulders, he thought about telling someone. Bringing in a new person, an adult might alleviate some of the stress building up on him. He thought about going over to her house, talking with her stepfather, maybe reason with him, try to get him to stop. Nothing was making sense to him right now. He was a mixing bowl of emotion; a new raw feeling would surface every few minutes. He was like a roll of the dice, and each new cast showed a different face and a different world of options. The common denominator in all of this was he needed to act and act quickly. He would sleep on it, and tomorrow would be the day he would start to put an end to this living Hell Amanda endured day after day. Tomorrow was the start of a new beginning. All he had left to do was figure out how he was going to make that happen.

CHAPTER 16

Morning rolled in like a wave crashing on an empty beach. The hour didn't matter to William; it would have been just one more in a sea of hours that passed while he stared up at his ceiling. He hadn't slept at all, not a single minute. His mind was racing way too fast to allow sleep to happen.

He was still in his bed, eyes open when his alarm clock sounded signaling his regular awakening time. His indecision time had expired; he was now on the precipice of making, or not making, the biggest decision of his life so far. He knew what he had to do.

He rose from the bed. Took a shower and ran through his normal progression of tasks to ready himself to face a typical day of school, but this would be anything but a "typical day."

He left the house in a hurry, grabbing his bike from the shed in the backyard. He took something else too from the shed to bring with him, the old wooden baseball bat his father had given Danny as a gift before his first season of Little League baseball. That bat had brought the boys hours upon hours of entertainment and fun both in their backyard and at the schoolyard a few blocks down. Today, William had other intentions for its use.

He knew that Kenny would be pulling his dilapidated Ford in front of his house any minute, he needed to make a fast escape before being noticed. He had a standing agreement with Kenny if he didn't emerge from his house by ten minutes past their scheduled pickup time that was the indicator that he would not be going to school that day. It was better than Kenny honking his horn at such an early hour and saved William or William's mother the trip outside to explain that a ride would not be needed that day.

William peddled his bike as fast as his legs could push him. His mind went back to the day he raced Kenny home from the lake. William hit the end of the street and made a right turn. His body was pushing him toward his location, and his mind was ready for anything. His actions were the exact opposite of what he should be doing, but it was what the situation called for, it was what he needed to do. He made peace with the decision and continued. Regardless of the outcome, William needed to live with himself, and for as long as he was breathing, this was the only way he could do that.

He brought his bike to a skidded stop in the dirt patch in front of a run-down ranch style house located about half way down the quiet street. The hour was early, but not too early. All the kids would have been on the bus heading to their respective schools by now, and all the working adults would have been heading to their respective places of work. He knew at least one adult who was home, the coward that was most likely still sleeping in a bed in the house that stood before him. It wasn't a massive structure, but given the circumstances that found William at this place made the residence feel larger than life, looming over him, intimidating him.

He didn't give himself any time to think. He knew that if he did the sea of second thoughts would overtake him, pulling him down

CHAPTER 16

and killing all the courage he had built to get himself to this point. He was close, and there was only one thing left for him to do. His first step toward the house was the hardest one, after that, each step taken got a little easier than the one before it.

His heart was racing now, his hands were shaking, his mouth was as if he had been sucking on cotton balls for the past three hours. He got to the door and without hesitation rapped violently on its face. There was a doorbell, but William didn't want to waste time figuring out if it was in working order.

The house remained still inside, "They are still in bed, the lazy fucks," William said aloud.

After three more sessions banging on the door, he could sense movement inside the dwelling. He had officially hit the point of no return. A rehearsed speech would have been a good idea at this point, but it was too late for that. He knew what he had to say, and he was going to let his raw emotions do the driving.

William heard the deadbolt lock click from its secure state, and a quiet creek sounded as the door slowly moved.

When the barrier moved from a closed position, William found himself eye to eye with the man he had spent so many years abhorring but never meeting.

He was a tall, slender man, almost unhealthy in his weight. The skin hung on a slight skeletal frame like old clothes thrown over the back of a chair. His hairline began at the very peak of his forehead, and it wasn't much of a hairline at that point. It didn't become a head of hair until it reached the back of his head; that's where it made up for lack of hair on the front of the head.

His face was not at all as William imagined; it was rough, hard and aged. Time and life were not kind to it. His eyes were sunken into his head like two black orbs living in the recessed holes where maybe eyes once lived. Under his eyes were two dark patches of skin that hung sagging. As if he knew what a grotesque sight his face had become the man made a poor attempt at covering what he could with the stubble beginnings of a beard. William would like to think he was trying to do the world a favor by covering his face, but he knew the reality of the unshaven appearance was due to pure laziness.

The rest of the man's body followed suit, there were no surprises, the body was just as abused and messy as his head and face. His clothes were only clothes by definition in that they were indeed items worn to cover the body, torn, stained and ill-fitting.

William must have been just staring at the man for some time because eventually, the man spoke, "Yeah?"

William was unsure of himself at first; he was still shaking, and his mouth was still lacking in any saliva.

After no reply, the man spoke again, "What da fuck ya want?"

"I'm Amanda's friend from school," William finally squeaked out in a broken tone.

"She ain't here," He said.

William's courage grew, "I know, I'm here to talk to you."

"Me? What da fuck you want with me?" The man asked.

"I know what you have been doing to her, the abuse. I'm here to make sure you never lay a finger on her again," William was firm in his tone.

"I don't know what da fuck you are talkin' about. Now get the fuck outta here," He went to slam the door shut, but William was quicker and jammed his foot in the path of the closing door. "Kid, you better get your fucking foot out of my fucking door."

William was bold, "Listen, mister, I'm not going anywhere until I know you will never touch Amanda again."

They were unreasonable terms, the reality of it was there would never be any way for William to have the guarantee he needed. In fact, there was no clear end game in his plan; he hadn't thought that

CHAPTER 16

far ahead.

The man was now out of his sleepy state and became more aware of the situation playing out on his front porch. When he looked down, he recognized the item in William's hand for the first time, "Is that a bat in your hand?"

William could feel the situation beginning to shift in a direction he was not prepared to go, "Yeah."

"Do you plan on usin' that thing on me?" The man was almost antagonizing William.

Time for William to show he could play with the adults, "I will if I have to."

He thought the response was appropriate, almost cool. The look on the man's face shifted from bothered and annoyed to angry with a hint of violence brewing up behind his eyes. He swung the door back open and pushed William free from the door frame. The entrance was now clear of any obstruction and could shut with no obstacle, but that's not what happened. The man stepped out of his house and stood toe to toe with William. William was tall for his age and had a larger frame than most kids his age. The dramatic effect of a grown man standing up to a high school kid lost its effect when the grown man was not towering over him. Amanda's stepfather underestimated William's size.

The man still had years and life experience to his advantage, "Well, go on then, use it," He said looking down at the bat in William's hand.

"Listen, asshole, just leave Amanda alone."

"I ain't got no idea what you are talking about kid. I ain't never touched that girl."

William saw right through all the falsity, "Fucking lies."

"Kid, I suggest you get the fuck off my lawn before I cram that bat so far up your ass, I ain't got no time for this shit."

PART ONE

William stood his ground, almost shuddering, the man could see the fear that lived just beyond William's eyes. He knew he had the upper hand on the young high schooler. The man stood and waited on William to act. He saw that the stalemate could go on all morning, so he finally gave up.

"Yeah, I didn't think you had the balls to swing that thing. Can't say I'm shocked, any friend of that stupid spoiled bitch can't be that bright," His words were meant to antagonize William, and it worked.

William's grip tightened on the bat, his heart was racing at full speed now, the rage boiled up inside him. That fear that once existed in his eyes dissipated and changed to anger and hate. The man witnessed the transformation taking place right before his eyes and knew he had stirred the boy to rage. He was aware that this kid was ready to act, and prepared himself for whatever may come next.

William pulled the bat back and squeezed his grip tighter than it had already been and began his violent swing of the childhood relic that was now a weapon. His movements were so predictable the man knew what was coming before it even began.

The bat felt light in his hands. It swung with ease. William hurled the fat end of it toward its target. He clenched his teeth and squeezed his eyes shut tight and prepared himself for the punishing blow that would serve as the long overdue retribution on a sick, twisted, abusive man.

As the bat cut the air, William knew where the moment of impact should be. That moment never came. The bat swung all the way through, never stopping and never finding it's intended target. It only came to a stop when it reached the end of its arc, which was the end of William's range of motion. He missed!

The man still stood. He might have been older than William and even slower in some respects, but he had lived a full life, full of experience, so much more than William. He knew that the bat was coming his way. He had anticipated it way before William knew he was going to do it. William had broadcast the bat swing and was so obvious that the man had more than ample time to dodge the would-be blow of the blunt object and remain standing on his feet.

The realization of William's missed swing coincided with his eyes opening, only to see the flat, broad side of the man's fist traveling at a high rate of speed towards him. Unlike his adversary, William was unable to dodge the strike, and the man's fist made contact with William's face, just below his left eye and to the left of his nose.

The punch wasn't particularly hard, but it did throw William from his feet and knocked him to the ground. The entire event was over in fractions of a second.

"Fucking pathetic," The man said in disgust as he still stood over William's downed body.

Slowly the realization of the morning's events made themselves real to him. He failed to do any of the things he set out to do. In fact, he was certain he had only succeeded in one thing, making Amanda's hellish life even worse. Before he could gather himself back and formulate a counter attack against this monster, the man was gone. His disappearance from the fracas was followed by the sharp slam of the front door as he retreated inside. It was the exclamation point on the entire confrontation.

William picked himself back up off the ground and for the first time began to feel the sting on his face, it hurt, but not nearly as bad as the bite in his pride. He failed to rescue his best friend; now he had to do something even more difficult, find Amanda and tell her what he had done.

He walked to the end of the driveway where his bike still lay; he left the bat behind; he didn't want it anymore, it would only serve as a cruel reminder of his failure. He picked up his bike he began his journey to the school. His peddling was a lot less vigorous than it had been earlier that morning. He was defeated, deflated and just overall beaten.

He arrived at the school oblivious to the time of day and what his next move would be. He knew he had to find Amanda, checking his watch he did the quick math in his head and knew that Mr. Mangatto's math class would be ending in about ten minutes. He raced to the classroom to wait. He was waiting for Amanda to exit the room. The bell rang just as he got to the closed door, a second later it opened.

The throng of students began to exit all the doors lining the hallway; Amanda was the last to exit Mr. Mangatto's class.

"Will, I thought you were out sick today!" She exclaimed.

"Listen, Amanda, I have to talk to you," William's tone was hurried, and out of breath.

"Jesus Will, what happened to your face?" Her tone changed.

"That's what I have to talk to you about," William was in panic mode.

"What did you do?" Amanda started to feel William's fear and began to adopt it as her own.

"Something dumb. Please, can we go somewhere and talk?" William was now pleading, almost begging.

"OK," Amanda's mind was racing, she had no idea what he was about to tell her.

They found a quiet space outside the school's side door, no one would know they were there, and no one would pass through there all day.

"OK, now you have me officially freaked out. What happened to you?" Amanda was trying her hardest to remain patient.

William wasn't sure how to start. He knew he was in too deep already to try to sweet talk or sugar coat his actions, so he opted for the straightforward approach, "Amanda, I went to your house this

CHAPTER 16

morning."

In a quick second, Amanda put the pieces of the puzzle together, all just based off of that single sentence.

"Will, you didn't, please tell me you didn't. Oh god, what have you done? Is that what happened to your face? Did Charlie do that to you?" She was beginning to breathe heavy.

"Charlie?" William questioned.

"My stepfather," Amanda answered.

Up to that point William never knew his name, he had always been referred to by so many other names, but never "Charlie."

"Yes, he did. I confronted him. I'm sorry Amanda. I needed to do something; he was never going to stop. He was going to keep going until he killed you, do you realize that? These people don't stop, they don't grow out of abusive tendencies, they keep going, getting worse and worse until something horrible happens, he would have killed you. Just look what he did to your arm," William did his best to rationalize the situation.

"Do you realize what you have done? Yes, you are right he will kill me. As soon as I get home, he is going to kill me!" Amanda's voice began to shake.

"I'm very sorry, I needed to do something, I wanted to help you, I wanted to rescue you."

"I didn't need to be rescued! I told you, one more year. One more year and I would be out, free and clear."

"You wouldn't have lasted one more year, don't you see? Today it's a broken arm, and it's a concussion then more and more hospital visits. Amanda, you would have been dead before your one-year timeline came up. You have to see that; you have to know that. He was never going to stop; he was going to kill you eventually. I couldn't have that on me. I love you too much to let that happen," William's eyes were now filling with tears.

Amanda joined him in crying, "I can't go back there, I can never go back to that house again."

William sunk in his stature, "I know. I didn't think it all the way through. I was furious I needed to act."

Amanda was quiet, the only movement she displayed were the tears that formed in her eyes and then rolled down her face.

"I'm sorry. I fucked up," William continued pleading with her.

After a few seconds of silence, Amanda spoke, "No. You didn't fuck up. I did. I brought you into this. What were you supposed to do? I know what I have to do now. I have to be as brave as you."

"What does that mean?"

"It's about time I act, and I need to talk to someone. I certainly can't go back to that house. I don't have a lot of options here," Amanda was growing calmer by the second.

"I messed up your life, didn't I?" William asked.

"No, my life was messed up way before today if anything, you might have saved my life today," Amanda was calm now.

"Now what?" William asked a simple but poignant question.

"Mr. Schroeder," Amanda said in a hushed tone.

Mr. Schroeder was a guidance counselor at the school. His primary duties were just to make sure the kids that fell under his responsibility, students with last names ending in A–M, made all the class and grade requirements to graduate high school. He always went far out of his way to help students with everything he could. He spent countless hours after school helping seniors research colleges and helped them fill out their applications. He showed them where to find financial aid. He spent his weekends volunteering at a youth crisis center, and so many other youth organizations geared to help troubled teens. He was a great man, a man dedicated to his work and even more dedicated to making the world he lived in a much better place for the generation coming up behind him.

CHAPTER 16

"Mr. Schroeder? The guidance counselor? What can he do?" William was feeling lost as if there was a missing puzzle piece that Amanda still had hidden away.

"I never told you this, but I had a long talk with him last year. I didn't tell him everything, but I let him know enough. I said the problem stopped, and there was nothing anyone needed to do. Looking back on it now I'm pretty sure he saw through my bullshit, but without me willing to press the issue there was nothing he could do. So, for the past year, he has been periodically checking in with my... um, 'situation.' He had a standing offer to help me whenever I needed it. Well, I think today is as good as any day to call him on that offer," Amanda was almost speaking light-heartedly about the situation.

William couldn't help but notice her almost joking approach to this life-altering crossroads. Through the years the situation at Amanda's house was wearing her down, emotionally, physically and mentally. She pushed all her strength into being strong and putting on the show that everything was OK. She thought she had a year of strength left, a year of hiding bruises, a year of telling herself that it wasn't so bad, she was wrong. She had nothing left, her tank had been on empty for some time now, she just refused to acknowledge it. Amanda thought if she never looked down at her fuel gauge she would never see how close to the "empty" line she was. She ignored her fatigue, her emotional strain, and physical bruises. She knew that giving in and quitting meant that evil won, and she was never going to let that happen.

What William did for her that morning saved her life. He set the actions into play, moves that would end with her getting out of a potentially deadly situation and into something safe and sane. He didn't know how close to the edge Amanda had been when he set out in the morning, but now he could see it in her eyes. The weight

PART ONE

lifted, the stress and tension left her body. All of those worries she carried with her for all those years were gone, none of it mattered. It felt amazing to be free of it all. She wanted to be angry at William for interfering, after all, she had a plan. She asked him to abide by her wishes, but she couldn't be mad at him, she loved him, and she knew his actions would eventually be the actions that guaranteed her a longer life.

A calmness resonated between them, unlike any that had ever been present in all the years the two wayward souls had been friends.

"Are you OK?" William asked in a more earnest tone than he had ever used. He wasn't asking to be polite he wanted to know.

Likewise, Amanda wasn't going to give the pre-rehearsed textbook reply; she was going to think about it. She reached down inside her gut, deeper than she had dared to go for so many years. She explored it and searched it for anything that would tell her that she wasn't "OK." Nothing existed, her gut was empty, for the first time in a very long time; she felt peace, calmness, and safety.

She drifted back to a time in her life; she was four, it was Christmas. Her mother sat on the floor with her in her lap. Her mother was beautiful; this was before she started drinking and before the drugs took their toll on her. Across the room in a high back leather chair sat her father. He had a smile on his face as he watched his daughter open the assortment of presents that lined the bottom of the decorated Douglas Fir tree that sat proudly in the front corner of the family living room. It would be the last time they would all be together as one complete and happy family unit. It would also be the last time Amanda would be truly happy. Time had a wicked sense about it, it warped and corrupted that little girl's dreams until they were faint pictures that would appear less and less often in the corners of her mind.

Her friendship with a young boy from Lake Ronkonkoma would

be the only saving grace in her life. He was young and naive but possessed a good heart. He did things and said things that had an actual impact on her life, an impact so deep it reached way beyond his understanding. He showed that girl that life didn't have to be ugly. It was beautiful at times, so many people flowed in and out of her life but this one person, this William McCabe flowed in and rescued her, and he would never even know it.

William feared that she didn't hear him or worse, things weren't alright repeated the question, "Are you OK?"

She looked up at him, the bruise on his face was losing its fresh red tint and shifting to a purple hue.

"Yes Will, I am OK. I'm going to be OK," She took a deep breath, pulled him in tightly to her and gave him a loving embrace, "Thank you, and I love you, Will McCabe."

She knew the severity of what was going to happen next.

They made their way down to the school's office and back in the corner where Mr. Schroeder's office was. He was sitting at his desk reviewing college applications when Amanda bypassed the traditional knock and just walked in.

"Mr. Schroeder, I need to talk to you," It was a sentence riddled with secret meanings, but Mr. Schroeder knew what it meant.

Without missing a beat, he replied, "Mr. McCabe would you be so kind as to wait outside? And please close the door on your way."

William looked at Amanda hoping for a reprieve, none came. He left Mr. Schroeder's office, closed the door behind him and sat down on the small salmon colored loveseat pushed up against the wall in the hallway outside the guidance counselors' offices. William slumped forward, pushed his face into his hands and felt the stinging pain from the bruise for the first time. Without any warning or control, he began to cry.

Over an hour passed before the door to Mr. Schroeder's office clicked and opened. William's head shot up, and he made instant eye contact with Amanda, her eyes were red, she had been crying, but her face didn't look forlorn, it looked happy, relieved.

"Come on Will, I need your help with something," Amanda spoke with in a liberated voice.

"Um… OK," William was confused but stood up and readied himself to offer any assistance he could.

Mr. Schroeder added, "Guys, please be careful."

"We'll be fine," Amanda answered.

William's mind was racing, what were they about to do? What task would warrant a "be careful" from a senior staff member of the education system?

Amanda didn't let William wonder for too long, "We are going to my house to get my stuff. I can't do much with one good working arm; I need your help."

"Your house?" William was shocked and spoke a little too loudly.

"Don't worry dumbass, they aren't there, I'll explain on the way, we got a bus to take us," Amanda looked confident and sure, it put William at ease.

Waiting out in front of the school was the short yellow school bus converted from a Ford van. It was the bus reserved for the special needs students and small class field trips. They boarded the bus and William noticed a box of black lawn and leaf bags on the first bench seat. Amanda grabbed the seat behind the one holding the bags and William slid in next to her.

"So what happened?" He finally asked. The anticipation was bubbling over.

"Well, I filed an official complaint of abuse against both of those assholes, and the county sheriff arrested them about thirty minutes ago. They will most likely make bail and be home tonight or tomorrow, but it doesn't matter, until further notice, I am the

CHAPTER 16

property of the state. Mr. Schroeder set me up in an all-girls home in Riverhead. He knows the lady who runs it, and she is a saint. She has done so much for girls just like me. I'm going to be safe and protected there."

William interjected, "Riverhead? But what about school?"

"I'm already enrolled, and Mr. Schroeder is sending all my transcripts over there as we speak," Amanda was missing William's concern.

"But, what about us? Who will I eat lunch with?" William realized that his concern was minuscule in comparison to what was on Amanda's plate.

"Oh, um… Will, I'm sorry. We are not going to be in the same school anymore," She answered.

When the words left her lips, it was the first time she had given it some thought. She began to get teary eyed and emotional but caught herself when the bus pulled up in front of her house. William shuddered at the thought of the incident that took place there just hours earlier. He could see his baseball bat still laying on the dead grass of the front lawn.

Amanda grabbed the box of bags and hollered, "Let's go, I need help taking everything I can."

The two worked at a rapid pace, bagging and loading up all the mementos of Amanda's life. She made on-the-fly decisions about what should come with her and what should stay behind, getting lost forever. When they had finished the task, they loaded four full black plastic bags onto the bus's back seats.

"Man, it's depressing when your entire life fits into four lawn and leaf bags," Amanda noticed.

"Not your 'whole' life," William corrected.

Amanda was quiet for a second, then spoke, "No, not my whole life. Thanks to you."

PART ONE

Amanda was eager to change the subject, "You had something to tell me yesterday, at school before you saw my arm. What was it?"

William thought for a minute; he couldn't recall anything.

"You said you had to tell me what happened yesterday, so something happened two days ago, you don't remember?" Amanda continued.

Suddenly it came back; he was going to tell her about the Melissa incident. Had that only been two days ago? To him, it seemed like a lifetime ago. So much had happened in that short span of time. He felt as if an entire lifetime took place in the course of those two days. So much had happened, so much innocence lost and so much peace attained. William realized at that moment that the burden he had been carrying around was also gone. His actions, despite how ill-advised they may have been, set in motion a series of events that successfully removed his friend from a looming dangerous situation. For the first time in a very long time, he felt at ease with the situation. His best friend was going to be all right. She now had a chance to live the life she deserved. There would still be some pieces left to be picked up, but things were on their way to finding their happy ending.

Amanda pulled William back from his drifting journey, "Well, what did you want to tell me?"

"Just some stupid story," William answered.

As the bus continued back to the school, he told Amanda the whole story involving Melissa, her teeth and Kenny's infatuation with Jackie and her well endowed upper half.

Amanda laughed hard at the story. It was a good laugh, a deep cleansing laugh. One that she needed to have, it pulled her out of the real situation she was entering into and let her live like a kid again if even just for a few minutes. William watched as she continued to laugh and thought how much he was going to miss her and miss these times when they just made each other laugh. She had been through more than anyone should ever have to endure and she still maintained her innocence and love for life. She was the greatest person he had ever known, and no one would ever come close to his heart like she did. He loved her so much he was willing to sacrifice their relationship to save her life.

The little bus pulled into the half circle driveway that lined the front of the school. Mr. Schroeder was standing out in front, talking with two females, one in a maroon skirt and blazer and the other in a tan pantsuit.

Amanda exited the bus leaving the bags of belongings behind; William stayed on the bus only because he didn't know what he was supposed to be doing. He watched as Amanda received a proper introduction to the two women standing with Mr. Schroeder. The meeting sealed with a handshake from maroon skirt lady and a hug from pantsuit lady. Amanda motioned to William to exit the bus and join her.

Amanda made the introductions, starting with pant suit lady, "Will, this is Mrs. Lawson, she is the one I was telling you about. She runs the home in Riverhead."

Mrs. Lawson extended her right hand, it was aged, it had seen some hard times, "Mr. McCabe, it's a pleasure to meet you. I've heard many great things about you."

William was confused. Ten minutes ago he didn't know this woman even existed; now she not only knew of him, but he also had a reputation with her. William was unaware he even had a reputation in general.

Amanda made an attempt to clarify the situation, "Will, Mr. Schroeder and Mrs. Lawson are friends. I told Mr. Schroeder all the stuff you have done for me, and he has been telling Mrs. Lawson."

"Oh… I see," William was less confused after Amanda's brief

summary.

Things had been happening at a record pace, and William couldn't help but feel a few steps behind everyone else. It was as if they were all in some elaborate plan together that had been in the works for the past few years and trying to bring young William up to speed in one morning.

William turned and looked at maroon skirt lady. Amanda, sensing his confusion about the second stranger in attendance, again made the proper introduction.

"Will, this is Mrs. Silvan. She works for social services. She is handling my case," Amanda explained.

William stuck out his hand for the ceremonial shake.

"Now William, Amanda has chosen to bring you into her situation against my best advice. I want to make this transition as easy as possible for her and if having you around does that, well… I can make an exception. I need something from you, however. A promise. I need you to promise that you will not share the events of today with anyone, not your friends, not your teachers not anyone. Where Amanda is going is to be kept secret, it's for her safety. Also, and I'm not prone to asking children to lie, but you need to make up a story about that bruise on your face. It was admirable, what you did this morning, but foolish too. You need to make sure you throw in an extra 'thank you' in your prayers tonight young man. A bruise on your face was probably the best case scenario for you. Consider yourself lucky," Mrs. Silvan lectured.

"Yes ma'am" William politely answered back.

Mrs. Silvan turned her attention to Amanda and continued, "Sweetheart, we will give you a moment to say your 'goodbyes' then we have to get going, OK?"

Amanda just gave a simple nod of acknowledgment. The adults peeled away and moved just out of the audible range of the two

CHAPTER 16

friends.

Amanda spoke first, "Will... this is the part that sucks, leaving you. You will never really know how much you have done for me. I love you, and I always will. I know I keep saying this, but you have to believe me, you saved my life."

William tried to muster together some string of words that would convey his feelings for her, nothing came out, only tears. He did his best to fight them back, but when he saw tears also welling up in Amanda's eyes, he couldn't find the strength to stop his. William hugged his friend and cried with her. He loved her, not in the normal high school crush way, this was deeper than any love he had ever felt. Losing her was like losing a part of himself. He was happy, relieved that she would finally be safe from the hands of that evil man, but he was hurt. The pain that struck him in places he never knew could hurt was unbearable.

As they broke their embrace, William couldn't help but wonder if that would be the last time he would ever hold her again. The thought made his stomach turn, and he pushed it out of his mind. The tears were running down both of their faces when William finally spoke.

"I love you, Amanda Flores," He confessed.

"I love you too William McCabe," She confessed back.

The three adults waiting to the side reappeared. Mrs. Silvan opened the passenger door of her state-issued social services vehicle, and Amanda climbed in.

Mrs. Silvan shook hands with Mr. Schroder and Mrs. Lawson before walking around to the opposite side of her tan four-door sedan and climbing inside.

William felt a hand on his shoulder, he looked up and saw Mr. Schroder giving him a broad smile, "William, what you did today may have been dangerous, but it was heroic."

"Mr. Schroeder, I'm losing my best friend today. I'm sorry, I just don't feel that heroic," William replied.

"Son, take the rest of the day off, go home, ice that face and tell your mother you fell. After that, tell her you love her," Mr. Schroder suggested.

Amanda rolled down the window of the passenger side of the Social Services vehicle. She had tears in her eyes when she looked back up at William.

"I'll write."

She wouldn't.

"I'll call."

She wouldn't.

"I'll come visit you."

She wouldn't do that either.

Amanda had all the intention in the world to do all of these things, but she quickly realized that keeping one foot in her old life was one foot too many. She understood the only break to make was a clean one. William was collateral damage.

PART TWO

CHAPTER 1

Lake Ronkonkoma, Long Island, New York.
April 14, 1999, 5:00 a.m.

The digital clock radio alarm let out its pre-programmed chime, it was designed to move its owner from a state of peaceful slumber to a state of acute alertness. The alarm clock had executed its duties with precision and reliability, but it wasn't needed. William had been wide awake for over an hour, just staring at the ceiling, trying to lasso in a million thoughts that had been racing through his head all night. Today marked the start of a new venture in his life.

It all started about three weeks ago when, in a turn of blind luck, he got a phone call from an advertising agency in Manhattan. They wanted to see him for an interview. William had received his bachelor's degree in June of the previous year. He had spent the last ten months working odd jobs to make some extra cash while waiting for that one call to come. The call that came three weeks ago signified the end of the odd job phase of his life and the beginning of his career phase. He was pursuing his goal of being a copywriter for a New York City advertising agency, and that goal was coming to fruition. Armed with only his student portfolio and an amateur résumé lacking in anything of substance or experience, he began a rigorous hunt for his first real job. He was so ambitious he wasn't going to wait for a position to be open. He opted for the blanket sending of résumés to every one of the advertising agencies listed in the registry.

Eighty-six résumés mailed out and three phone calls back for an interview. William thought it was a raw deal at the time, little did he know that sending résumés out blindly rarely got a response. In a remarkable swing of good fortune, he got an offer from one, and today was his first day of work. A small upstart agency located on West 14th Street in the Greenwich Village section of Manhattan. They had just landed a new micro-brew beer client and needed a young writer to work on the account, and William found himself in the right place at the right time. Truthfully, the agency could have offered William virtually no pay for the job, and he still would have accepted. He was young, had no experience and no expenses, he was still in the basement bedroom in his parent's house.

No matter which path or how rocky or smooth the road was, William was now an actual working writer, and working in New York City and today was his first day.

His plan was to catch the 6:20 AM train to Manhattan's Penn Station. From there he could jump on either the 2 or 3 train to 14th Street and walk three blocks to his new office. He left himself plenty of time as a pad, just in case something went wrong, like a delay in the train's arrival or a wrong turn on his walk to the office.

William was up, ready, out of his house and on his way to the train station even earlier than he anticipated. With his extra pad of allotted time, he decided to make a quick stop at the local 7-Eleven for a cup

CHAPTER 1

of coffee. Drinking coffee was still relatively new to William. It was something he picked up in his college years while pulling all-nighters studying for his exams, or just trying to remain somewhat awake and attentive after a long night of drinking with his college buddies.

The 6:20 train was right on time and William settled himself into a window seat, and just looked out into the dimly lit sky that covered the early morning hours of the Long Island landscape. The sun was just beginning to break through and expose all the hidden secrets usually safe under the cover of night.

The commute into Penn Station went smoothly, as smooth as the steel wheels of the train. Those same steel wheels danced gracefully on the steel rails that lay beneath them. William was still too young and caught up in his affairs to truly appreciate the engineering marvel of his morning ride. The early hour saw slightly fewer commuters than normal, but still more than any one city should ever be host to on any given weekday morning. Penn Station was nothing short of a menagerie of the human species, all running in different directions with different purposes and different destinations. William found the entrance to the subway; it was right at the end of the corridor where his train dispensed with its passengers like a cement truck dumping its contents. Passing through the turnstile and onto the waiting subway, he felt his transition from one train to the other went quite smoothly. A good sign that he was destined to master the art of the New York City commute.

William's new office building was still quiet at this hour. The rest of his co-workers were not scheduled to wander in for another hour. This down time left William with some time to kill. He decided to take a stroll around the block, giving the neighborhood a quick once-over.

As he turned the corner, he stumbled upon a remarkable find, or at least he felt it was. A small cafe/coffee shop sat wedged between a nail salon and a vitamin shop. It was one of the very few neighborhood establishments open at this hour. He opened the glass door, and the small bell tied to the handle on the inside of the door gave a welcome chime. No one seemed to notice even the bell's announcement that a new patron had entered the establishment, or if they did, no one paid it much attention. Not waiting to be seated, even as a rookie New Yorker William knew that the best course of action was always just to assert yourself, don't wait to be invited.

He took up residence at an empty stool bolted to the floor in front of the counter. This cafe was a nostalgic trip back to a time when coffee shops had personality. William thought that this attempt at being retro was a clever marketing scheme until he realized that it wasn't a scheme at all, it was the real deal. Buzz's Coffee Shop had been a neighborhood staple for the past fifty years, and the dated interior decor wasn't some ironic attempt at being chic or clever. The dated interior was due to Buzz's, or the current lease holder's, lack of willingness to spend money for any upgrades. So there it stood, this gem from the past, serving up the best coffee south of 59th Street, and had been doing so long before William stumbled upon it while killing time.

Settling into his seat, he grabbed a used, dispensed newspaper that sat on the counter next to him and flipped it over to immediately check out the sports pages. He figured the less eager he looked for service, the quicker the offer of assistance would come, and sure enough he was right.

"What'll it be?" Was the question asked by the voice behind the counter?

Without looking up from his newspaper reading, William answered, "Coffee, cream, two sugars."

"Anything else?" The voice followed up with.

Still not breaking character William kept his focus on the

CHAPTER 1

newspaper. He wasn't actually reading it but using it more as a prop. He was playing the role of a Manhattan business type who was way too busy to peel himself away from the compelling words printed on cheap newsprint. William finally answered, "Nope, just the coffee will do."

Still staring at the black print, he waited for some acknowledgment that never came. Finally, he peered over the top of the newspaper and saw nothing, the waitress had retreated to another part of the café to resume her role co-starring another leading man.

His first screen test as an official New Yorker was over, and he felt he was convincing in his role. He immediately went back to reading his paper, this time for real. The Yankees season was still fresh and new, and they were coming off the best season William could remember them having. A staggering record of 114-48 and it was capped off with an impressive World Series win, a sweep against the San Diego Padres. He was halfway through the box scores when he heard his coffee being delivered on the other side of his constructed newspaper barricade. He broke character and dropped his paper to thank the waitress, this time face to face. Thanking her was his intention, but it's not at all what transpired.

With the newspaper peeled back, he was free to view the scene playing out in front of him it was like a curtain pulled back revealing a magical scene set for a Broadway play. That's when he first saw her. Seconds ago she was just the faceless waitress bringing him coffee; now she was so much more. He had been struck; a lightening bolt of emotion ran through his body. A white hot heat burned from the inside of his chest, his face, getting equally hot, turned flush. He tried to conjure up any string of words he could, something that resembled a cohesive sentence. She was beautiful, not in the usual classic sense of the word, something a lot different. This time it was personal. It was a beauty that resonated deep with William, but he could see where the rest of the viewing public might only see her as above average. She was tall, slim, almost a dancer's body, very lean. She had olive skin, skin that looked so soft to the touch, like a silk dress. Her hair was pulled back for practical reasons, but William knew that once unleashed it was a gorgeous mane of hair, equal parts wavy and curly. Pulled back it showed off the most perfect face William had seen in his young life. It had a radiance about it, cute but not childish, elegant but not dainty. She was real, not like those women in the ads for which he would soon be writing headlines and taglines. Her eyes were brown but wide, showing them off like a prized possession. Her lips were full, pouty, but this was genetics not of any surgical or medical means. She had one small dark mole that lived just above her upper lip and off to the left. It was the kind of imperfection that she hated her whole life, but others found so appealing. It was her trademark, her calling card. Her neck was long and around it lived the most subtle golden chain holding up a cross of the same color. Her posture was perfect as if a pole had been inserted into her back for permanent support. Her hands were the hands of a woman who worked, still young in texture but showing signs of wear and tear. Her nail polish had been barely applied. It looked like it had been fresh and new at one time, but life and time had worn it down. Now it was just a scattering of paint chips arranged on her small nail surface similar to the way a collection of exotic islands appears on a topographic map. What William noticed about her hands is what wasn't there, a ring.

William was infatuated with her, not in his normal way of looking at girls. This time it was her face that paralyzed him. The face of perfection, he thought to himself. Her body came secondary to him, in fact, he didn't even notice it at this point, it could have not been there, and he might not even know. He would come to see it eventually, and it also would not disappoint him.

CHAPTER 1

William caught her eye and stammered through something he thought was a "Thank you," but it wasn't. Thinking he blew his only shot to make a good first impression he hung his head, accepting defeat. Instead, the waitress smiled, she had been hit on and flirted with a million times a day, this was the first time she could recall feeling flattered by it. She quickly took mental stock of her appearance and thought, as often girls will, that she was a mess. Without saying another word to her admiring customer, she quickly scurried away.

William, thinking he chased her away, tried to concentrate on anything else, but failed. Her face had been permanently etched into his mind. That was a face he would not soon forget and, as fate would have it, he would not have to forget it. Just minutes later the mystery waitress returned but looking a little different. It took William a second to realize that during her absence, she had done a quick round of maintenance, like a race car pulling into a pit stop. Her hair was now released from the tight bun of captivity and let free to flow like the waves that crashed on the Long Island beaches of his youth. A quick touch up of makeup had also been applied, and William couldn't be sure, but he thought maybe even one more button on her waitress blouse was undone. Nothing distasteful, there were still more than enough buttons clasped to maintain the air of decency.

She approached slowly when she noticed William watching her, a smile spread across her face. As she got closer to him, almost too close she spoke in the most cheerful of tones, "Will there be anything else, sir?"

"Just your name," William replied. He couldn't believe he said it, it was out of his mouth before his brain and reason could stop it.

"Jessica," She answered in the sweetest of southern accents. "And yours?" She asked.

"William, but I'm thinking about going with Billy," William

answered, again surrendering more information than he intended to.

"Na, I like William," She said not losing eye contact with him.

"OK, William it is," William relented.

"Do you work or live nearby, William?" Jessica prodded.

Even Jessica had to admit to herself that this was more forward than she had ever been with a customer or anyone she just met. Something just felt welcoming about William, maybe it was his blue eyes or just the way he made no attempt at hiding his interest in her.

William had a smile on his face when he answered her inquiry, "Yes, I work around the corner… well, I will be working around the corner. I'm a copywriter for an ad agency, today is my first day."

"So I reckon I will see you for coffee more often then?" Jessica danced her tones somewhere between asking and telling.

William felt Jessica's flirting being kicked up a notch and figured he had better keep up or be left behind and lose out to some smooth, quick talking Manhattanite. He thought for a minute and finally gave his reply, "If you are serving it, I will be back every day."

William cringed at the cheesiness of his last line and thought for sure he blew it. Jessica looked at him for what seemed like hours until finally, she broke out in laughter, almost uncontrollably. When she settled herself down, she looked into William's eyes and quietly said, "Sweetheart, that was the worst line ever, but bless your heart for trying."

William blushed, he figured he ruined whatever chemistry was starting to unfold in this secret cafe. He began to surrender hope, then Jessica slid his check to him and written in purple ink was her name and right below it, her phone number!

Typically William would think that was an excellent way to start his career in New York City. The first City girl he met he got her number, it was going to be city girls galore from here on, but not this time, this time was different. William wasn't thinking about the

CHAPTER 1

scores of beautiful women walking the streets of Manhattan right at that moment, and how many of them were willing to surrender their phone numbers. No, he was thinking about Jessica and how maybe the first number he got would be the only one he would ever need.

CHAPTER 2

"This is your desk William, or is it Bill, or Billy, or Will?" Asked Mr. Henry Trask, everyone in the office called him Hank. He was pointing to a small cubicle that was situated right next to the entrance to the back office space.

"Everyone usually calls me William, but Billy is OK too," William answered his new boss.

"OK, Billy it is. We have a William in accounting, and honestly, two William's would just fuck things up for me," Hank Trask so crudely put it.

William had never actually heard a grown up in a position of authority curse before. He felt a little put off by it but liked it at the same time. He felt it was a nice introduction to the adult world he had heard so much about.

Taking a seat, Billy adjusted his chair and computer screen to his liking. Hank Trask started to walk out without giving Billy any direction as to what he should be doing, then he stopped. He laughed to himself and turned back to Billy, "You have no idea what you are

PART TWO

supposed to be doing, do you?"

The question was rhetorical, but Billy answered anyway, "No, not a clue."

"OK," Hank Trask offered up a suggestion. "Read the paper, for now, IT guys get in around 9:30, they will be up here to get you up and running on your computer. In the meantime, I am going to get you the case studies and the marketing plan for Great Creek Brewery, that will be your first client. See how you do on that, and we will start to give you more. Listen, kid, we are a small agency here, we got our foot in the door on a few cool little clients that could really propel us to the next level. You're in a good spot, ground floor and all. Keep your head out of your ass and out of my way, and you will do great."

Hank started to walk away, again stopped and turned to offer one more piece of sage advice, "And kid... welcome aboard."

No sooner was Hank Trask out of the room then a short weasel-faced man appeared out of the recess' of the maze of office cubicles.

"Hey, New Guy," His weasel voice matched his face. "I'm Spencer, people just call me Spence."

"Hey Spence, I'm Will... I mean Billy," Billy was still adjusting to his new name.

"Cool. Well, Billy, it is good to have you on board, I could use the help. They got me buried over here. Which whatever, it's not a big deal. I am the senior copywriter, so I guess it just comes with the territory," Spence said offering up a helping of fake modesty.

Just as quickly as he appeared, Spence disappeared back into his hovel made of half height movable partition walls. Billy, finding the exchange odd at best, returned to reading his newspaper. He wasn't two pages in before a tall well built, and sharp dressed man entered the room. He made direct eye contact with Billy and spoke in a fast moving pace and a distinct Brooklyn accent.

"McCabe, right?" Not waiting for an answer he continued. "You like coffee?" Once again not waiting for a reply, "Let's take a walk."

No words were shared between the two men as they crossed the office space and into the elevator. The closing elevator doors served as a cue for the fast talking man to do what he did best, talk.

"I'm Eric Wright, the senior creative director here. Just call me Eric, I don't need that Mr. Wright bullshit…"

Eric paused and looked blankly ahead as if an epiphany had just hit him, "Mr. Wright? I like that."

Playing out a verbal scenario out-loud he continued, "Hello ladies, are you looking for Mr. Right? Well, your search is over. Ha! I like that!"

He turned and looked at William with a big smile on his face. William smiled and nodded back, a sign Eric understood to mean that Billy approved of his joke.

Eric continued, "Where was I?" Again not waiting for an answer. "So I did six years at McCann, Hank and I go way back, he started this place with one client and brought me on board to help it grow. We are a creative juggernaut here, we aren't the biggest or the best, but one thing we are is 'Best bang for your buck.' We pride ourselves on that. I liked your shit, you can write, not great, not super creative, but you got the foundation."

The elevator stopped in the lobby and almost before the doors opened Eric began walking out, timing his debarking perfectly with the opening of the elevator doors. He continued through the lobby of the building never breaking his stride.

Eric continued, never missing a beat, "We pitched a few small companies last year, businesses that were a lot like us. Good products but no corporate budgets. We landed about 70% of what we pitched."

Billy chimed in with what he thought was an appropriate response, "That's good."

"Good? McCabe that's fucking top notch, excellent is what it is.

We started getting more work than we knew what to do with."

"Hey, Carl," Eric greeted the security desk guy almost mid-thought. "Carl is a fucking prince, the guy would do anything for you. Make friends with Carl, and you're set. Anyway, as I was saying, we were growing, and, to be honest, we were short on talent. You meet Spence yet?"

Billy didn't answer expecting Eric to continue talking but this time Eric paused, he really did want a reply.

"Yes," Billy finally answered.

"Good, nice enough guy but a fucking schmuck, and looks like a weasel. He is an OK copywriter, but not great, kind of a hack who thinks he is better than he is. Listen, my point is we have work, tons of it. You can really make your bones here and learn a lot."

They continued walking down the street and talking simultaneously until they appeared at a neighborhood cafe. The two men walked in and grabbed an open booth. It wasn't until they sat down that Billy realized they were in the same cafe he had visited just that morning, the one with the waitress, Jessica. His eyes began scanning the room looking for her, suddenly Eric broke Billy's concentration, "What the fuck you looking for McCabe? It's a coffee shop, don't they have these in… where are you from?"

Billy again, not sure if this was a question Eric wanted to be answered, "Long Island?"

Eric's eyes got wider, "Are you asking or telling me? Jesus, Long Island? Where about?"

"Ronkonkoma," Billy said with almost a little too much pride.

"Holy shit, that's far! I know we are probably paying you shit right now but once you start making some cash, move your ass into the city; that commute will eventually kill you if you don't. Anyway, back to what I was saying, the work is good the experience is phenomenal and the people, for the most part, are good guys."

CHAPTER 2

Billy was locked in on every word coming out of Eric's mouth, he knew he had to be. If he let his mind wander for even just a second, he would be searching the cafe for Jessica. While his attention remained on Eric, a waitress stood over them and asked, "What'll it be boys?"

Eric ordered for them both as if they were on a date, "Two coffees, sweetheart."

Billy's heart raced as he broke eye contact with Eric to look at their order taker. She wasn't Jessica, she was just some other nameless waitress that Billy didn't care about. Billy had taken a quick pan around the cafe one more time before Eric started up again. A quarter of the way around the room he saw her, on the other side refilling patrons empty coffee mugs. This was the first time Billy saw her out from behind the counter. He could see her entire body, long muscular legs that seem to go on forever. Billy always fancied himself as a connoisseur of women's legs. Even Amanda, in High School, had toned legs.

Jessica sensing she was being watched gave a casual look Billy's way and when she saw him her face lit up with delight while also showing signs of confusion. Billy made a subtle facial gesture towards Eric hoping Jessica would understand that he was here on some morning business meeting type thing and not the creepy stalker that maybe he appeared to be. Billy was surprised when she smiled back and nodded, understanding his poor excuse of visual communication. Eric was still talking, and Billy hoped he hadn't missed anything important and rejoined the conversation. Although the word "conversation" was used very liberally in this instance. There was very limited, if any, back and forth between Billy and Eric. This was more of a lecture than a conversation.

The two men finished their coffee, Eric only breaking from his fast cadence of speech to take the occasional sip of coffee from his mug. Billy's head was spinning, Eric was feeding him an overload of information, more than Billy could ever hope to retain.

Eric threw a ten dollar bill down on the table, more than covering the two coffees. He turned and said to Billy, "Let's head back to the office. Those morons in IT should have your computer up and running by now."

They stood up from the table, and Billy looked back at the ten dollar bill on the table wondering why Eric was not going to wait for his change. But Eric, sensing his confusion, put it to bed with one simple statement, "These girls make shit money here."

Billy started to see Eric as a good-hearted guy. A young man who through hard work, pure talent, and a little luck found himself in sound financial standing. Eric always believed in helping young talent get their start in the business. He always felt that enough people stepped up and helped him when he was a young Graphic Designer from Bay Ridge. Eric now saw it as his duty to always go out of his way to help the younger talent coming up behind him. The circle of life as he liked to call it.

The two men left the cafe about thirty minutes after they had entered it, except now Billy exited with a better understanding of his future and his career and a second cup of coffee in his belly. They walked along the sidewalk back to the office, Eric seemed a little slower paced on the return trip, almost as if the added caffeine slowed him down instead of accelerating him. There were actually a few seconds of silence between them, but that didn't last long.

Eric, not breaking stride again or turning to face Billy asked, "Did you know that waitress back there?"

Billy weighed the brevity of the question, "I had a cup of coffee there this morning before coming into the office."

"She had eyes on you like stink on shit. I think you had more than just a cup of coffee in there this morning."

"Well, she gave me her number," Billy shared. That wasn't

something he would usually share with people, he was generally a very private person when it came to his dating life. Eric stirred something in him, he felt that he could open up to him and tell him things that might not be appropriate to say to a boss. Eric resonated a friend vibe more than a boss vibe.

Eric began to share more pearls of wisdom, "Listen, kid, this city can eat you up and spit you out when it comes to the ladies. They are the smartest and most beautiful women in the world. New York's 'C' list of women beat any other city's 'A' list. But mark my words. They will rip your heart out, piss on it and let their friends piss on it, then let their new boyfriends piss on it before handing it back to you in a pint-sized coffin. Ruthless doesn't begin to describe a New York City woman. But, if you keep your head on straight and stay sharp you will do just fine, who knows, you might find love, I guess anything is possible."

Eric paused then added, "Word of warning. You fuck things up with the coffee girl in there you will never be able to go in there again, and that place has the best coffee in the neighborhood. You don't want to have to drink the sludge from those street cart vendors."

CHAPTER 3

The first week of Billy's new job was a whirlwind of activity. It raced by faster than a child tearing through his mound of gifts on a Christmas morning. Eric kept him busy with creative pitches for new clients and re-writes and body copy edits for existing ones.

Friday rolled around, and Spence leaned in on Billy's cubicle. With his rodent face, he asked, "Hey new guy, some of us are going to grab some drinks after work today, you want to come?"

Billy had no plans for the night. He was always eager to bypass the evening rush of business suits and skirts. They were always pushing and shoving their way through the full subway cars and filing into the passenger cars of the Long Island Rail Road in anything but an orderly way.

Without much of a hesitation, Billy replied, "Sure. Thanks that sounds great."

Spence made one more offer that set Billy's mind into a whirlwind of thoughts. He added, "You can bring someone if you want, 'the more, the merrier' I always say."

The words were barely out of Spence's mouth when the idea rushed into his head like water being released from behind a broken dam wall.

"The waitress girl. Jessica!" Billy thought to himself.

Or at least he thought it was to himself. His ability to inner dialog must have been sacrificed during his moment of extreme excitement. He only realized this when Spence replied, "Whoever you want to bring man, it doesn't matter to me."

He was looking for the perfect opportunity to call her and invite her out, and this could be it.

Gathering the nerve, he picked up the receiver of his phone and slid down in his chair. It was as if the lower he sat, the more privacy he afforded. The cubicle setup was enough to give him ample privacy, but his confidence was still shaky at best when it came to the phone call he was about to make. He stared at the phone number written on the check Jessica had given him earlier that week. The paper in one hand and his phone in the other he waited for that wave of nerve to sweep over him and give him the "fuck it, just do it" attitude. That's all Billy would need to punch the collection of numbers into his desk phone. Being the careful planner and a skilled writer, he opted to plan ahead for a voice message option. Billy scribed a well thought out statement on a piece of office stationery and laid it out on the desk space in front of him. He sat in the quiet cubicle waiting, and then it came. That rush of confidence that usually arrives out of lack of patience, as if the brain is tired of sitting idle, so it creates this false assurance just to elicit some activity. Once the faux courage is enacted, the brain usually shuts off and becomes a spectator for the events that follow.

Equipped with his high dose of courage and his carefully written statement Billy slowly and methodically punched in the corresponding numbers into his phone. Hitting that last digit was

CHAPTER 3

like hitting the point of no return button. The phone in his ear began relaying ringing sounds that Billy assumed matched the ringing of Jessica's phone on the other end. After three painstaking rings, there was a click, and Billy's pulse jumped up an extra forty beats per minute. He inhaled and waited for a voice to connect at the other end. A voice never came. Instead, three melodic chimes sounded followed by a speech from a prerecorded female explaining to him that the number he was trying to reach was no longer in service. Confusion fell over Billy's face, had he been duped? Did she give him a false number? Was the playful banter between them all a show for a larger tip? Did she just see him like every other creep in New York who wanted to live out some fantasy of a one night stand with the cute waitress from the corner cafe? Was any of this possible? Had he really read the situation so incorrectly?

While all of these thoughts raced through his head, his emotions ran the gamut. He went from confusion to embarrassment to anger, all the while he was locked in on the purple ink that spelled out the false phone number, thinking to himself how he could be so stupid? Was Eric right? Had New York women been that ruthless and cold? That's when he saw it, staring at the mysterious phone number he saw it. That wasn't a seven, it was a one with a slight curl at the top! Was this just his way to justify the rejection or could it be that simple a mistake?

Billy quickly picked up his phone and this time went right to punching in the numbers, he didn't need to wait for the confidence build up again. He pushed the last button once again, and again the digital ringing tones played out in his ear, and once again a click on the other end of the phone. Waiting for those tones, Billy held his breath. The tones never replayed. Instead, a sweet sounding Texas-accented melodic voice almost sang on the other end. It clearly said, "Hello?"

Still not convinced he had actually reached the attractive young waitress from the coffee shop he asked, "Jessica?"

Once again a sweet sounding voice on the other end responded, "Yes, this is Jess, who am I speaking to?"

Billy froze as if he forgot his name, "Um… it's Billy, you uh, served me coffee on Monday and gave me your number."

"William! I was beginning to give up all hope of hearing from you. It's not every day I give my phone number to a patron."

"I know, I'm sorry about that, I just got busy with my new job and lost track of the days," Billy was lying through his teeth, the real reason for his hesitation in calling Jessica was based solely on fear, nothing else.

"So Mr. William, what can I do for you this Friday afternoon?"

Billy stammered through one long run-on sentence of a proposal, "Well, the thing is… um, some guys I work with at this new job and stuff, they are sort of going out to do this happy hour thing tonight and since I'm kind of new at this place. I don't really know anyone and I sort of figured it would be really helpful if you came out with me to help kind of break the ice with my new co-workers."

"Bless your heart, that is the sweetest cover story for a date I have ever heard. William if you want to ask a lady out for a date, four hours before the date is not the time to do it," Jessica reprimanded in the sweetest Texas accent Billy had ever heard.

This was not the reply Billy was expecting, but Jessica was not the kind of girl Billy expected either. She was a straight shooter, not afraid to call out bullshit when she saw it. She could be dainty as a flower and as abrasive as saw blade in the same sentence.

Sensing her response was more unorthodox than Billy was used to she retreated slightly back into her southern charm, "I'll tell you what I will do. I will accompany you tonight for your little work gathering on one condition. Next Friday night you treat me to a

CHAPTER 3

proper dinner, at the restaurant of my choosing."

Billy realized that this was the best deal he was ever going to get, he didn't even consider attempting a counter offer. He merely said, "Deal!"

Billy rattled off the details to her before thanking her again, the two exchanged formal good-byes and hung up. Billy knew the conversation could have gone better for him, but he was more impressed with Jessica's calm demeanor than his own shortcomings.

After taking some time to collect himself, he jettisoned to the men's room. He splashed some cool water on his face to regain his composure and alleviate some of the blushing redness that was now infecting his entire face. After a few minutes in the men's room, he returned back to his desk to finish out his day, especially now that he had something to look forward to. Something more than just seeing Spence's weasel face sucking down beers for the better part of a Friday evening.

Work ended at the usual time, and Billy ran back to the men's restroom to quickly freshen up. The scheduled plan was for him to meet Jessica outside the cafe at 6:00 p.m. Still very much shaken and nervous from the phone conversation earlier that day he needed to give himself a small pep talk. Billy stood in front of the bathroom mirror. He moved in way too close to be using the mirror to check his overall appearance. He looked his reflection in the eye and began, "William, you can do this, you have done this before, a million times. Just stay cool, stay calm and relaxed. Just be funny and charming, and everything will turn out great."

Billy would have continued his speech for way longer than he should if only he weren't interrupted and surprised by the flush of water that came from behind the closed stall door behind him. Realizing for the first time that he wasn't alone embarrassment began to set in. Billy knew there were only seconds to make a decision.

Should he leave the bathroom? Hoping the occupant behind the closed stall door would not be able to place his voice and Billy would remain anonymous. Should he stand tall and face his mystery bathroom counterpart? Billy chose the latter. He stayed still until the lock of the fiberglass stall door turned, and the door swung open. Standing there with a confused look deeply etched on his face was Mr. Hank Trask.

Hank broke the silence first, "Jesus McCabe, I hope you are talking about meeting a girl and not taking a shit."

Billy was left speechless while Mr. Trask washed his hands and stepped out of the bathroom without saying another word.

Normally this exchange would have been a lot higher on Billy's devastation scale, but he had something a lot bigger on his mind right now, his first date with a real New York City girl. Sure he understood that Jessica wasn't even from the city, but he saw that as a small technicality not even worth mentioning.

Billy finished freshening up and grabbed his bag and told Spence he would see him at the bar later and headed for the street. Turning the corner he saw Jessica was already waiting there for him, he checked his watch as he approached her.

Jessica saw his concern and addressed it right away, "You're not late, I'm early."

The two began walking toward the bar, the conversation was light and infrequent. Jessica did most of it, she wanted to avoid any and all awkward gaps in conversation. This is where last names were exchanged. Jessica's last name was Martin. She made the obvious assumption that Billy was Irish when she heard his last name. She told Billy she had grown up in a quiet suburb of Houston, Texas called League City. She explained that her father, David Martin, was an engineer for the Grumman Corporation in Bethpage, New York and was part of the team that built the first LEM (Lunar Excursion

Module). This was the spider looking craft that brought the astronauts safely to the surface of the moon all throughout the Apollo Program. He was subsequently hired by NASA to continue his work after the Apollo Program had ended. He was employed at the Johnson Space Center on the outskirts of Houston. Within a month he and his new bride, Jessica's mother, Kathy, had relocated themselves to the Lone Star State and a long thirteen years after that, Jessica was born. She was an only child but lacked the typical only child personality traits. Her parents were older than most when they began a family and didn't succumb to the regular child spoiling rituals that so many younger parents make. She moved to New York City three years ago to pursue an acting career. After only three call backs for roles, she didn't get she knew she needed a paying job. She took the cliche route and landed a waitressing job. She didn't do the acting thing as much anymore, the work just wasn't coming in enough, and she lost the interest. She was currently taking classes at LaGuardia Community College in Queens. She eventually wanted to be a teacher, as her mother was in Texas. Presently, she shared an apartment with a friend from school in the Prospect Heights neighborhood in Brooklyn. She still had a few aunts and uncles living out on Long Island who she got together with on holidays.

Billy was so entranced by Jessica's biography. He didn't even notice that they had not only reached the bar but entered it, sat, ordered drinks and were half way through their second round when she finished her story.

Spence eventually showed up with two other girls from the office. Realizing that it was just them with him, the two girls graciously left after just one drink leaving Spence to jump into Billy and Jessica's conversation. The couple dropped every subtle hint that they could think of that they wanted time alone, but Spence was not picking up on any of them. He continued to talk about himself, and he continued to bore and frustrate his audience. Seeing a small break in Spence's monologue, Jessica took the opportunity to bust through it like a running back piercing a hole in the offensive line.

She quickly spoke, "Well gentlemen, this has been an amazing experience, thank you both for the company. I have an early day tomorrow, I'm working the breakfast shift. I must be getting going. William, would you mind walking me to the Subway?"

Billy gave an almost too enthusiastic, "Sure!"

Without any hesitation, he turned to Spence and added, "Thanks for the invite. I had a splendid time, I'll see you Monday morning."

Jessica and Billy were out the door before Spence could say a word. For the first time all night and maybe even the first time in his life, he was left speechless.

The two took the stroll down Lexington Avenue to the 14th Street/Union Square Station. Billy was playing out all the scenarios in his head, kiss or no kiss. If he was going to opt for the kiss should it be a cheek or lips? The zero hour had arrived as they approached at the station entrance. Billy tried to think of something clever, but the creative caverns of his mind were closed for the night. All he could get out was, "Well, I guess this is you."

Jessica, again quick to respond, "Oh no Mr. William. You are not getting off that easy, this night is still young, and I am starving. You are taking me to the best pizza place in all of New York. DiFara's on Avenue J, in Brooklyn."

Billy was confused, "I thought you had to work in the morning?"

"Come on, I would have said I was doing mission work in Uganda to get out of there, that guy was so annoying."

Billy just smiled, he already knew, he was going to like this girl.

The ride on the Q line out of Manhattan and into Brooklyn was a quiet one that time of day. Arriving at DiFara's Billy soon realized Jessica was right, it was the best pizza Billy had ever tasted, and even

CHAPTER 3

better than the pizza was the company he had with him. Time seemed to run at a different pace when he was with Jessica. Hours felt like minutes and minutes felt like seconds. After they finished their pizza Jessica, who wasn't eager for the night to end, wanted to show Billy the best view of Manhattan. She navigated the city's transit system with such ease; Billy felt impressed. He was never the macho type, it never meant much to him to always know the best and fastest way to get somewhere, and he was never above asking for directions. After a transfer or two and a short walk, they ended up at Brooklyn Bridge Park overlooking the East River and the most beautiful view of the Manhattan skyline. The centerpiece was the two towers of the World Trade Center that rose out of the ground on the southern end of the island. Block-shaped and not very ornate in their design they remained stunningly beautiful. Their sheer size alone commanded respect and awe. Sliding across the landscape almost directly above their heads was the span of the Brooklyn Bridge, opposite in virtually every way to the World Trade Center. The bridge was horizontal, the towers vertical. The bridge was classic, intricate and brick, the towers, built of steel and glass, were simplistic in design. The two debated for hours over which style they liked better. Billy was siding with the bridge and Jessica with the towers. That's the way they were, Billy was an old soul, and Jessica was new, young and innovative.

They sat together on a vacant bench in the park sometimes talking, sometimes just enjoying the silence between them. It was a perfect moment, the best Billy had felt about a girl in a very long time. His confidence was at a whole new level than it had been just that afternoon when he first called her. Riding this wave of fearlessness he slowly slid his arm around Jessica's shoulders and pulled her in close. She was now comfortably nestled under his arm, and her head lay on his chest where she had front row seats to the intense beating of his heart inside as a gentle nervousness fell over him. Having very little control over his actions, he leaned down and gently kissed the top of her head. Jessica seemed surprised at first but then pushed herself just slightly closer to him, increasing the level of the snuggle just enough to let her new suitor know the kiss was not only all right but appreciated.

This was the anti-date for Jessica. Since moving to New York, she had her fair share of dates, and they all turned out bad. The majority of them were horrible within the first ten minutes. Jessica was starting to think that all the men in New York felt a date in any form was an open invitation for sex. It was an odd turn of events that the one guy she felt was worthy of first date sex wasn't even trying for it.

Jessica felt herself reach such a state of relaxation with Billy, at one point she nodded off while resting her head on him. Billy took this as the biggest compliment a girl could give. Sure sex with a girl is a big step in a relationship, but this was something more, this was a high level of trust, comfort, and peace. He smiled and stared out at the smattering of buildings that lined lower Manhattan.

The park was not known for high levels of criminal activity, but this was still New York City and still Brooklyn. They remained there, not being harassed for what seemed like hours as if a protective bubble had been placed on them making them impenetrable to any outside force looking to do ill will. It wasn't much longer before the dark skies over the city began to change in tint to a lighter blue. Billy had heard about marathon dates like this, ones that lasted all night long. He never thought he would be on one.

The new day had begun for New York and for both Billy and Jessica. He walked her home and sealed the perfect night with a gentle kiss on the lips, to which Jessica was happy to oblige. She climbed the steps of her building and once inside the door of her apartment collapsed on the couch and let out a big sigh and just simply said, "Wow!"

CHAPTER 4

Billy loved his new exciting life as a genuine career man. He was no stranger to the big city that lay just to the west of his childhood home. His parents would methodically drag the entire McCabe clan in, once a year, to see the spectacle that was the Rockefeller Center Christmas Tree. Ever since childhood, the city held a special splendor for him. It was a place filled with wonder and amazement, and it held so many mysteries in all of its hidden cracks and corners.

Now he found himself as a young adult, climbing aboard that commuter train every morning and making that pilgrimage into the towering city. The city was his second home, he longed for the day where he could call it his first home. He started dreaming of the day he would have his first Manhattan apartment, he felt city living brought a higher level of cultural existence.

He began spending more and more time inside the city's boundaries. He would finish work and find some eclectic coffee shop down some small secluded street in the West Village and just sit and write. He was writing anything his mood dictated; short stories, poems, song lyrics, anything to make himself feel more in tune with the city's culture. He fancied himself on par with all the greats, Fitzgerald, Salinger and even Vonnegut, who was his favorite and was living in New York at that time.

Often he would finish work at 6:00 p.m. and not be on the train back to Long Island until past 11:00. On pleasant days he would find a small square of park space and just sit and watch the flow of New Yorkers move through the obstacles like the water of a swift moving stream. He found himself more and more amazed at the native New Yorker species, he envied their survival skills and their ability to always adapt to whatever the situation dictated. If a New Yorker didn't feel their coffee was stirred enough, they would place their finger over the drink spout and give the paper cup a violent shake. When an unannounced rain shower would begin to fall, a real New Yorker just grabbed any number of discarded newspapers to make a makeshift umbrella for their head.

This was New York, a city that no one outside could ever understand, and most inside didn't understand either, they were just better at ignoring the things that would confuse anyone else. They were the most helpful and rudest people on the planet. They were people who understood what good pizza was, what a real bagel tasted like and that the deli with the most outdated interior offered the best food.

New York was a living thing, she had a pulse, she loved and hated, she was kind and cruel, and William loved every second he spent in her company.

After graduating High School, Danny joined the NYPD. He was working rotating shifts as a uniformed patrolman in The Bronx. It was hard for Billy to remember from week to week which shift his brother was currently working. Billy's relationship with him was a close one, they would often meet for drinks or to take in the occasional Yankee game after they finished their respective jobs.

Most times they would just meet at a small Irish pub on the Upper East Side, it was a nice halfway point from both of their work locations. A week after Billy's marathon date with Jessica, he had met Danny at their normal spot.

Billy sat and waited for the question he knew was coming and he didn't have to wait too long. Danny walked into the bar and gave his brother a hug and asked, "What's new brother?"

Billy was busting at the seams to tell the story of Jessica, he almost exploded with a verbal onslaught when Danny finished his question. Danny was sitting on a loaded bomb, and those words were the trigger to set it off, all of this was unbeknownst to him of course.

"I met someone!" The bomb exploded.

"Oh, yeah?" Danny was trying to decipher his brother's over-enthusiastic response.

"My first day at work she served me coffee, then later that week we went on a date. Guess what time the date ended?" An overly excited Billy asked.

Danny was not at all interested in playing his brother's teenager guessing game, "Will, I don't know, 2:00 a.m.?"

"Nope, went all night."

"You fucked her all night?" Danny now sounded impressed.

"No, I didn't fuck her at all," Billy protested.

"What? What do you mean?" Now Danny was confused.

"I don't know, she was cool, and fun and we just hung out all night until the sun came up. It was actually kind of cool," Billy was trying to sell it to Danny, but even he could hear the exaggerated level of corniness as he told the story.

"Will, listen to me. You just started working in the city. Right now you should not be focusing on finding a best bud to share

Hallmark moments with, you need to concentrate on getting some ass, and as much as possible," Danny was in lecture mode.

"She's not breaking the band up or anything Dan, I just like her," Billy was now pleading his case as if he were before a judge.

Danny realized that he wasn't going to convince his younger brother that he was making a mistake. It was pretty obvious he was passionate about this new girl. He figured it was young, naive love. It would run its course and eventually fizzle out. Danny would have bet any sum of money that his brother would be heartbroken and single in four months time, and back in love again in five months time. That's just the way Billy was.

Surrendering to the notion that Billy knew best, he just simply said, "Well Will, if you're happy then I am happy for you."

"Thanks, Dan, I doubt you meant that, but I'll take whatever kind word I can squeeze from that emotionless head of yours."

Danny just smiled at Billy's remark and moved on, "When are you seeing her again?"

"Tomorrow night," Billy quickly answered.

"Where are you taking her?" Danny asked.

Billy did not agree with the way Danny phrased his question. He didn't like to see it as him taking her someplace. It implied that location and activity planned for the evening were Billy's to plan and not a joint venture. He wanted Jessica's input on all date locations and activities. He wanted to be as unselfish as he possibly could. Whatever the adventure the two would take on, he wanted everything about it to be shared. If it was a great night, it was their great night, if the date were a bust, the blame would be theirs to share. He felt that made it more romantic and a lot less chauvinistic.

Danny's question still lingered in the air like an almost deflated helium balloon, having just enough gas to keep it hovering off the ground but not enough to let it fly free.

CHAPTER 4

"You know, I don't know," Billy finally replied.

"You don't know?" Danny was now more confused than he had been all night.

"Yeah, I was thinking about dinner, but now that I think about it, I think that should be something we agree on together, right?" Billy asked his older brother.

"Sure, and then you can pick out window treatments together and before you know it you can pick out wedding venues together and then divorce attorney's together and…"

Billy cut his brother off, "All right, I get your point. Maybe I'm a little further down the road on this than I should be."

"A little? Will, she is passing the sign that reads 'ninety-six miles to the next rest stop,' and you are already at that rest stop. Move over to the right lane and follow the speed limit for a little while," Danny spoke in highway travel analogies for some reason.

"OK, but that was a very odd way to present your point," Billy added.

"Yeah, I know. Sorry, I had nothing else."

CHAPTER 5

The rendezvous with Jessica had been set and planned, as far as a date and time. Billy was going to be picking her up at her apartment on a Saturday night at 8:00 p.m. Billy decided to drive his car into the city and pick her up in style. "Style" was a relative term, however. Some people might not agree with Billy's definition of the word. He was still new to the working world, and since the majority of his travel was done on the Long Island Rail Road, Billy never saw any reason to invest in a new automobile. He was still getting the mileage out of his High School and College vehicle, a 1981 Buick Skylark. It was of the four-door sedan variety. The car wasn't much to look at and even less in the reliability department. All it needed to do was make sure it could jockey Billy to and from the Ronkonkoma train station where he would board his more luxurious form of travel, the train. He figured the less appealing the car looked sitting in the station parking lot, the less likely it would be broken into or stolen.

Billy was never one to care too much about the level of sophistication his cars had. To him, they were simply a means to get from one point to the next. He recalled when Kenny saved for years to buy himself a black 1988 Camaro Iroc Z only to completely destroy it in an accident three months later. Luckily Kenny was unhurt, but his beautiful Camaro never saw the road again.

Billy arrived in Jessica's Brooklyn neighborhood fifteen minutes early. He feared he would appear too eager being so early, so he circled the block a few times, just to chew some minutes up. On his fifth pass around the block, Billy noticed a set of headlights suddenly appear, in what felt like inches from his rear bumper. Billy began to panic; he had heard about stuff like this, car jacking or mugging or whatever it had been called, either way, he started to worry. Before his paranoia could get the best of him, the top of the trailing car lit up like a holiday festival. The light show had been immediately followed by a quick, abrupt chirp of a siren. He was being pulled over. He felt an immediate relief fall over his entire body. He wouldn't be ending up in an abandoned construction site, dead and in the trunk of what remained of his beloved Skylark, at least not tonight. Soon the relief gave way to a new panic; he wasn't in danger, but he was still in trouble. He slid his car over to the side of the road, pushed the column shifter up into the park position and quickly played through all of his driving decisions from the past five minutes. What had he done wrong? Did he make an illegal right on red? Failure to stop? Speeding? What was it?

The NYPD officer approached his driver's side window from behind slowly. He could see through the side view mirror that the man had his hand rested on the handle of his service revolver, still housed in its holster, for now.

"Sir, please put your hands on the steering wheel where I can see them," The officer called out in a very aggressive tone.

Billy did as he had been told. He had a brother on the job and knew that too many times a mere non-compliance with a police

CHAPTER 5

officer's wishes could end badly.

The bright Mag-lite flashlight blinded Billy as it was being aimed at his face.

"Where are you headed, son?" The voice from behind the bright light sounded.

"Um... I was just picking up my date, sir," Billy had a tremor of nervousness in his voice.

"Are you lost?" The police officer asked.

"Um... no, sir?" Billy replied, but his inflection made it sound as if he was asking the policeman a question.

"No?" The officer asked, "You got a few people in the neighborhood a little nervous. They say you have been circling around here for the past few minutes."

It suddenly became apparent to Billy why he was pulled over. He felt relief and embarrassment at the same time.

"I apologize, officer, I was a few minutes early and just circled the block to kill some time. I didn't mean to cause a stir in the neighborhood," Billy pleaded his case and was hopeful it would get dismissed as just a big misunderstanding.

The officer outside his window picked his head up and spoke across the hood of Billy's car, "What do you think Rog? Believe the kid is telling the truth?"

Up until that point, Billy was completely unaware that a second police officer was standing outside the window on his passenger side as well. His incognito presence was probably the point, Billy wasn't supposed to know he was there.

"Yeah, I'm sure he is, but let's run his license just in case," Officer "Rog" spoke from the other side of the car.

Billy knew his license was clean and started to feel a wave of relief. As a precautionary measure, Billy would keep his brother's PBA card tucked in his wallet directly behind his license, for easy access, just in case it was ever needed.

The PBA card was an identification type card given to any police officer in good standing with the Patrolman's Benevolent Association, in other words, in the union. Police officers would commonly give these cards out to close family members and at times were granted some courtesies for minor infractions. Once Billy removed his license from the wallet, the PBA card became visible within the transparent plastic window that typically housed his driver's license. Not missing much, due to the ungodly strength of his flashlight, the first officer asked, "What's that?"

Billy was feeling too embarrassed to pull the card due to the non-issue, and his more than likely excusal from the situation tried to play dumb, "What's what?"

"The PBA card, whose is that?" The policeman asked.

Again Billy attempted to play dumb, "Oh that… it's my brother's."

The officer was not buying his dumb routine but was so numb to the game he just played along, "Your brother got a name?"

"McCabe, Danny McCabe," Billy replied.

"No shit? From Long Island?"

"Yes, Ronkonkoma."

"Small fucking world, I went to the academy with your brother, good guy. What's he up to?"

Billy wasn't sure if the unexpected turn was a good thing or a bad thing, "He's up in The Bronx now, I forgot the precinct number."

"Wow, The Bronx, guess he drew the short straw," Billy wasn't sure if that last comment was directed at him or Rog, still lurking in the shadows on the other side of the idling car.

The policeman handed Billy his license back feeling no need to run a check on it, "Tell your brother I said 'Hi.'"

"Um… OK, I will," Billy answered.

The police officer just stood there, not leaving. Billy began to

CHAPTER 5

wonder, was there a step he forgot, something he forgot to do. Surely he wasn't looking for a tip or anything. But the officer just sat there, perched like a raven on a telephone wire, waiting. He had this smirk on his face like he knew the punchline that Billy obviously didn't.

Finally, he spoke, "You will tell your brother I said 'Hi' right?"

"Yes, sir," Billy was now getting nervous, what was happening to him?

"Might be helpful to you if you knew who was saying 'Hi,' right?" The officer spoke in a lecturing tone.

"Oh!" It finally occurred to him why the police officer was still standing there. He was waiting to give his name.

"Yes, your name. What is it?" Billy finally asked the question that would appease the uniformed man standing next to his car.

"Matt Collins, we were in the academy together, and occasionally carpooled, I'm from Medford," Officer Collins, now identified, spoke.

"Matt Collins, you got it. I'll probably see him this weekend, I'll tell him I ran into you."

"Thanks, tell him to give me a call, we'll grab a drink… and kid, good luck on your date," Collins laughed as he looked up at "Rog" and gave a nod of his head to motion him back to the squad car illuminating the entire block behind him.

They walked back to their patrol car leaving Billy sitting in his vehicle thinking to himself, "What a strange exchange that was."

As he began to put his wallet back into his back pocket he noticed the digital time displayed on the aftermarket stereo he had installed, it read "8:20." His fifteen-minute early arrival had quickly changed into twenty minutes late. He was just around the block from Jessica's apartment and got there as fast as his Skylark, and the intrusive traffic signals would let him.

The tires of the mighty Buick screeched as he made the turn onto her block. The noise they made was more of an indication of their age and lack of any suitable tread than it was due to his uncontrollable speed.

Billy almost sped right past Jessica's building; it was only the last minute sighting of her sitting on the front steps that caused him to hit the breaks sending the car into a miniature skid.

"Slow down there 'Speed Racer.'" Jessica teased.

Billy was now in full panic mode. He wanted desperately to make a great second date impression on her, and here he was, twenty minutes late.

He left the car double parked and swung the creaky door open and began to run his words together in a rapid-fire string of gibberish, "Was early, cops pulled over, knew Danny, I didn't ask his name, sorry."

"William, I have no idea what you are trying to tell me. I'm going to assume it has something to do with you being late. I'm sure you have a good reason; I won't hold it against you. Well, maybe I will, depends on how the rest of the night goes," Jessica said in a teasing tone.

Finally calming down Billy spoke in a reserved manner, "I do have a good reason. I'll explain it all on the way to…" it suddenly hit him, he had no plans for the evening. He immediately felt his idea of making the night's activities a joint decision was a bad one.

"Where are we going, William?" Jessica asked.

"Well, that's the thing, I didn't want to make plans on my own. I felt it was rude to just assume you would want to do what I want to do. So, I figured we could decide on something together," Billy tried to rationalize.

"That is very sweet. Of course due to a lack of planning you realize we won't get into any decent restaurant. Any movie or any other activity that requires a reservation or a ticket is also going to be

CHAPTER 5

slim pickings," Jessica spoke with a big smile on her face.

She enjoyed Billy's innocence, and it only encouraged her to feel she had the task of "fixing him."

"Well, if you are interested, my roommate has two tickets to see a band at Irving Plaza tonight. She can't use them, and they are sitting upstairs on her dresser. But we have to both be in agreement," Jessica offered.

"I'm intrigued, what is the band?" Billy questioned.

"Do you like Canadian Folk Rock."

"Is there any other kind of Folk Rock?" Billy sarcastically inquired, "I love live music, and that sounds like a lot of fun. I vote yes."

"Perfect, wait here, your car is double parked, and I'll get the tickets and be right down," Jessica jumped up from her seated position on her front step and darted back into her building.

She appeared seconds later with a white envelope in one hand and a sweater in the other.

"Let's go!" She yelled.

"Driving?" Billy asked.

"Sure, it will be quicker if you don't mind."

"Not at all."

Jessica skipped around to the passenger side and got in quicker than Billy could get there to open the door for her. Billy was left to just surrender his chivalrous act but wanted to make sure she was aware.

"You were supposed to let me open the door for you," He said as he slid into the driver's side seat.

"Supposed to? I am capable," Jessica almost sounded irritated by his comment.

"I didn't mean it like that, I just meant I was trying to be a gentleman," Billy attempted to remove his foot from his mouth.

"I know, William, you don't have to treat me like I'm some

delicate buttercup, I am from Texas. I know how to ride horses and shoot guns, and I didn't even grow up in the country. I'm an only child, and my father always wanted a son. I'm a lot tougher than you might be used to," Jessica had a huge smile on her face as she delivered her soliloquy.

Billy pulled away from Jessica's building to begin his navigation through Brooklyn. His plan was to take the Brooklyn-Queens Expressway, more commonly known as the BQE, to the Williamsburg Bridge into Manhattan, a plan that looked perfect on paper.

He was passing the Fort Greene section by the Brooklyn Navy Yards when the old Buick Skylark started to sputter and buck like an angry rodeo bull trying to eject the rider off its back. Billy was an expert at piloting broken cars; it was all he ever owned. He slid the dying vehicle over to the right lane and was able to exit the BQE. He found an empty lot ominously situated at the end of the ramp, the Skylark lumbered into the lot and came to a dead stop. The engine was still running, but the car would not move, in any direction. Billy used his limited knowledge of automobile functionality to deduce that the trouble was transmission related, not the engine. The cause didn't matter at this point, what did matter was he had been stranded in an unfamiliar neighborhood, and on a date with a girl he very much wanted to impress. He was not off to a good start.

He noticed an FDNY Firehouse across the street from the lot and figured that was a good place to start looking for a solution plan.

"I'm so sorry about this Jess, I feel like an idiot" He finally spoke to Jessica.

She began laughing, slightly at first, but it grew into a more hearty laugh. She eventually stopped and said, "Are you kidding, this is great."

Billy was unsure if she was serious or if this was a very thick layer of sarcasm.

CHAPTER 5

"Are you serious?" He had to ask.

"Yes, when you said you wanted to make this date a shared adventure you never had this in mind, but this is better than anything we could have planned. Come on, let's go see what kind of help we can get from the firehouse over there," Jessica said.

Billy began to relax, Jessica was right. Billy was so uptight about this night that maybe he just needed to pull back, relax and just enjoy where the night would take them.

At a desk located just inside the front door of the station sat a rotund, red-faced fireman. He had his face buried in the daily newspaper when Billy and Jessica walked in.

"What can I do for you two?" He asked without looking up from his paper.

Billy was amazed that he was aware that anyone walked in, much less how many people walked in, "Yes, How are you doing? My car died, and I got it into that lot across the street. I was going to call for a tow but was just curious if anyone here might be able to look at it?"

The question made the large man not only look up from his newspaper, but he also placed it down on his desk.

"Son, you are aware that you wandered into a firehouse and not an auto repair shop aren't you?" Not giving Billy time to answer he continued, "We can light it on fire for you and then proceed to put it out, but we aren't any good at getting them running once they stop. Now that lot across the street is ours. We use it for training purposes. You are more than welcome to leave the car there until you can get it running and drive it off or find someone more equipped than a fireman to fix it," Upon completion of his dissertation, he picked the newspaper back up and continued reading.

"Thank you, sir," Jessica replied, then she tugged on Billy's arm signaling to him that he was fighting a lost cause.

Admitting defeat, Billy asked the seated man, "Do you have a phone I could use?"

"Yep," The red-faced man looked over their shoulders at a pay phone attached to the wall.

"Let's just call a tow truck and have it picked up," Jessica offered.

"OK, wait, let me call my brother first, he is usually pretty good at fixing these things," Billy suggested.

He pulled the phone from its cradle and dropped a quarter into the slot before dialing his brother's number.

"Hello?" The voice at the other end spoke.

"Danny, It's William, my car died I need your help."

"Where are you?" Danny asked.

"Somewhere in Brooklyn, by the Navy Yards, I think."

"What the hell are you doing over there… wait a minute, you're on a date with that chick you were telling me about, aren't you?" There was a particular joy radiating from Danny's voice.

"Yes Dan I am, we were on our way to Irving Plaza to see a show, the car just stopped moving, the engine is still running, but it won't move," Billy explained.

"OK, sounds like a transmission thing. Listen here's what you are going to do, grab a cab or something, go to your show. I can't get out of here for a couple more hours anyway. I am meeting Zeus after work, and I'll pick you up at Irving Plaza then we will go fix your car. No reason you should miss your show over this. Go have fun," Danny laid out his well-thought-out plan.

Zeus was one of Danny's childhood friends; he could pull any mechanical device apart and reassemble it without any instructions. His real name wasn't Zeus, of course; it was Mitchell. "Zeus" came about one day when a neighbor's lawnmower wouldn't start, Mitchell was ten years old, he popped open the air filter and propped open the choke and started the mower up. The neighbor was so impressed with young Mitchell's skills that he said something about him being the "God of Engines." When Mitchell told his friends that story, they associated it with the only god they had known at that time, Zeus. The name stuck, and so did his reputation for building and fixing anything with moving parts.

Billy felt confident that if there was any human on the planet that could get his Buick back up and running, it was Zeus. They hailed a cab and headed to downtown Manhattan to see Canadian Folk Rock.

Still feeling the date was a disaster Billy spoke volumes with his body language as he slid down in the back seat of the cab.

Jessica reached over and picked up his limp hand and held it in hers, she smiled at him and said, "Thank you, William, so far this has been the best date."

Either she was overly sweet and kind and lying or demented and telling the truth. It didn't matter, the gesture made Billy feel a lot better about the comedy of errors that had so far unfolded.

The cab ride to the concert and the show that followed went perfectly. It was a welcomed departure from the night's past activities and a much-welcomed change. After the show, Billy and Jessica stood pensively in front of the theater sharing the silent space that lived between them. Billy cherished the idea that neither one of them felt the need to fill that space with the mindless clutter of meaningless talk. Billy was leaning against the wall with Jessica immediately to his right. They were waiting for the calvary of Danny and Zeus to arrive. Billy purposely kept his hands out of his pockets so they could dangle unattached to anything along his side. He was flying the flag and sending out all the signals he had in his arsenal that said it was OK to grab hold of his more than available hand. Jessica, oddly enough, was doing the same thing. Their hands shared a space so close you could almost feel the energy radiating off one hand to the other like two magnets that get so close they eventually pull each other closer on their own.

Billy wouldn't wait for the hands to act like magnets and work on their own, he had decided it was time to take a little charge of the evening. This was one of the few elements that he felt he could control, so he reached over and grabbed her hand. He didn't exhale until he knew Jessica was all right with the new physical contact. It was a small gesture of intimacy but a milestone one. When Jessica offered no resistance, Billy could finally let out the air that he was holding captive in his lungs.

He was just beginning to slide into a more relaxed mode when Jessica broke the silence, "Nervous?"

"Um... No, not really. Why?" A confused Billy asked.

"Your hand is like a wet sponge," Jessica teased.

Billy felt so embarrassed, he started to pull his hand away to wipe it off. Jessica gripped it tighter, refusing to let him retract the physical sentiment.

"No, leave it," She said, "I don't mind, in fact, it's sweet. You're a really good guy William McCabe, I'm glad we did this."

On cue, Danny's blue Monte Carlo pulled up in front of the theater and gave two short friendly blows of the car's horn.

Billy approached the car and made the proper introductions. Zeus was sitting in the passenger seat and spoke first to Jessica, "I'd offer you the front seat, but I'm pretty sure you would rather be sitting in the back seat with Willy."

"The back seat is just fine, thanks," Jessica answered in her sweetest Texas accent.

"Smart move, Danny is a real creep, and he cuts farts that smell like dead turds," Zeus was not one to play the charmer in the presence of a lady.

Billy spoke first once all the parties were present and accounted for, "Thanks for doing this, I owe you huge."

"No problem bro, if we weren't doing this, we would be sitting in a bar, drinking and meeting lots of hot chicks who would invite us back to their place. But this is better, I'd much rather be doing this," Danny's sarcastic tone was thick with flavor.

Realizing that there was a new female in his audience he added a small rider at the end of his badgering, "I'm kidding of course."

"OK, so where are we going?" Danny asked.

"BQE, over by the old Navy Yards," Billy instructed.

"OK, what exit?" Danny asked a very poignant question. It was simple enough, but Billy realized he didn't know the answer.

"Um… I don't remember. The car acted up, I exited. I didn't look to see what exit," Billy explained.

"OK, what street did you leave it on, we can look it up on the map?" Again Danny asked a very logical and straightforward question so one would think.

"Um… I don't remember Danny. It's in a lot across the street from a firehouse in Brooklyn, close to the BQE, at least I think we were still in Brooklyn, maybe it was Queens? Jesus, I have no idea where I left my car!" Billy was beginning to panic.

He looked over at Jessica, who was watching the exchange unfold in front of her like a scene in a movie.

She laughed and finally spoke, "Don't look at me, I have no idea where we were."

Zeus was also getting a kick out of what was now resembling a Laurel and Hardy routine, "So, we just drive around Brooklyn and Queens close to the BQE looking for firehouses. How many could there be?"

The question was rhetorical, but the answer turned out to be a lot more than any of them had imagined. The four adventurers trolled the two boroughs for a few hours, once or twice drifting into parts that seemed a little rougher than they would have liked. It was during those times when Danny made his off-duty service revolver a bit more accessible to him.

It was close to 2:00 a.m. when they drove down a street that looked vaguely familiar to Billy. He wasn't sure if they had finally reached their desired firehouse or were so lost that they now had begun checking the same areas more than once.

Suddenly it appeared, still parked under the high yellow street light in an empty lot across the street from a quiet firehouse, Billy's Buick Skylark.

"There!" Was all Billy had to yell to bring a collective sigh of relief to all the inhabitants of Danny's car. Phase one of the quest was now complete, now on to phase two, could Zeus administer field triage and get the old Skylark back and street worthy?

It took about an hour and two quick trips to a nearby gas station for some improvised parts for Zeus to complete his successful operation. They fired up the engine, Zeus slid the column shifter down and the transmission engaged.

"Good as new," He proclaimed.

Jessica had been relaxing in the back seat of Danny's car stealing a few quick sleeping moments while the men worked on the troubled automobile. Zeus closed up the hood, wiped down his hands and returned the used tools back to their home in the metal case that was inside the trunk of Danny's Monte Carlo.

Jessica hearing that the Buick was resurrected emerged from the car and lifted her hands above her head to stretch. When she did that her shirt lifted exposing just a small portion of her midsection.

Zeus and Danny caught Billy staring, and Danny teased, "Easy big cat, the poor girl has had a long night, approach with caution."

Feeling embarrassed Billy just simply said, "Shut up."

Jessica approached the waiting men now standing over the idling car like it was some trophy they won.

CHAPTER 5

"Well boys, you did it. Thank you so much, it has been a pleasure meeting you and thanks again for the help," Jessica now turned and faced Billy, "William, if it's all the same to you, I am so tired and would love it if you could drive me home in your perfectly working automobile."

Zeus leaned over to Billy and spoke softly, "Car is tip top, should be no problem getting you guys home. Your brother and I are going to grab a quick bite at this late night place we know so we will be around for like another hour or so, call us if you have any problems," Zeus paused. "With the car," He and Danny were still laughing when they got into their vehicle and drove off.

The digital clock on Billy's Buick now read 3:26 a.m. as he slowly pulled up to Jessica's apartment.

"Why are you driving so slowly, Zeus said it was good as new," Jessica spoke in a very groggy voice as if she were dancing carefully between the worlds of sleep and awake.

"I don't want to alarm the neighbors again," Billy responded.

Jessica let out a small chuckle. The moment deserved a much larger laugh, but she lacked the energy needed to deliver it.

"Next time, we stay in and watch a movie," Jessica joked.

"Next time?" Billy asked. He thought for sure that there would never be a sequel to this date.

Jessica just smiled as she leaned over and gave Billy a very significant kiss on his un-expectant lips.

She pulled her head back, looked him deep in the eyes, and with her most honest tone said, "Thank you, William. This night was perfect, and I mean that. I couldn't have asked for anything more."

Jessica seemed a lot more awake now as she smiled at Billy one last time before getting out of the car. When she was securely back in her building, Billy drove off. His mind was racing. He kept replaying what Jessica had said to him. He was flush with adrenaline. He also was not paying attention and made a right turn while the traffic light was still red, a non-infraction in the neighboring counties of Long Island but still illegal within city limits. Immediately a band of red and blue pulsating lights appeared behind him.

Looking up through the rearview mirror Billy yelled, "You have got to be shitting me!"

CHAPTER 6

The days flowed into weeks and the weeks rolled into months, all of which were flying by at breakneck speeds. The relationship between Billy and Jessica was flourishing and growing, the dates became more frequent, and the gift giving became more personal, and the language between them grew as well. Words like "Boyfriend" and "Girlfriend" danced very dangerously close to the edge of their tongues. They were locked into an unspoken game of chicken to see which one would use the word first.

The game would finally reach its apex one afternoon while Billy was enjoying a grilled cheese sandwich at the coffee shop. He enjoyed eating there, not for the reason Jessica suspected. She would tease Billy about only eating there, so he had an excuse for her to wait on him. The truth was, Billy loved her company, and the food wasn't half bad either.

Jessica's boss had made his way over to them. Billy was seated at the counter, and Jessica assumed her proper position behind the counter with a coffee pot in her hand.

"Are you going to introduce me to your boyfriend? The guy spends enough time and money in my establishment I think it's worth learning his name," The Boss said.

"Yes... I'm sorry Jeff, this is William, William this is Jeff, he sort of owns this place," Jessica nervously waded through the introduction.

Jeff offered his hand to Billy for the ceremonial handshake that two people traditionally took part in upon meeting.

"Nice to officially meet you, Jeff," Billy offered.

Wanting to avoid the awkward lull that sometimes follows a new introduction Jeff didn't linger. He turned and headed back to the kitchen to check on the staff and the ongoing food preparations.

Billy waited for Jeff to disappear before he said what was brewing in his mind, and once Jeff turned the corner Billy erupted, "You just called me your 'boyfriend'."

"I did nothing of the sort," Jessica tried to maintain her most proper composure.

"Yes, you did," Billy said correcting her.

"No, Jeff called you my boyfriend."

"And you didn't correct him, therefore consenting to the notion that I am indeed your boyfriend," Billy was giddy now, more than anything.

There was something about being in a new and fresh relationship that made him act like a High School kid.

Jessica was quiet, she was thinking about the idea. Finally, she asked, "Does that bother you? Being my boyfriend?"

Billy was a little surprised at the turn in the conversation and how quickly it went from playful banter to serious relationship decisions.

"I won't lie, it's been something I have been thinking about a lot lately. I have a lot of fun with you, I don't think becoming exclusive would be such a bad thing, do you?" Billy remained very non-committal about the whole thing.

CHAPTER 6

"William, I think I have made my feelings very clear."

Billy didn't feel she had.

"No," He said. "You really haven't."

"I think we are both looking for the same thing here and neither one of us has the balls to jump in and be the first to say it," Jessica explained.

Billy wasn't going to let her steal this moment from him before she could finish her thought he cut her short, "Jess, I love you and want to be your boyfriend!"

"Love? I was hinting at the boyfriend thing, you blindsided me with that love thing," Jessica spoke in a soft tone, still in a state of surprise.

"Oh shit, I screwed this up, didn't I?" Billy asked.

"No, not at all, I'm just not sure how I respond to that. You might be a little further down the road than I am, but I definitely see myself getting there. Just slide over to the slow lane and let me catch up."

"What's with all the traffic analogies?" Billy asked.

"I don't know I had nothing else," Jessica explained.

Billy just laughed at the joke that Jessica would never get. He knew she was right, he was speeding way too fast. Billy also knew that even if he didn't move over to the slow lane, she would catch up, probably sooner than later. He just had a gut feeling about her, and he knew she felt it too.

It didn't take long for Billy to prove to himself that he was right in his assumption. It was almost two months to the day since he had made his courageous proclamation when he found himself alone with Jessica in her apartment. Her roommate was visiting her parents in Michigan, and they had the place all to themselves. Billy would be lying to himself if he weren't prepared to be asked to spend the night. He would be even further lying to himself if he thought that the invitation to spend the night was just a gracious gesture to avoid having to go back to Long Island at such a late hour.

Billy had the game plan all worked out in his head, like a High School football coach who spends days watching the upcoming opponent's game footage. He had everything planned. Which in this case only meant sitting back and doing nothing. He was going to wait for Jessica to give the green light to the next step, but he still had a box of condoms in his jacket pocket just in case.

The night moved on at the regular pace, like a metronome clicking off the beats, keeping time. The couple lay cuddled up on the couch, under a blanket watching a movie on cable. It was some nameless feature that Billy couldn't differentiate from any other countless films. The tale of "boy meets a girl, boy falls in love, boy loses the girl, boy gets the girl back," Billy's mind was elsewhere. He had been in two other relationships in the past. One during his senior year of High School that carried on to his first year of college. The second was his college girlfriend who eventually broke up with him because she felt he was too immature, she finally told him "It's like I'm dating my younger brother."

Billy was not a virgin, but he wasn't wealthy with sexual experience either. His nervousness was warranted. He wondered if Jessica was feeling the same anxiety that he was. He kept stealing quick looks at her to see if he could read her face. Was she stiff with a nervous energy? She didn't appear so, in fact, she looked as if she were watching the movie.

"How the hell could she be watching this mindless drivel?" Billy wondered to himself.

The movie came to it's over predictable conclusion, and the credits began rolling on the screen, spanning from bottom to top.

Jessica looked over at him doe-eyed and spoke, "That was a sweet movie, wasn't it?"

CHAPTER 6

Billy had no idea, he hadn't paid attention to any of it but lied anyway, "Yes it was. I liked it."

The movie could have ended with the boy killing the girl in a gruesome ax murdering scene for all he knew, but judging from Jessica's reaction he understood his response was an acceptable one.

Jessica could sense the tension thick in the air. She knew what inviting Billy to stay the night implied. Jessica was well aware of it when she extended the invitation. It was a decision that she did not take lightly. She was a confident woman who made her own choices. She didn't believe in the wait until you are married philosophy but also kept her sex partners limited to a select few she felt had earned her trust. Billy had more than exceeded all the expectations she had set. Besides, she was still human and had needs.

Not waiting for Billy to gather the confidence he needed to make the first move she slid over and grabbed his shirt front and pulled him toward her pushing her lips firmly onto his. The move took Billy by surprise at first, but he quickly relaxed and let the moment dictate itself. Their tongues intertwined as the passion between them grew. Billy felt his hand sliding up the loose fitting T-shirt back and began to gently rub the smooth bare skin of Jessica's back. He was gauging her reaction as he made nervous circles on her back with his slightly shaking hand. With each pass, the coverage area got wider and wider until his hand came in contact with her bra strap. Playing the innocent role he stopped as if he was surprised to find the apparatus located there. Without missing a breath or a tongue kiss, she slid her own hand past Billy's. Like a master magician practicing the art of sleight of hand, she undid the clasp that held the bra and so much more in place. Once the fastener was free Billy felt he was free to slide his hand under the warmth of her armpit to the front of her torso where his eventual goal awaited. That goal was her soft, young breasts, still so full of life as their principal purpose dictated, to give nourishment.

Jessica slowly pulled back and whispered, "Let's move to the bedroom."

What followed next was a dance of physical and emotional connections. Two bodies coming together, at times very clumsily. This was the physical embodiment of two people taking their relationship to a higher level. It wasn't a beautifully orchestrated ballet of movement and grace, but what it meant far surpassed that. They were in love, and the time leading to this moment only served as the catalyst that ignited their true feelings. Feelings that could no longer hide behind the shield of modesty and embarrassment. This joint gesture put their feelings in the spotlight. There was love between them, there was no hiding it anymore, it had exposed itself in the most intimate way possible.

Neither Billy nor Jessica took this lightly, they were serious, and they were in love. Maybe it was premature when Billy professed his love earlier, but now it didn't matter. No one had to say the words anymore, it was all exposed and understood. They both felt it, the feeling was now mutual.

Jessica still felt it needed to be solidified, "I've fallen in love with you William McCabe."

The words danced off her tongue like the pleasing melody of a song that strikes some inner emotion, so deeply hidden that when it's heard it brings instant joy and elation.

Billy needed to say something to assure her that he too felt it, "You make me so happy Jess, I love you."

The two new lovers sat in silence for what seemed to be an eternity, bodies cradled together, basking in the moment. They shared the electricity of love and emotion and sex that still lingered in the air above them.

After a few minutes, Jessica spoke first, "I have a confession, I was so nervous, I have no idea what that movie was about, and I have no idea how it ended. It wasn't until you agreed with me that it was sweet that I knew it had a happy ending."

The confession made them both laugh. Years later while channel surfing, they would come to the same movie, and this time watched it. Sure enough, the movie ended with the boy's love interest dying, not from an ax swung by him, but by a car driven by someone else. Unbeknownst to both of them at the time, the actual ending was far from happy.

CHAPTER 7

The sun had only been up a few minutes before the rented cargo van gently rolled down East 81st Street. What lay packed inside was more than just the collective belongings of two people, it was their future and the start of their new chapter.

Billy and Jessica had found a perfect Upper East Side apartment that still worked nicely into their budget. The timing of it had been almost too perfect, after an exhausting two months of apartment shopping they began to accept the idea of not living in their desired neighborhood. It was an early Sunday morning when the phone in Jessica's apartment rang and the locator service representative on the other end informed Jessica that there was hope. A new listing had just become available, and if they could get over to the building within the hour, they might be able to get it.

The lease was signed shortly after fifty minutes of hurried travel through the city's subway system. It was done, they had their first Manhattan apartment together. It was a bold step and one that they both took feet first, never looking back or having any second thoughts about. In New York, getting an apartment together was more of a commitment than marriage. Their status as an exclusive couple was now scribed on a legally signed lease for a one-bedroom apartment on 81st Street between 1st and York.

Billy was still amazed that they were able to fit all the contents of their respective lives into one rented plain white, windowless cargo van. He was proud of his lack of material things but embarrassed at the same time.

They would both be living very spartan lives until they could save up and get some nicer furnishings. This also made their initial move-in process easy and able to be done by just the two of them.

It was late afternoon when the last of the van's contents had been moved out and into their new home on the fourth floor.

The apartment living room was a menagerie of missed matched items. An old futon with a worn mattress stood solidly against the back wall. Alongside the futon, there was a red plastic crate designed to transport cartons of milk which had since found a new purpose, holding up a lamp. This lamp was salvaged from Billy's house, it had stayed in the basement among the items marked for discarding. It was cracked and lacked a shade, so the bulb sitting atop it lay bare and exposed.

The television was the exception, it was new and modern. A 31 inch Sony that weighed more than almost all the other furniture in the room combined. It took the two of them and the help of a handcart and a friendly neighbor to relocate it from the van to the wall opposite the futon.

The bedroom furniture was all Jessica's, it was a queen bed that almost touched the walls on either side of the bedroom and a dresser. Billy agreed to abandon his bedroom set for one main reason, he slept in a full-size bed, which was smaller than Jessica's queen sized bed. The idea that her furniture was not overly feminine served as

CHAPTER 7

the only excuse Billy could hold on to for giving in to her wishes and using her bed.

The one room of the spread that lacked any attention was the kitchen. After the van had been emptied, it still remained just as bare as it did when they first unlocked the door and stepped in for the first time. They would have to make special arrangements to begin to populate the kitchen with all the proper and useful accouterments. Neither Billy nor Jessica fancied themselves as a master of the culinary arts so the first few months would consist of a lot of take-out. They both knew that to remain budget-savvy some cooking would have to be learned and executed a few nights a week.

When the hectic day began to settle down in conjuncture with the sun setting Billy and Jessica sat stoic on the futon staring at a blank TV screen, the cable had not been hooked up yet.

"It's only a one-year lease, even if you grow to hate me within the next two weeks, that's only fifty weeks left that you have to put up with me," Billy was trying to cut the tension with some ill-timed humor.

"Stop it, William, it's not that. This place is expensive, I'm still going to school, and you are still relatively new at your job. Maybe we should have gotten something cheaper, perhaps in one of the outer boroughs," Jessica was wearing her logical thinking hat.

"Listen, Jess, I know you are concerned about money, but we will be fine, I'm kicking ass at work, and I'm going to get a raise any day now," Billy was reassuring in his tone.

"William, I can't help it if I'm worried, but I'm trusting you on this. Worst case I will drop out of school and pick up extra shifts at the cafe. Jeff told me he has a friend who runs a catering business and is always looking for extra help on some of these high profile type cocktail parties. He said the tips are fantastic and the work is easy. I could take a few of those on," Jessica was already planning for the worst case scenario and the first day hadn't even closed out yet.

"If it will make you feel better, grab some of those catering gigs when you can, but do not drop out of school or skip class to do it. I'm counting on you to get your degree and start making the big bucks around here, I need me a sugar mamma," Billy teased.

Jessica started laughing, she knew Billy was right. He always had a calm demeanor about him. Even in the most stressful of situations he always seemed calm, relaxed and focused. Jessica admired this in him, but at times it would be the cause of her added stress and frustration. Sometimes she just needed Billy to be worried or panicked as she was. She needed to know that she wasn't overreacting when something went wrong, and Billy's calmness always made her feel that way.

This was a beautiful moment they were sharing, and she was thinking about the financial ramifications of it. She wanted to just enjoy it, to live in the moment they were in at that exact second. To Billy, this was a more significant emotional step than it was financial. If there was any panic or worry to be found on him, it was that he just moved in with a girl he had only been seriously dating for eight months.

"Everything is going to work out, we love each other too much for it not to," Billy felt assured.

This was his fantasy life, and he was living it. He kept wondering when would he wake up and see it was a dream, or worse, when would it all come crashing down on him in real life. He couldn't help himself to always dwell on the negative thoughts that broke into his subconscious like a burglar committing grand larceny in his home. He pushed the thoughts out of his head and forced himself to just enjoy the moment.

CHAPTER 8

The systematic and ritualistic routine of Billy's workday became increasingly easier for him to manage. He was getting more and more adept at his job, in fact, he was getting very good at it. Writing had always come easy to him, it was second nature, he just enjoyed doing it. He worried that making a career out of writing would be killing his passion for it, but he found he was happy to be making a living in it.

Billy had been instrumental in landing a few new minor accounts, and his work was constantly being chosen over Spence's, who still carried the senior copywriter title. Billy wasn't looking to step on toes or make any sort of power play for Spence's job, he was content with his current position. He thrived on the attention he was getting for his cutting edge and successful work.

As the time passed and Billy continued to prove himself as a viable asset to the company and not just a "beginner's luck rookie" as Spence would often refer to him in an angry or jealous tone. His skills and abilities began to draw attention from everyone in the agency and he was quickly becoming the copywriter people preferred to work with, again drawing the ire of Spence.

It was a crisp cold December morning, one of those days where the weather was a static field surrounding the city. It wasn't snowing, it wasn't even supposed to snow, but the air felt thick with it like a blizzard was hiding behind the fence prepping for a sneak attack. Billy was at his desk working, as was customary for him at this time of day. The phone on his desk gave off its melodic chime, Billy lifted the receiver to his head, "Hello, this is Billy McCabe."

"McCabe, it's Eric, you busy?" Eric didn't let Billy answer, "Fuck it if you are, I'm your boss, come into my office," Without ending the conversation with a proper sendoff the line went dead, Eric had hung up.

It was always hard to read Eric's mood by his tone or his words, they were always the same. He spoke fast, he got to the point, he didn't mess with things he felt irrelevant. Billy ran his mind quickly over the last few days of work, he was searching for a reason to be in trouble, nothing came to mind. He grabbed a small steno pad from his desk and his favorite black roller ball pen and made his way to Eric's office.

The office was tastefully decorated for a single professional man whose only relationship was with his career. Eric struck Billy as the type who never paid attention to anything in life that was not related to his work. He figured either Eric hired an interior decorator for his office or there was a hidden side to him that no one within the office walls had ever seen. A side that loved Pottery Barn and spent weekends shopping at Pier 1 and visiting wineries on Long Island's North Fork.

"Come in, sit down," Eric half whispered while on the phone with someone else.

Eric punched a few buttons on his phone and waited, listening.

CHAPTER 8

Then pressed two more buttons and listened. This dance with the phone lasted for a minute or two more before Eric returned the receiver back to its original home.

"Sorry, just checking on some investment accounts I have," Eric had explained before he continued with Billy, "McCabe, how long have you been here? Has it been a year yet?"

"Coming up on it next month," Billy kept his answers short and to the point, just the way he figured Eric would like them to be.

Sensing some nervous tension in Billy's face Eric broke the mood, "Relax kid, this is a good meeting, one you want to have. Listen, you are doing really well here, we are all pleased with the work you are pushing out. Truth be told we brought you in on the cheap, we were still a new agency and to be even more honest we knew you would take whatever shit pay we offered. You were fresh out of school, I could have paid you in walnuts and you would have agreed just for the experience. Well, I think so far things have worked out, for both of us, so now I want to keep you. I shouldn't tell you this, but people in the business are noticing your work. I'm getting that question I never like to get 'who's your new guy?' That's always the first question someone asks before they try to steal that 'new guy' away from me. Believe me, I understand that telling you this gives you a huge upper hand to grab me by the nuts and squeeze everything you can out of me, well… that sounded gay, but I think you get my meaning."

Eric looked at Billy but didn't wait for a reply, as had become customary, "My point is I want to give you more money. Do you want more money? Of course you do, who doesn't want more money? Don't answer that McCabe."

Billy wasn't about to try to push an answer into any of Eric's questions, even if there was a space in the conversation to do so.

"McCabe, we are building something big here, I want you to be a part of it, you are the type of young talent we need here," Eric was being very complimentary. Billy liked hearing the kind words, maybe even more than he liked hearing about the more money he would be receiving.

Billy was at an age where he saw his entire life laying out ahead of him. There was very little he cared to be looking at in his rear view mirror. His youth was his best asset, he would never know how to use that until he no longer had it. It was a common tale.

He was overly eager to work, and the fiscal reward was second to the experience he was getting, and rightfully so. He often heard the twisted tale of those kids with degrees who could not find work due to lack of experience. He knew that every day he walked through the doors of that agency was another day of valuable experience, that experience would get him into his next gig and the one after that. He wanted to remain loyal to Eric, but the reality of the working world would play heavy odds against his staying with one company for his entire career, it just wasn't done.

He had seen his father dedicate his life to the same company only to be phased out five years before he was retirement eligible. He vowed never to let himself fall into that complacent trap.

He shook Eric's hand and thanked him for the kind words and the increase in pay, but all he was thinking about was Eric's confession that there were other companies interested in Billy's talents. He was still very early in his career trek to make any moves, but it was a nice round of ammunition to have in his possession.

The thought was burrowed deeply into his head. It was so deep that when he got home later that evening the first message he told Jessica was not of the increase in pay. That news would have gone a long way toward padding their very tight budget, but instead he wanted to tell her about the growing interest other companies seemed to have with him and his skills.

"You would leave Eric?" Jessica questioned.

CHAPTER 8

"Jess, I'm not saying I will, I'm not even saying I want to, all I'm saying is that if there is interest in me I need to look into that. Even more so, if there is an offer made I have to pursue that. I am trying to make a career here. Spence is still the senior guy over there. He's a good person and all, but he is ten years older than me, it's not like I can sit around and wait for him to retire so I can move into the senior spot," Billy explained his thinking.

"Isn't it too early to be looking into making a move?" Jessica seemed concerned.

"Again, I'm not looking to make any move anywhere. All I am saying is that if someone makes me an offer or another agency makes an inquiry about my willingness to jump ship, I'm going to listen. I'm going to have that conversation with them," Billy seemed to be getting visibly frustrated.

"William, don't get angry at me, I'm just saying that maybe you need to put some years in at one place before looking to move on."

"Put some years in? Is that what you have been doing at that dead end cafe job? Putting years in? Is that the kind of person I should be?" Billy regretted the words as soon as they left his lips.

"I'm going to school William, the cafe is not my career," Jessica snapped back.

Billy knew he could still retreat and save face and maybe salvage the night from this pending argument. He weighed his options and took the safe path, "You're right, I was wrong, I know you are going to school and the waitress thing is temporary."

Jessica let out a deep exhale, she was happy to avoid the argument, "Thanks, William."

Billy sat at the small kitchen table for two to finish eating his pork fried rice dinner in silence. A million things raced through his mind. He wanted her to understand that he was looking for her to be supportive of him and not hold him back. He wanted to continue that argument; he wanted her to see his point of view. Her support was paramount to the success of their relationship. He began to hate himself for backing down and giving in. Worse was the growing feeling of resentment that started in his gut and worked its way up to his throat like a pot of boiling water on the stove that spills its contents all over the range. The feeling worked its way past his throat and into his head where it made a quick slide back down to his tongue, and before he could think better of it, his mouth released all that build up.

Looking up from his meal that was placed before him on a plate with his fork still firmly in his grip Billy looked right at Jessica and said, "Excuse me, waitress. My fork seems to be dirty, can you get me a new one?"

"Fuck you!" Jessica screamed as she slammed down her glass into the sink breaking it into countless smaller pieces. Then she burst into an exaggerated stomping walk to take her into their shared bedroom. For added dramatic effect, she slammed the door causing a movement of all the contents of the shelf on the wall next to the door.

"I'll be sleeping on the couch I guess," Billy retained his sarcastic tone just for an additional insult.

He waited for an answer or any sign of life to come from the other side of the closed bedroom door, it never came. He still had his confidence that he was right, if Jessica were going to be in a relationship with him, she would need to support him in everything. That was a two-way street, and Billy began to realize that the cheap shot he fired after the buzzer sounded epitomized exactly what he was upset with Jessica for. He had not shown her support in her choice of path.

He considered apologizing, but that would only be half honest, he still felt strongly that Jessica shared the blame. After some internal debating he figured it was best to let tempers cool overnight like an extinguished campfire whose once hot coals lay cool and safe by morning's light. The theory of never going to bed angry was not one practiced by the McCabe's, one may even argue that it was not even known by them.

Billy's parents were not prone to large fights. Arguments would happen, but they were rare, mostly kept hidden from the children and over within a few hours. This wasn't a testament to the strength of the McCabe's marriage as much as it was due to Billy's dad's unwillingness to engage in any level of confrontation.

Billy, taking a cue from his father finished his dinner, washed his plate and plopped himself down on the futon in front of the television. He began his nightly routine of scanning the programming that was being fed to him by his television. He never had an aim or a purpose with his search; it truly was random. He couldn't tell you what it was he was looking for, not even a genre. He would stop at a basketball game until they would break for commercial, then it would be some old syndicated sitcom until they broke for commercial and the routine would continue for some time. He would almost always end up with some movie he had seen numerous times before. If the movie were on one of the premium channels, he would stay, mostly because it didn't have commercials to break up his attention. It didn't even matter to him if he joined the movie already in progress, odds were he had already seen it once, and if not, the plot lines were never convoluted enough to confuse him.

Tonight's routine didn't stray too far off course, even with the earlier battle with Jessica. He had made peace with the idea of letting things settle for the night and revisit the issue under the umbrella of a new day's light. As sure as his plan had been, he kept a watchful eye at the slice of bright light that radiated from under the bedroom door. As long as that illuminated line was there, resting in that tight space between the door and the floor he knew Jess was still up and awake.

He thought maybe she was waiting for him to make that bold first step and go to her. He wouldn't.

When patience ran out on the other side of the door, the light went out. Now there was nothing to differentiate between the bottom of the door and the top of the floor, just darkness. Billy let out a sigh, he knew he had failed, he knew what Jessica wanted was to work this out immediately, he was aware that all of this but still chose to ignore it. It was laziness, he certainly didn't feel the altercation put their relationship in jeopardy and using simple battlefield triage methods this was a patient who would pull though and could be worked on later.

It was only forty minutes later when Billy was suddenly awoken from sleep by a dark shadowed figure that standing him. The figure didn't make a noise or any physical contact with him, it was the figure's sheer presence that alerted Billy out of his peaceful slumber and into an instant state of panic.

Jessica didn't make him panic too long, she quickly took one step closer to the couch and spoke, "William, I want to talk to you."

Her sweet calming voice revealed to Billy that it was his girlfriend standing over him and not some intruder with a harmful purpose.

Billy was still groggy from whatever remained of the state of sleep he hadn't lost in his startling wake-up, "Yeah, sure Jess, we can talk."

Billy knew what it was going to be about, it was the conversation he was putting off until the next day. He couldn't hide from it anymore, it came and found him, sleeping on the futon of his Manhattan apartment.

"I don't like what happened before," Jessica began as she sat on the edge of the futon.

The word "before" confused Billy, he had only fallen asleep for forty minutes, but to him, the incident in question happened yesterday. Inside Billy's trained head, any night time sleep served as the demarcation line between one day and the next. It took him a few seconds to process the time and the day before he answered.

"I don't either Jess, and I was wrong to make that stupid crack about you being a waitress. I'm sorry about that. I know you are working to better yourself and I need to support that. But, that said, I didn't like what I heard from you. I have no intention of changing jobs at this point, I still very much like my job. It was just a passing thought. If there is a genuine interest in me, I will consider it. That's all I was saying, and I would have hoped that when I said that I would have gotten your full support, and I didn't so I got pissed off," Billy was surprisingly coherent and articulate for just being pulled from sleep.

Jessica was silent. Billy could tell she had a whole speech worked out in her head. She was eager to deliver this lecture and Billy's admission of guilt, and the subsequent challenge to her support put her speech in a tailspin, and it was no longer relevant.

She was stubborn at times, but she also understood when a point wasn't worth making. Billy had admitted his wrongdoing and even apologized for it, he also made a very valid point defending his own anger.

"You're right, I'm sorry," Jessica felt as if she was conceding defeat, but this wasn't a battle for supremacy, it was relationship growing pains with the man she loved.

The quick surrender was a little surprising to Billy, he didn't expect a big push back, he felt he did make a strong case for himself.

"Jess, I love you, I will support you in anything you want to do, even if that means waiting tables for the rest of your life," Billy reassured her.

"If I'm waiting tables for the rest of my life, my life better be a short one," Jessica teased.

"Can I come back into the bedroom now?" Billy asked.

"Yes, but don't think you are getting back to sleep right away, this waitress has one more patron to serve if you know what I mean," Jessica made an attempt at being coy.

"Jess, although I do appreciate the sexual connotation you delivered, it was anything but subtle. We will work on that, in the meantime, I'll take an order of two eggs, sunny side up," Billy made his own joke which got lost on Jessica.

"What? You want me to make you eggs?"

"No, two eggs... sunny side up? Your tits? Get it? Jesus, forget it, you are just too sweet and innocent to joke with like that."

"OK, but after we make love I am making some eggs, you got me craving that now."

"And you'll want sausage with that too, right," Billy made another attempt at the sexual humor with her, again it failed.

"I don't think we have any sausage, but I can look."

"Never mind."

"Oh, were you saying... oh god, you are gross William."

Billy just laughed and followed her back into the bedroom, the first fight had come and gone with very few casualties.

CHAPTER 9

The mail arrived as it always had, too many parcels stuffed in the miniature mailbox that stood in line with its counterparts in the building's lobby. Jessica was always first home in the afternoon, and by default, it had become her responsibility to be the retriever of the mail.

She would sift through the pile of bills, and junk advertisements addressed to "current occupant" hoping for that one oddball piece that would break up the daily monotony. Carefully placed amidst the phone bill and a Macy's flyer was a thicker than usual envelope, cream in color and adorned with decorative calligraphy on the front. Its odd appearance made Jessica stop and give it a more thorough look.

It was her name on the envelope, there hadn't been a mistake in the delivery of such a fine looking parcel. The return address revealed its purpose, it was sent from her aunt in Texas. It was a wedding invitation. She was aware of her cousin's engagement last year but had put the event so far from her active mind that the idea that a nuptial would be following shortly had escaped her consciousness.

Immediately her thoughts turned to more selfish ones, this would mean a trip back to Texas, she could bring William with her, he could meet her family. The thought train moved so quickly like the high-speed variety that would glide along the tracks through a European countryside. What would William think? Was it still too early in the relationship to move to the "meet the family" phase? To her the answer was obvious, she loved him and was anxious for her family to meet the man who was occupying her every thought, but was it equally as obvious to William? She would carefully broach the subject when he arrived home from work later that evening.

Jessica was preparing a chef's salad for dinner. She enjoyed the healthier eating whereas Billy was more of a steak and potatoes type guy. She saw chef's salad as an agreeable compromise. The salad satisfied her taste while the assortment of meats that adorned it pacified Billy, a real compromise indeed. The locks on the apartment door began their succession of pops and clicks, Billy was on the other side of the door releasing them from their locked state with the turn of his keys.

Jessica readied herself for the looming conversation she was prepping for since first seeing that decorative envelope. Billy crossed the barrier between the hallway and their shared living space and officially the game was afoot.

"How was your day, sweetheart?" Jessica asked in her innocence.

Billy was a little confused at Jessica's break from protocol, "Fine, I guess."

Jessica had a rehearsed list of questions intended to "put him at ease" before she broached the precarious topic. She ran through them in her head, trying to reach each one before checking it off and heading to the next one. She tried, but her patience ran to its inevitable end somewhere between question two and three. Her

CHAPTER 9

anxiety bubbled over like a pot of boiling water left unattended.

"Let's go to Texas, I want you to meet my family!" She blurted out with an uncontrolled sense of vigor.

"What?" Billy asked although it was more of a stall tactic to gather himself after the blind-side attack. He heard her perfectly but had no idea where this was coming from and needed the extra few seconds it would take Jessica to repeat the question for him to calculate an appropriate response and assess the situation better.

"My cousin is getting married in June, the invitation came today. I have to go back to Texas for the wedding. I want you to come with me, as my boyfriend. I can introduce you to my family," Jessica took the extra time to fully explain her angle.

"Oh, I see," Billy did in fact clearly understand everything Jessica had just said. It was a legitimate reason to initiate the formal introductions between boyfriend and family. He had no reason, besides his own adolescent fear, to say no. So he said the only thing he could, "Sure, I guess. I just need to check with work about taking time off, but I can't see any reason why not."

The truth was, he had a million reasons why not, but not one of them was reasonable, and they all involved putting his relationship at risk. He knew he loved Jessica and was accepting that any future with her would entail meeting her family, or at least her parents. None of that meant he had to jump into that with both feet, willingly. He would move forward, but it would come with a lot of nauseous anxiety. Billy wasn't socially inept. As long as the other parties in the social setting weren't the people who gave birth to and raised the woman he was now having sex with on a two-to-three-times-a-week basis.

Any option he planned on exercising to get out of the unavoidable trip was quickly squashed when Jessica jumped on him and threw her arms around his neck with a childlike giddiness.

"Oh my god, I can't believe you are going to come down to Texas with me," She exclaimed.

"I can't believe I'm going to leave New York," Billy added. He had been on a plane once in his life, a spring break trip to Florida with some college buddies. He had only left the Northeastern United States three other times by car, once to Toronto and two more trips to Florida as a kid with his family.

Billy was prepped for the emersion into Jessica's family during the next few weeks. He learned names of aunts, uncles, cousins, even close family friends that had no blood relationship but still carried the "aunt" or "uncle" title.

The wedding weekend would span a little longer than the traditional two days that everyone else called the weekend. Billy and Jessica would be flying out of New York's LaGuardia airport late Wednesday night after they finished work for the day. The plan was to land at Houston's George Bush Intercontinental Airport late and stay in a hotel by the airport. Thursday morning they would drive the rental car out to Jessica's childhood home. Thursday and Friday would be the see the old friends and tour the neighborhood days, leaving Saturday completely free for the wedding. Sunday was earmarked as a relaxing day, a day to spend with Jessica's parents mostly, this is where Billy found the bulk of his stress living, it would be anything but relaxing. They would fly back first thing Monday morning.

The time between the decision to go to Texas and the date of the trip moved quicker than any other time in Billy's life. He would often find himself wishing some horrible incident would occur just to give him a non-disputable excuse to not go. No matter how hard he wished it would not change anything, this was going to happen. He was going to board a plane, fly to Texas and meet his girlfriend's parents, some unforeseen incident would not be recusing him from

CHAPTER 9

this one.

Travel day had arrived, just as the calendar dictated. Billy and Jessica finished their respective jobs and met back at the apartment, they grabbed a quick bite to eat before heading out the door. The evening hour would bring with it a heavy load of traffic clogging the arteries between Manhattan and LaGuardia Airport out in Queens. They walked down to the Avenue to increase their chances of finding an available unoccupied cab, their plan worked. Their timing was impeccable. Just as they reached the corner, a taxi was stopped at the curb, unloading an elderly couple. Their disembarking left the cab ready for new patrons to embark, and Billy and Jessica were at the right place, at the right time.

It was an early start for Billy, earlier than he wanted to leave. Just getting to the airport from his Manhattan apartment could prove to be perilous, loaded with countless obstacles and delays that no one could account for.

The timely cab arrival, lighter than expected traffic, curbside check-in, and a swift moving security line made them over two hours early for their flight. Billy was unaware of the extremely early hour until he finally got to their assigned gate and sat down in the thinly padded metal row of seats. Upon his realization, he gave Jessica a profound look of disapproval. He spoke in a very sarcastic tone, "Thank God we are here early, this is so much better than relaxing on the couch for another hour. In fact, can we get rid of the apartment and just live here?"

"Shut up William. I'm not a big fan of planes or flying so I just wanted to get here early enough to relax before we boarded."

Billy realized he was being selfish and quickly changed his demeanor, "You're right, I'm sorry Jess."

Then he slid his hand across the cold metal seat divider and clasped Jessica's hand and gave it a gentle squeeze to show he was supportive. Jessica squeezed back and gave a subtle smile showing she appreciated his support. It was the silent language that couples begin to develop after spending a serious amount of time together.

Jessica gave Billy another rundown of the roster of family members and friends that he would most likely be meeting. He wanted to be prepared, he didn't want to be the guy who made the gay joke to her homosexual cousin or ask the aunt who just buried a child if she has any kids. He wanted to be armed with as much knowledge and back story as was available to avoid making any social faux pas.

The history lesson continued as they began the boarding process and quickly wrapped up shortly after they found their seats and got settled in with seat belts securely fastened as instructed for them to do. Billy was beginning to feel confident in his knowledge of Jessica's family, extended and otherwise.

The flight was uneventful, with the slight exception of the elderly woman who began sobbing when the plane was flying through a rough patch of turbulence. She quickly stopped when the flight leveled off and returned to its smooth movement across the sky. Billy felt people took the technology of flying for granted, he thought the woman's reaction to turbulence was silly and unfounded. Was she not aware that there were at least a million other things that could bring down a plane? For instance a complete instrument failure causing the plane to plummet to the ground 30,000 feet below, that were a lot more feasible than slight sudden adjustments in air pressure?

Billy wasn't afraid of flying, he understood how it worked. He understood the accepted risks that came with it. He knew that driving his car on the Long Island Expressway brought more risks than flying in a vacuum sealed aircraft moving at almost 500 miles an hour at 30,000 feet in the sky.

The real cause of people's fear lie in the misguided notion that they were in control of their fate in those other situations, but being

CHAPTER 9

a passenger in an aircraft they felt helpless. This is where Billy was different, he enjoyed not feeling in control of his fate or his life. He loved the idea of a pre-determined destiny. He wasn't reaching for a higher power, his thinking was based more on a sense of laziness. If he was going to leave this planet, he didn't want it to be because of some ill-advised or even downright stupid thing he had done. He figured a plane crash would be perfect, no matter how hard one tried there was no way blame could be shifted to some lonely passenger seated in seat 26C.

This was the way Billy's mind worked. Moments like these he felt his thoughts were morbid or he was suffering from some minor depression. He felt fine otherwise and figured his unconventional way of thinking made him good at his job, so why fight it?

The plane touched down in Houston fifteen minutes ahead of its scheduled time. There was no rush for them to get anywhere, in fact, due to the late hour the plan was just to get to the Marriott located at the airport, check in and get to bed.

Jessica had done her best to warn Billy about the extreme levels of heat that exist in Houston. Even at night, long after the sun had gone to bed, things were still hot, not having enough time to properly cool off from the previous sun-drenched hours. It was a big misconception that Houston had a dry heat like Dallas. It was still a coastal city, and that meant humidity and lots of it. The wave of heat first smacked him in the face when he left the controlled air comforts of the plane and moved into the suspended passageway that connected the aircraft with the adjacent building. It hit him like that heat wave that emanates from a hot oven when you first open its door. It's a strong punch to the face. It's the kind of heat that one only feels in manufactured circumstances, like cooking, or in a dryer, it's not the heat one normally associates with basic weather systems.

Jessica could see the shock on Billy's face and interjected, "Wait until tomorrow when the sun is up."

"Is that when people start to spontaneously combust?" Billy joked.

Once having settled into the room, Jessica gave Billy a look. In a bizarre role reversal she said, "You realize we won't be able to do much at my parent's house, we need to get a few days worth of sex in tonight."

Billy was feeling tired from the long day of travel, but he was still a young man in a relationship with a beautiful woman. It would take a lot more than just your basic lack of energy to reject that proposal.

The couple made love before passing out into a deep slumber. The sleep had hit them so fast and hard that they didn't even attempt to redress leaving them both sleeping exactly as they had done in the womb, naked. This also made things a lot easier in the morning hours to get in one more passionate session in before the period of temporary celibacy began.

CHAPTER 10

The happy vacationing couple took advantage of the hotel's extra dense curtains that kept the room dark no matter what the light situation was outside and slept in late. The car rental facility was located back at the airport, but there was an electric rail shuttle that connected the hotel to the airport terminals so patrons could mitigate their exposure to the searing Houston temperatures. This arrangement kept Billy in air conditioned comfort all morning. It wasn't until he exited the car rental office that he got his first taste of Texas heat, and it went down like a tall glass of rusty nails. The heat he felt the night before was almost refreshing compared to what he was feeling now. Immediately beads of sweat began to form on his forehead, and as he lifted his hand to wipe them, he could feel the wetness of his t-shirt sticking to his back. The car was pulled in front by the car rental agent. This was a feeble attempt to keep the customers from spending too much time exposed to the relentless, unwavering heat that attacked its prey in the open cement parking lot.

"Jesus Christ! This damn heat" Billy gathered the strength to blurt out.

Jessica just laughed. It had been a while since she had experienced the Houston summer, but the scorching heat brought back a lot of childhood memories for her, and in its own sadistic way made her feel right at home.

Jessica would be handling the driving duties, it was easier, she knew her way around the vast twisted collection of concrete that was the Houston freeway system. She made her way south on the Eastex Freeway until the pocket of buildings punching into the sky came into view. Downtown Houston wasn't anything like Manhattan, it was big in other cities standards, but Billy had been spoiled, looking at the Manhattan skyline everyday ruined the beauty that lived in other cities' skylines. Once passing through downtown, they picked up Interstate 45 heading toward Galveston. The morning rush hour had passed, so traffic hadn't been too bad so far. Downtown was now in their rearview mirror, so Billy assumed they had escaped the clutches of the infamous traffic snarl that Jessica had warned him about, he was wrong. The freeway looked almost empty when they rolled past downtown, but now at the intersection of the Gulf Freeway and the 610 Loop there was a sea of cars, just stopped. The pace had moved from a breakneck speed to a snail's crawl in a matter of seconds.

The car's air conditioning was working harder than any other part of the car, Billy wondered how much longer it could hold on. Surely these things could collapse under the strain and pressure of the unrelenting Texas heat. It was to Billy's surprise that the vehicles interior cooling system withstood the test, Jessica still seemed unfazed by the whole thing.

Jessica's childhood home lay nestled in the tree-lined streets of the historic section of League City, Texas. The mammoth live oak trees had spiderweb-like branches. They not only reached upward to the heavens but in some cruel twist of nature's fate, some branches turned away from the sun-rich sky and headed back down to the cooler safe haven of the ground from which they sprang.

The house was almost Victorian in design, ornate with a wrap-around porch, complete with a swing. It was a vision of Americana that Billy had never really seen, and something about it struck a happy chord with him. He felt invited, comfortable and not at all out of place.

Kathy Martin came barreling out of the house like a bullet shot from a gun, leaving the screen door to slam in her wake.

"Jessie, my little buttercup. You're here!" She yelled loudly in a put-on Texas accent.

"Mamma!" Jessica ran to her mother and threw her arms around her in a genuine loving embrace.

Slyly looking over her daughter's shoulder Mrs. Martin asked in her most rhetorical tone, "And who might this young man be who has seen it fit to escort my daughter home?"

"Mamma, this is William, the man I have been 'living in sin with' as you so casually put it," Jessica played her best defiant role.

"Now pumpkin, let's not start your visit off with silly quarreling. I'm just glad you're here and if this young man accompanied you… well, he is welcome in my home," Mrs. Martin played her best reasoning role, almost as spurious as her daughters that preceded hers.

Billy stepped forward and offered his hand to Mrs. Martin, "Honored to meet you, ma'am."

Jessica had prepped him on the usage of "sir" and "ma'am" in Texas etiquette. It followed one rule, always use it when talking to anyone at any time.

The sun still lay heavy in the sky, beating down its unrelenting heat rays on any mortal foolish enough to expose themselves to its immense power. They retrieved their bags from the rental car and retreated into the house. Once inside, Billy could feel the cooled air that offered immediate relief from the heat. Mrs. Martin offered Billy a glass of tea, to which he instantaneously accepted.

The absence of Mr. Martin didn't seem to be registering with anyone including Billy, who was still recovering from the near heatstroke he felt he had just endured.

Finally, it was Mrs. Martin who revealed the whereabouts of the missing family member, "Your father ran to the market. He had to pick up some burgers and some extra beer for Mr. William here, he should be back shortly."

Almost on cue, the oversized red Dodge pickup truck pulled into the driveway. A tall, slender man with pressed jeans and a "Made in Texas" t-shirt materialized from the driver's side of the truck. His shirt had been neatly tucked into the jeans showing his zero body fat, impressive for a man his age Billy thought. The clothing was cinched in the middle with a belt that displayed a fist-sized buckle that was systematically positioned in the direct center of the man's lower abdomen. The man was everything Billy thought a Texas man should look like, almost too cliche. The only thing left were the animal skin boots. No sooner did that thought enter his mind did Billy get a closer look at the choice of footwear Mr. Martin had adorned, and sure enough, cowboy boots. Was this guy for real? Billy remembered Mr. Martin was born and raised in New York. Why the determined attempt to appear so genuinely Texan? Was he trying to put on a show for Billy? Was it the "Don't Mess with Texas" cliche? Or more accurately "Don't Mess with the Daughters of Texas."

Mr. Martin retrieved two grocery bags from the bed of the truck and made his way up the driveway and into the house. Immediately Billy rose to his feet to greet the man, Jessica and Mrs. Martin remained seated.

CHAPTER 10

"You must be William. I have heard a lot about you, all good things, so no need to worry. Not all Texans carry guns... I leave mine upstairs next to the bed," Mr. Martin joked.

Billy squeezed out an uncomfortable laugh as he squeezed out an awkward handshake, "Pleasure to meet you, sir."

Mr. Martin looked pleased with the New Yorker's grasp of the word "sir" and its proper use. That was one lesson Billy learned that seemed to be paying off its weight in gold.

"Come on son, I got us some beer," Mr. Martin was leading Billy out of the living room and into the kitchen.

Billy could tell right away that Mr. Martin was from a different generation, he still believed in an unyielding division between the sexes. Men had their role in life, and likewise, women had theirs. The lines were thick and defined, not thin and vague, in his eyes there was no "gray area."

Mr. Martin firmly placed a can of beer into Billy's hand. Billy popped the top back and took his first sip of the cold lager that rushed down his throat and felt like liquid gold to him.

"So, Jessie tells me you are a writer. You write anything I would have read?" Mr. Martin asked breaking the uncomfortable silence that was living in the air between the men and their cold ale.

"Well, sir. I don't write books or stories or anything like that. I'm a copywriter, I write headlines and body copy for ads. I work at an ad agency," Billy did his best to explain his career.

He always felt apologetic when he had to explain to someone that he wasn't the next Hemingway, that the writing he did was nothing like the writing authors did. He liked his job, he liked what he did, why should he feel the need to apologize for not being the guy who would write the next great American novel? None of that mattered, he still took an apologetic tone when talking about his work.

"I see," Mr. Martin replied.

Billy was under the impression that he still didn't really understand what it was that he did but was far from eager to continue the explaining portion of this conversation. After all, the only concern Mr. Martin had was that the man his daughter was shacking up with had the means to support her.

Billy had known this before Mr. Martin asked his next question, "You make decent money doing that kind of work?"

"Yes sir, I do all right," Billy gave his uncomfortable reply.

"Good," Mr. Martin's reply was short and to the point.

The two men continued to drink their beers in the cool air conditioned comfort of the old house on 3rd Street.

The silence didn't last too long before a shrill call from the next room broke it up.

"David! Jessie wants Mexican for lunch," Mrs. Martin yelled across the two room span.

"OK, where?"

"I was telling her about that new place they just opened up on Bay Area Boulevard and Highway 3. Let's go there."

Billy quickly saw that it was Mrs. Martin who ran things around the house. She made all the decisions, and Mr. Martin was nearly furniture there. He provided the financial and transportation support but brought very little else to the table. Billy didn't want to perceive Mr. Martin as weak; he wasn't. Maybe the term that best fit him was "beaten down." He was advanced in age, older than Billy's father. He had worked a long full and prosperous career. He provided for his family every day of his life. He was a successful and intelligent man in all aspects of society, yet it was his wife who told him what he would be eating for all three meals every day. She would tell him he was tired, and it was time for him to go to bed. She would instruct him that his toenails needed to be cut or his old slippers needed to be thrown out. In essence, she treated him like a child. Perhaps it was to fill some void that formed when Jessica, their only child, moved half way across the country. She was left without a role in life, no direction and misguided as to what her next step would or should be. She was a smart woman, educated, but exited any career path she may have been on once she got pregnant with Jessica. The only path for her now was playing the role of mother, nurturer, and caregiver. It was all she ever knew. The absence of a child was not enough to deter her from this role. She would just simply shift the recipient of her parenting from her vacated daughter to her husband, who was still very much "living at home."

Billy thought to himself that he would never let that happen to him.

The rest of the evening carried on with no real incident worthy of note. Mr. and Mrs. Martin played the game of serving up the not so subtle hints that they expected their only child to be well along on her career path and maybe even on track to giving them a grandchild. Jessica played the game of deflecting them using every weapon in her arsenal. It was clear she was well prepared for this treatment and was ready with the response that would only fuel the next question or jab. This cold war waged on all through dinner and continued until it was time for everyone to retire to sleep.

Billy rested on the awkwardly placed cot that sat wedged tightly between the couch and the coffee table. He couldn't help but think that this life, marriage, kids, a house in the suburbs, all of it, scared him. He loved Jessica, and he felt being married to her would be great, but maybe he just wasn't ready for it yet. He knew she would be looking for that question followed by the exchange of that special shiny diamond encrusted piece of jewelry. One thing was clear, he had some soul searching to do, he had watched his parents carry out their version of the sick twisted, dysfunctional dance but never dreamed that their relationship was the norm. Maybe it was; maybe marriage was not just a lover's dream filled with "I love you's" and flowers, date nights and cuddling. Maybe the idea of maintaining a loving relationship after having kids was a fool's dream. Maybe the idea of maintaining any level of tolerance for each other once those kids left the house was an exercise in futility. Billy just assumed he would go down that road, marriage, kids and a house, the script written for him from the template used in so many canceled sitcoms.

Billy didn't get much sleep that night. It wasn't completely due to the restless nature of his wondering mind. That had a lot less to do with it than the obtrusive metal cot spring that was strategically placed to align with the small of his back. No matter which way he positioned himself, the stabbing was relentless and refused to let him get any sleep at all.

The evidence of his all-night battle with the defiant bed spring was clearly visible in his face the next morning.

"Jesus babe, you look horrible," Was the way Jessica greeted him in the morning.

"Damn cot spring was piercing my spine all night long," Billy was clearly agitated.

Jessica tried to retain her laughter, but it was no use. Like a water balloon being filled with water, eventually it would burst, and she did.

Her laughing only further infuriated Billy, and he waited for her to stop so he could tell her so. The problem was she wasn't stopping, or even slowing down. The cot spring situation wasn't the culprit causing her laughter, it was the miserable look on her boyfriends face that was the real cause of her uncontrolled laughter.

Her outburst carried on for such a prolonged period of time that it gave Billy pause enough to realize the ridiculous nature of his anger and he joined in with her in laughing.

When Jessica was finally able to compose herself, she assured

CHAPTER 10

him, "We will get a new bed or something else to sleep on. I'm sure it's no problem. Why didn't you just go on the couch?"

"Because I didn't know if your parents wanted me on there or not."

"Christ William, our dog used to sleep on there."

"Terrific, I think I'd rather the violent spring over old dog ass."

This made Jessica start laughing all over again. Billy joined her again. All of his compounded fears of marriage and his future life just seemed to melt away. He loved her and would be a fool to not spend the rest of his life in the company of such a wonderful, fun, caring and beautiful woman.

"I love you, William McCabe," Jessica had an uncanny way of speaking the words he was feeling at the exact moment he was feeling them.

"I love you more," He replied.

CHAPTER 11

Thursday carried on in an uneventful way. Jessica showed Billy all the steps of her formative years and where they took place. The elementary school, the middle school, and the high school. The trip down memory lane reached a lot further than just academia. Her first dance school, the town pool where she learned to swim and the park where she chipped her tooth. Each turn of the car's steering wheel revealed a new milestone, some accomplishment in Jessica's life. There were periodic checks with Billy to make sure his interest level hadn't faded, it hadn't. He found himself engrossed in Jess's tales of yesteryear and the stories of her childhood. For the most part, the quiet suburb of Houston didn't differ that much from the quiet suburbs of Billy's own childhood. A few more retail franchises then he was used to, but he was learning that, with some minor variations, a suburb was a suburb.

The rest of the day was peaceful, relaxing. Jessica promised that she would not toss Billy into the pit of strangers that were her friends without a good day of rest and relaxation. Since he was functioning on very little sleep due to his all-night battle with the cot spring, she saved the night out with friends for Friday. This left Thursday free for just the two of them to enjoy a peaceful dinner alone.

Billy could see the glimmer in Jessica's eye, she was home, she felt at ease here, this was where she longed to be. Thoughts began to swirl inside Billy's head. Could a marriage work? He would never leave New York, he knew that he couldn't survive outside of the city's outstretched arms. He always assumed Jessica was now a New Yorker. It was in her blood, and she considered it home, but the look on her face and the tone of her voice spoke volumes as to where her heart really resided. This was a conversation that Billy registered in his subconscious and knew he would have soon.

When they arrived back at the Martin house to retire for the night, Billy saw a brand new cot had replaced the old Ironsides that just one night earlier waged war on his lower back.

"See, a new bed, just for you. Now you can get a decent night's sleep," Jessica was reassuring in her tone.

Billy was feeling brave in the quiet house in the late hour, "What do you say we break this thing in?"

"William! No! My parents are just upstairs, I told you, we have to be good, just for the few days we are here. Don't worry, we will make up for it as soon as we get back to New York," Jessica was always reasoning with him.

"Jess, let me ask you something. Do you miss living here?" Billy, accepting defeat on one front, decided to shift gears.

"William, this was my home for most of my life, it's familiar to me. I know it, and it knows me. I think I can be happy in New York, and right now I am, but this place will always be my home. Just like Long Island is for you."

"But Long Island is just a quick train ride away for me, this is a lot different for you. Do you think you would ever want to move

CHAPTER 11

back here?" Billy asked.

Jessica saw the reason behind Billy's line of questioning, "Listen, William. New York is my home now for one reason and one reason only, it's where you are. All I need to make me happy is you, and if I have you it doesn't matter if I'm living in Antartica, I'm happy, and more importantly, I'm home."

"Fair enough, but let me ask you this. Would you be even happier if I wanted to move here?" Billy posed yet another cheaply disguised question.

"I'm not going to get caught up in rhetorical questions with you. Let's just enjoy the time we have and take everything day by day. You are going to worry yourself sick thinking this far into the future," Logical Jessica had spoken again.

Billy took a moment to let her words sink in, "You're right. Now I'm tired, and I'd like to get some sleep that doesn't involve Jack the Spring Ripper stabbing me in the spine."

Jessica gave a sweet chortle and kissed him gently on the lips before heading up to her old bedroom for her own deep sleep.

Friday night had snuck up on them quicker than they had anticipated. This was mostly due to them sleeping in way past 11:00 a.m. catching up on their missed sleep from the previous nights. They were meeting a collection of Jessica's old school mates at an old tavern close to the NASA campus. In the early days of the Apollo missions, the bar was a local hangout for astronauts. It was a real fly-boy type place where the burgers were fat, and the beer was just cold enough to say it wasn't warm. In the years since the old pub had gone through a metamorphosis. Apollo ended, and the Space Shuttle Program started. Astronauts were family men (and women) now, and nights out drinking with the guys became less and less frequent. Eventually, the local kids just hitting drinking age began to use it as their regular place, more for nostalgic reasons than for its exquisite selection of brew and food. Every now and then, when the stars aligned, an astronaut could be seen sitting at the bar enjoying a bottle of beer and reading the sports page of the Houston Chronicle.

The pub had changed its target demographic, but one wouldn't know by looking at the decor. The walls were still adorned with head shots of space travelers of the past all with the black congratulatory scribble to "Buck," the establishment's faithful owner. Any wall space not occupied by an eight by ten glossy was filled with other agency paraphernalia. Such as mission patches, Saturn 5 rocket models and even a full-sized replica of a launch suit that was carelessly fastened to the faded peeling faux wood paneled walls.

Just inside the main door stood a secondary entrance that was a pair of saloon-type swinging doors that were fashioned to look like a woman bending over showing her bloomers. When one pushed through the mini hanging dividers, they would split open and swing right where her biological split would be. It was crude and lacking in taste, but Billy still loved it and laughed when passing through them. The thick haze of cigarette smoke hovered over the entire interior of the bar like a storm cloud hanging low over a city, waiting to dump its rain upon the waiting people below. Country music played on the jukebox. Billy felt that was a little too cliche until wedged between two country classics was an old Ozzy tune that Billy hadn't heard since his years riding his bike to the ball field next to the lake. This pattern continued all night. After about four or five country songs, some classic rock gem would break up the flow before the jukebox would go back to its twang and slide guitar medley of the familiar country music.

It was unlike any bar Billy had seen in New York, but something about it appealed to him. It had a rustic nature. The yellowing of everything from the years of being barraged with tobacco laced smoke to the thick film of grease that caked the once white drop ceiling tiles

CHAPTER 11

above the kitchen area representing a certain fire hazard. The thin layer of sawdust on the floor was not placed there symbolically it was just the years of residue that emanated from the shuffleboard table in the corner, the floors were just never swept.

"Jessie!" A call rang out from across the bar over the latest Garth Brooks hit playing over the aged, crackling sound system.

A group of about eight people gathered at the bar's edge. Some standing, some seated on the worn and ripped bar stools with the wad of yellow foam pouring out the side of the once-padded top.

Jessica immediately moved across the bar to join her friends with Billy in tow. A quick round of introductions followed, and names were thrown back and forth, names that Billy would never retain, at least not in the first attempt.

He did, however, notice some firm looks being pushed his way from one of the members of the gathering. A young man, short in stature with a thin build. He kept his eyes locked on Billy, no matter where the conversation was directing the attention of the rest of the group. It became so noticeable to Billy he finally had to say something.

"Do we know each other?" Billy asked in a friendly way.

"Don't think we do," The stranger replied.

Billy didn't like where this was heading. He wasn't afraid to take things to a physical level if it became necessary. He had had his fair share of scrums and was able to hold his own in them.

"You just kept looking over at me like maybe you thought I looked familiar, that's why I asked," Billy was being stern but doing his best to keep things civil, these were Jess's friends, and he didn't want to start a war.

"Nope," The man answered again, this time adjusting his gaze elsewhere.

Billy knew he had him beat, like a dog that breaks eye contact with his master as a sign of obedience.

Jessica grabbed Billy by the arm and started to lead him away from her group of friends, "Come on William, help me pick some songs on the jukebox."

Billy knew this was a ploy to get him isolated to chastise him for starting some friction with one of her friends. He knew it and still went willingly. He felt he was right, the guy was staring at him for an awkwardly long time.

Bracing himself for the scolding, he stopped in front of the glowing music player, "Listen, Jess…"

"Hold on, before you say anything I owe you an apology," Jessica interrupted.

Billy was shocked but let her continue.

"That guy, sizing you up is Jerry. He was my boyfriend when I left for New York. I broke up with him when I left. He took it real hard. To be honest, I didn't really even consider him my boyfriend. He was this guy who would just hang out with my friends and me, and once or twice I hung out with just him. He started to refer to me as his girlfriend, I just never corrected him. I guess I didn't see the harm in it. He means well, but he is probably a little jealous of you. Just ignore him."

Billy paused before voicing his many concerns, "You brought me to some backwoods country bar to meet your ex? Jesus Jess, you know how shitty these situations always turn out. I guarantee this dick will get drunk and will try to fight me. He stands four foot nothing and weighs less than my shoes so unless he is a master ninja or is packing a gun, the latter of which could be very possible, I will drop this asshole. Then all your friends, and most likely you, will hate me and think I'm some nutball from New York who likes fighting, probably because I'm Irish. I can't win in this situation at all."

"I know, I'm so sorry. I really didn't know Jerry would be coming

CHAPTER 11

and couldn't imagine a scenario where he would want to come. Just be the bigger man here," Jessica pleaded.

"You do realize what you just said, don't you?" Billy added.

"Yes, be the bigger… oh, you asshole, yes, I get it, and yes he is very short," Jessica was laughing.

The night continued without incident, mostly because Billy was taking the higher road and ignoring the constant stares from Jerry. He was more than happy to stay in the background and give Jessica the night to play catch up and reminisce with her old friends. As the evening started to wind down, the remaining girls were getting their last drinks and last stories in before having to call it a night. Out of the corner of his eye, Billy spotted Jerry making his way through the circle of giggling girls and heading directly toward Billy.

"Oh Christ, this guy is going to start something," Billy thought he said to himself, but it was actually out loud, although no one heard.

"Can I have a word, buddy?" Jerry asked.

"Sure thing Jer, what's on your mind?" Billy replied in his most condescending tone.

"The thing is, Jessie and I, we were an item before she went to fancy New York and met you. I was going to marry her, we were happy together. Then she ends up with you, you obviously brainwashed her into thinking you're something special, but you're not, I'm special, you understand?"

"Jerry, you do realize 'special' is a term people give to disabled kids to not be mean?" Billy was calm.

"What? What the fuck are you talking about?" Jerry was not calm.

"Forget it, Jerry, listen I understand your frustration, Jessica is a beautiful girl. I mean gorgeous. You will never get a shot at something like that again. And did I mention how stunningly beautiful she is?

You would think someone that perfect has to have a flaw somewhere, right? Guess what Jerry, she doesn't. Believe me, I have explored every inch of that body looking for it, it doesn't exist. So I know what you are thinking now, hot girls are shallow, you would be wrong again. That is the most giving person I have ever known. She gives and gives and gives. And when I say gives, I mean gives. You know what I mean Jerry?" Billy was antagonizing him.

Jerry was struck silent, Billy continued, "Jerry, I'm saying she fucks like a champ. That beautiful, perfect-bodied woman standing over there comes home from work every night and does things to me that I didn't know were possible. She makes me reach levels of pleasure that no man or animal has ever reached before, and I hear that pigs have some awesome orgasms."

Billy continued without giving Jerry a chance to speak, "Now you say you and her were happy. But Jerry a woman who is happy or content with a man does not move 2,000 miles away from him and begin a new relationship with someone else. That really defies any logic. Now I guess by pure ratio and biology that my dick is bigger than yours, so my balls by default would also be bigger. Now I'll admit, you walking over here to say that shit to me takes some balls, but as we just discussed my balls are bigger. So, if you don't turn around and walk back to the place from which you came, I will cram my fucking fist down your fucking throat. You fucking rodent of a man!"

Jerry was shocked, Billy could tell by the look on his face this was not at all how he envisioned the confrontation going down. Billy knew Jerry played this whole thing out in his head a million different ways before making it happen and what just transpired was never one of those pre-thought out scenarios. Jerry was rendered speechless and turned to walk away. He took two steps and then stopped.

"Fuck," Billy said out loud because he knew what was coming

next.

Jerry turned, leaped toward Billy and took a swing at his face. His coordinates were way off, the blow landed somewhere between Billy's shoulder and his collarbone. Without taking the time to react Billy swung and landed his fist squarely on Jerry's face. Jerry landed on the floor with a thud that was louder than a person his size should make. With some delay, a pain rose up in Billy's fist.

"Fuck Jerry! Why the hell would you do that?" Billy was angrier at the situation then the pain in his fist.

Jerry was squirming on the floor like a worm just pulled from the moist soil. He pulled himself up to his knees and was muttering, "You asshole I'm going to kick your ass."

Billy shaking the pain from his fist was still standing above him, "Jerry, come on. Just stay down, don't do this, you won't win this one."

"You don't deserve her," Jerry said in a broken tone.

Billy could hear him sobbing. He bent down and helped Jerry back on his feet and sat him down on the closest bar stool. This was the first time Billy noticed everyone was staring at them, up until that moment he had forgotten they were in a public place.

"You're right Jerry, I don't deserve her, she is an amazing person, and you almost had her. That's something. Be proud of that. I love her, Jerry and I will kill anyone that ever tries to take her away from me."

Billy grabbed a handful of ice cubes from a waiting glass on the bar and handed them to Jerry, "Put this on your face, it will keep the swelling down."

"Thanks, man," Jerry spoke in a hushed tone.

He was embarrassed and heartbroken all at once. Billy looked up at the bartender who was ready to throw them both out and asked him to pour Jerry a fresh beer, and that they would be leaving now.

Billy threw $20 on the bar and turned to Jessica, "I think we should get going."

Billy looked at Jessica and was expecting a different expression than the one he saw. There was no anger in her face, no rage, no embarrassment, just a smile and a gleam in her eye. Her chin was held high, everything in her body said, "This is my boyfriend."

Billy reading Jessica's expression said, "Really? You're happy about this? I told you this was exactly what was going to happen."

"I love you too William McCabe," Nothing was going to ruin her moment.

"I don't get you, Jess can we leave now?" Billy asked.

"Yep, let's make one pit-stop first, there is this dead-end by my parent's house we could go and park the car there for a little bit, no one will bother us."

CHAPTER 12

"I do," The words are simple in nature, but when used during nuptials they mean so much more than the three letters could ever imagine. It's a commitment, a vow, and a promise. Jessica's cousin, Jason, and his bride to be stood in front of a full church and made this decree. They swore allegiance to each other in all sorts of positive and negative situations. Sickness or health, richer or poorer, until they die. What a morbid ceremony practiced by two people to commit themselves legally to each other for the foreseeable future.

Billy personally found the whole thing to be a sham. People got married when they found themselves in a relationship at the same time they found themselves economically viable. If money weren't an object, most people would marry their prom date. Love is an easy thing to start, but it eventually becomes work, and that's when it breaks down. People meet, they have a connection and fall in love, and when those people change, like they are destined to do, they find they don't love that person anymore.

The legal commitment the bride and groom participated in was done a few hours before the actual ceremony. It was when they both signed the state legal document and had it witnessed by the best man and maid of honor. It was at that point they were married in the eyes of the state. It wasn't when they stood in front of the pastor in front of the church and declared that they indeed "do" promise all of those things asked of them.

Jason Martin was the son of Jessica's father's brother. He was a young, good looking kid and his bride was even more stunning. They were a beautiful couple.

"If there is any justice in the world their kids will be ugly," Billy whispered to Jessica.

"Stop it!" She yelled back in a hushed whispered tone.

The cynical side of him couldn't help but picture the happy couple ten years down the line. One of them would be fat, and the other would be involved in an illicit affair to help compensate for the love lost due to their spouse's weight gain. Soon after the affair would start so would the divorce proceedings. The way Billy saw it the marriage was doomed before they even left the church.

One would think that he was anti-marriage, but nothing would be further from the truth. He loved the idea of it, he just felt it was executed poorly by most of its participants.

Of course, this brought him to his own internal dilemma, would he ever engage in that rite of passage, could he ever see himself being a "married man"? In his younger years, the answer was easy, "yes," followed with an "of course"! These days it wasn't so simple, there was no black and white on this debate. The debate itself was riddled with all varying shades of gray.

He knew it was on Jessica's radar and he couldn't run from it forever. He saw the question burning in her eyes when the topic would poke its head out of its hole like a groundhog searching for its shadow.

CHAPTER 12

Playing out in front of them and a whole collection of friends and family was the ultimate groundhog shadow search. The question was being asked again, this time in a ritualistic performance taking place on a stage in front. It was a play, with actors and a script worthy of Mr. Shakespeare himself. A wedding was always a prime occasion for anyone to wax nostalgic about their own future nuptials, and Jessica was no exception. Billy felt her hand on his during the entire ceremony, but it was during the emotional exchange of vows that he felt her grip tighten and could hear the sporadic sniffle from her nose. He knew if he looked over at her and saw the tears in her glassy brown eyes it would be enough to send him dropping to one knee and make his own proposal there between the church pews. He wasn't a cold hearted man. He loved romance and was a sucker for an emotional woman, he could never refuse the damsel in distress routine or a woman shedding a tear at a wedding, it all made him a big emotional mess.

Billy managed to keep his focus on the arrangement of burning candles perfectly aligned along the alter's edge. Watching those miniature flames dance in the air above the robust ivory candles was the only thing keeping him from losing control of his own emotions.

He loved Jessica and marrying her wasn't such a bad idea, in fact, it was a very good idea. He knew all of this in his heart, but his head was still questioning it. Was he ready for this? Was he too young? He wanted to shut his mind down for the rest of the day and just let his heart do the driving.

The ceremony ended with a thunderous applause from the throng of well-wishers in attendance. Billy, in his attempt to not get caught up in the emotions, missed the whole scene that played out right in front of him.

The entire crowd gathered outside the church doors to catch the first glimpse of the new bride and groom and throw bird seed, which replaced the traditional rice, at them. Billy knew this tradition probably had a sensible explanation and origin, he just couldn't fathom what it was.

The caravan of limousines and cars left the church parking lot and headed just a few miles down the road to the reception hall for the post-ceremony celebrations.

Billy and Jessica were rewarded for their blood lineage connection to the groom by getting a table close to the front of the room. Billy didn't see this as too much of a reward, it was furthest from the bathrooms, the bar, the kitchen and the exit out. The wedding reception carried on like most do; the obligatory group dances, the tossing of the garter and bouquet and the ever predictable ritual of smashing cake into your new spouse's face. Billy always thought that was a horrible way to partake of their first shared dessert. It was an aggressive gesture and a terrible waste of food, this was no way to begin a union of love and devotion.

Billy's distaste for the traditional wedding ceremony began to surface. He felt the whole dog and pony charade was silly, but he didn't let this taint his opinion of the institution of marriage as a whole. In fact, as the day moved on, and he witnessed the joy of the people involved in this shared celebration, the idea grew in his mind. The idea flooded over him like a wave crashing on the beach, he wanted to propose to Jessica.

He scanned the room quickly, he was looking for someone in particular, he knew exactly what and who he was looking for.

He stood up from his chair and made a straight line across the dance floor parting the sea of bad dancers wearing Hawaiian leis and oversized neon plastic sunglasses.

Reaching his target he paused and waited to be noticed, "Mr. Martin, I'd like to have a word with you if you don't mind sir."

"Sure William, let's step outside, it's a little too loud in here," Mr.

CHAPTER 12

David Martin was an accommodating man and a very astute man. He had a good idea what this talk with his daughter's boyfriend was going to be about. He had been preparing for it for a long time.

"Well, sir..." Billy ran on, taking a pause to try to make his mouth a little less arid, "the thing is I know you are just meeting me here this weekend for the first time and you are probably thinking 'who is this little shit my daughter brought home'..." The swear word had just spilled out, Billy immediately felt embarrassed, this was not going at all how he envisioned, "I'm sorry about that, it just slipped out. So like I was saying, I love your daughter very much, and I see myself spending the rest of my life with her, she makes me very happy, and I think I make her happy too. I have a good job, and I can provide for her... I'm not chauvinistic, I will support her too, and she can follow her career dreams too. I don't even know how I feel about kids yet, that can come later. Basically what I'm saying is that I'm not going to make her be one of those 'stay-at-home' women... well, not unless she wants to be. I don't think there is anything wrong with that."

Billy stopped but only to take the breath he hadn't taken since he started his nervous ramble.

Mr. Martin interjected, he couldn't bear to see Billy struggle like that anymore, "William, relax. This clearly isn't very easy for you, and I respect that you are making this ill-fated attempt, but let me help you out here. Jessica is an adult, she makes her own decisions in life, and if you want to ask her to marry you and she says yes then that's good enough for me. You don't need my blessing, I trust my daughter's decision."

The tension in Billy's face immediately dissipated. He was all out of words, he just nodded his head and headed back inside the reception hall.

When he arrived back at the table, Jessica had a perplexed look on her face, "Why were you just talking to my father out in the hallway?"

"I'll tell you later," Billy was still pale with fear and the saliva had not quite returned to his mouth, he would need a few more minutes.

Similarly, when Mr. Martin returned to his seat, his doting wife asked, "Was that what I think it was?"

"Yep, it was," Mr. Martin kept his response short and to the point, at first.

He then added, "You know for a boy who makes his living putting words together he sure isn't that good at it."

CHAPTER 13

The door would not be released from its locked state without the proper approval from the suit-donning man inside. When the audible buzz went off, Billy gave the door a slight pull, and it opened. He stepped inside the plush carpeted jewelry store and was immediately greeted by the man in the suit, "How can I help you today?"

Billy got the impression that this man just wanted to get the exchange over with and didn't really have a genuine desire to "help" him in any way.

"I'm looking for an engagement ring," Billy finally spoke.

"Ah, well a preemptive 'congratulations' might be in order for you young man," The sales clerk said in an overly rehearsed tone.

What followed next was a lengthy lecture on diamonds and rings and financing options. It was all flying at Billy faster than he could process it, he was retaining none of it and understanding even less.

Somewhere between the explanation of a "princess cut" and ring settings, Billy interjected, "Listen, buddy, I appreciate all this. I have to be straight with you, this shit is way over my head. What I'm looking for isn't so much a ring but a salesman I can trust to not fuck me over on the purchase of a ring. Can you be that salesman?"

The man in the fine pressed three-piece suit was taken aback with his customer's honesty and straight forward nature, "Um… yes, I can be."

"Good, then you and I can do business together," Billy took the man at his word, it may have been naive or foolish on his part, but he did still believe in the goodness of humanity and people's desire to do the right thing.

Billy explained what he wanted and what he wanted to spend and in less than one hour he left the establishment with the ring he wanted. He felt unstoppable, his confidence soared, and his self-esteem grew tenfold during the negotiations and purchase of the ring.

Billy was walking along Lexington Avenue with his head held high, he had set out to get engaged and now it was almost done. Only one step remained, one step between him and his "mission complete" status, asking Jessica for her hand in marriage and her accepting. Maybe that was two steps. Either way, Billy figured that was the easy part or was it? A blanket of panic covered him all at once. How was he going to do this? He had the pressure to create a moment that would be forever scripted into their lives. It would be the story they would tell their future children, and if the story wasn't good, maybe they would tell no one at all. How could he create this Hollywood scene? He wasn't working from a script, he didn't have a set designer, or a soundtrack or a lighting technician. He was doomed, it was like acting in a play where he was the only one who had actually read it. There were a million variables and a million deviations from the planned script and he had control over none of them. The panic blanket began to tighten its grip on him forcing his breathing to become more labored. The cold sweat began its full

CHAPTER 13

frontal assault next, and it was relentless. Just when Billy began to formulate a defense plan against it, the next barrage began to descend on his fragile psyche, the dizziness and nausea. It was a double fronted attack and he was still too weak from the previous ones to mount any sort of defense. He had lost this battle, he knew it. The best he could hope for was a successful retreat and the buying of some time to lick his wounds to return to battle another day. He immediately worked out the plan of retreat and tried his best to execute it, but to no avail, it was too late.

The dizziness began to close in his vision. The first casualty was the peripheral vision, it met its demise right away. Billy was now left with only the small range of sight that only included what was directly in his line of fire, "tunnel vision" as it was called. That didn't last too long, and soon the tunnel was tightening its grip. Billy retained some of his composure, enough to realize that once the tunnel closed, it was going to be lights out for him. This is where he made a crucial error. The safe bet would be to lay up, grab a seat and close his eyes and wait for the moment to pass. Instead, he tried to muscle through it. He kept his gait and pace down the avenue just trying to clear his mind. He was determined to beat this mentally, not by giving in physically.

It would prove to be a fatal miscalculation as Billy's last strand of consciousness lost its footing, and he passed out, right on the sidewalk of Lexington Avenue, somewhere between 61st Street and 62nd Street.

The voices in the room were the first thing Billy remembered, there was a swirl of background chatter, nothing he could make out or understand just yet. Slowly he opened his eyes and then things started to fall back into place. He started to remember the sequence of events that brought him to this state. His vision was extremely blurry at first, then it began to become more focused. It didn't matter that his vision was clear, now it was still hindered by the blinding lights that filled the room. The lights pierced his head with such a sharp, angry pain that he winced and released an audible grunt of discomfort. This alerted the spectators in the room that he was there, in case they forgot.

"William, it's me, Jessica. Don't move. You took quite a spill honey and knocked your head pretty good," She spoke in a soft, soothing tone.

"Is that why my head feels like it's been pounded like a hooker on a Navy base?" Billy's fall didn't deaden his ability to make the most inappropriate statements at the most inappropriate times.

"Jesus Will, there are other people in here, that was out loud," Danny spoke up from the corner of the room.

"Dan? What are you doing here, what the hell happened?" Billy's confusion was evident.

Jessica spoke first, "Well, it seems you passed out on the sidewalk on Lexington Avenue and hit your head. Someone called the ambulance, and the hospital called your brother. You had him on your emergency contact card in your wallet, I didn't even know people still used those, but anyway, he called me, and we got here as soon as we could. You had a severe concussion, but the doctor said you will be fine after a couple days' rest. He's going to release you tonight."

Billy took a moment to process all this new information, his mind began to trace his steps. Why had he passed out in the first place? What could have caused it? Then it all hit him at once. The ring!

"Um… Jess, where are my belongings?" Billy carefully phrased his question. The only thing worse than spoiling the surprise of the engagement ring would be for it to now be in the hands of a greedy ambulance attendant or the "Good Samaritan" who called the ambulance. Who knows, maybe they were splitting the profits.

"Don't worry sweetheart, I have everything. It's all safe, not to worry at all," Jessica had a huge smile on her face that stretched her lips to almost comical proportions.

"You mean, you know?" Billy still playing his cards close to the chest, just in case he was misreading the signals.

"I do," A clever choice of words for her to use.

"Shit, this was not at all how I wanted to do this Jess. You deserve something bigger, better and so much more romantic," Billy began to rant, ignoring the glaring pain growing behind his temples.

"I do," Jessica repeated again.

"I know you do, that's what I'm saying. You deserve better," Billy was starting to feel confused over Jessica's unorthodox replies.

"William, I'm not listening to you, I'm saying 'I do' because I want nothing more than to be your wife. I'm answering the question before you ask it," Jessica was giddy with excitement and unable to control her emotions.

Billy had just realized at this time that the room emptied out, it was just the two of them. He didn't know if this was planned or just happenstance.

Billy's tone dropped, "I can't believe I messed this up. This was supposed to be special."

"It was, in fact, it was perfect. William, I want you to understand something about me. Marriage is something so much more than jewelry and elaborate weddings. It's about a partnership, a union between two separate souls becoming one. We enter this and become two halves of a whole. I know that sounds cliche, but it's how I feel. Today, rushing to the hospital to be by your side and take care of you and worry about you and make sure you are getting the attention you need, well… that was the first time in my life I felt like a partner with someone. I felt your well-being was my well being, I had such a connection with you today, I saw my future, and it was with you. I want to do this with you until we are old and gray. Then, that nurse brought me that bag with your clothes and stuff in it and I saw that box and it was fate, destiny or whatever else you want to call it. It wasn't some über rehearsed proposal down on one knee after an expensive dinner, it was so much more. It was you, laying in a vulnerable state, needing me and from your concussed state you proposed to me, at the perfect time in the most perfect way. William McCabe, you pulled off the most romantic and poetic marriage proposal in the history of marriage proposals, in your sleep. I love you and my answer is, without any doubt, yes! Yes, I will marry you."

There were tears in her eyes when she finished her speech. Billy took it all in, Jessica had a wonderful way of always finding the beauty in everything, but she was right, and she understood it. Marriages didn't succeed or fail based on its wedding or on how elaborate the proposal was. A marriage succeeded because of the people, their understanding of self-sacrifice and devotion and making someone who was not blood-related closer to you than any other relative. It was the deepest most meaningful relationship any two people could share.

Finally, Billy spoke, "Oh… so I guess you found the ring? Shit. Um, not sure how to tell you this Jess, that's not for you. I've been seeing someone else for a while now. I think it's getting pretty serious," Billy teased.

"Why the hell would you ruin a beautiful moment like this with some childish joke?" Jessica still had the smile on her face showing that she really wasn't mad.

"Because sweetheart, I want you to be fully aware of the level of immaturity you are willing to spend the rest of your life with."

"Oh, trust me, I'm aware, and after a lot of careful consideration and going against my parent's wishes, I decided to do it anyway."

CHAPTER 13

"Your parents don't want you to marry me?" Billy lost all of his sarcastic tones and really felt jaded by his future in-law's nonacceptance of him.

"No, of course they want me to, they think you're fabulous. I just wanted you fully aware of the level of immaturity I can throw back at you."

"Touché" Billy replied.

"We have a lifetime to talk, just get some rest now, you need it. I'll be here, and I'll take care of you. Forever."

CHAPTER 14

The man at the counter eating his lunch had a familiar look to Billy, but nothing that would alarm him too much. He continued eating his lunch and stealing a quick chat with Jessica when she was between customers. They had a standing agreement; Billy was allowed to have his lunch at the cafe where she worked as long as he understood that her customers came first.

He finished his club sandwich, gave his fiancé a kiss and grabbed his coat and headed for the door. As he stepped out into the bustling city and began his quick paced walk back to his office, he felt a slight tap on his shoulder. He turned immediately and saw the man from the cafe standing before him.

"Yes?" Billy asked.

"Billy McCabe?" The man asked back.

"You know I am," Billy shot back.

He now remembered why he felt this man looked familiar. Billy had met him last year at a local advertising awards dinner. His name was Saul Lieberman; he was a partner in one of the most aggressively growing ad agencies in New York City. They were still young but landing new clients by the day.

"Do you know who I am?" Mr. Lieberman asked.

"Yes, I do Mr. Lieberman," Billy replied.

"Then I'm sure you can guess why I've hunted you down in an attempt to steal a minute of your time to invite you out for a drink," Mr. Lieberman offered.

"I think I have an idea," Billy returned.

Mr. Lieberman slipped Billy his beautifully designed business card, "Please son, do me and yourself a huge favor, call me. Soon."

"Thank you, Mr. Lieberman, I will," Billy said.

"Please, call me Saul."

The rest of Billy's day continued; it rarely strayed from its scripted routine. He was still writing great ads and still watching as Spence was getting all the accolades. In the past, he was content to accept that this was the price of the business, just the way it was. Now he felt different, today he felt he had options. He was going to meet with Saul, but he would not settle for anything less than a Senior Copywriter title. The money would be secondary, if he wanted any growth in this business, he needed that Senior title.

A week had passed before he set a meeting with Eric; he was going to press him about his future role in the agency. He needed to give Eric and the company every opportunity to make the right move before he would ever consider taking a meeting with Saul Lieberman or anyone else.

Billy knocked on Eric's door, "You got a minute?"

"Sure," Eric replied.

Billy took a deep breath and began, "Eric, I just want to let you know that I am happy here, you have given me the opportunity to break into this business. You took a shot on me when no one else would without experience. I'm very grateful for that."

CHAPTER 14

"But?" Eric interjected.

Billy knew his purpose was thinly veiled, "But… I need to know where I stand with this agency. I have given you two years of amazing service, half of the clients we landed in the past year we got on my creative. The other half request that I work on their accounts, not Spence. I'm not trying to make this about Spence, but he has the Senior title and pay, and I'm doing the Senior title work."

"You want to be the Senior Copywriter?" Eric asked.

"Eric, what I'm saying is that excluding the title and pay I am the Senior Copywriter," Billy was quick to respond.

"McCabe, listen, you may be right about that. In fact, I know you are right about that. You are better than Spence, and you have been an integral part of this agency's growth."

"But?" Billy now interjected.

Eric appreciated the ironic twist of using his own witty retort against him, "But… You have been here less than two years, and Spence was here on the ground floor with me. Demoting him and promoting you over him puts me in a hell of a tight spot. Plus you are like ten years younger than he is."

"So, I guess that leaves me asking my original question again. What's my role in the future of this agency?" Billy prodded.

"Listen, McCabe. You have a very valid point. You warrant a raise, no doubt in my mind that you deserve that. Starting next week, you will see a 10% increase in your salary. But the title thing? My hands are tied on that one. Sorry kid, I can't fuck over Spence like that."

Eric could see the disappointment on Billy's face, "Listen, kid, hang in there, we will do something for you. Maybe split it up into two different creative teams you can lead one and Spence can lead the other, I don't know. You're doing great work, keep it up, and I know we will find something for you long term."

Accepting defeat in Eric's last reply, Billy stood up from the leather seat that sat opposite Eric's desk and began his retreat, "OK, I understand. It's cool. Don't worry about it."

The quick concession should have been a dead giveaway that Eric was on the verge of losing his top creative talent, and he almost saw that, but his conscience was quickly swept away by his ringing phone.

Eric picked up the receiver, "Hello, it's Eric, hold one second."

He looked back up to say something else to Billy, but it was too late he had already vacated the office. Eric pushed the meeting with Billy to the back of his mind and continued with his phone call.

After his day had ended, Billy looked at the business card of one Mr. Saul Lieberman and rolled it between his fingers like some fancy Las Vegas card dealer. He wanted to call him, but some underlying sense of loyalty was preventing him from pressing those buttons on the face of the phone. He hated the way the meeting with Eric went earlier that day, but maybe that wasn't reason enough to make a rash decision.

He began to weigh the logic. He started to convince himself that there was nothing rash about calling Saul and just having a drink with him. Maybe just hear him out. He wasn't going to sign any long term contracts, it was just a drink.

Before he could debate his own conscience any longer his phone was to his ear, and he was pushing the numbers, it was settled, he was having drinks with Saul Lieberman in less than one hour.

Delmonico's was one of New York's oldest restaurants, so many a deal played out inside the darkened interior. These deals that ranged from the illegal kickbacks of the New York mob to the slightly more legit ones of the Wall Street broker. It rested secretly at the intersection of Beaver Street, William Street and Hanover Square, a less famous five-cornered junction in lower Manhattan.

Mr. Saul Lieberman was already sitting at the bar when Billy arrived. He jumped up from his stool and extended his chubby hand out for Billy, "Billy my boy, thanks for meeting up with me. What can I get you to drink?"

Billy was strictly a beer guy, but when drinking in the most upscale watering holes, he always felt a little too second class ordering a bottle of beer. Jameson Irish Whiskey on the rocks was his fall back drink for such an occasion.

It was no surprise what Saul wanted to meet with Billy about, so he didn't waste time with too many formalities and cut right to the chase.

He was there to offer Billy a job, and not just any job, the senior copywriter position at his agency. He was dangling the much-desired fruit in front of Billy. He somehow knew what Billy wanted to be offered and gave it up right away.

Billy told himself that there was a tough decision he had to make here, but there wasn't. He wanted the job, and he was going to accept it. It was a tremendous growth opportunity for him and his career. He had a good gut feeling about Saul; he seemed trustworthy and honest. Billy would be trusting his career in his hands and wanted to make sure that it would be handled with the utmost care. Saul also seemed hungry, like Billy. Ready to grow his company and go after the larger more lucrative accounts, this also appealed to Billy's ambitious side. The relationship felt right, there wasn't much left to discuss.

By the third round of drinks, Billy had agreed to be Saul's new Senior Copywriter. Two years ago this young, eager kid from Long Island was searching for his first job out of college, now he was already heading to his second job, as a senior creative. It was a fast track career, very unorthodox.

Billy always felt that the creative field offered a small window of relevancy. There weren't any 50-year-old copywriters or any junior creative staff in the business. By that age, you were either in management or off on your second career. He felt a slight paranoia about being phased out before he could reach his full potential. Getting the Senior title was a huge step up in securing his future worth and brought him closer to his dream position of Creative Director.

The subway ride and subsequent walk home were a blur, Billy was walking on air the entire trek. When he reached his apartment and unlocked the door, Jessica was standing in the living room, staring at him with anger in her eyes.

Billy was confused, "What?" It was all he could think to say.

"Where have you been?" Jessica asked in a tone just below a yell.

"I had an after work meeting. Wait until I tell you the good news," Billy was hoping the new job would smooth over his four hours of not being accountable for.

"William, I called your brother, he checked to see if you were in any of the New York City hospitals. That's how worried I was. I tried to call, you didn't answer your phone. Why didn't you call?" There was a genuine worry on her face.

"Babe, I'm sorry. I just didn't think, but wait until I tell you what happened," The news was bubbling over inside Billy, he needed to tell her before he exploded from the pressure building up.

"What? What happened?" Jessica still had an annoyed tone.

"I got a new job! I'm the new Senior Copywriter for this great agency downtown. More money and the senior title I always wanted. I met with this guy, Saul, he offered me the position, and I accepted. Isn't that great?" Billy's excitement came to its full potential.

"You got a new what?" The news didn't seem to pacify Jessica's anger at all, in fact, it only seemed to stir it to a higher level.

"You're not happy about this?" Now Billy was very confused.

Jessica took a calming breath, "You didn't think to talk to me about this before making any decisions?"

Any fool would have seen the loaded question and answered accordingly, but Billy's deadly combination of elation and confusion overtook him, "No, I didn't."

"You didn't?" Jessica asked for dramatic effect.

"No babe, I guess it never crossed my mind, I just figured you would be happy."

"William, I am happy for you, but I need to ask you something, where do you see yourself in five years, ten years, even twenty years?"

"I don't know, I guess working," Billy lumbered through his reply.

Jessica readied herself for the lecture she was about to give, "William, do you know where I see myself at those very same intervals? With you. Married to you. Sharing my life with you. The key word there is 'sharing.' If during that time I want to make a career move or any other major life decision I would make sure I talk to the person who will be my partner in life for, what I hope is, the rest of my life. Are you following me?"

Billy was silent for a few seconds, he was really processing what Jessica had just said. Finally, he spoke, "You're right. I didn't think about it that way. I guess I was just so focused on living my life with only me in mind. I'm just not used to being in a relationship like this."

"William, sweetheart, this isn't just some 'relationship.' We are engaged, that means sometime shortly we are going to get married. We are going to be husband and wife, that brings us to a whole new level here. You need to understand that. There is no more you and me, it's us. Every decision made from here on affects the future 'us.' I need you to see that."

"Jess, I swear, I wasn't trying to do anything behind your back or anything I just didn't think of it that way," Billy reasoned.

"I know it wasn't malicious, but I worry that you don't fully see the gravity of the situation we are in. I'm not sure you fully appreciate what it really means to be married. It's not like dating on steroids, it's a whole new world. A world of trust and partnerships and shared experiences and living as one joined mind. I need to make sure you really see that before I walk down that aisle with you," Jessica's anger dissipated and was replaced by genuine concern. She was really driving her point forward.

"Jess, I'm not afraid to marry you. I know it's what I want. I'm just not used to all this yet. I will get there, just bear with me, it will take me some time, but I am committed to this, I'm committed to you," Billy was honest with her.

Jessica was in full lecture mode, "So, let me ask you again. What does your future look like? What do you want in life? Are we on the same page here William?"

Billy took a while to think about it. He was partly hoping Jessica would lose patience and move on, but she didn't, she waited for his reply, he would have to answer and hope he was answering correctly.

"Well Jess, I see myself married, to you, maybe two kids. I'm working, maybe I make Creative Director, and you are working too. Just because we have kids doesn't mean we both can't have careers unless you don't want one. Then I will support you on that too. Maybe we are still living in the city, but maybe not. Maybe after we have kids we decide a house out in the suburbs is better, maybe Long Island, maybe New Jersey, but preferably Long Island. Kids grow up, have families of their own. We get old, retire down to Texas where it never snows and live our golden years as that happy cute old couple that sometimes gets experimental with their sex lives," Billy's humor was always his fall back to lighten a tense situation.

Jessica smiled. Billy wasn't sure if she was amused at his joke or if she was pleased with his future plan.

"That was perfect, thank you. Just please, no more major life decisions without at least bringing my opinion to the table, please." Jessica pleaded.

"Of course, and I'm sorry I was self-centered on this one, I just wasn't thinking," Billy offered.

"I know, this is why you need me around for the rest of your life. Someone has to do the thinking for you," Jessica joked.

The tense moment between them passed. It was one of the so many obstacles that they would face in their relationship. It was a minor obstacle, but they came out the other end just a little but stronger in their relationship. Each roadblock, misunderstanding or fight would be the same. They would be forced to muscle through it and come out the other side just a little stronger in their commitment to each other. They were the building blocks to a long and successful marriage, and this young couple had already begun to figure that out.

CHAPTER 15

The morning of September 11, 2001, began just like any other morning for Billy, and everyone else in the world. It would end very differently. The lives of every New Yorker, every American, and everyone around the world would be changed forever. The early morning hours were the last anyone would know of this way of life. No one knew this, if they did, everyone would have taken the extra minute to tell the people in their lives how much they loved them. They would tell them how much they meant to them and how much they needed them. Even those who would see the next sunrise unaffected were still affected.

Billy always like to keep things in perspective. He knew life was a fragile balance of events and situations. He had experienced some loss in his life. He knew the importance of declaring that constant reminder that he did indeed love and think about those people in his life that mattered most to him.

He had been working at his new job for a few months and was fitting in very well. He liked the staff, he liked the work and even loved the neighborhood in which he was working. His building was on Fulton Street near Broadway. It was in the heart of New York's financial district. It had personality and an attitude. The post 80's had not been kind to the Wall Street broker, but they still had a swagger to their step and a pompous arrogance. This modern beast was working and socializing in one of the oldest and most historic parts of New York City. Trinity Church, Bowling Green, and the Old Customs House all within a stone's throw from the financial epicenter of the free market world. It was an exciting blend, and Billy was right in the middle of it all.

As was customary, Jessica woke first, very early, she was up hours before the sun awoke from its slumber. She had an early shift at the cafe. She also had class later that night, so she was not looking forward to a long full, hectic day ahead of her.

She was able to slide out of bed and into the shower without waking Billy. In fact, she had managed to dress and finish all her final preparations without stirring him at all. She gave him an extra few minutes to see if he would wake before she left. She didn't see the need to wake him, they had plans to meet for dinner later that night after her class, she would see him then. As Jess took one last look at the sleeping Billy in the bed, she smiled to herself and turned to leave. Without any other warning noise, a voice came from under the sheets.

"Were you really going to leave without saying, 'goodbye?'"

Startled at first Jessica turned to see Billy sitting up in bed, "I didn't want to wake you."

"You didn't," Billy replied, "I was just lying here watching you. You are beautiful when you think no one is watching."

"Am I ugly when I know someone is watching?" Jessica asked in a mocking tone.

She moved over to the bed and sat on the edge. She leaned over and gently kissed Billy's forehead.

"I love you, William," She professed.

"I love you more," Billy answered back.

She stood up and headed for the door, she looked back one last time and saw Billy still staring at her, smiling.

She reminded him, "Remember, we are doing dinner tonight after I get out of class."

She liked to give Billy constant reminders of things that she knew he already knew.

He watched her walk out of the room and across the living room. He could almost see the door to the apartment from his bed and followed her with his eyes all the way until she slid out of his line of sight. He heard the door unlock, open, close and then lock again.

Billy had some time left before he was scheduled to get up, but he decided he didn't need the extra time. His new job was going great. He was excelling and making all the senior partners happy. He loved his new position and the company that came with it. Getting up for work was never a dreaded chore, he looked forward to going into the office every day. He executed the most perfect of stretches accompanied by a growl that made him sound more like a bear awakening from hibernation than a human just getting up for work.

Years of distrust of the local weather reports created a habit for him. The first thing he would do, after peeling his body off the mattress, would be to look out the window to confirm what he felt the reports would have wrong. This day he couldn't remember what the reports were calling for, and with the sun yet to show its cheery face it was hard to tell what the day's weather would be.

Billy brewed a pot of coffee and plopped himself down on the couch to catch up on the only news he felt inclined to follow, the sports news. The Yankees were scheduled to play the Red Sox the night before, but bad weather won that contest. After the Yankees, there wasn't much else he followed in September.

Billy took a minute to run over his schedule for the day. He tried to convince himself that he was the ever concerned employee, but the reality of it was, no client pitches meant it was acceptable to wear jeans to work. After a thorough inquiry into his mental calendar he was able to confirm it, jeans it was.

By the time Billy left his building the sun had awoken from its slumber and was making its presence known to all the residents of New York City. The weather was so agreeable that Billy opted to get off at the Brooklyn Bridge/City Hall station, one stop early and walk to his office on Fulton Street.

Billy usually meandered into work at 9:00 a.m., but today he was surprisingly early, about fifteen minutes early. In his old office, he would take advantage of those fifteen minutes and go see Jess and have a cup of coffee with her, but now he had nothing to do but actually go to work early.

Billy was just sitting down at his desk to read the morning paper when it happened. "It" was a jolt, a bang, and shake that rattled his office and the world. He jumped up from his chair more confused than scared.

He said aloud to no one in particular, "What the fuck was that?"

A buzz began to stir around the office; everyone had the same exact question Billy had, and they were all asking it. One thing was sure, no one knew "what the fuck" it was. An earthquake? No, it was too short and sudden. An explosion was the only viable answer. But where was it and what exploded? Billy made an attempt to keep the staff calm.

"It was probably a gas leak explosion. We are all fine, I don't smell gas here, so we are not in danger," Billy explained.

No sooner were the words out of his mouth before a man that he had never seen before poked his head into the door and exclaimed,

CHAPTER 15

"A plane just smashed into the Trade Center!"

Just as quickly as he appeared, he disappeared.

There was no clear sight line to the Twin Towers from any window in Billy's office. They were only a few blocks away, but their view had been obstructed by the other large buildings of the financial center. What Billy did see when he looked out of his window was a scattering of people on the street below, like ants who just had their mound crushed by a mischievous child.

"This isn't good," Billy thought he said to himself but when a junior Graphic Designer behind him replied, "Oh God, we are all going to die in here," He knew he spoke it out loud.

Trying to mitigate the damage he assured the staff that everything was going to be fine, and it was probably just a freak accident. It was too late, TV's in the conference room were on, phones ringing, radio's broadcasting all delivering the same tragic news, this was not an accident.

Billy was scrambling to find Saul or one of the other partners. He needed something, some word from them. Should everyone remain in the building, should everyone leave? No one knew what to do, and the chaos only increased when it all happened again. An exact repeat. A jolt, a bang and a shake, but this one a little more intense, it almost knocked Billy to the floor. Allowing for the delay on the TV there was a collective scream from the people glued to it in the conference room. It was almost as if the real life shake they just felt didn't register until they saw it on TV. A second plane, the second tower.

This was real, it was more real than real, it was the most real anything had ever been to Billy in his entire life. Everything he took for granted was now in question. Was this an attack? How big was this going to get? Was it just planes into buildings? Was it more? Were there bombs in the streets? Armed soldiers on the streets of Manhattan shooting civilians?

Up until this point, war to Billy was something he saw on the news, something that happened to other people in countries he couldn't pronounce. Everything had changed, the war was here, it was happening in his country, in his city, and about two blocks away.

Not waiting for anyone else to make a decision Billy spoke, "Um... Everyone, listen up. I don't think it's safe here. We should probably leave the building. If you can get home to your families, I suggest you do that."

Billy was not in a position to cancel work for the day but given the catastrophic events going on no one cared who gave the order, just that the order had been given. People began calling people. Checking in on them, and letting them know they were safe, then one by one grabbed their belongings and started to file out the door.

Billy began to second guess his unofficial leadership call. Should he have sent those people out into the street? God only knows what was waiting for them out there. Did he just send all of his co-workers to their deaths? Why weren't any of the partners in yet? Why were people looking for the Senior Copywriter to make life and death decisions? None of that mattered now, he did what he did, he was willing to stand by it, and even follow it. So he grabbed his coat and left too.

He didn't know what he was going to see when he stepped out into the street, and that worked to his advantage. It was the worst chaos he had ever seen, a pell-mell of people screaming, crying, all looking up and pointing. Paper and other unidentifiable debris were circulating in the soft winds of southern Manhattan. Billy walked a block north and for the first time had a clear sight line to the towers. Gathered on the street, literally on the street, no one was concerned with vehicle traffic at this point, he saw a large throng gathered all with an upward gaze. Some were pointing, some had their hands over their mouths, but all had a look of horror. Billy thought about not looking, he thought he should just keep his head down and walk north, keep walking north until he got to his apartment. He thought this but didn't act on it. He turned and looked up at the sight at which everyone else on the corner was looking. Nothing could have prepared him for the gruesome sight he saw. Two gaping gashes tore into two architectural giants, someone, something, cut the two largest structures in the city like a butcher cuts into a slab of beef.

None of what he was looking at felt real. For the first time in his life, he questioned his sanity. Was this some super-realistic dream, or some hallucination? There was no way what he saw was real, it wasn't possible. None of what he saw was possible, none of it could register into his understanding of the real world. This just didn't happen. This was a movie special effect, not a real thing.

Unable to cope with the severity of the situation he turned to leave, but before he did, he grabbed the arm of a woman standing next to him. He made sure she looked at him and not the wreckage above and said to her, "This isn't real, it's fake, it's a movie. I'm dreaming, aren't I? We need to all go home and wake up from this nightmare. So let's all just go home and wake up, OK?"

The woman on the other end of his grip became nervous and pulled her arm away from him. She pushed him away and yelled, "You have got to get a grip, this shit is really happening!"

Billy didn't want to continue the debate, so he turned his eyes away from the chaos. He directed his gaze away from the reality playing out in front of him and began to push his way through the mob that was now clogging all the major arteries of the city.

Billy knew the walk from his office to his apartment was about five miles, a very doable walk in most situations, this was not most situations. He was never going to find a cab and given the current state of the city's stability he knew that going underground in the subway system was not a smart option. Left with no other choices, he began his long walk home. He figured once inside the safe confines of his apartment he could start to figure things out.

Once he got a few blocks away from the hysteria, his head began to clear. The rational thought began to come through. It was at this moment he first thought of Jessica. She was going to be worried sick about him. He figured she would be calling his office over and over and with every passing telephone ring that went unanswered her panic would rise to a higher level. He needed to see her, put her fears to rest. Her cafe was on 14th Street, and he knew he could get there in about thirty minutes on foot.

Billy pulled on the glass door, the tiny bell tied to the handle announced his arrival. No one inside the cafe heard the chime or heeded its call, they were all fixated on the television mounted to the wall in the main dining area. Billy took a quick scan of the faces in the cafe, he didn't see Jessica.

Finally, he asked of no one in particular, "Where's Jessica?"

Janice, the most senior waitress on the staff, turned to see who was asking. Her face went pale, and her mouth went slightly open as if she wanted to say something, but no words came out.

Repeating his question, he asked again, "Where is Jess?"

Janice, without breaking her stare at Billy, tapped the arm of the man standing to her immediate right. The arm belonged to Jeff, the cafe's owner. When Jeff turned and saw Billy standing there his face became a carbon copy of Janice's. Billy's mind began racing too fast to process the billions of thoughts that started to race through it. Something had happened; that's all he knew. It was only five seconds before Jeff spoke, but it might as well have been five hours, and so much was processed in Billy's mind in that time. Of all the scenarios he played out, her being in the Twin Towers was not one of them. There would be no reason for her to be there, but he did consider everything else. Hit by a car. Burned in a grease fire. Had she been

CHAPTER 15

shot during a botched robbery? Abducted by aliens. Every thinkable possible and impossible scenario ran through his head in those five seconds. All he knew was something wasn't right.

"Where is Jess?" He repeated, this time sounding a little agitated.

Jeff spoke first, "Billy, listen, I got a phone call this morning from a friend of mine. He was looking for some waitresses to work a breakfast event he had going on."

Billy didn't wait for him to finish his explanation, "What event? Where is it?"

"Bill we just don't know anything for sure just yet, we have been calling her. Phone service has been shit."

"Where the fuck is Jess?" Billy asked, more enraged now.

Jeff and his staff all paused. Jeff took a hard swallow but it was useless to swallow, his mouth had been bone dry since he first saw Billy in his cafe.

"Bill, the event, the breakfast thing, it was at Windows on the World," Jeff finally revealed thinking that was a clear enough explanation for his worry. It wasn't.

"What the fuck is Windows on the World?" Billy knew the answer, he just needed to ask it.

Jeff had a sullen look on his face. He did not want to be the one to say what needed to be said next, but no one else was going to speak, "It's a restaurant. It's on the 107th floor of the North Tower of the World Trade Center."

Billy's vision went dark, he didn't faint or pass out, it just went dark. Everything around him stopped. He began to break out in a cold sweat, vomit began its journey from his gut, up his esophagus and headed for his mouth for an untimely jettison. He held it in, he needed more clarification. Somewhere in the background of his consciousness, the entire wait staff of the cafe released a collective gasp. The South Tower had just collapsed.

Not making any sense Billy looked at Jeff and repeated again, "Jeff, where is my fucking fiancé? What are you saying to me?"

Jeff wasn't sure how to answer the question. Apparently, Billy was dealing with some sort of denial, and Jeff was ill-equipped to handle it. Billy looked up at the TV for the first time since entering the cafe. He watched as the news replayed the South tower's collapse over and over again. The look on his face went from confusion to anger, to hurt, to complete devastation all in a matter of seconds.

He looked up at the stained drop ceiling of the cafe and whispered, "Now what?"

His chest began to tighten, his breathing became labored, his head got light, and the room began to spin, slowly at first then gradually picking up speed until it became a vortex of blurry colors.

Billy lost consciousness and fell to the floor only after striking his head on a table. He would eventually awaken, but he wasn't sure he really ever wanted to again.

When he finally came to Janice had a cold rag on his forehead and some gauze on the cut over his right eye. She was blurry at first, but his focus began to sharpen as he took deep breaths. He had let out a huge sigh of relief, it had been a dream, thank God it was only a dream, what a horrible nightmare. He cherished the feeling that Jess was still alive, but it was short lived. He quickly noticed his surroundings, and it all came back again. It hit him in the chest like a sledgehammer swung at full force producing a blow with enough vengeance to knock him down, but not enough compassion to kill him.

He looked up at Janice, her eyes were red and had tears in them. All Billy could gather the strength to ask was, "The North Tower?"

One word from Janice was all it took to describe Billy's life, "Gone."

PART THREE

CHAPTER 01

June 24, 2008, 9:36 a.m.
414 East 74 Street, Manhattan, New York

The digital alarm clock/radio combo sounded for the fourth or maybe even the fifth time. All the previous attempts to get Billy out of bed were failed ones at best. He knew that there was no recourse coming. No cup of water poured on his head by his scolding mother. No job to be late for, and worst of all not a single person in the world awaiting his arrival at any place.

None of this mattered to him, he was not only unaware of the time of day, but also unaware of what day it actually was. Billy was now self-employed, a term he stretched to its furthest reach of credibility. The reality was he wrote just enough headlines and taglines for the lowest bidder so he could pay the rent. His friends, old and new, eventually gave up trying to get him to break out of this depressive state. He had moments of clarity, moments where he began to enjoy life again. Smiles on his face were in diminished supply and only came in short spurts.

There was a period of seven months in 2005 that everyone thought Billy had finally shaken the ghost of Jessica. He had met and begun dating a very attractive woman. They had met while Billy was on line buying milk. She stood in place in front of him and found herself short seventy-three cents for her purchase. Billy in an unprovoked act of kindness handed the cashier a dollar to cover her shortfall, telling her to keep the change. Her name was Lisa. She was essentially the anti-Jessica. She was tall, standing five feet nine inches. Shoulder length hair, light brown with a subtle kiss of a golden glow, like that single bright beam of escaped sunlight that slips past the oppressive rain cloud. Lisa had pale skin, freckles on her cheeks and shoulders. Her eyes danced beautifully between the world of blue and a light gray. She had a simple sense of humor; the most childish things would make her laugh.

She doted on Billy, he meant the world to her. It was hard to imagine anything going wrong. Billy was happy again. Attending social events, laughing, singing, all the things a happy guy will do.

Then something happened. It started innocently enough, a slip here and a slip there but when Billy was calling Lisa "Jess" more than once a week Lisa needed to confront him. It didn't go as cordially and maturely as she had expected. The yelling finally came to an abrupt end when Billy finally broke down and muttered the words Lisa had always dreaded hearing, "I'm just not ready to move on yet. I still love Jess. I still think about her all the time."

That was three years ago, and Billy disappeared into extinction. He would make random appearances at the occasional birthday party or wedding. By this stage in his life, Billy relegated himself to his apartment on Manhattan's Upper East Side for the majority of his days.

CHAPTER 1

His freelance writing was keeping him occupied enough; he was still an excellent copywriter, and writing still brought him joy. It was the only time he could escape himself, leave his surroundings and move to a clean, unaffected corner of his mind. A place free from sadness and worry, it was a bright white space devoid of anything bad, no distractions just Billy and his words. He could stand in this space, and see the words float around him like a child playing in a cascading sea of bubbles. Billy was free to pluck the best words carefully out of the air like seasoned oranges from a tree in a peaceful grove. He assembled his ripened words together, constructing the purest of sentences. To Billy, words were perfect, they only did what they were told to do, there were no bad words, only misused words.

The months following that harrowing day were a blur to most people, and Billy was not above its reach. He too sped through the collections of "I'm so sorry" and the "How are you holding up?" and all other forms of well-meaning condolences.

Mr. & Mrs. Martin made the trip up to New York. There was no body to collect, and all of her belongings could have been mailed down to them in Texas. It was more a pilgrimage for them, a weak attempt at achieving closure. Billy put them up in the apartment, that space that would no longer exist between him and his fiancé.

Jessica's parents were kind to him. They tried to sympathize with the loss he was going through, but no matter how hard they tried they just could not feel Billy's loss was on the same plane as theirs.

There was going to be a memorial service for her back in Texas. The town was going to add a plaque to the park that lay nestled among the row of live oak trees that lined Main Street. Billy would attend. It would be the last time he would ever be in that part of Texas again. It would also be the last time he would ever see or talk to Mr. & Mrs. Martin. It was unspoken, but both parties knew that remaining in contact was no way to let the wounds heal. That's how easy it went, one day these people were slated to be his extended family, and then one cruel twist of fate pushed them out of his life forever.

Billy had been left with a few simple items that served only as a simple reminder that Jessica did, in fact, exist in his life and on this earth. He tried to keep photos and memories displayed, trying to honor her memory but after too many emotional breakdowns he packed it all in a box and threw them all out.

Now time found him living in this state of nothing, just barely existing. He quit his job after the failed relationship with Lisa and slowly slid into a state of seclusion.

Billy's cell phone chimed and then chimed again. He always kept the phone close to him, it was an old habit he picked up back when Jessica worked late. He could never really sleep until he knew she was home and safe. He picked up the phone, looked at the number displayed on the screen. It was Kenny Springer, his childhood friend. Kenny and Billy reconnected in the days following Jessica's death and since then have remained in contact, mostly through phone calls.

"Ken, what's up?" Billy, barely audible, spoke into the phone.

"Will, listen… not sure what you got going on this Saturday, but we are having this big sort of BBQ thing at my folk's house. The old man is finally retiring. Forty-two fucking years on the job and he's finally had enough. Imagine forty-two years punching tickets on the LIRR? God, I'd kill myself, but God bless him, the son of a bitch loved the job. Anyway, he's done, retired and we are doing this big thing for him. You were always like family to us, so I want you there. If anything the old man would love to see you again. That guy loves telling stories about all the stupid shit we did as kids, at least give him that."

Billy let Kenny finish his sales pitch, "What time?"

Kenny shocked that Billy's immediate answer wasn't "No."

CHAPTER 1

Paused, "Um… well, officially it starts at like noonish, but I'll be there at 10:00, so stumble in whenever you want."

Billy took a minute to think, then finally spoke, "Sure Ken, your old man was always good to me, it's the least I can do. Besides I could go for getting out of the city for a day. Can you pick me up at the train station?"

"Yeah, what time?"

"I don't know, figure like 11:00 at the Ronkonkoma station. I'll text you when I get there."

"OK Will, and hey, thanks, this means a lot."

Billy didn't acknowledge that last remark in fear it would strike up old emotions he was trying so hard to bury in the ground forever. Instead he just simply replied, "Cool, I'll see you Saturday."

Billy stayed in bed for what seemed like an eternity. He finally mustered the courage to look at the clock on his nightstand and saw that only twelve minutes had passed. Such was life for Billy these days, time moved as slowly as the colorful kaleidoscope of cars that lazily meandered down the Long Island Expressway each weekday morning.

"Coffee will do the trick," Billy said aloud to no one.

Swinging his feet out and rising up to them Billy gave his back a quick stretch and headed to his kitchen to start brewing his coffee.

Billy knew he was borderline depressive. He knew that seven years was a long time to still be grieving the loss of his fiancé. He knew all of this, but it didn't change anything. He felt the way he felt, and nothing was making it better. His routine had become a series of muscle memory tasks. He never put any thought into anything outside his writing. Eating, sleeping, reading the paper, even watching TV, it all became mindless tasks that he blindly walked through. He knew that there was a cure for this, a solution to all of his problems, he just hadn't met her yet.

PART THREE

Sitting down on the couch Billy started to flip through the channels, one after another, all with nothing to offer. He started to contemplate why he was paying money to the cable company. They were supposed to be keeping him entertained, needless to say, they were failing at that task. He finally stopped on some old war movie showing on one of the less frequently visited channels. He stopped pressing the "Channel up" button not because he was particularly interested in the gray monotone action playing out in front of him, but because his mind started to wander.

He started to realize that he hadn't been back on Long Island in almost six years. "God," he thought to himself, "Has it been that long?"

Suddenly feeling nauseous just thinking about going back to the place where his life started, back where his life had endless possibilities. A place and time where he felt whole, and not broken. The more he thought about it, the more nauseous he became until he hit his breaking point. Lunging up from the couch he barely made it to the bathroom before letting off two dry heave spasms followed by one more spasm, this one brought with it the added gift of returning last night's dinner.

He rinsed his mouth out with a capful of mouthwash. After dispensing the used liquid, he looked up and came eye to eye with face in the mirror that slightly resembled a face he used to own. He leaned in tight, he could see every line on his face and every pore in his skin. He pulled the skin back on his face in an attempt to reveal a younger version of himself, a version with vigor and life. He let the skin go loose again when he saw that small indented scar above his right eye. The scar he gained when striking his head on the table after receiving the worst news of his life. That slight outward mark would always be the symbol of that day. The inward scar was much deeper and hideous, but no one would ever see that one.

CHAPTER 1

Billy gathered himself, cleared his mind using breathing techniques he learned by studying Zen Buddhism. After Jessica's death, Billy searched for something to hold on to, anything that might help alleviate some of the pain he was experiencing. He turned to Zen Buddhism for answers. His courtship with the philosophy and way of life only lasted ten months. He committed to certain television shows longer. One thing he was able to take from it and retain were methods of breathing meant to clear the mind of all thought. The idea of emptying one's mind at any given time appealed to him. Billy often thought if he could achieve this level of enlightenment he could control his thoughts and block out the bad and focus on the good. He never could figure out how one stops thinking about everything. He always found himself trying to think of not thinking about anything, which in turn made him realize that he was still thinking about something. Around and around the paradox went until Billy just gave up and turned on the television.

Certain thoughts about Jessica's death haunted Billy. They were the thoughts that made him shake at night, they put a fear so deep in him, and worst of all filled him with an unbearable level of guilt. The scene played out over and over in his head. The black room, void of light, the dark smoke creeping in like death himself. He sat up in his bed at night, dripping in a cold sweat imagining the fear Jessica felt knowing that this was more than just a horrible situation; this was the worst situation imaginable. Did she hold on to the hope of a rescue all the way until she took her last breath? Did she give up hope early on, facing reality and the inevitable outcome that lay ahead of her? Did she take stock in her life, counting up all the things she accomplished and all the things she never would? Did she think of Billy? Did she cherish the few years they had together? Did she reach for God in those moments, or did she curse him? What about the fear, was she scared, did she call out for Billy in those moments?

Waiting for him to come and save her. Was she angry at him for never coming? For never calling? For not scaling the wall of the tower kicking in the window, grabbing her by the waist and pulling her out of danger and into his arms forever?

The magical Billy rescue would never come, neither would any other form of rescue, not the FDNY, not the NYPD, not God himself, nothing. Just blackness, just the waiting arms of death.

In the months after Billy would read these stories about people finding their inner hero and helping someone else in their final moments. He wanted so badly to find someone, anyone who could offer an account of his sweet Jess doing some heroic deed. Not because he needed her to leave this world a hero, he thought that was a bullshit notion, he just wanted her to be doing something productive. Something to help curb the fear that was swirling around all of those floors.

If Jess had been someone's ray of light in the otherwise black situation that person perished with her and the story, whatever it was, perished too.

There had been many times Billy attempted to visit the site, ground zero as it had become known. He never made it past his old office on Fulton Street.

The days that followed September 11 were filled with support for people like Billy, not just from his family and friends, but the entire nation it seemed was there for anyone who lost someone in the attacks. Billy tried to avoid watching the horrible footage of the planes or the building collapse, but it was everywhere. On every television, in every newspaper, on the tongues of everyone he passed. For Billy, the real pain started after. After the family members stopped calling, and after the rest of the world began their transition back into a state of normalcy. This is where he felt truly alone.

One of these lonely nights Billy was brushing his teeth before

CHAPTER 1

bed. Needing a fresh new tube of toothpaste, he looked under his sink and saw the shiny aqua green plastic of the backside of Jessica's favorite brush. He picked it up, cradled it in his hand like a newborn baby. He pressed it against his chest. It wasn't Jessica, he knew this, but right now it was the closest thing he had to her. He pushed it so hard against his body that it left tiny indented marks where the plastic brush bristles pushed violently into his skin. This was Billy's way of hugging Jessica, one more time.

He sat there on the cold tile floor of the bathroom floor holding that brush for hours. He was just sitting in silence, slightly swaying like the way an old rocking chair on the front porch of a house might sway when the gentle autumn breeze sweeps in and gives it a gentle nudge.

While he sat there something began to stir up inside him, raw emotions reaching a level he had never experienced before. Suddenly tears appeared in his eyes. They were not just gentle tears that pool up in the corner of your eye before being released to slide gently down your cheek before jumping for freedom at the edge of the jaw line. This was more uncontrolled, almost violent. Sobbing, weeping, crying, whatever the name people wanted to use, it was all happening to Billy. It came at him with such a powerful rush that holding it in was not an option. It would have been as futile as trying to stop the raging waters of a river just released from behind broken dam walls.

This fit of crying lasted all night, until the outside sky went from a deep purple hue, sliding through a range of dark blues and eventually landing on the light blue end of the spectrum. Billy was spent, all his energy drained from his body. His all night crying episode took him through all the levels; the gentle sobbing accompanied by spasmed breaths all the way to the uncontrollable full force cry that was a lot less graceful looking. This level is where the body expelled fluid not only from the eyes but the nose and mouth as well. None of it was

PART THREE

pretty, but it was necessary.

By the time his emotional purge had ended Billy felt clean and baptized. There was a stockpile of emotion that had built up so large behind his exterior shell that when it finally saw the slightest break of daylight to escape it seized the opportunity. The emotions rushed the gate, tearing it down in its wake. Leaving only bent damaged remnants in its wake.

Billy, sitting with his back up against the bathtub, turned and reached behind him. He gave the water spigot a turn to release the water for a hot shower, one he so desperately needed. When the water reached a temperature hot enough to boil an egg, he pulled himself up to his feet. He gently placed the hairbrush down on the sink and slid out of his clothes and into the awaiting steam filled shower. The hot water cascaded over his head and down his body relaxing every muscle it touched. He stood under the shower head letting the water stream over him for almost an hour. He reached such a high level of relaxation he closed his eyes and cleared his mind. He made peace with the idea of never holding Jessica again, never touching her soft skin, never smelling her perfumed neck or shampooed hair. He accepted that he would never taste the cherry lip balm that she would so liberally apply to her red lips all year long.

When Billy finally reached down to turn the rainfall of water off the entire bathroom was thick with fog, almost nothing was visible. He pushed the curtain back and just stared at the frosted over glass pane that used to be a mirror before being bathed in hot water vapors.

His gaze turned downward. Sitting on the edge of the sink, waiting for him like a mother waits for her child to exit the school bus after the first day of kindergarten, was Jess's brush. He cracked a smile. He couldn't help but think about all those poor souls who suffered a loss that same day. They would cling to the misguided hope that their loved one was alive somewhere. They would come

CHAPTER 1

in droves with brushes holding hair samples in their worn bristles. They wanted so badly to match the DNA of some nonexistent person wandering around New York City, not knowing who they were. Just knowing that they just climbed out of the rubble of the two largest buildings in the city. It was a silly notion but one that Billy even caught himself buying into at one of his lowest moments. He understood why these people did that, they needed some sliver of hope, something that would make their wives, husbands, children, or parents not dead.

The twin towers crumbled to the ground, Billy knew that. He also knew that anyone inside them met the same fate the buildings did, they would not exist on this earth anymore. Chasing ghosts was not on his list of coping mechanisms.

The realization and acceptance of Jessica's death and the cleansing all-night cry went a long way toward Billy's recovery. One fact remained, his fiancé was still dead and gone and was never going to come back. He still had a lot of healing to do, but he had taken his first step.

CHAPTER 2

The shining silver train with the blue emblazoned Long Island Rail Road seal on its side glided down its steel rails with effortless movement and a quiet reserve. Billy sat in the window seat, his ticket wedged in the seat back in front of him. This granted him the convenience of showing his paid fare without actually interacting with the conductor. He was free to stare out the window, watching the passing whirl of trees and the back of strip centers fly past in a kaleidoscope of blurry colors and shapes. Not much had changed on Long Island, ever. The few times Billy snapped out of his comatose state to reconnect with the world around him he immediately recognized some landmark that gave him a general idea of where he was.

Ronkonkoma sat almost at the geographic center of the island. It was a working, middle-class town, no one really too rich and no one really too poor. It was home to the Ronkonkoma train station, which was a large transit hub for the Long Island Rail Road. This station, this hub, was going to serve as Billy's welcome mat home.

PART THREE

It was an unseasonably hot June day. Billy stepped off the train and onto the white cement platform that started just beyond the yellow stripe of paint that signified the edge of the train's staging area. The warning "Watch The Gap" was written at intervals along the floor. This served as a cautious reminder that there was indeed a small space between the train car and the platform, and one needed to be mindful of it.

Billy worked his way to a shady spot on the raised surface to check his phone for any messages. He had sent Kenny a text message when he was about two stops away, giving him ample time to get to the station to orchestrate a successful pickup. Just as Billy took his cell phone from the pocket of his cargo shorts, it buzzed with the alert of a message. He looked at the screen, "Parked by the garage" it was Kenny's text reply.

The parking garage was located on the North side of the station and reaching it meant climbing a large flight of stairs up and over the Westbound tracks before descending the stairs again on the other side. When Billy got to the bottom of the stairs, he could see Kenny's black Toyota Camry parked on the side of the road. It was neatly located between the ticket office and the parking garage. Kenny was waiting, leaning on the rear passenger quarter panel. Once he had visual contact with Billy, his arm shot up, like a kid in a classroom who knows the answer to the question the teacher just asked. Billy acknowledged Ken with a simple nod of his head. Slinging his gym bag, that for today was doubling as luggage, over his right shoulder and made his way to a patiently waiting Kenny.

"Hey man," Kenny called out once he felt Billy was in earshot.

"What's up?" Billy replied.

The exchange was never filled with pomp and circumstance. It was always short and right to the point. The two friends exchanged a combination handshake and hug before Billy tossed his bag into the

CHAPTER 2

Camry's back seat and climbed into the passenger seat.

"I hope this shit-box has air conditioning," Said Billy, throwing out the first playful verbal jab.

Kenny laughed and without making eye contact pushed the power window button releasing the passenger side glass from its raised state, and lowering down inside the door, "There, that's your fucking air conditioning."

The two shared a collective chortle, as Kenny put the car in drive and headed up the road to his parents' house.

The Springer's house was a modest one, a high ranch that sat just on the cusp of the cul-de-sac circle that was home to so many sporting events of the young boys' life. Cars had already begun to fill the street. They were the vehicles of the out of town family members who had arrived early this morning or, in the case of Kenny's two uncles from New Jersey, arrived last night. Kenny's spot in front of the house was no longer vacant as he left it. Some cousin or other family member had come while he was picking up Billy. There was still plenty of space available on the street and Kenny slid into one of the available spots along the sidewalk curb.

The two exited the vehicle. Kenny spoke first, "Listen, something I forgot to tell you."

Billy stopped in his tracks, slowly turned to meet Kenny's eyes, "Yes?"

"Jason Cosimo is coming. The thing is he helped my dad a lot with the retirement funds and investing and shit. I kind of had to invite him."

Billy took a minute to wonder why Kenny thought this would be a problem. He always found Cosimo annoying at best, but they got along all right. Billy even recalled seeing him coming out of Madison Square Garden after a Ranger game once. The two chatted for a few minutes. It was all Billy could spare and given Cosimo's severe alcoholic state the conversation was not destined to last any longer. Finally, Billy asked, "Why is that a problem?"

Kenny paused, then shrugged his shoulders, "I guess it's really not a problem. He was just always such an ass in High School I just figured I would warn you."

"Na... it's fine. I'm sure he has matured a lot," Billy reasoned.

Kenny, again paused, "Nope, no he has not."

The two friends shared a laugh. Kenny realized that he hadn't heard Billy laugh like that in a very long time. It felt good to hear, but he was not about to spoil the moment by drawing attention to it. It was better to just let it be.

They entered the house and right away Billy got smacked in the face with the wonderful aroma of Mrs. Springer's home-cooked meatloaf. Meatloaf was never considered a delicacy to most people, but to Betty Springer, it was a religion. She took more pride in her "secret" meatloaf recipe than she did in the accomplishments of her children. It was the one thing that could bring any neighborhood kid to the Springer house. So many evenings spent playing stickball would always end with each of the neighborhood boys quizzing Kenny on what his mom was serving up for dinner. If the answer were meatloaf, the kids would always try to conjure up some reason why they needed to eat dinner at Kenny's. Needless to say, Mrs. Betty Springer's meatloaf was legendary.

"William! Oh God, I haven't seen you in so long! How are you, my dear?" Mrs. Springer called out, turning from her science lab spread of spices and ingredients.

"Hey, Mrs. Springer. Thanks so much for inviting me. Can't wait to have some of that meatloaf."

Mrs. Springer was always trying to downplay the effect her magical chopped meat in a loaf form had on people. She turned to look at the magnificent display of craftsmanship that lay on the counter before her. Cracking just the slightest of smiles as if holding back the biggest of secrets she replied, "Oh this, it's just something I throw together every now and then."

Nothing could have been further from the truth.

Passing through the house stirred up a litany of old memories of sleepovers, and long summer afternoons of watching MTV for hours on end, fantasizing about becoming rock stars. Billy felt at home at the Springers house, it was the closest thing he had left to tie him to his childhood. His own parents had sold their Long Island home years ago and taken part in the New Yorker's rite of passage and relocated to the sunny shores of Florida's east coast, Ft. Lauderdale to be exact. There was a certain feel, a particular smell that came with a suburban Long Island home. They all had that in common, there was no way to effectively describe it. If he were blindfolded and placed in any number of houses scattered throughout the United States, Billy would always know when he was in a Long Island home. It just had a feel to it, an electricity about it.

Sliding the screen door partition open and stepping out into the second story back deck that overlooked an expansive back yard Billy saw Mr. Springer sitting in a folding lawn chair under an oversized deck umbrella.

"William my boy," Mr. Springer bellowed, rising to his feet.

"Sir," Billy replied.

Billy reached out and grabbed hold of Mr. Springer's hand and engaged in an unspoken battle of strength played out through a handshake. John Springer, or Jack as his friends called him, was a large, barrel-chested man. Never finishing high school, his greatest assets was his brawn and strength, not his mind or wit. He took pride in causing a wince of pain in the face of the counterpart of his handshakes, and Billy did not disappoint. Once seeing he had bested his son's childhood friend in the handshake feat of strength he smiled and asked, "How are you, son?"

Billy, recovering from the boa constrictor grip of a handshake, answered, "Fine sir. Congratulations on your retirement. Any big plans?"

"Plans? Sure, get fat."

Mr. Springer had been using that same joke his whole life. It ranged from describing weekend plans to vacation plans and always the far off retirement plans. Now that the retirement was finally here he could consolidate the joke to just the one occasion, and he was more than happy to use it, as often as possible.

"Still in the city?" Mr. Springer asked after waiting for a laugh that never came from his predictable joke.

"Yes, sir, Upper East Side of Manhattan. Been there a while now."

"Like it?" Mr. Springer asked.

"Sure," Billy replied, "it's nice."

Mr. Springer was missing the obvious hints and clues that Billy was not eager to talk about his deceased fiancé. He lowered his voice and took a more serious tone, "William, I just want to tell you, we were all crushed to hear about your lady friend. That must have been so hard for you. You know I lost someone too, in the towers. My supervisor's son worked up there, one of the big financial places, young kid, a real shame."

Billy never understood the strange infatuation people had with trying to force a connection with a real life tragedy. If given his choice he and everyone he ever knew would have been so far away from the World Trade Center on the morning of September 11, 2001. Yet he consistently met people who always felt the need to bring their story closer to this tragic event. Billy's response was always the same, he nodded in agreement and said nothing, but inside he was screaming, "You have no idea what living through this is like. You have no idea how privileged you are to not have someone you love perish that way.

CHAPTER 2

You have no idea how stupid you sound. You don't know what kind of Hell this leaves for those who are left behind. Don't wish you were connected to this. Don't pretend that you are more affected than you really are. Be happy, be thankful that something like this didn't touch you, didn't get you or anyone you love!"

He thought it but never said it.

As the sun continued to track its way across the sky and the hands on the old Springer family grandfather clock continued to move, more and more people showed up to the Springer house. Suddenly from inside the house, there was the collective sound of laughter. It continued in short bursts until finally the screen door on the deck slid open. Billy was standing right in the line of sight and was easily the first person seen when exiting the house. So it was no strange occurrence that he was the first person addressed by the party's newest attendee.

"McCabe? Is that really you? You have got to be..." Jason Cosimo very obviously wanted to use a different word here but given the surrounding company opted for the safer and cleaner, "you have got to be kidding me!"

Billy stuck out his hand for Jason to shake, "Hey Jason."

Cosimo looked down at Billy's hand puzzled like it was a complicated equation that filled the entire chalkboard of an advanced college mathematics class.

"Put that thing away, bring it in here for the real thing you schmuck," Jason said as he grabbed Billy and gave him a forceful hug.

"And what's with this 'Jason' shit, you never use my first name."

Billy struggled to not smile, he didn't want to give Cosimo the impression that he found him amusing. Something like that would only inflate his already inflated ego.

The boys gathered in the backyard in a semicircle taking turns talking about each of their lives. Kenny followed in his father's footsteps and joined the MTA. He was working as a Human Resources representative at their administration offices on Livingston Street in Brooklyn. His father was proud that he took the civil service road but thought his job was a little soft. It was a desk job, a "pencil pusher position" as he called it, even if Kenny's starting salary was twice what his father made at retirement. Kenny left the old neighborhood but didn't stray too far, settling into a modest house in the town of Deer Park, just a few miles away from his childhood home. Kenny was married to a sweet girl named Rachel. Rachel was an ER nurse at the same hospital Kenny's mom worked at, Stony Brook University Hospital. It was Kenny's mother who orchestrated the initial meeting between the two. For Kenny, it was love at first sight, but then again it always was with him. A girl would say hi to him in the grocery store, and he was already talking about what their kids would look like. When Kenny fell in love, he fell hard. He had his heart badly broken too many times to count all throughout college. Rachel was different, she reminded him of his mother, doting and caring. She spoiled him and their two children, both boys. Liam, the oldest was named after his best friend and best man at his wedding, Billy, or William as those who knew him as a child still called him. Liam was the Gaelic version of the American name William. Their second child, Matthew followed two years after Liam. They were well-behaved children, respectful and kind to people. Kenny and Rachel took pride in them, displayed them like trophies on a mantle piece. They had their crazy moments of rambunctiousness, but they were kids and more importantly they were boys, so that was to be expected.

Rachel was a tall, slender woman, beautiful in every way a person can be. Kenny at times would tell Billy of varied sexual escapes, and Billy always found himself aroused by his best friend's wife. Feelings he never shared with his friend. He would never act on it, and would always feel shame when it entered his head. He did everything to bury it deep in a box in his mind, never lifting the lid to look inside.

"So, Ken, when are you going to let me bang that hot ass wife of yours?" Cosimo crudely blurted out.

That was Jason Cosimo, always saying what he shouldn't but what everyone else was thinking.

Jason Cosimo followed a very different path than Kenny. He was the perpetual bachelor, never settling down with a woman for more than a month at a time. Most relationships he had never lasted to sunrise the next day. He really grew into his body. Like a majestic butterfly breaking out of its cocoon leaving behind the old ugly caterpillar shell. He was tall and sported a very muscular build. Girls loved to look at him but hated to talk to him. Cosimo's verbal filter just didn't exist, the crass comments he made among his friends were the same ones he would make in front of a girl he just met. He had done very well for himself financially, making the majority of his money as a broker on Wall Street in the years immediately following college. In fact, he never actually got his college degree. His freshman year at Hofstra University, he caught the eye of his economics professor who saw a raw talent in him. He introduced him to some old Wall Street colleagues of his. Jason was immediately struck by the cockiness and high level of self-esteem these men possessed. These were people he felt a kinship with, he had found his home, his new family. He didn't drop out of college immediately, it was more a tapering off approach. He attended fewer and fewer classes and spent more time with his new friends in Lower Manhattan's financial district. Cosimo's world only existed in the space between Broadway and William Street, and Beaver and Pine. Eventually, he would trade in his college world. The world filled with Hackey Sack in the quad and smoking weed in the dorm rooms, with the occasional class attending and test taking sprinkled in. His new world was an exciting one. A fast paced world of cocaine, energy drinks, and meaningless sex with women who lacked any kind of identity. Most importantly his world had money, so much money. He was making money faster than he could spend it, which only led to trouble. Trouble first found Cosimo in a drunken, cocaine-induced frenzy in Times Square where he punched a tourist in the face for walking too slowly in front of him. A tourist, on vacation with his wife and children. This occurred at a time where the mayor of New York was trying hard to clean up the tainted image of the city left in the wake of the 1970's and 1980's. There were a series of other run-ins with the law and the court system of New York City. This behavior was never reprimanded in his new profession if anything arrests were worn as a badge of honor for those in the high-stakes, high-stress game of Wall Street. This reckless lifestyle continued on for Jason for five years. He was still working in Downtown Manhattan on September 11, 2001. No one knows what it was that actually affected Jason to react the way he did. Some speculate he witnessed one of the bodies falling to their death from the upper stories of the towers. Whatever it was, he walked away from the life, forever. He moved back out to Long Island, started his own financial advisory company and helped blue collar workers save for their retirement. He still had more money saved and invested than he would ever need, so he bought himself a beautiful house in Belle Terre overlooking Port Jefferson Harbor and pulled back the throttle of his high-speed, reckless life.

The three boys now reunited in the Springer's backyard began to reminisce about the old days and the old neighborhood. It was actually Cosimo who first brought her up.

"Whatever happened to that crazy chick you were friends with McCabe?"

Billy froze, with his beer halfway to his mouth. He knew exactly who Cosimo was talking about. To say he hadn't thought about Amanda every day would be a lie, but he did just that, lied, "What chick?"

"Oh man, I forgot her name. That short little spark plug that kicked me in the balls," Cosimo lamented.

It was Kenny who finally ended the Inquisition, "Amanda, Amanda Flores."

"That's it!" Cosimo exclaimed. "Do you still keep in touch?"

Billy looked down at the bare patch in the grass, "Na, we lost touch when she left the school."

"That's a shame, you two were attached at the hip. She had like a fucked up home life, right?" Cosimo asked.

"Yeah, step dad was an asshole," Billy hadn't spoken out loud about what actually went down with Amanda to anyone, ever. Kenny didn't even know the whole story.

Cosimo sensing that Billy didn't want to rehash that old memory ended the topic almost as quickly as he started it, "Well, it's a shame either way. You guys ready for another beer?" He asked on his way to the cooler parked under the tree and out of the direct punishing blows of the sun.

The rest of the BBQ carried on like a scripted play, each of the characters playing their specific role, just as it was written out. The estranged uncle getting a little too forward with some of the younger teen girls in attendance. Telling them how much they had "matured." The oddball aunt having too many Jim Beams before engaging in a slurred tirade of verbal passive aggressive punches at various family members that she felt had slighted her in some way.

As the sun began its ritualistic retreat behind the horizon, the party began its dissension into a small gathering. The three boys were left sitting at the patio table sipping the last of the beer while the trophies of their alcohol conquests were proudly displayed on the table in front of them.

"McCabe, listen, I have an extra ticket to the Yankee game next

Wednesday night. Why don't you come with me, I'm tired of taking boring ass clients who only want to talk about making money. You obviously don't give a shit about making money, so it's a step up already," Cosimo offered up his best cordial invitation.

Billy thought about it. His normal routine would have been to say no, even with no other plans scheduled. He had stepped outside his normal routine and ended up at the Springer's retirement party, and so far was having a great time. Maybe this was time to start a new routine.

"You know what Cosimo, I'll go. Thanks," William had some life in his voice, even at the late hour and in an intoxicated state.

"Perfect, I'll call you, we will work out a meeting place."

"Cool, thanks. Now Kenny, if you could kindly show me where I will be sleeping it would be much appreciated. I would like to lay down before I pass out and give myself a scar over my other eye," William slurred.

The other two boys were slightly shocked, it was the first time they had ever heard William make light of anything about that day, especially the physical reminder that permanently lived above his right eye. William could see the awe on their faces.

"Oh come on boys, I'm not that fragile, am I?" William asked.

Cosimo spoke first, "No, not at all, just slightly more durable than a tissue."

Kenny cringed, had Cosimo gone too far, he held his breath for what seemed like minutes, but it was barely a second before William laughed.

Kenny and Cosimo looked at each other, it had been a long time since they all shared a moment like this, it just felt right.

CHAPTER 3

William had been up since 6:30 a.m. He had some freelance work to get done and enjoyed the quiet peace that lay over New York City at that early hour. On nicer days, he would sit on the fire escape outside his bedroom window with his coffee in his hand and just listen to the city breathe. She was a magical place, she was bigger than life. It always fascinated him that nothing was ever bigger than she was. He remembered how amazed Jess would be when the President of the United States would be just a few blocks away at the UN and life was carrying on the same as any other day on their block. She would spin tales of how the entire city of Houston went to shut down when George Bush would come back to town. Billy would always tell her the same thing, "New York City is bigger than the President."

Jess would still be shocked when she would see the famous celebrities riding on the subway, just like every other New Yorker. Or when the latest starlet would pass her on the street like she wasn't just on the cover of every magazine the month before. Billy's response was always the same, "They aren't bigger than New York."

The city was truly larger than life. Nothing got in her way, Presidents, Senators, movie shoots, movie actors, professional athletes, billionaire business owners, billionaire stock brokers, snow, rain, hurricanes, floods, blackouts, nothing was ever bigger than she was. She would always be the most important person in the room, she was New York City.

Only once did she surrender her larger-than-life title, just once, Billy knew the exact date, so did every other New Yorker, so did every other American. She was knocked down, but she wouldn't stay down. She pulled herself back up, like a phoenix rising from the ashes. Billy often thought if she could do it why couldn't he? Sure she was older and had experienced life, and she was a lot bigger, but she also lost a lot more than he had. He wanted so much to be like that majestic girl, he wanted to be more like New York City; strong, resilient, full of life, larger than life.

It was a little past 10:00 a.m. when Billy's cell phone gave off its melodic chime. It was a call he was expecting. Tonight was the night he was going to the Yankee game with Jason Cosimo. The Texas Rangers were in town, and the Yankees were once again in playoff contention. If nothing else, the game would be a good one, and Billy was trying to remain optimistic that Cosimo would be good company, entertaining at best.

Billy answered his phone with a greeting personalized for the recipient at the other end, "Yes, Mr. Cosimo?"

"McCabe, you ready to get tanked and maybe catch a few innings of baseball in-between beers?" Cosimo asked in his never ending sarcastic tone.

"Well, I have some work to do tomorrow, so I'm not sure about the 'tanked' part, but the rest of it sounds like fun," Billy returned Cosimo's serve.

CHAPTER 3

Cosimo had one word that served as his kill shot, "Pussy."

Game, set and match, Jason Cosimo.

Admitting defeat and restarting the verbal volley Billy kept it safe with an easy question, "So, what's the plan?"

"Meet at the big bat? Say, 6:00?"

The "Big Bat" was a 120-foot replica of Babe Ruth's bat jutting out of the pavement in front of the hallowed grounds of Yankee Stadium. It even brandished his super-sized signature and the Louisville Slugger logo. Its real purpose was to cover a boiler vent but gained notoriety as the default meeting place for those joining other parties at the stadium before heading inside.

This was an acceptable plan, and Billy acknowledged it by a simple repeat of it, "Six o'clock, big bat, you got it… and Cosimo, don't forget the tickets."

"You sound like my mother, McCabe."

"Probably because I've been fucking her for so long," Sneak attack by Billy.

"Nice! Well played McCabe, well played," Cosimo conceding defeat.

Game, set and match, William McCabe.

Billy got to the stadium early; he was still a quick subway ride away on the 4 train, Cosimo was coming from Long Island, so his trek was a lot more involved and time-consuming. The stadium was a bustle of activity. Billy had visited other professional stadiums in his life and was still looking for one that could give Yankee Stadium a run for its money when it came to baseball appeal and atmosphere. He realized that there were better stadiums out there, nicer, newer, better amenities but what they could never match was the feeling you got standing on the sacred grounds of the ballpark in the Bronx. So many baseball names played here, names like Ruth, Gehrig, DiMaggio, Mantle, Maris, Berra, Mattingly and the list goes on and

PART THREE

on. There was an aroma in the air; it was hard to describe, but if the game of baseball were ever going to have a smell, that would be it. The experience wasn't just of the nose; it touched all the other senses too. The sound of the elevated four train rumbling overhead like thunder cloud and the street musician playing a constant loop of "Take Me Out to the Ballgame" on his tenor sax. The sight of the swells of people milling about outside the stadium. Fathers with sons, packs of friends, guys taking their girlfriends on dates, it didn't matter, everyone was there for the same thing, to watch the New York Yankees play baseball.

"McCabe!" A voice called from within the throng of pin-striped jersey wearing people.

"Yo!" Billy called back to the unseen voice assuming it was Cosimo and he would soon appear.

Sure enough, the slender figure of Jason Cosimo emerged from the sea of fans, "You been waiting long?"

"Nope, just got here a few minutes ago," Billy assured him.

"Cool, we got sick tickets, few rows off the field on the third base side. They're mint!"

The two friends made their way through the crowd sidestepping the photo takers and street vendors selling all sorts of Yankee paraphernalia. None of the goods were sanctioned by the New York Yankees or Major League Baseball, which is why it was priced substantially lower than the official merchandise sold inside the stadium walls. Billy swore he passed a vendor selling T-Shirts that read "New York Yankers" He just shook his head at the obvious typo and continued following Cosimo through the crowd.

Once through the ticket checkpoint and inside the stadium they scouted the closest beer vendor, grabbed two each and made their way to their seats. All of this was done with very little chatter and instructions. It was as if the two men had a mission and it was strictly business until that mission was met with a satisfactory conclusion. Within fifteen minutes of entering the stadium gates, they were seated in their proper, ticketed seats. They each had two beers in their possession, to cut back on the trips back to the vendor cart located in the mezzanine, it was a successful mission.

Now the small talk could begin. Cosimo sent up the first attempt, "How's work?" He asked.

"It isn't exactly 'work' these days. To tell you the truth, it's shit. I get these god awful freelance jobs and churn out a god-awful product and get paid a decent amount for it. It sucks, but to be honest, it's all I have the heart to do at this point," Billy was surprised to hear himself share that deeply with Cosimo, especially this early in the evening.

"Bill, listen. I know everyone is getting on you to get your shit together and all that crap, I'm not going to tell you that. You have to do what you have to do. No one else can make you happy, only you can," It was a rare moment of sensitivity from Cosimo.

Billy was a little surprised but glad to hear Cosimo's reasonable side, "Thanks, Cosimo."

The game began with its normal round of tradition and fanfare. The "Bleacher Creatures" shouting out each player's name until acknowledged. This was a fairly new stadium tradition. The "Bleacher Creatures" were the inhabitants of the outfield bleacher seats. It was a general admission area, no assigned seats. No alcohol was served in that area, and yet it was home to some of the rowdiest and drunkest people inside the stadium. It was a great place to be if you were a die-hard Yankee fan, but it was hell on earth if you were anything else. At the start of the game, the "Creatures" would chant each position player on the field and not stop until that player turned and signaled to them that he did indeed hear them. This signal was usually a wave of the glove or a tip of the cap. The crowd would cheer then move on to the next player. It quickly became a time-honored tradition in the stadium and even the newly acquired players enjoyed being indoctrinated into it.

The two old friends exchanged the normal play by play in each of their lives. Cosimo had a lot more to share, it was only natural, he was doing a lot more than Billy was. Listening to Cosimo speak about the various activities that filled his days made Billy feel empty. He had been idle for such a long time now. He never felt it was an acceptable way to live, but he chose it anyway.

Billy wanted to return Cosimo's offering with his own busy life details, but he had none to offer. His talk of work in the first few minutes was all he had going on in his very uneventful existence. It was true, his life was empty.

Billy tried to offer some fodder of activity or action about his own life, he could see the look on Cosimo's face, he wasn't buying the rehearsed bit. Eventually, Billy gave up.

"Cosimo, I don't do anything these days. I do just enough work to pay the rent, and after that, I sit around and do nothing."

Cosimo was speechless, for one of the very few times in his life and it would only last a few seconds. He appreciated Billy's honesty and wanted to be constructive with his next words, so he took his time to pick them carefully.

"Listen, Will, it was a shitty thing that went down, I could never begin to understand it. I know everyone is on your ass about picking up your life and moving on like it never happened. I got to be up front with you; they are all crazy. There is no way you or anyone else picks up and moves on from that. You are doing just fine, grieve the way you want to grieve, take as much time as you need. You got friends and family around you, you will be fine, I know that, and deep down you know that too. You're a smart guy, and you will figure all this out eventually. In the meantime, just take it one step at a time. You can't go back to where you were before you lost your girl, that world doesn't exist anymore, don't even look for it, it's gone. You got to make a new world and new life, and maybe that life is you barricaded in that beautiful Upper East Side apartment, writing slogans for the retail world until you die and they find you weeks later naked and surrounded by jars of your own piss, like Howard Hughes. Or, just maybe something comes along, like your awesome friend Cos and delivers the best pep talk speech you have ever heard, and you start making changes. Either way, it's no one else's life, so live it the way you want to… just maybe ring my phone once a week, just so I know you aren't dead in a sea of your collected urine."

Billy was locked into what Cosimo was saying, so much so that he had no idea what was going on with the game. It wasn't until Cosimo who just wrapped up his speech yelled, "Come on. These fuckers are giving up runs like they are served at an all you can eat buffet."

Billy wanted to thank Cosimo, not just for what he said but how he said it. It was the first time someone didn't play with words with him. He wanted to thank him, but the moment passed, and he felt it was understood. He never would have guessed that Cosimo would be a voice of reason, but life stopped making logical sense to him a long time ago.

The innings passed almost as regularly as the beer. The game ended with a Yankee win, 18-7, and the two friends found themselves a little drunker than they had initially wanted to be.

Billy made a friendly proposal to his friend, "You want to crash at my place? You can stay on the couch and head back out to the Island tomorrow."

Cosimo gave a slurred laugh, "Thanks, I appreciate the gesture. I'll have a car service come get me from the station. I got a guy out there that owes me, he sends his driver to get me whenever I need it.

Don't worry McCabe, I don't drive when I drink anymore. I learned that lesson a while ago."

The lesson Cosimo was referring to was his third DWI arrest because it was clear the first two did not offer a learned lesson. That was a different Jason Cosimo from a different time.

"I wasn't trying to say... you know what I meant," Billy struggled to administer some damage control on what he thought was perceived as an insult.

"McCabe, I'm fucking with you, it's fine really."

The two had made their way out of the main gate and were heading towards 161st Street. Billy was headed to the elevated 4 train and Cosimo would be on the underground B train to take him down the West side where he could transfer to Penn Station to catch the train back to Long Island. His trip was substantially longer than Billy's, but that was the price of living in the peace and quiet secluded world of suburban Long Island.

As they neared their point of separation, Billy stopped, reached out his hand to Cosimo, who once again only used it as a means to pull him in closer for a hug.

"McCabe, you're a good guy, thanks for coming out tonight, don't be a stranger, call me. I'll have you out to the house out on Long Island."

Cosimo began to loosen his grip signaling the hug had reached its conclusion, but Billy stayed, he held on a little extra. Typically Cosimo would insert some stab at Billy's sexuality here, but even he just let the moment be, it was the right thing to do.

When they finally broke apart, Billy spoke, "Cos. Thanks, I really needed this, it means a lot that you invited me."

"Pleasure was all mine, McCabe."

Jason Cosimo turned to leave and slid his hands into the pockets of his shorts, he stopped dead in his path, quickly spun around and

CHAPTER 3

catching Billy before he got too far.

"McCabe!" He yelled.

Billy turned to see him standing still with a small rectangular flat sheet of plastic in his hand.

"I completely forgot, I have something for you," Cosimo said reaching out his hand with the flat plastic in it.

Billy took the necessary steps toward him to see what it was that was being offered to him. Before he could examine it, Cosimo slapped in into his hand. Billy looked down to see what the mystery item was that was now in his possession. When his eyes adjusted to the light reflected on the plastic, he could make out exactly what he was holding. Slipped into a hard protective sleeve was an Autographed Gary Carter rookie card. The same card he had given to Cosimo as a bribe to protect Amanda so many years ago. He felt his eyes well with tears but knew he could never show that kind of emotion to Cosimo so relied on deep breathing to keep his emotions in check.

"I would have given it back to you sooner, but I wanted him to sign it first," Cosimo said.

He could sense the overwhelming emotions that were beginning to win their battle with Billy. Knowing that he would not want his emotions seen by him, Cosimo turned and continued walking to the subway leaving Billy speechless with his mouth ajar.

Without turning around again to face him, Cosimo yelled out, "You should look her up."

Billy finally mustered the ability to orate one syllable, "Who?"

"The girl who used my testicles for a fifty-yard field goal attempt," He yelled as he disappeared down into the subterranean hole that housed the massive complex of rail and trains.

CHAPTER 4

The sandwich shop was tucked away, hidden between so many other retail outlets, one would think it was the owner's intention to go unnoticed. It was one of the million secrets that the city kept only for those worthy enough to do the necessary legwork needed to uncover these hidden gems. The food there was nothing short of divine, the delicacy served between two slices of freshly baked bread was enough to make anyone question eating anywhere else, ever again.

When Billy walked in, he saw that Kenny had beat him there and was already seated at a table near the window with a sandwich in front of him and a second one on a plate across from him. Billy assumed that Kenny took the pleasure of ordering for him and not that they were being joined by a third, invisible party.

"Hey buddy," Billy called out once he was officially in an audible range.

"Will, hey man. Thanks for meeting me. I was in the city for this meeting thing and figured what the hell, I'll give you a call," Kenny had explained this all before Billy took the seat across from him.

"I took the liberty of ordering you a roast beef melt, your favorite," Kenny continued after Billy sat down.

"Thanks."

Kenny kept the conversation light, "So buddy, how have you been?"

"You know Ken, I have to say, I've been doing pretty good. Did Cosimo tell you we went to a Yankee game a few weeks ago?" Billy asked.

Kenny gave a quick laugh. The idea of Billy spending three hours in a tight space with Jason Cosimo amused him, "He mentioned that you guys were going, but I haven't seen him since."

"You know what that prick did?" Billy asked understanding that his question could have returned any number of plausible answers ranging from the idiotic to the insane.

"Not sure I want to know," Kenny knew it had the potential to be a loaded question.

"Well, remember back in High School when Amanda kicked him in the balls?" Billy began.

"Oh sure, how could I forget?"

"Well, to bribe him out of ratting her out I gave him my Gary Carter rookie card. I had completely forgotten all about it until after the game he gave it back to me, except when he did it was signed, by Gary Carter!" Billy's voice got higher with excitement when he relayed the story.

"Jesus, Will. That's an incredible gesture," Kenny was just as shocked at hearing the tale as Billy was telling it.

"Odd thing was he just handed it to me and walked away. But he said one thing, it really got me thinking. He said I should look her up. He was talking about Amanda. A crazy thing to say, right?" Billy was looking for some confirmation from Kenny.

CHAPTER 4

"No, not really," Kenny wasn't going to confirm anything for Billy.

"What? What do you mean?" Billy was confused by his friend's response.

"Well, Will, you guys were so close to each other back then, almost inseparable. You refused to have a serious girlfriend all throughout high school because you were so in love with her and to be honest she did the same. I honestly have never seen two people so right for each other as the two of you were. We were stupid kids and had no idea what love was, but there was something so profound between you two. I swore to myself I would never marry anyone unless I had what you had with Amanda. It was that strong. Listen, I'm sorry I never said any of this to you before, talking about relationships and love has never really been our thing, and then you met Jess. Well, Will, you know I thought the world of Jess and I have no doubt that you loved her, but I never saw that look in your eye with her that you had with Amanda. I'm not sure if there is only one right person for us out there, maybe there are a few right people, and if we miss out on one we can still find another. Maybe that's what you had with Jess. You have an opportunity here to make this right. If you found her and finally did what you should have done twenty years ago and ask her out, you might see I'm right," Kenny finished his speech and took his first bite of his waiting sandwich.

"Jesus Ken, how long has that been bottled up?" Billy wanted to keep things light to avoid the emotions he could feel rising up from his gut.

"Not that long, I just thought of most of it now, just sitting here," Kenny also kept it light.

Kenny's words rang true to Billy, he took a few minutes to digest them. How would he even begin to find someone he hadn't seen or heard from in over twenty years?

Kenny broke the silence and Billy's deep train of thought, "Or maybe living in the past is bad advice. Maybe I should tell you to get out there and start dating again and find that next perfect match."

Billy appreciated his friend's honesty, "No Ken, I know you're right, I appreciate it. I know it doesn't look like it, but I am really getting my life back on track. I'm not doing myself any good living like this. I'm not too sure about the Amanda thing, but finding someone, even if it's just for some conversation and company doesn't sound like such a bad idea."

Kenny added one last morsel for Billy to chew on, "You know Will, you saved her life, I'm sure she hasn't forgotten that."

CHAPTER 5

The phone on the nightstand rang. There was a caller ID display on it, but Billy didn't even bother looking, no one but family called that number. He rolled over just enough to reach the phone receiver, lifted it and in his most unenthusiastic voice grumbled, "Hello?"

"Ass-munch, are you still sleeping?" The voice on the other end sounded off.

"Um… No," Billy was clearly stalling until he could figure out who it was on the other end of this call.

Noticing the obvious stall, the voice on the other end spoke again, "It's your fucking brother, Danny. What the fuck is the matter with you?"

"Nothing" Billy answered, "What's up?"

"Some of the guys from the precinct and I are going to get some drinks after my tour tonight. I want you to get your lazy ass out of that shit-hole apartment and come down and have a beer with us."

Billy paused, clearly looking for an excuse, "I got work to do."

"Bullshit!" Danny yelped back almost before the excuse had left Billy's lips.

Billy tried his most convincing voice, "It's true, it's a client thing, big pitch, a bunch of headlines."

"Listen, Will, you're my brother, I love you, but you got to stop this shit. Just come out, there is a new cute detective in my squad, I want you to..."

"Dan, no, come on with that. I don't do that blind date set up shit anymore."

"OK, forget the girl, forget I mentioned it. Come out anyway, I want to see you, have like two brews then you can get the fuck out of there and go back to your shitty apartment and write for your made up clients."

Billy stopped, his older brother was showing his soft white underbelly. Anyone on the outside would never know it, but this was about as open as Danny would ever get. There was a genuine concern in his voice. Billy knew his brother was there for him when Jess died. He called almost every day, he did everything he could and called in all of his favors to make sure Jessica's parents got the best treatment from the department when they flew in from Houston. Danny acted like Jess was a wedge between them, but once she was gone, he felt his duty to protect his kid brother, to ease the pain as much as his ability would allow. All of this weighed on Billy's mind, he never forgot what his brother did in those days after. Danny was a saint to Billy, in his way the only one Billy knew he could turn to and now here he was, like a carnival barker on the other end of his phone line. Selling him a good time and a few beers for a bargain. Billy must have been contemplating this longer than he thought because eventually, Danny's voice at the other end of the line chimed in, "Will, you still there?"

"Yeah, I'm here. Listen, I'll come for one drink, one drink only.

CHAPTER 5

Then I have to get back to work. OK?"

"Deal, one drink and I'll throw you out myself. 9:00, at the Salty Dog, 72nd and Lex. See you there."

Danny hung up quickly, not giving Billy a chance to change his mind.

Billy had a little less than twelve hours to kill before his rendezvous with his older brother. Subtracting the travel time he would need to get to the Salty Dog, and the prep time he would need before leaving, he figured he still had about ten hours to kill off. He thought about a movie, but there was only so many times a guy could go to the theater alone before the very thing he was doing to feel less depressed and alone started to add to the depression and loneliness.

It was April, and the winter cold had begun to give way to the outset of the spring temperatures. Today was exceptionally pleasant. Billy knew he needed some outside time. After a quick shower, he popped his head out the front door of his building, like the groundhog looking for his shadow. Billy grabbed his coat and his New York Islanders ball cap and started down the street. His destination was not immediately clear to him, his plan was just to walk. The Upper East Side of Manhattan was still holding on to its German roots. He passed a few German bakeries and German butcher shops. He ended up walking into a Starbucks coffee shop. Ever since Jessica's death, he could never find it in him to go back to her cafe. This left him in an ongoing search to find that perfect cup of coffee that he had gotten so used to. He wandered into every small coffee shop he would pass in Manhattan, they all reminded him of his lost love. The chain stores had a much different feel to him, they never affected him. So he was content with getting his daily caffeine fix from any of the city's Starbuck's or Dunkin' Donuts.

Sitting at a table in front of the window he watched the people passing by, going about their day. A woman dropped her MetroCard and looked very agitated in having to bend down to pick it up. Billy thought to himself that if that was the worst thing to happen to that lady today, she's had a very good day. Billy thought stuff like this a lot. He felt he had some higher enlightened perspective on life and priorities. He had experienced a loss, a tragic loss, but what he failed to realize at times was that he was not alone. Everyday people just like him lose someone they loved, sometimes even tragically.

Sipping the last of his dark roast coffee, he stood up. He had no place he needed to be, he had no aim, no purpose. He felt he was just destined to wander. Roam the streets of New York City until his uneventful demise finally caught up to him.

He had walked west, and before he realized how far he had gone, he found himself at the entrance to Central Park. He had come this far he figured he might as well keep going. The park in April was still relatively quiet. The tourists had not started their annual summer pilgrimage to invade all of the city's landmarks. He walked until he found an empty bench, sitting alone off a secluded path. He felt a connection to that bench, it was alone, in an empty, quiet space, just like he was. He approached it and carefully sat down as if it were some frightened animal.

A peace fell over him, a calming blanket wrapped around him. It wasn't the private bench, it wasn't the warm sun piercing through the trees, it wasn't even the tranquil nature of the park; it was all of it. Everything was working in unison. This was as close to peace as Billy had felt since losing Jessica. He relished it, took it all in, cleared his mind and just let himself be in the moment. He felt himself smile, he didn't force a smile, the smile just happened on its own.

Billy was raised as an Irish Catholic, his faith had started out like anyone else raised the same way. He believed in God, but mostly out of fear of him. Jessica had a strong faith and was raised a Baptist from Texas. During Billy's years with her, his faith grew. His belief in God grew. It was important to her, so it became important to him. When Jessica was taken from him, he cursed God at first. Then after some time, he lost his faith, so cursing a deity he didn't believe in anymore was senseless. He gave up on religion, gave up on all of it.

Now here he was, in the park, sitting and something came over him. He felt it in his chest, a burning. It wasn't necessarily a pain, but it didn't feel right either. Then just as uncontrolled as his smile had been his eyes began to tear. Then his breathing became labored, he was sobbing. Not as uncontrolled as the day in his bathroom but a good cry. His body was acting on its own accord. He had surrendered control of it. He let go, let the cry happen, it was therapeutic for him. He hadn't cried for a very long time. He wasn't even sure this time it was about Jessica, in fact, he was sure it wasn't. This was about him, about his life here on earth, not about his fiancé or her life ending here on earth.

With no one around he let the raw emotion take control. It was civil, it was a coming to peace cry. He felt somewhat renewed after it. It was something he needed. He sat back on the bench, tilted his face toward the sun in the sky, took in a big deep breath and with its release felt his whole body reach a state of relaxation. It was almost as if he was sinking into the wooden slats of the bench itself. He was light and heavy at the same time. His thoughts were like helium holding up a balloon, and yet his body, thick with relaxation was too heavy to move. He just needed to sit and stay for a while, which he did.

His peaceful state remained uninterrupted for an extended period of time. It was finally broken when the cell phone in his pocket began to chime. He had forgotten he even had it with him. These days he rarely took it anywhere, but then again these days he rarely went anywhere.

Pulling the phone from his jacket pocket, he flipped it open and spoke into the miniature communication device.

"Hello?" He asked.

"McCabe? Is this Billy McCabe?" The digital voice on the other end inquired.

"Yes, this is he," Billy thinking this was a call for some new freelance work and had already begun working on his rejection speech.

"McCabe! How the fuck are you? It's Eric, Eric Wright. Your old Creative Director."

Billy didn't need the title to remember Eric, he still held him in high regard, "Oh yeah, Eric. How are you?"

"Shitty! I need my copywriter. Listen, we are booming here I need you back. The agency is on the move, we are getting big, I mean gigantic. Spence can't do it. He never could, we need you. I want to bring you back in, give you the senior title."

"Eric, that's generous and all, but I don't know. I'm kind of just doing this freelance stuff for now…"

Eric didn't wait for Billy to finish his sentence, "McCabe, stop. I know you're writing shitty headlines and taglines for schlock clients. It's fucking mindless bullshit writing. You don't need that. Listen, I also know that your girl, Jess, she died in the towers. Tough break, that's a hard one to recover from. Let me tell you something, something I never talk about. My brother, my twin brother, he was FDNY, went up those stairs, never came back down. Went out a hero that guy, my fucking hero. It was a shit storm, killed my mother, I mean the woman is still around, but a piece of her died that day too. She will never bounce back, I accept that. But for me? I know my brother is looking down on me and he would kick the shit out of me if, for one second, I stopped moving forward. This fucking circus we are in, this life we live, we get one shot to make it great. My brother did. He lived, still does, in my sister and me. I owe it to him to make this ride a fucking great one. You see what I'm saying? You can't sit by idly and wait for death or whatever the fuck it is you are waiting for. It's bullshit. You need to get off your ass and start doing something. Listen, you know I thought the world of Jess, she was great, served me the best coffee in New York for years. I also know she was not the kind of chick to want her guy to sit around mourning her. She will be waiting for you on the other side and man, you are going to have to explain to her why you wasted every day after she left. I'd hate to be you in that situation. She will kick your ass worse than my brother would have kicked mine. Now, do what you got to do, you have my number. This is a once in a lifetime opportunity, don't pass on it. Get on living your life, you have too much talent to piss away like this."

Billy realized that all the rehearsed speeches in his arsenal could never serve as an adequate response to what Eric just said. He paused, but not for too long, he knew Eric was not the type of person to let the silence sit for too long.

Finally, Billy spoke, "Monday, give me until Monday to make up my mind, OK?"

"You got it, stay strong, you will make the right move, you always have."

"Always?" Billy asked, an apparent reference to his leaving Eric's firm in the first place.

"Always. Leaving me was a brilliant career move, took balls and actually made me admire you," Eric was quick to pick up on Billy's hint.

"You admire me?" Billy sounded confused.

"More than you may ever know my man," Even in this humbling moment Eric radiated confidence.

Before Eric could hang up Billy squeezed in one last thing, "Eric?"
"Yeah?"
"Thanks."

PART THREE

Eric laughed on the other end of the phone, "Someone gave me that exact same speech once."

"Who?" Billy wondered.

"My brother, after our father died," Then without an official sign off Eric hung up.

CHAPTER 6

The Salty Dog was your typical townie bar, not much for the bridge and tunnel crowd. The bridge and tunnel bars were the overly commercialized bars, pubs, and lounges of Manhattan that targeted the suburbanites who wanted to come into the big city for a night out. All the locals knew to stay far away from a bridge and tunnel place, especially on a Friday or Saturday night.

Billy showed up a little late. He wanted to assure himself that he would not be there, alone, sitting at the bar waiting for his brother to show up. His plan paid off, he walked in and was immediately grabbed and hugged by his older brother who had, by the strong stench of alcohol, been there for a while.

"William, you sexy animal. You made it! Thanks for coming out," Danny yelled into Billy's ear while keeping him in a tight bear hug embrace.

Danny was drunk, that much was clear. That didn't matter to Billy, he was happy to be seeing his brother. Danny introduced him to the collection of NYPD detectives that were all gathered around.

Each one sporting a mustache that revealed their profession, the only way they could have been more obvious would be to pin their badge to their foreheads.

Danny turned to the direction of the bar and yelled at no one in particular, "Someone get my kid brother a beer! He's empty handed."

Just like magic, before Billy could protest a cold bottle of a Yuengling beer was placed into his palm. Billy turned to thank whoever placed the beer there, but no one was around. That's how it worked with Danny and his cop buddies. Everyone was always looking out for each other, it was a good feeling, a camaraderie between men.

Billy, not really feeling too social just yet, made his way to the bar after his initial introduction to the group. The collection of New York's finest included the usual cast of characters that Billy had met before. Sprinkled in were some new faces that he had never seen, or if he had, he didn't remember them.

Danny approached Billy, still sitting at the bar, "Get you another brew?"

"Not just yet, I'm still working on this one."

Danny contemplated walking away and back to his circle of friends, but stopped and turned to look Billy in the eyes, "Listen to me Will, I'm really glad you came."

"Me too Dan, thanks for inviting me. I really needed this," Billy continued. "Eric, my old boss, called me today. He offered me the senior position at the agency. Said they are getting busy and they need me."

"Are you going to take it?" Danny interrogated.

"I wasn't sure when he offered it, but I've been thinking about it all day. I think I am. I want to get back to work, get back to the agency experience and be in the mix with a good creative team again like I used to be."

CHAPTER 6

A feeling of intense relief cascaded over Danny, he had thought his brother was going to say something very different. He thought Billy was going to deliver a drawn out diatribe about never working in an office setting again, but he didn't. This time Billy was different, he seemed alive and reborn. Danny really started to allow himself to believe again that his kid brother was on his way back. Things may return to normal.

Feeling proud of his younger sibling Danny turned to the crowd gathered in the bar, he raised his glass and spoke loudly enough so that even the passersby on the street could hear, "A toast. To my kid brother Will on his big promotion and reestablishing himself in the corporate world of advertising. My brother, William McCabe, senior copywriter! Sláinte!"

A long-standing drinking tradition with the McCabe's had always been to end the toast with the Irish blessing word "Sláinte."

Just as Danny was proclaiming his brother's accomplishment for the entire upper east side of Manhattan to hear, the newest detective in Danny squad was walking through the door. She was short, cute and gave off a presence of "don't mess with me." Danny's detective squad were all males, a virtual "Boys Club." They were a very close and closed circle of friends. It was difficult for any new detective transferring over to make a good impression. Their newest addition had the added obstacle of being the only female in this pack of alpha men. She needed to be hard, and she needed to be tough, and most importantly, she needed to be the best. On her first week on the job, she pulled down a man twice her size who was smacking his girlfriend around on the subway platform at the 125th Street Station in Harlem. She was able to accomplish this Herculean task by squaring herself face to face with the perpetrator and kicking him squarely in the testicles. This sent him crumbling to the dirty cement subway platform like a precariously built house of cards. When teased about it later, she was asked if that was a new technique they were now teaching in the academy she simply replied, "Nope, soccer camp."

She was a good cop, had a keen wit about her, she was always able to see any situation from the outside. She had a soft spot for victims of abuse, she detested domestic abuse. Loathed the idea that she lived in a world where much larger and stronger men would prey on weaker women and children. She made a vow to do whatever she could inside and sometimes outside her abilities to stop all domestic abuse. The intensity and vigor she displayed in dealing with these cases won her a lot of respect from her male counterparts. She was someone to be respected and taken seriously.

Her career path was impressive, after graduating from the police academy she found herself working as a uniformed patrol officer in the 81st Precinct in Brooklyn's Bedford-Stuyvesant neighborhood. Her career with the NYPD began to get recognition after an incident at the intersection of Utica Avenue and Fulton Street. A thirteen-year-old girl was crossing Jackie Robinson Park when a man claiming to be her father stopped her. When the girl claimed she didn't know the man, he pulled out a crowbar and smashed the girl in the head, sending her to the ground with a thump. A pool of her blood began to form slowly around her. The girl was laying in the grass unconscious but still breathing. His failed first attempt to end her life was reason enough for the deranged man to take a second swing at her. When he cocked the crowbar back to get a second, more violent hit, a loud pop rang out from across the park. Before the man could bring the bar down to his helpless victim, something punched him in the chest and sent him flying backward. It hit him with so much force that his feet left the ground and didn't rejoin it until after his body had. That's when the stinging, burning feeling in his chest began, eventually spreading throughout his entire body, then a warm liquid began to soak his shirt. It must have seemed like the whole process took hours

CHAPTER 6

for the man, but in reality, it was over in a second. His realization of what happened didn't reveal itself to him until he saw a young, short uniformed police officer standing above him with her service revolver drawn and pointed at his confused face. The heroic actions displayed by this young officer fast-tracked her career. Now here she was, out with the old guard, the "Old Boys Club" of seasoned detectives, and they were the ones inviting her out for a drink, to be one of them.

She had entered the bar just as Danny McCabe was finishing up his drunken speech singing the praises of his younger sibling. The first words she could make out when entering the bar was a name, and that name was preceded by the words "My brother." She hunted down a familiar face in the room and locked into Detective Robert Weaver. She pushed her way through the crowd gathered around the bar and parted the sea of people just enough to reach him.

"Bob, what's going on up there?" She asked.

"Danny's giving some speech about his kid brother getting a new job. He's just drunk, typical McCabe."

"McCabe?" She always knew Danny's last name but never gave it too much thought, it wasn't that uncommon a last name.

Detective Weaver was now giving his full attention to her, "Yeah, Danny McCabe. You know him."

"Yes, I know him, did he say his brother William McCabe?"

Detective Weaver looking more confused now, "Yeah, I think that's his kid brothers name, Will or Billy or something like that. Why? You know him?"

Not answering she continued to push her way through the crowd of people that had begun to dissipate now that the ruckus was over. When she got to a clearing in the patrons, she was rewarded with an uninterrupted line of sight to the man sitting at the bar next to Danny.

Her eyes began to fill with tears, her pulse skyrocketed, her face became pale white while a feeling of nausea overcame her. Everything in her head told her to turn and walk away, this wasn't the time or place for this to happen. However, her body moved on its own, one step at a time closer and closer to the unexpected man now sitting alone at the bar with just his bottle of beer to keep him company.

When she finally reached him she could feel her pulse racing, she hadn't worked out exactly what she was going to say, poor planning on her part because now she couldn't muster any words. Finally, something came from her lips, "Are you, William McCabe?"

Billy, thinking this was the mysterious girl Danny wanted to set him up with answered with a very uninterested tone, not even making eye contact with her, "Yep, that's me."

She paused, looked at him deeply. It was him, it was the same William McCabe she knew, she was sure of it. She took a deep breath and continued, "I work with your brother, my name is Amanda…"

Billy, not processing anything going on, cut her off, "Listen, I'm sure you are a great person, and my brother had nothing but the best intentions in telling you to come talk to me, but I assure you, I'm fine. In fact, I'm going to be better than fine. It's just not a good time for me right now. I know you can understand, I'm sorry, but it was nice meeting you anyway."

The emotional strain of the interaction was too much for Amanda to bear. It had been almost twenty years since she had come face to face with her best friend. Although there was an ocean of time between them, Amanda never stopped thinking about William. He had encouraged her to get out of the dangerous situation she had been in. He gave her the strength to stand up and act. William McCabe had saved her life. If not for Will McCabe, she would not have survived.

Amanda turned and bolted for the door before her emotions got the best of her. As she moved through the bar and toward the door all the memories of her young teen years replayed in her head. Every one of them involved William. The companionship he offered her, the genuine friendship he so unselfishly gave, all of it, it all still meant so much to her.

Unaware of what just transpired, Billy remained seated at the bar. It was somewhere between his second and third lift of the Yuengling bottle to his lips that Danny came and sat down next to him.

"Why were you talking to Flores?" He asked.

The name he just heard uttered from the lips of his brother struck him. It took him a second to put the pieces of the puzzle together. He hadn't even had the decency to turn and look at the face of the girl introducing herself to him. That name, could it be her? Why didn't he look up? Why didn't he ask? His mind raced faster that an atom smasher. Thoughts flashed through his mind like a sped up slide show. He took a deep breath and began to slow down his brain just enough for him to start to collect his thoughts. He spun around on his bar stool and scanned the interior of the bar, but had no idea what he was looking for. The girl he had been looking for was just inches from his face, and he had no idea what she even looked like. All he had was his memory of a girl he last saw almost twenty years ago. How could he have let his pride get in the way? All he had to do was look up from his half empty bottle of alcohol, and he would have known. He would have seen her eyes and known, the eyes never change, brown orbs that carried so much love and yet seen so much pain. The emotions rose inside him like a shaken can of soda, just waiting for some unknowing target to pull the tab back and release the build-up trapped inside. When Billy was finally able to regain his composure, he realized that looking for a face he had not seen in so long in a crowded bar was useless.

Facing defeat, he threw his head back and yelled way too loud the only word he could think to accurately illustrate the emotional severity of the situation, "Fuck!"

All at once anyone within twenty feet of him turned and looked. Most seeing there wasn't much to see quickly retreated back into the social activities they were engaged in before. Danny's confusion began to grow.

"What the hell was that about Will?" Danny asked.

"Amanda Flores," Billy mustered the strength to say her name out loud, admitting defeat.

Danny looked confused and after a slight pause asked, "Yes, that's her name."

"She was just here, I didn't see her," Billy said.

All of this was causing a great deal of perplexity for Danny. He didn't know the backstory, or that his brother not only knew the latest addition to his detective squad but had a deep and meaningful history with her.

Finally, Danny confessed, "Will, I have no idea what you are talking about."

Realizing that the entire story was only playing out inside his own head, Billy took exactly thirty seconds to give Danny the very abbreviated version of the William and Amanda tale.

Danny stood for a second, processing the information he was just exposed to. Finally, he spoke, "Small fucking world!"

Still staring into space Danny gave a quick laugh to himself before turning to Billy, "So… go talk to her."

"She left, and I don't even know what she looks like now, I didn't even look up at her when she was talking to me," Billy lamented.

"You really are an insensitive prick, you know that? She went outside, I think she is still out there, talking to Bob Weaver," Danny offered up the slightest ray of hope that all was not lost.

Without saying another word to his brother, Billy shot up from his bar stool and bolted for the door. He flung it open jumped out to the sidewalk that ran parallel to Lexington Avenue. He shot his head north then south on the Avenue. He had repeated this maneuver three more times before a voice spoke from behind him.

"Will?"

Billy spun around so quickly and violently he almost hurt himself. Standing behind him, leaning up against the outside wall of the bar was the treasure at the end of his map, the finish line ribbon at the end of his race. It was the person he had been looking for his whole life. He didn't know it until that very minute, but everything that happened to him was just leading him to this moment. It was her, Amanda, his classmate, his lunch partner, and most importantly, his best friend.

He stood frozen in time, he didn't know how to react next, but he didn't have to. His body responded on its own as if being controlled by a force greater than him, and when Amanda took one step off the wall toward him, he did the rest. He took the remaining two steps to bridge the gap between them and grabbed her, he pulled her so close to him and hugged her so tightly. He swore to himself he was never going to let her go again. Her face, buried in his chest, just savored the moment. She was holding on to him just as tightly. Both of them clung to each other as if it meant their lives. Billy could feel her shaking in his arms, her grip tightened, and he began to hear her cry a gentle sob.

Amanda finally broke the silence, "I've missed you."

Billy could feel a tear drop gather in the corner of his eye, "I've missed you too."

He was a range of emotions. He was experiencing feelings he had not had in so long. He knew what he felt had a name. He was still acting on instinct when he was finally able to process his feelings and put them into words.

"I love you," He professed.

When the words left his mouth and reached Amanda's ears, her grip tightened, and the gentle sob turned into a cry. She pushed her face deeper into his chest.

"I love you too."

For the first time in her life, Amanda was home.

Made in the USA
Middletown, DE
30 January 2017